Black
Sheep

Author of over fifty books, Georgette Heyer is one of the best-known and best-loved of all historical novelists, making the Regency period her own. Her first novel, The Black Moth, published in 1921, was written at the age of seventeen to amuse her convalescent brother; her last was My Lord John. Although most famous for her historical novels, she also wrote twelve detective stories. Georgette Heyer died in 1974 at the age of seventy-one.

Also available by Georgette Heyer

Black
Sheep

Georgette Heyer

arrow books

17 19 20 18

Arrow Books
20 Vauxhall Bridge Road
London SW1V 2SA

Arrow Books is part of the Penguin Random House group of companies
whose addresses can be found at global.penguinrandomhouse.com.

Penguin
Random House
UK

First published in Great Britain by The Bodley Head in 1966
First published in paperback by Arrow Books in 2004
This edition reissued by Arrow Books in 2019

www.penguin.co.uk

A CIP catalogue record for this book is available from the British Library.

Typeset by SX Composing DTP, Rayleigh, Essex
Printed and bound in Great Britain by Clays Ltd, Elcograf S.p.A.

Penguin Random House is committed to a
sustainable future for our business, our readers
and our planet. This book is made from Forest
Stewardship Council® certified paper.

One

A little before eight o'clock, at the close of a damp autumn day, a post-chaise entered Bath, on the London Road, and presently drew up outside a house in Sydney Place. It was a hired vehicle, but it was drawn by four horses, and there was nothing in the appearance of the lady who occupied it to suggest that a private chaise, with her own postilions, would have been rather beyond her touch. She was accompanied by a middle-aged maid; and she was attired in an olive-green redingote of twilled silk which so exactly fitted her admirable figure that any female, beholding it, would have recognised at a glance that it had been made for her by a modiste of the first stare. It combined the simplicity of a garment designed for travel with an elegance only rivalled by the hat which becomingly framed Miss Abigail Wendover's face. No curled plumes or bunches of flowers adorned this confection: it was made of *gros de Naples*, bound with a satin ribbon; its poke was moderate, and its crown shallow; but it was as fashionable as the redingote.

The face beneath it was neither that of a girl in her first bloom, nor that of an accredited beauty, but it held an elusive charm which was centred in the lady's eyes, and the shy laughter which lurked in them. They were gray, and they held a great deal of intelligence; but her other features were not remarkable, her mouth being too large for beauty, her nose too far removed from the classical, and her chin rather too resolute. Her hair was neither fashionably dark nor angelically fair, but of a soft brown.

I

It was not cropped, after the prevailing mode; she wore it braided round her head, or in a knot from which curls fell about her ears. Occasionally, and in defiance of her niece's vehemently expressed disapproval, she tied a lace cap over it. Fanny said that it made her look like an old maid, and cried out indignantly when she answered, in her pretty, musical voice: 'Well, I am an old maid!'

It seemed as if her arrival had been eagerly awaited, for hardly had the chaise drawn up than the door of the house which was her home was flung open, and a footman came hurrying out to let down the steps of the chaise. He was followed by an elderly butler, who handed his mistress down, beaming a welcome, and saying: 'Good-evening, Miss Abby! Well, and it *is* a good evening which brings you home again! I am very happy to see you, ma'am!'

'Oh, and so happy as *I* am, Mitton!' she responded. 'I don't think I was ever away for so many weeks before! Is my sister well?'

'Pretty stout, ma'am – barring a touch of rheumatism. She was a trifle down pin when you first went away, and took the notion into her head that she was of a consumptive habit –'

'Oh, no!' exclaimed Abby, in comical dismay.

'No, ma'am,' agreed Mitton. 'It was no more than an epidemic cold, which left her with a little cough – as the *new* doctor was able to convince her.' His tone was one of bland respect, but there was a twinkle in his eye, which drew an involuntary chuckle from her. The twinkle deepened, but all he said was: 'Very glad she will be to see you, Miss Abby. Quite on the fidgets she has been for hours past, fearing that there might be another put-off.'

'Then I must go up to her immediately,' Abby said, and went with a light step into the house, leaving Mitton to extend a gracious welcome to her attendant.

Since the struggle for position between the butler grown old in the service of the family, and the one-time nurse to its three younger daughters, was unremitting, Mrs Grimston took this in bad part, detecting a note of patronage, and merely adjured him never to mind how she did, but to take care of Miss Abby's jewel-box.

Meanwhile, Abby, running up the stairs, found her sister awaiting her at the top of the first flight. Miss Wendover, enfolding her in a fond embrace, shed tears of joy, and begged her, in one tumbled speech, to retire instantly to bed after the fatigue of her journey; to come into the drawing-room; not to put herself to the trouble of uttering a word until she should be perfectly rested; and to tell her at once all about dear Jane, and dear Mary, and dear Jane's sweet new baby.

Sixteen years separated the sisters, for they were the eldest and the youngest members of a numerous family, three of whom had died in infancy, and one, the first-born son, when his only child was hardly out of leading-strings. Between Selina, on the shady side of forty, and Abigail, with a mere eight-and-twenty years in her dish, there now intervened only James, Mary, and Jane. It was with Jane, married to a man of considerable property in Huntingdonshire, that Abigail had been sojourning for the better part of the past six weeks, having been summoned to support her sister through the disasters which had befallen her. Measles had attacked her youthful family, and at the very moment when Nurse, falling down the backstairs, had broken her leg, and while she herself was in hourly expectation of presenting Sir Francis with a fourth *petit paquet*. In a letter heavy with underscorings, Lady Chesham had implored her dearest Abby to come to her at once, and to bring Grimston with her, since nothing could prevail upon her to abandon her beloved children to a strange nurse's care.

So Abigail had posted away to Huntingdonshire, where she had remained for five weeks, under trying conditions, all three children having succumbed to the measles before her arrival, her sister being brought to bed within two days of it, and her brother-in-law, at no time remarkable for amiability, apparently labouring under the conviction that this unfortunate con-catenation of circumstances had been designed for the express

3

purpose of causing him to suffer the maximum amount of undeserved hardship.

'You must be worn to a thread!' Selina said, leading her into the drawing-room. 'And then to be obliged to go to London, in all that racket and bustle! I don't think Mary should have asked it of you!'

'She didn't: I invited myself, as a reward for *not* having got into a quarrel with Sir Francis. Never have I known a more glumpish, disagreeable man! I sincerely pity Jane, and forgive her all her peevishness. You can't conceive how glad I was to see George's good-humoured countenance when I reached Brook Street, and to be made so welcome by him and Mary! I enjoyed myself very much, and did a vast deal of shopping. Only wait until you see the bonnet I've brought for you: you will look charmingly in it! Then I bought ells of the prettiest muslins for Fanny, besides a quantity of fripperies for myself, and – But where is Fanny?'

'She will be so vexed not to have been here to welcome you!'

'Fiddle! why should she be? It's Thursday, isn't it? Then I collect she is at the cotillion-ball?'

'I thought there could be no objection,' Selina said, a little defensively. 'Lady Weaverham invited her to dine, and to go to the Upper Rooms afterwards, in her party, and I consented to it, having then no apprehension that you would be with us again today.'

'Why, of course!' said Abby. 'Very uncivil of Fanny it would have been to have cried off!'

'Exactly so!' said Selina eagerly. 'With Lady Weaverham, too – such an amiable woman, as I know you must agree! Besides having two daughters, which makes it so particularly kind in her to have invited Fanny! Because it can't be denied that our dearest is the prettiest girl in Bath!'

'Oh, out of cry! As for Lady Weaverham, no one could be more amiable – or more shatterbrained! I wish – No, never mind! I'm glad she *has* taken Fanny to the ball on this occasion, for I must talk to you about Fanny.'

'Yes, my love, of course! But you are tired, and must be longing to go to bed! A bowl of broth –'

'No, no, just a little thin gruel!' said Abby, laughing at her. 'You goose, I stopped to dine in Chippenham, and I'm not in the least tired. We'll drink tea together, as soon as I've put off my hat, and enjoy a comfortable prose.' She added mischievously: 'You look the picture of guilt – as though you were in dread of a scold! But how should I dare to scold my eldest sister? I'm not so brassy!'

She went away, leaving Selina to ring for the tea-tray, and mounted the stairs to her bedroom, where she found Mrs Grimston unpacking her trunk. A look of disapproval had settled on this formidable dame's countenance, and she greeted Miss Wendover with the information that she had known at the outset how it would be if Miss Fanny were left with only Miss Selina, and Betty Conner (who had more hair than wit, and was flighty into the bargain) to take care of her. 'Jauntering about all over!' she said darkly. 'Concerts, and balls, and theatres, and picnics, and I don't know what more besides!'

Abby had her own reasons for suspecting that her niece had been enjoying far more licence than had previously been granted to her; but as she had no intention of discussing the matter with Mrs Grimston she merely replied: 'Well, how should you?' which effectually reduced her old nurse to offended silence.

The Misses Wendover had virtually had charge of their orphaned niece since she was two years old, when her mama had died in giving birth to a still-born son, and her papa had confided her to the care of her grandmama. His own death, three years later, in no way affected this arrangement; and when, in Fanny's twelfth year, her grandpapa had met with a fatal accident on the hunting-field, and his widow had chosen to retire to Bath, instead of continuing to endure, in her Dower House, a climate which had never agreed with her frail constitution, his surviving son, James, who was Fanny's guardian, had been only too glad to leave Fanny in her care. He was himself the father of a hopeful family, but his wife, a lady of forceful character, had no wish to assume the charge of his niece. When Mrs Wendover died, three years later, Fanny was bidding fair to become an uncommonly beautiful girl, and Mrs James Wendover had even less desire to include her in her household, where she would not only outshine her cousins, but might even teach them to be as light at hand as she was herself. So James, steward and tenant of the estate of which Fanny was the owner, graciously informed his sisters that they might, for the present, continue to act as the dear child's guardians. It would be a pity (as his Cornelia pointed out to him) to interrupt her education at one of Bath's exclusive seminaries. James, adhering to the custom of his family, was determined to arrange an advantageous marriage for Fanny; but he thought there was time enough before it would become Cornelia's duty to launch her into society, not foreseeing that when Fanny was ripe for presentation Cornelia would be more than ever determined to leave her with her aunts. Cornelia confessed that she could not like Fanny, in whom she detected a sad resemblance to her poor mama. It was to be hoped that she would not grow into one of these modern hurly-burly females; but for her part Cornelia considered that her vivacity led her to be far too coming. But what could one expect of a girl reared by a couple of doting old maids?

The younger of the doting old maids went downstairs again to the drawing-room, where her sister was already seated behind the tea-table. Miss Wendover, after one glance at her carriage-dress, with its rucked sleeves and its little winged ruff of starched muslin, greeted her with instant approval, exclaiming: 'I never saw you look so becoming! London, of course?'

'Yes: Mary was so obliging as to take me to her very own Thérèse, which I thought excessively good-natured of her.'

'Thérèse! I daresay it was shockingly dear, then, because Cornelia once said to me – so spiteful of her! – that it was to be hoped George might not be ruined by Mary's extravagance, and that *she* couldn't afford to have her dresses made by Thérèse.'

'Could, but won't,' said Abby, sipping her tea. 'How happy James must be to have a wife who is as big a nip-farthing as he is himself!'

'Oh, Abby, how can you? Remember, he is your brother!'

'I do, and never cease to regret it!' retorted Abby. 'Now, don't, I beg of you, recite me a catalogue of his virtues, for they don't render him any more lovable – less, in fact! Besides, he's an incorrigible busyhead, and I'm quite out of charity with him.'

Selina had been uttering soft clucking sounds of protest, but they ceased at this, and she demanded quite sharply: 'Has James written to you too?'

'Written to me! He actually came up to London to read me one of his pompous lectures! My dear, what *have* you been doing here? Who is this ramshackle youth who has been making up to Fanny?'

'No such thing!' declared Selina, her colour much heightened. 'It was a case of love at first sight – and a very pretty-behaved young man! Only think of his running out of the Pump Room, with no umbrella, to procure a chair for me, and becoming drenched, because you know what it is in Bath when it suddenly comes on to rain, there is never a chair or a hackney to be had, and I was persuaded he would take a chill, which would settle on his lungs, but he made nothing of it – so very obliging! And he had not then exchanged one word with Fanny, because she wasn't with me, and although *I* remembered that I had seen him in the Upper Rooms two – no, *three* – days before, *he* did not, and Fanny *was* with me on that occasion, so if you are thinking that he got the chair for me because he wished to become acquainted with her you are quite mistaken, Abby! If that had been his object he would have desired Mr King to have introduced him to us, at the Upper Rooms. *And*,' she concluded, with the air of one delivering a clincher: 'he is not a *youth*! I daresay he is as old as you are, and very likely older!'

Abby could not help laughing at this tangled speech, but she shook her head as well, and sighed: 'Oh, Selina, you goosecap!'

'I collect you mean to reproach me,' said Selina, sitting very straight in her chair, 'but why you should do so I haven't the least guess, for Fanny had a great many admirers before you went away, and when *I* said she was too young to be going to balls, *you* said I was *Gothic*, and also that she would enjoy her London come-out much more if she had previously been into society a little, which is *perfectly* true, because there is nothing so – so *agonising* as to be fired off from the schoolroom, no matter how many dancing and deportment lessons one has had! Particularly if one is a trifle shy – not that I mean to say that Fanny is shy – indeed, I sometimes wonder if she is not a little *too* – though never unbecomingly! And if James has been tattling to you, depend upon it that odious woman who is Cornelia's bosom-piece – which is just what one would expect of Cornelia, to make a crony of a backbiting creature like Mrs Ruscombe! – well, you may depend upon it that it was she who set him on, because Mr Calverleigh never greets that tallow-faced daughter of hers with more than common civility, in spite of having been regularly introduced, and receiving every encouragement to dangle after the girl!'

'Yes, very likely,' agreed Abby.

'There, then!' said Selina triumphantly.

There was no immediate response to this, but, after a few moments, Abigail said: 'If that were all – but it isn't, Selina! George isn't a backbiter, and he spoke of Calverleigh with the greatest contempt, because he thought it right to warn me that the young man is not at all the thing. Besides being a gamester, it seems that he is what they call a gazetted fortune-hunter. In fact, the on-dit is that Fanny is not the first heiress he has made up to: there was some silly girl who was ready to elope with him, if you please, only last year! Fortunately, the plot was discovered, and the whole affair hushed up.'

'I don't believe it!' declared Selina, trembling with indignation. 'No, and I wonder that George should repeat such – such steward's room gossip! *Not the thing*, indeed! I consider him most truly the gentleman, and of the *first* respectability, and so does everyone else in Bath!'

'Oh, Selina, what a bouncer! You know very well that Lady Trevisian didn't hold him in high esteem. Indeed, she told Mary that she had warned you, just before she left Bath, that you would be wise to hint Calverleigh away. That was how George came to know about the business.'

Much flushed, Selina said: 'I wonder that she could think of nothing better to do than to go tattlemongering all over London! Making a mountain out of a molehill, too, as I very soon discovered – not that I mean to say that it was not very wrong of Fanny, and I assure you I told her so – and all because she saw Fanny walking with him in the Sydney Gardens, quite by accident – meeting him, I mean, and Betty with her, of course – at least, she was *then* – so I gave Fanny a *severe* scold, and told her how shocking it would be if people thought she was *fast*. Yes, and I said that I was surprised at Mr Calverleigh, which I collect she must have told him, because he paid me a morning visit the very next day, to beg pardon, and to explain to me that this was the first time he had ever been to Bath, which accounted for his not knowing that it was quite improper for a young female of breeding to wander round the gardens – to say nothing of the labyrinth! – without the vestige of a chaperon, not even her maid, because Fanny had sent Betty home, which was very naughty of her – most thoughtless, only she is such a child still that I'm persuaded she had no notion – and *he*, I promise you, felt it just as he ought!'

'Did he?' said the younger Miss Wendover rather dryly. 'Well, you can't suppose that I mean to make a mountain out of a molehill! But the thing is, Selina, that however engaging Calverleigh may be he will not do for Fanny. If George, who is far too good-natured to abuse people merely because he doesn't like them, calls him a *loose fish*, which I fancy means a libertine –'

'Abby! Oh, *no*!' exclaimed Selina, outraged.

'Well, there must be something very undesirable about him to bring James posting up to London in the greatest fuss imaginable!'

'Yes, because he wants poor Fanny to make a brilliant match! I hope I know how to value my brother as I ought, but I must say that I think he has a maggot in his head on *that* subject!'

'It was more than that,' Abby said slowly, a frown creasing her

9

brow. 'He seemed to me to be almost overpowered! Indeed, he couldn't utter the name without shuddering! I could have laughed, if he hadn't put me so much out of temper. For what must he do, when I asked him *why* he held Calverleigh in such violent dislike, but prim up his mouth, and say that it was not a matter fit for my ears! I must be content to abide by his judgment, and if I did not nip the affair in the bud there would be nothing for it but to remove Fanny from our care.'

'*What?*' Selina gasped.

'Don't fall into despair, my love!' said Abby, smiling at her. 'He may *talk* of removing Fanny to his – or, rather, *her* – own home, but I fancy he would meet with some sturdy opposition from Cornelia! If he overbore it I'm sure it would be for the first time in his life!'

'It would be the cruellest thing! She would be miserable!' uttered Selina, in palpitating accents.

'Oh, she would run away!' replied Abby cheerfully. 'I told him so, which gave him the chance to deplore her upbringing. However, before we got to actual dagger-drawing –'

'You should not! Oh, dear, oh, dear, how often has dear Mama begged you not to be so – so *impetuous*?'

'No, of course I should not, but there was no harm done, because Mary was there, and I defy anyone to brangle in the teeth of her placid good sense! She said, in her sweetly comfortable way, – *you* know, Selina! – what a to-do was being made over a flirtation, which would never grow to serious proportions if James would but refrain from turning it into a grand tragedy, and so putting it into Fanny's head that she was a modern Juliet. James was a good deal struck by this, and so was I, too!' She broke off, perceiving that her sister did not share her sentiments. 'You don't agree?'

Her mild eyes filling with sentimental tears, Selina said, in a trembling voice: 'How can you be so unfeeling? When you have said I don't know how many times that our darling should never be sacrificed as *you* were! When I recall your sufferings – when I think of your – of your blighted life –'

'Selina, have you run mad?' interrupted Abby, regarding her in astonishment. 'What sufferings?'

'You may try to hoax me, but you won't make me believe that you have forgotten your anguish when Papa forbade poor Mr Thornaby ever to approach you again! *I* shall never do so!' declared Selina.

'Good gracious!' The anxious look in Abby's eyes was put to rout by one of irrepressible merriment. 'My dearest goose, do *try* to forget it! I have, I promise you! Indeed, I haven't any very clear recollection of what he even looked like, though I do remember that I believed myself to be brokenhearted at the time. At seventeen, one does, only to discover that one has quite mistaken the matter.'

This sad want of sensibility daunted Selina for a moment, but she made a recover, saying, with an air of boundless understanding: 'You were always so brave, my dear one! But if you had forgotten Mr Thornaby why did you refuse Lord Broxbourne's offer? So very flattering, and such an excellent man, with a most superior mind, and *every* quality to render him acceptable!'

'Except one! He was a dead bore!' Abby's eyes began to dance again. 'Have you been picturing me nursing a broken heart all these years? My dear, I do beg your pardon, but it is quite useless to make me the heroine of a tragic romance: I must always disappoint you.'

'Next you will tell me that you too are determined to arrange a splendid match for poor little Fanny! I hope I know you rather too well to believe that!'

'I hope you do. I may own that Papa chanced to be right when he sent Thornaby packing, but I still hold to it that this resolve he had – and my grandfather before him, and James after him! – to arrange only the most advantageous marriages for every one of his children was nothing short of an obsession! And you may be sure I won't allow Fanny to be sacrificed as you and Jane were! Mary was so compliant as to fall in love with George, but only think of Jane, positively *forced* into marriage with that odious creature who had nothing but his wealth and his title to recommend him!'

Selina, who had derived consolation all her life from the inculcated belief that Papa must know best, said feebly: 'No, no! How can you say such things, Abby? One would think – not but what – perhaps sometimes he may have been a *trifle* – But I am sure he did only what he believed to be *right*!'

'But for Papa,' said Abby inexorably, 'you would have married that curate – I forget his name, but I daresay you would have been very happy, with a quiverful of children, and – Oh, dearest, forgive me! I didn't mean to make you cry!'

Selina had indeed dissolved into tears, but she wiped them away, saying: 'No, no! It was only *remembering*, and even dear Mama, who entered into all my feelings, couldn't conceal from me her apprehension that he would become bald before he was forty! It is *you* who should be pitied!'

'Not a bit of it! I don't regret Thornaby, and I was *not* sacrificed, as Jane was! No, and I won't let James make a burnt offering of Fanny either: that you may depend on! But, on the other hand, my dear, I won't – if I can prevent it – let her throw herself away on the first fortune-hunter who makes up to her!'

'But I am persuaded he is no such thing!' expostulated Selina. 'He is possessed of *considerable* estates in Berkshire, and he comes of a most *distinguished* family. I believe he can trace his lineage back for *hundreds* of years!'

'Well, I know nothing about his ancestors, but from all I have been able to discover the present family is distinguished for profligacy, and nothing else! *This* man's reputation is bad; and, according to James, his father was far from respectable; while as for his uncle, *he*, after having been expelled from Eton, seems to have gone his length in every extravagant folly until he was packed off to India, under orders never to show his face to his family again! As for the estates, George says they are grossly encumbered. And if you think all these circumstances make Stacy Calverleigh an eligible suitor –'

'Oh, no, no, no!' Selina cried distressfully. 'Only I *can't* believe that poor Mr Calverleigh – and it always seems to me *most* unjust to visit the sins of the fathers upon the children, and when it comes to an *uncle* positively wicked! Such engaging manners, and feels just as he ought, besides showing delicacy of mind, and – oh, I don't believe it!'

'Well, it was what George said, and you must allow that he is not at all prudish, as James is.' She paused, her brow wrinkled in thought. 'And I should suppose, wouldn't you, that a libertine *must* be engaging?'

'Abby!' gasped Selina. 'I must *beg* of you to guard your tongue! If anyone were to hear you – !'

'Well, no one but you can hear me,' Abby pointed out. 'And all I said was –'

'I know nothing about *that* class of person!' interrupted Selina hastily.

'No, nor do I,' said Abby, on a note of regret. 'Except what I've read, of course, and that diverting man who came to a ball the Ashendens gave – oh, years ago! Papa said he would not permit a daughter of his to stand up for as much as one dance with *such a fellow as that*, only I had already done so, and very agreeable it was! I don't know that he was a libertine, but I do know that he was a shocking flirt – and *not* because Rowland told me so! In that consequential way of his, which made him look just like Papa – *you* know!'

It was evident that whatever Miss Wendover might have known she was determined to forget. Summoning to her aid all the authority of her years, she said, in a voice of the gravest reproof: 'Must I remind you, Abigail, that dear Rowland is dead?'

'No, and you need not remind me that he was our eldest brother either. Or call me by that detestable name! Whatever else I might forgive Papa, *that* I never could! *Abigail*! Mashams and maidservants!'

'*Some* people think it a charming name!' said Selina, casting an arch look at her. '*One* of them is Canon Pinfold, who thinks *you* are charming too! He says that it is from the Hebrew, and means *father rejoiced*.'

After a stunned moment, her unregenerate sister went into a

peal of laughter. It was several minutes before she could do more than wail: 'Papa c-can't have kn-known that! He w-wanted another son!' and when she did manage to stop laughing Selina's look of pained reproach very nearly set her off again. She bit her lip, and said, a little shakily: 'Don't mind me! You know what I am! And what in the world has all this to do with Fanny? Selina, I realise that you have a decided *tendre* for Calverleigh, but if he were the biggest prize on the matrimonial mart I still should not like it! Good God, do you wish her to plunge into marriage with the first man she has met who is neither middle-aged nor a youth she has known since he was a schoolboy? At seventeen!'

'I told her she was too young to be talking of having formed a lasting attachment,' answered Selina, thrown upon the defensive again. 'Yes, and I said that her uncle would never countenance it, and that she must put it out of her mind!'

This effectively banished any lingering desire in Abby to giggle. She exclaimed: 'You didn't! Oh, Selina, I wish you had not!'

'You wish I had not?' echoed Selina, her voice as much as her countenance betraying her bewilderment. 'But you have just said –'

'Yes, yes, but don't you *see* –' Abby interrupted, only to break off her sentence abruptly, as she realised the folly of expecting Selina to perceive what was so obvious to her own intelligence. She continued, in a gentler voice: 'I am afraid that it may have put up her back – roused the independence of spirit which you have so often deplored. Yes, I know that you think she ought to submit meekly to the decrees of her guardian, but recollect that she hasn't been reared as we were, to regard the lightest pronouncement of a parent – or an aunt! – as something it would be sacrilege to question, and *unthinkable* to disobey!'

Roused to indignation, Selina retorted: 'Well, I *must* say, Abby! For you to talk in such a way, when you never showed the least respect for Papa's judgment! And when I recall how often you came to cuffs with him, casting dear Mama and me into agonies of apprehension – *Well*! Not, dearest,' she added hastily, 'that I mean to say that you ever actually disobeyed Papa, for that I know you didn't!'

'No,' agreed Abby, in a flattened tone. 'A very poor honey, wasn't I?'

The mournful note startled Miss Wendover, but in a very few seconds she realised that it had its origin in fatigue, aggravated by anxiety. It was incumbent upon her to divert poor Abby's mind, and with this amiable intention she first told her, with an indulgent laugh, that she was a naughty puss; and then launched into a recital of the various events which had lately occurred in Bath. Her rambling discourse embraced such topics as what her new doctor said about Russian Vapour Baths; how eagerly dear Mrs Grayshott was awaiting the return of her son from India – if the poor young man survived the voyage, so ill as he had been in that horrid country; how much she was obliged to poor Laura Butterbank, who had spared no pains to cheer and support her during Abby's absence, coming every day to sit with her, and always so chatty and companionable, besides being charmed to execute any little commission in the town. But at this point she broke off, to accuse her sister of not listening to a word she said.

Abby had indeed been allowing the gentle stream of inanities to flow past her, but at this reproach she recalled her thoughts, and said: 'Yes, I am! Mrs Grayshott – Miss Butterbank! I'm glad she bore you company while I was away – since Fanny seems not to have done so!'

'Good gracious, Abby, how you do take one up! No one could have been more attentive, the sweet child that she is! But with so much of her time occupied by her music-lessons, and the Italian class, besides having so many of her friends living here, who are for ever inviting her to join them for a country walk, or some picnic-party – *perfectly* unexceptionable! – I'm sure it is not to be wondered at – I mean, when Laura gave me the pleasure of her company every day there was no reason why Fanny should have stayed at home, and very selfish it would have been in me to have asked it of her! Yes, and most unnatural it would be if she didn't wish to be with girls of her own age!'

'True! Or even with the fascinating Calverleigh!'

'Now, Abby – !'

'Well, it would be,' said Abby candidly. 'Any girl would prefer the company of a taking young man to that of her aunt! But it won't do, Selina.'

'I am persuaded that when you have made his acquaintance – not that I would for a *moment* encourage her – oh, dear how very affecting it is! *You* will have to tell her, for I know I could never bring myself to do so!'

'Dearest, it isn't so dreadful that you need fall into affliction! It's certainly unfortunate, and I wish with all my heart that she might have been spared such a painful disappointment, but she'll recover from it. As for forbidding her to see Calverleigh, or telling her the things that are said of him, I'm not such a widgeon! She would fly to his defence! But if *he* were to draw off? Not compelled to do so, but because he discovered her to be not such a rich plum as he had supposed? She might suffer a little unhappiness, but not for long. She's not the girl to wear the willow for a mere flirt!' She added thoughtfully: 'And she couldn't, under those circumstances, fancy herself to be a star-crossed lover, could she? I do feel that that should be avoided at all costs, for although I've never been star-crossed myself I can readily perceive how romantic it would be. Selina, I never knew Fanny's mother at all well, but you must have done so. Was she high-spirited, like Fanny? Rather too dashing, perhaps, to suit the Wendover notions of propriety?'

'Celia? Good gracious, no!' replied Selina. 'She was very pretty – quite lovely, when she was a girl, but she went off sadly, which I do hope and pray Fanny won't, because she is very like her in *countenance*, and Mama always was used to say that *fair* beauties seldom wear well. But Fanny isn't in the least like her in disposition! She has so much liveliness, and poor Celia was a very quiet, shy girl, and *most* persuadable! What makes you ask me about her?'

'Something James said. I wasn't paying much heed, but it was something about Fanny's too close resemblance to her mother.

And then he stopped short, and when I asked him what he meant he fobbed me off, saying that Fanny was as foolish as her mother. But I didn't think he did mean that, and nor did Mary. She remembers more than I do, of course, and she tells me that you elder ones always thought that *something* had happened – some indiscretion, perhaps –'

'I never thought any such thing!' intervened Selina firmly. 'And if I had I should have considered it most improper to have pried into it! If Mama had wished me to know anything about it, she would have told me!'

'So there *was* something!' said Abby. 'A skeleton in our respectable cupboard! I wish I could know what it was! But I daresay it would prove to be no more than the skeleton of a mouse.'

Two

Not long after eleven o'clock that evening, a gentle tap on the door of Abby's bedchamber was followed immediately by the entrance of Miss Fanny Wendover, who first peeped cautiously into the room, and then, when she saw her aunt seated at the dressing-table, uttered a joyful squeak, and ran to fling herself into the arms held out to her, exclaiming: 'You aren't in bed and asleep! I told Grimston you wouldn't be! Oh, how glad I am to see you again! how much I've missed you, dear, dear Abby!'

It would not have surprised Abby if she had been greeted with reserve, even with the wary, half-defiant manner of one expectant of censure and ready to defend herself; but there was no trace of consciousness in the welcome accorded her, and nothing but affection in the beautiful eyes which, as Fanny sank down at her feet, clasping her hands, were raised so innocently to hers.

'It's horrid without you!' Fanny said, giving her hands a squeeze. 'You can't think!'

Abby bent to drop a kiss on her cheek, but said with mock sympathy: 'My poor darling! So strict and unkind as Aunt Selina has been! I feared it would be so.'

'*That's* what I've missed so much!' Fanny said, with a ripple of mirth. 'I am most sincerely attached to Aunt Selina, but – but she is not a great jokesmith, is she? And not a bit corky!'

'I shouldn't *think* so,' responded Abby cautiously. 'Not that I know what *corky* means, but it sounds very unlike Selina – and, I

18

may add, sadly unlike the language to be expected of a girl of genteel upbringing!'

That made Fanny's eyes dance. 'Yes – slang! It means – oh, bright, and lively! Like you!'

'Does it indeed? I collect you mean to pay me a handsome compliment, but if ever you dare to attach such an epithet to me again, Fanny, I shall – I shall – well, I don't yet know what I shall do, but you may depend upon it that it will be something terrible! *Corky*! Good God!'

'I won't,' Fanny promised. 'Now, do, do be serious, beloved! I have so much to tell you. Something of – of the first importance.'

Abby knew a craven impulse to fob her off, but subdued it, saying in what she hoped was not a hollow voice: 'No, have you? Then I will engage to be perfectly serious. What is it?'

Fanny directed a searching look at her. 'Didn't Aunt Selina – or Uncle James, perhaps – tell you about – about Mr Calverleigh?'

'About Mr – ? Oh! Is he the London smart you've slain with one dart from your eyes? To be sure they did, and very diverting I thought them! That is to say,' she corrected herself, in a ludicrously severe tone, 'that of course they are very right in thinking you to be far too young to be setting up a flirt! Most forward of you, my love – quite improper!'

She won no answering gleam. 'It isn't like that,' Fanny said. 'From the very first moment that we met –' She paused, and drew a long breath. 'We loved one another!' she blurted out.

Abby had not expected such an open avowal, and could think of nothing to say but that it sounded like a fairy-tale, which was not at all what she ought to have said, as she realised an instant later.

Raising glowing eyes to her face, Fanny said simply: 'Yes, it is just like that! Oh, I knew you would understand, dearest! Even though you haven't yet met him! And when you do meet him – oh, you will dote on him! I only wish you may not cut me out!'

Abby accorded this sally the tribute of a smile, but recommended her ecstatic niece not to be a pea-goose.

'Oh, I was only funning!' Fanny assured her. 'The thing is that he isn't a silly boy, like Jack Weaverham, or Charlie Ruscombe, or – or Peter Trevisian, but a man of the world, and *much* older than I am, which makes it so particularly gratifying – no, I don't mean that! – *so wonderful* that in spite of having been on the town, as they say, for years and years he never met anyone with whom he wished to form a *lasting* connection until he came to Bath, and met *me*!' Overcome by this reflection, she buried her face in Abby's lap, saying, in muffled accents: 'And he must have met much prettier girls than I am – don't you think?'

Miss Wendover, aware that her besetting sin was a tendency to give utterance to the first thought which sprang to her mind, swallowed an impulse to retort: 'But few so well endowed!' and replied instead: 'Well, as I'm not acquainted with any of the latest beauties I can't say! But to have made a London beau your first victim is certainly a triumph. Of course I know I shouldn't say that to you – your Aunt Cornelia would call it *administering to your vanity!* – so pray don't expose me to her censure by growing puffed-up, my darling!'

Fanny looked up. 'Ah, you *don't* understand! Abby, this is a – a lasting attachment! You must believe that! Has my uncle told you that he is a desperate flirt? *Such* a sad reputation as he has! He told me so himself! But I don't care a rush, because, although he has frequently fancied himself to be in love, he never wished to *marry* anyone until he met *me*! And if my uncle said that he is a trifle rackety he might have spared his breath, for Stacy told me that too. He said – oh, Abby, he said he wasn't fit to touch my hand, and no one could blame my uncle if he refused to give his consent to our marriage!'

She once more hid her face in Abby's lap, raising it again to add: 'So you *see* –!'

Abby thought that she did, but she only said, stroking the golden head on her knee: 'But what is there in all this to cast you into agitation? Anyone would suppose that your uncle had already refused his consent, and had threatened you both with dire penalties into the bargain!'

'Oh!' breathed Fanny, looking eagerly up at her. 'Do you mean that you think he won't refuse it?'

'Oh, no!' said Abby. 'I am very sure that he will! And although I have no very high opinion of his judgment I give him credit for not being such a niddicock as to accept the first offer made to him for your hand! A pretty guardian he would be if he allowed you to become riveted before your first season! Yes, I know that sets up all your bristles, my darling, and makes you ready to pull caps with me, but I beg you won't! Your uncle may dream of a splendid alliance for you, but you know that I don't! I only dream of a happy one.'

'I know – oh, I know!' Fanny declared. 'And so you will support me! Best of my aunts, say that you will!'

'Why, yes, if you can convince me that your first love will also be your last love!'

'But I have told you!' Fanny said, sitting back on her heels, and staring at her in rising indignation. 'I could never love anyone as I love Stacy! Good God, how can you – *you*! – talk like that to me? I know – my aunt told me! – how my grandfather repulsed the man *you* loved! And you've never loved another, and – and your life was ruined!'

'Well, I thought so at the time,' Abby admitted. A smile quivered at the corners of her mouth. 'I must own, however, that whenever that first suitor of mine is recalled to my mind I can only be thankful that your grandfather did repulse him! You know, Fanny, the melancholy truth is that one's first love very rarely bears the least resemblance to one's last, and most enduring love! *He* is the man one marries, and with whom one lives happily ever after!'

'But you have not married!' muttered Fanny rebelliously.

'Very true, but not because I carried a broken heart in my bosom! I have fallen in and out of love a dozen times, I daresay. And as for your Aunt Mary – ! She, you know, was always accounted the Beauty of the family, and you might have reckoned her suitors by the score! The first of them was as unlike your Uncle George as any man could be.'

'I thought that my grandfather had arranged that marriage?' interpolated Fanny.

'Oh, no!' replied Abby. 'He certainly approved of it, but George was only one of three eligible suitors! He was neither the most handsome nor the most dashing of them, and he bore not the smallest resemblance to any of your aunt's first loves, but theirs is a very happy marriage, I promise you.'

'Yes, but I am not like my aunt,' returned Fanny. 'I daresay she would have been as happy with any other amiable man, because she has a happy disposition, besides being very – very conformable!' She twinkled naughtily up at Abby. 'Which I am *not*! My aunt is like a – oh, a deliciously soft cushion, which may be pushed and pummelled into any shape you choose! – but I – I *know* what I want, and have a great deal of resolution into the bargain!'

'More like a bolster, in fact,' agreed Abby, with an affability she was far from feeling.

Fanny laughed. 'Yes, if you like – *worst* of my aunts! In any event, I mean to marry Stacy Calverleigh, whatever my uncle may say or do!'

Well aware that few things were more invigorating to high-spirited adolescents than opposition, Abby replied instantly: 'Oh, certainly! But your father, you know, was an excellent dragsman, and he was used to say that you should always get over heavy ground as light as possible. I am strongly of the opinion that you – and Mr Calverleigh – should refrain from declaring your intentions to your uncle until you can also present him with proof of the durability of your attachment.'

'He wouldn't care: you must know he wouldn't! And if you mean to say that I must wait until I come of age – oh, no, you couldn't be so heartless! Four whole years – ! When you have met Stacy, you will understand!'

'I shall be delighted to meet him, and wish it may be soon.'

'Oh, and so do I!' Fanny said eagerly. 'You can't think how much I miss him! You see, he was obliged to go to London, but he said it would only be for a few days, so he may be in Bath again by the end of the week. Or, at any rate, next week: that you may depend on!'

This was said with a radiant look, and was followed by a shyly ecstatic account of Fanny's first meeting with Mr Calverleigh, and a description of his manifold charms. Abby listened and commented suitably, but seized the first opportunity that offered of turning Fanny's thoughts into another channel. She directed her attention to the pile of dress-lengths she had procured in London, and bade her say if she liked them. This answered very well; and in going into raptures over a spider-gauze, wondering whether to have a celestial-blue crape trimmed with ribbon or puff-muslin, and arguing with Abby over the respective merits of Circassian or Cottage sleeves for a morning-dress, Fanny temporarily forgot Mr Calverleigh, and went off to bed presently, to dream (Abby hoped) of fashions.

It seemed, on the following morning, as though she had done so, for she visited her aunt before Abby was out of bed, eager to show her several fashion-plates from the latest issue of the *Lady's Monthly Museum*, and hopeful of coaxing her to sally forth before breakfast on a visit to the dressmaker on South Parade. In this she failed, Abby pointing out to her that her Aunt Selina, no early riser, would be very much hurt if excluded from the expedition. She added a reminder that in all matters of taste and fashion Selina was infallible.

Fanny pouted, but submitted, knowing the truth of this dictum. She might stigmatise many of Selina's notions as fusty, but no one had ever cast a slur on Selina's eye for the elegant and the becoming. In her youth she had been the least good-looking but the most modish of the Wendover girls; in her middle age, and endowed with an easy competence, she enjoyed the reputation of being the best-dressed woman in Bath. If Fanny did not, like Abby, seek her advice, she was shrewd enough to respect her judgment; so that when, presently, she showed Selina the sketch of a grossly overtrimmed walking-dress her secret longing to be seen abroad in this confection was nipped in the bud by Selina's devastating criticism. 'Oh, dear!' said Selina, wrinkling her nose in distaste. 'All those frills, and tucks, and ribbons – ! So – so *deedy*!'

So nothing more was seen of that fashion-plate, and in due course all three ladies set out in Miss Wendover's new barouche for South Parade, where Madame Lisette's elegant showrooms were situated.

Madame Lisette, who was born Eliza Mudford, enjoyed Royal Patronage, but although she was the particular protégée of the Princess Elizabeth, in whose service she had started her career, and rarely failed to receive orders from Bath's noblest and most fashionable visitors, the Misses Wendover ranked high amongst her favourite clients: they were rich, they were resident, and they set off to the greatest advantage the fruits of her genius. By no means all her customers were honoured by her personal attention, but no sooner had her head saleswoman caught sight of the barouche drawing up outside the door than she sent an apprentice scurrying upstairs to Madame's office with the news that the Misses Wendover – *all* the Misses Wendover! – were about to enter the shop. So, by the time the Misses Wendover had enquired kindly after Miss Snisby's health, and their footman had delivered into the care of an underling the package containing the silks, and the gauzes, and the muslins purchased in London by Miss Abigail, Miss Mudford had arrived on the scene, suitably but exquisitely gowned in a robe of rich silk but sober hue, and combining with the ease of an expert the deference due to ladies of quality with the chartered familiarities of an old and trusted retainer. No less skill did she show in convincing the youngest Miss Wendover that the style of dress, proper for a young matron, for which that damsel yearned, would not make her look dashing, but on the contrary, positively dowdy. Such was her tact that Fanny emerged from the salon an hour later with the comfortable persuasion that so far from having been treated like a schoolroom miss her taste had been approved, and that the resultant creations would set her in the highest kick of fashion.

This satisfactory session being at an end, the ladies betook themselves to the Pump Room, where it was Selina's custom (unless the weather were inclement, or some more agreeable diversion offered itself) to imbibe, in small, distasteful sips, a glass of the celebrated waters. Here they encountered a number of friends and acquaintances, prominent amongst whom were General Exford, one of Abby's more elderly admirers, and Mrs Grayshott, with her daughter, Lavinia, who was Fanny's chief crony. The two girls soon had their heads together; and while Abby gracefully countered the General's gallantries Selina, who was sometimes felt to take more interest in the affairs of strangers than in those of her family, engaged Mrs Grayshott in earnest conversation, the object of her sympathetic enquiries being to discover whether Mrs Grayshott had received any news of her only son, last heard of in Calcutta, but living in daily expectation of embarking on the long journey home to England. The look of anxiety on Mrs Grayshott's rather care-worn face deepened as she shook her head, and replied, with a resolute smile: 'Not yet. But my brother has assured me that he has made every imaginable arrangement for his comfort, and I'm persuaded it can't be long now before he will be with me again. My brother has been so good! Had it been possible, I really believe he would have sent his own doctor out to Oliver! He blames himself for that dreadful sickness, you know, but that is nonsensical. Oliver was very willing to go to India, and how, I ask him, could *he* have foreseen that the poor boy's constitution was so ill-suited to the climate? *I* did not, for he has always enjoyed excellent health.'

'Ah!' said Selina mournfully. 'If only it may not have been ruined by this sad misfortune!'

Her tone held out no hope for the future; and as she went on to recount the dismal story of the sufferings endured by just such another case – not *personally* known to her, but he was a cousin of one of her acquaintances, or, if not a cousin, a great *friend*, not that it signified – Mrs Grayshott could only be thankful that the arrival of Miss Butterbank on the scene interrupted the disheartening recital before it had reached its death-bed climax. She was able to escape, and lost no time in doing so. Perceiving that the younger Miss Wendover had just shaken off her elderly admirer, she went to join her, forestalling a gentleman in a blue coat and Angola pantaloons, who was bearing purposefully down upon her. Aware of this, she laughingly begged Abigail's pardon, adding: 'I only wish you cared, Abby!'

'I do, and would liefer by far talk to you, ma'am, than to Mr Dunston! How do you do? Not in very good point, I'm afraid – but don't doubt you will assure me that you're in high force! This is an anxious time for you.'

'Yes, but I know that if – if anything had happened – anything bad – I must have had news of it, so I won't let myself fall into dejection, or post up to London, until my brother sends me word. When *that* happens, I shall cast Lavinia on your hands, and be off. I was so very much obliged to Miss Wendover for offering to take charge of her! But it is you who will do that: you don't object?'

'My dear ma'am, how can you ask? I am naturally cast into the greatest agitation by the very thought of having so onerous a burden thrust upon me! It is only civility that prompts me to say that I shall be charmed to take care of Lavinia.'

Mrs Grayshott smiled, and pressed her hand. 'I knew I might depend on you. I don't think she will be a trouble to you. What I do think – Abby, may I speak frankly to you?'

'If you please! Though I fancy I know what it is that you do think. Fanny?'

Mrs Grayshott nodded. 'You know, then? I'm glad you've come home: I have been feeling a little anxious. Your sister is a dear kind creature, but –'

She hesitated, and Abby said coolly: 'Very true! A dear kind nodcock! She seems to have fallen quite under the spell of this Calverleigh.'

'Well, he – he *is* very engaging,' said Mrs Grayshott reluctantly. 'Only there is something about him which I can't quite like! It is difficult to explain, because I haven't any cause to take him in dislike. Except –' Again she hesitated, but upon being urged to continue, said: 'Abby, no man could be blamed for falling in love with Fanny, but I don't think that a man of principle, so much older than she is, would wish her – far less *urge* her! – to do what might easily set people in a bustle. His attentions are too particular to suit my old-fashioned notions. That makes me into a Bath quiz, I daresay, but you know, my dear, when a man of fashion and address makes a child of Fanny's age the object of his attentions it is not to be wondered at that she should be dazzled into losing her head, or be easily brought to believe that the rules of conduct, in which she has been reared, are outmoded – quite provincial, in fact!'

Abby nodded. 'Such as the impropriety of strolling about the Sydney Gardens with him? Give me a round tale, ma'am! – Have there been other – oh, clandestine meetings?'

'I am afraid so. Oh, nothing of a serious nature, or that is generally known, or – or that you will not speedily put an end to! I might not have spoken to you, if that had been all, for it's no bread-and-butter of mine, and I don't relish the office of being your intelligencer, but I have some reason to think that it is not quite all, and am a great deal too fond of Fanny *not* to tell you that certain things I have learned from what Lavinia – in all innocence! – has let fall, I apprehend that this unfortunate affair may be rather more serious than I had at first supposed. To what extent Lavinia is in Fanny's confidence I don't know, and – I must confess – shrink from enquiring, because perhaps, if she thought I was trying to discover a secret reposed in her, she would fob me off, even prevaricate, and certainly, in the future, guard her tongue when she talked to me. That may seem foolish to you: the thing is she has been so close a companion to me, so open and trusting in her affection –' Her voice became suspended. She shook her head, saying, after a moment's struggle: 'I can't explain it to you!'

'There is not the least need,' Abby responded. 'I understand you perfectly, ma'am. Don't fear me! I promise you I shan't let Fanny so much as suspect that Lavinia betrayed her confidence. Let me be frank with you! I've every reason to suppose that Calverleigh is a fortune-hunter, and it has been made abundantly clear to me that Fanny believes herself to have formed a lasting passion for him. I don't know if Calverleigh hopes to win my brother's consent to the match, but I should very much doubt it. So in what sort is the wind? Does he hope to enlist my support? Is he indulging himself with a flirtation? Or has he the intention of eloping with Fanny?' Her eyes widened, as she saw the quick look turned towards her, and a laugh trembled in her throat. 'My dear ma'am – ! I was only funning!'

'Yes, I know, but – Abby, sometimes I wonder if our parents were right when they forbade us to read novels! It is all the fault of the Circulating Libraries!'

'Putting romantical notions into girls' heads?' said Abby, smiling a little. 'I don't think so: I had a great many myself, and was never permitted to read any but the most improving works. I might be wrong, but I fancy that however much a girl may admire, or envy, the heroine of some romance, who finds herself in the most *extraordinary* situations; and however much she may picture herself in those situations, she knows it is nothing more than a child's game of make-believe, and that she would not, in fact, behave at all like her heroine. Like my sister's children, when they capture me in the shrubbery, and inform me that they are brigands, and mean to hold me to ransom!'

Her smile was reflected in Mrs Grayshott's eyes, but she sighed, and said: 'It may be so – I don't know! But when a girl falls in love, and with – oh, with what they call a man of the town! – who is practised in the art of seduction – ?'

'Well, I don't know either,' said Abby, 'but it occurs to me, ma'am, that your man of the town, assuming him to be in search of a fortune, would scarcely choose a girl four years short of her majority! Indeed, eight years short of it, because Fanny will not come into full possession of her inheritance until she is five-and-twenty. I'm not very well informed in such matters, but would not that be rather too long to – to live on the expectation?'

'Is he aware of this?' Mrs Grayshott asked. 'Does Fanny know it?'

Abby's eyes, swiftly raised, held an arrested expression. She said, after a moment's pause: 'No. That is, the question has never arisen. I don't know, but I should suppose she doesn't. I see that it must be my business to enlighten Calverleigh – if it should be necessary to do so. Meanwhile, –'

'Meanwhile,' said Mrs Grayshott, with a significant smile, 'Mr Dunston is advancing towards us, determined to wrest you from me, and so I shall take my leave of you! Don't think me impertinent if I say how much I wish I could see *you* happily established, Abby!'

She moved away as she spoke, leaving the road open to the gentleman in the blue coat and Angola pantaloons, who came up, saying simply: 'You have come back at last! Bath has been a desert without you.'

She turned this off with a laughing rejoinder; and, after enquiring politely how his mother did, and exchanging a little trivial conversation with him, said mendaciously that she saw her sister beckoning to her, and left him.

Miss Wendover, who had observed with satisfaction the presence of Mr Dunston in the Pump Room, sighed. Like Mrs Grayshott, she wished very much to see Abby happily established, and could think of no one who would make her a better husband than Peter Dunston. He was a very respectable man, the owner of a comfortable property situated not many miles from Bath; his manners were easy and agreeable; and Miss Wendover had it on the authority of his widowed mother, who resided with him, that his amiability was only rivalled by the elegance of his mind, and the superiority of his understanding. Such was the excellence of his character that he had never caused his mother to suffer a moment's anxiety. One might have supposed that Abby, in imminent danger of dwindling into an old maid, would have welcomed the addresses of so eligible a suitor, instead of declaring she had never been able to feel the least tendre for men of uniform virtues.

She certainly felt none for Peter Dunston, but Miss Wendover was mistaken when she suspected, in moods of depression, that her dear but perverse sister had set her face against marriage.

Abby was fully alive to the disadvantages of her situation, and she had more than once considered the possibility of accepting an offer from Mr Dunston. He would be a kind, if unexciting husband; he enjoyed all the comfort and consequence of a large house and an easy fortune; and in marrying him she would remain within reach of Selina. On the other hand, no romance would attend such a marriage, and Abby, who, in her salad days had declined the flattering offer made her by Lord Broxbourne, still believed that somewhere there existed the man for whom she would feel much more than mere friendly liking. She had once believed, too, that she was bound, sooner or later, to encounter him. She had never done so, and it had begun to seem unlikely that she ever would; but without indulging morbid repinings she was disinclined to accept a substitute who could only be second-best in her eyes.

At the moment, however, her mind was not exercised by this question, being fully occupied by the more important problem of how best, and most painlessly, to detach Fanny from the undesirable Mr Calverleigh. Mrs Grayshott was no tattlemonger; and since she had a great deal of reserve Abby knew that only a stringent sense of duty could have forced her to overcome her distaste of talebearing. What she knew, either from her own observation, or from the innocent disclosures of her daughter, she plainly thought to be too serious to be withheld from Fanny's aunt. At the same time, thought Abigail, dispassionately considering her, the well-bred calm of her manners concealed an over-anxious disposition, which led her to magnify possible dangers. The tragic circumstances of her life, coupled as they were with a sickly constitution, had not encouraged her in optimism. Married to an officer of the Line, and the mother of three hopeful children, she had endured years of separation, always looking forward to a blissful reunion, until her dreams were shattered by the news of Captain Grayshott's death, during the Siege of Burgos. This blow was followed, less than a year later, by the illness, and lingering death of her younger son, and the break-down of her own health, so that it was hardly surprising that she should be readier to foresee disaster than a happy outcome.

Not that she ever betrayed her lowness of spirit. If she could be brought to speak of her trials, which was seldom, and only to a few trusted friends, she said that she was by far more fortunate than many soldiers' widows, because she had been supported throughout by her brother, of whose affection and generosity she could not speak without emotion. He was an East India merchant – but, as the highest and most antiquated sticklers in Bath acknowledged, a most gentlemanly person – and a bachelor, commonly said to be rolling in riches. Not only had he coaxed and bullied his sister into accepting an allowance from him which enabled her to establish herself with modest elegance in Edgar Buildings, but he had claimed the right to maintain his surviving nephew at Rugby, and his only niece at Miss Trimble's select seminary in Bath. It was generally supposed that Oliver Grayshott was destined to be his heir, and although there were those who thought it rather too bad of Mr Balking to have sent his poor sister's sole remaining son to India, it was almost universally agreed that she would have been culpably in the wrong had she refused to be parted from him.

She had not done so, and now, as several persons had foreseen from the outset, he was returning to her, if not at death's door, at the best in a state of total collapse.

Abby, blessed with a cheerful mind, took a more optimistic view of Oliver's case, but she did realise the anxiety which Mrs Grayshott must be feeling, and was inclined to think that the consequent agitation of her nerves might well have led her to exaggerate the strength of Fanny's infatuation.

The following three days did nothing to promote such a comfortable notion. There could be no doubt that Fanny, dazzled by the attentions of a London beau, had plunged headlong into her first love-affair, and was ripe for any outrageous folly. Wholly unpractised in the art of dissimulation, her spasmodic attempts to appear unconcerned betrayed her youth, and might, under different circumstances, have amused

Abby. But it was not long before Abby found much more to dismay than to amuse her. She was herself impulsive, often impatient of convention, and, in her girlhood, rebellious, but she had been reared far more strictly than Fanny, and it came as a disagreeable shock to her when she discovered that Fanny watched for the postman every day, and, at the first glimpse of his scarlet coat and cockaded hat, slipped out of the room to intercept the delivery of letters to the house. Never, at her most rebellious, had Abby dreamed of engaging in clandestine correspondence! Such conduct, if it were known, must sink Fanny below reproach. Every feeling was offended; and had she not been tolerably certain, from Fanny's downcast looks, that no letter from Mr Calverleigh had reached her she thought she must have abandoned caution, and taken the girl roundly to task. At first inclined to give Mr Calverleigh credit for propriety, a little quiet reflection made her realise that if marriage was indeed his object he would scarcely commit an act of such folly as to write letters to Fanny which would be more than likely to fall into the hands of her aunts. His aim must be to propitiate Fanny's guardians; and in his dealings with Selina he had shown that he knew it. Abby thought that he had succeeded all too well. Selina had been very much shocked by the disclosures made to her, but she hoped, in a nebulous way, that perhaps, after all, they would be found to be untrue; and she was moved to what Abby considered an excess of sensibility by the spectacle of her niece running to look eagerly out of the window every time a vehicle drew up outside the house. 'Poor, poor child!' she mourned. 'It is so very affecting! I do not know how you can remain unmoved! I had not thought you so – so *unfeeling*, Abby!'

'I'm not unmoved,' responded Abby crossly. 'I am most deeply moved – with a strong desire to give Fanny the finest trimming of her life! I'd do it, too, if I didn't fear that it would encourage her in the belief that she is a persecuted heroine!'

In this noble resolve to abstain from gratifying her desire she was strengthened by Fanny's reception of the only piece of advice she permitted herself to give that love-lorn damsel: that she should not wear her heart on her sleeve. Chin up, eyes flashing, flying her colours in her cheeks, Fanny said: 'I am not ashamed of loving Stacy! Why should I dissemble?'

Quite a number of pungent retorts rose to Abby's tongue, and it said much for her self-control that she uttered none of them. Intuition had made Fanny suspect already that her favourite aunt was ranged on the side of Stacy Calverleigh's enemies; she was slightly on the defensive, not yet hostile, but ready to show hackle. No useful purpose would be served by coming to cuffs with her, Abby thought, and therefore held her peace.

Three

*M*r Calverleigh did not reappear in Bath that week, nor did he write to Fanny. Abby began to entertain the hope that a mountain had indeed been made out of a molehill, and that he had merely been amusing himself with a flirtation; and could have borne with tolerable equanimity Fanny's wilting demeanour had it not been disclosed to her by the amiable Lady Weaverham that her ladyship had received a very proper letter from him, excusing himself from dining with her on the following Wednesday, but stating that he would certainly be in Bath again by the end of the next week, when he would call in Lower Camden Place to proffer his apologies in person.

This piece of news applied a damper to Abby's optimism. Her spirits were further depressed by the announcement by Selina, in the thread of a voice, that she had contracted a putrid sore throat, accompanied by fever, a severe headache, and a colicky disorder. She had not closed her eyes all night, and could only hope that these distressing symptoms did not presage an illness which, if not immediately fatal, would leave her to drag out the rest of her life between her bed and a sofa. Abby did not share these gloomy apprehensions, but she lost no time in sending for the latest practitioner to enjoy Selina's favour. She begged him not to encourage the sufferer to think herself hovering on the brink of the grave. He promised to reassure Selina, and very nearly lost his most lucrative patient by telling her, in hearty accents, that nothing worse had befallen her than what he was tactless enough to term a *touch of influenza*. Before he had time to prophesy a speedy recovery he realised that he had fallen into error, and, with a dexterity which (in spite of herself) Abby was obliged to acknowledge, retrieved his position by saying that, although he would ordinarily consider the illness trifling, when it attacked persons of such frail constitution as Miss Wendover the greatest care must be exercised to ensure that no serious consequences should attend it. He recommended her to remain in bed; promised to send her within the hour a saline draught; approved of such remedies as extract of malt for a possible cough; goat's whey, to guard against consumption; laudanum drops in case of insomnia; and a diet of mutton-broth, tapioca-jelly, and barley-water, all of which she had herself suggested; and left the sickroom tolerably certain that he had restored her wavering faith in his skill. He told Abby, apologetically, that neither these remedies nor the depressing diet would do any harm, and with this she had to be content, resigning herself to the inevitable, and deriving what consolation she could from the reflection that for some days at least there was no danger that while she danced attendance on her sister Mr Calverleigh would be strengthening his hold on Fanny's youthful affections.

The eldest Miss Wendover showed every sign of enjoying a protracted illness, for although the fever soon abated she maintained a ticklish cough, and, after an attack of heart-burn, threw out so many dark hints to her entourage about cardiac nerves that Fanny became quite alarmed, and asked Abby if poor Aunt Selina's heart had indeed been affected.

'No, dear: not at all!' responded Abby cheerfully.

'But – Abby, I have sometimes wondered if – Abby, does my aunt *like* to be ill?'

'Yes, certainly she does. Why not? She has very little to divert her, after all! It makes her the centre of attention, too, and how unkind it would be to grudge it to her! The melancholy truth is, my love, that single females of her age are almost compelled to adopt dangerous diseases, if they wish to be objects of interest. Not only spinsters, either! You must surely have observed how many matrons, whose children are all married, and who are so comfortably situated that they have really nothing very much to do, develop the most *interesting* disorders!'

Her eyes as round as saucers, Fanny asked: 'Do you mean that my aunt will lie on a sofa for the rest of her life?'

'No, no!' said Abby. 'Sooner or later something will happen to give her thoughts a new direction, and you will be surprised to see how quickly she will recover!'

In the event, this happened rather sooner than could have been expected. Shortly after noon one day, Abby entered her room to find her seated bolt upright on the day-bed, to which, supported by her maid, she had tottered an hour before, eagerly perusing the crossed sheet of a letter just delivered by the post.

'Oh, dearest, *whatever* do you think?' she exclaimed, in accents startlingly unlike those with which she had greeted her sister earlier in the day. 'The Leavenings are coming to spend the winter in Bath! Good God, they may have arrived already! Mrs Leavening writes that they mean to put up at the York House while they look about them for lodgings, and depend upon us to advise them, for they were never in Bath before, you know! I wonder if the lodgings the Thursleys hired in Westgate Building – but they are in the *lower* part of the town, of course, and though it is a broad street – and anything *here*, or in Pulteney Street, or Laura Place, *might* be above their price – not that Mrs Leavening tells what is the figure they have in mind, but I shouldn't suppose Mr Leavening's fortune to be more than *genteel*, would you?'

'My dear, since I haven't the least guess who the Leavenings may be, I can't answer you!' replied Abby, her eyes alight with laughter.

Miss Wendover was shocked. 'Abby! How *can* you have forgotten? From Bedfordshire – our *own* county! Almost our neighbours! *He* had a wart on his left cheek – such a pity! – but in all other respects *quite* unexceptionable! Or am I thinking of Mr Tarvin? Yes, I fancy it was he who had the wart, which makes it even more delightful, for there is something *about* warts, isn't there? Dearest, I wish you will go to York House this afternoon! So unfriendly not to welcome them immediately, and I wouldn't for the world have Mrs Leavening suspect that we had forgotten her! You will tell her how happy I am to hear of her arrival, and explain how it comes about that I am unable to visit her myself – not but what I am a great deal stronger today, and I daresay I may be able to come downstairs tomorrow. And if you were to walk up Milsom Street, Abby, you could pop into Godwin's, to discover if they haven't yet received that book Mrs Grayshott told me I should enjoy. It is called the Knight of something or other – not, of course, that I am an *advocate* for novel-reading. Perhaps Mrs Leavening would come and sit with me for a little while tomorrow. What a lot she will have to tell us about our old friends, which James and Cornelia *never* do! I declare, it has put me in spirits only to think of it! We must hold one of our evening-parties, dearest! I shall occupy myself in making out a list of the people to be invited while you are in the town.' She added kindly: 'Such a fine afternoon as it is! It will do you good to take a walk, dearest. You have been cooped up with me for too long.'

Abby was too glad to promote these cheerful plans to raise any objection to Miss Wendover's disposal of her afternoon, which she had meant to have spent in quite another manner. Fanny had been persuaded to join a party of her friends on an expedition to Claverton Down, so Abby presently set forth alone on her two errands. Neither was successful: Godwin's Circulating Library was still unable to supply Miss Wendover with a copy of Mrs Porter's latest novel; and although Mr and Mrs Leavening were expected to arrive that day at York House they had not yet done so, and were scarcely looked for until dinner-time. Abby declined a civil invitation to await their coming in one of the hotel's lounges, began to deliver a verbal message for them, and then thought that Selina would say that she ought to have written a note. She went into the lounge on one side of the hall, and sat down at one of its two writing-tables to perform this duty. There was no one in the room, but just as she was about to seal her brief letter with a wafer found in one of the table's drawers she heard the sounds betokening an arrival, and paused, wondering if it could be the Leavenings. But only one person entered the hotel, a man, as she perceived, catching a glimpse of him through the open doorway. She fixed the wafer, and was writing the direction on the note when she saw, out of the corner of her eye, that he had strolled into the room. She paid no heed, but was startled, the next instant, by hearing someone in the hall command the boots to carry Mr Calverleigh's portmanteaux up to No. 12.

Taken thus by surprise, it was several moments before she was able to decide whether to make herself known to him, or to await a formal introduction. The strict propriety in which she had been reared urged her to adopt the latter course; then she remembered that she was not a young girl any longer, but a guardian-aunt, and one sufficiently advanced in years to be able to accost a strange gentleman without running the risk of being thought shockingly forward. She had wondered how she could contrive, without Fanny's knowledge, to talk privately to Mr Calverleigh, and here, by a veritable stroke of providence, was her opportunity. To flinch before what would certainly be an extremely disagreeable interview would be the act, she told herself, of a pudding-heart. Bracing herself resolutely, she got up from the writing-table, and turned, saying, in a cool, pleasant tone: 'Mr Calverleigh?'

He had picked up a newspaper from the table in the centre of the room, and was glancing through it, but he lowered it, and looked enquiringly across at her. His eyes, which were deep-set and of a light grey made the more striking by the swarthiness of his complexion, held an expression of faint surprise; he said: 'Yes?'

If he was surprised, Abby was wholly taken aback. She had formed no very precise mental picture of him, but nothing she had been told had led her to expect to be confronted with a tall, loose-limbed man, considerably older than she was herself, with harsh features in a deeply lined face, a deplorably sallow skin, and not the smallest air of fashion. He was wearing a coat which fitted too easily across his very broad shoulders for modishness, with buckskins and topboots; his neck-tie was almost negligently arranged; no fobs or seals dangled at his waist; and his shirt-points were not only extremely moderate, but even a little limp.

She was so much astonished that for a full minute she could only stare at him, her brain in a whirl. He had been described to her as a young, handsome town-beau, and he was nothing of the sort. He had also been described, by her brother-in-law, as a loose fish, and that she could far more readily believe: there was a suggestion of devil-may-care about him, and these deeply carven lines in his lean countenance might well (she supposed) betray dissipation. But what there was in him to have captivated Fanny – and Selina too! – she found herself quite unable to imagine. Then, as she continued to stare at him, she saw that a look of amusement had crept into his face, and that a smile was quivering at the corners of his mouth, and she perceived very clearly why Fanny had allowed herself to be fascinated by him. But, even as an answering smile was irresistibly drawn from her, it occurred to her that Selina, even in her sillier moments, would scarcely refer to a man of her own age as *a very pretty-behaved young man*, and she exclaimed, with that impetuosity so frequently deplored by the elder members of her family: 'Oh, I beg your pardon! I mistook – I mean, – I mean – *Are* you Mr Calverleigh?'

'Well, I've never been given any reason to suppose that I'm not!' he replied.

'You *are?* But *surely* – ?' Recollecting herself, Abby broke off, and said, with all the composure at her command: 'I must tell you, sir, that I am Miss Wendover!'

She observed, with satisfaction, that this disclosure exercised a powerful effect upon him. That disturbing smile vanished, and his black brows suddenly snapped together. He ejaculated: 'Miss *who?*'

'Miss Wendover,' she repeated, adding, for his further enlightenment: 'Miss *Abigail* Wendover!'

'Good God!' For a moment, he appeared to be startled, and

then, as his curiously light eyes scanned her, he disconcerted her by saying: 'I like that! It becomes you, too.'

Roused to indignation, Abby, losing sight of the main issue, allowed herself to be lured into retorting: 'Thank you! I am excessively obliged to you! It is an outdated name, commonly used to signify a maidservant! *You* may like it, but I do not!' She added hastily: 'Nor, sir, did I make myself known to you for the purpose of discussing my name!'

'Of course not!' he said, so soothingly that she longed to hit him. 'Do tell me what it is you *do* wish to discuss! I'll oblige you to the best of my power, even though I don't immediately understand why you should wish to discuss anything with me. Forgive me! – I've no social graces! – but have I ever met you before?'

'No,' replied Abby, her lips curling in a contemptuous smile. 'You have not, sir – as well you know! But you will scarcely deny that you are acquainted with another member of my family!'

'Oh, no! I won't deny that!' he assured her. 'Won't you sit down?'

'I, sir,' said Abby, ignoring this invitation, 'am Fanny's aunt!'

'No, are you indeed? You don't look old enough to be anyone's aunt,' he remarked.

This piece of audacity was uttered in the most casual way, as though it had been a commonplace instead of an impertinence. He did not seem to have any idea that he had said anything improper, nor, from his general air of indifference, could she suppose him to have intended a compliment. She began to think that he was a very strange man, and one with whom it was going to be more difficult to deal than she had foreseen. He was obviously fencing with her, and the sooner he was made to realise that such tactics would not answer the better it would be. So she said coldly: 'You must know very well that I am Fanny's aunt.'

'Yes, you've just told me so,' he agreed.

'You knew it as soon as I made made myself known to you!' She checked herself, determined not to lose her temper, and said, as pleasantly as she could: 'Come, Mr Calverleigh! let us be

40

frank! I imagine you also know why I did make myself known to you. You certainly contrived to ingratiate yourself with my sister, but you can hardly have supposed that you would find *all* Fanny's relations so complaisant!'

He was watching her rather intently, but with an expression of enjoyment which she found infuriating. He said: 'No, I couldn't, could I? Still, if your *sister* likes me – !'

'My sister, Mr Calverleigh, was not aware, until I enlightened her, that you are not, as she had supposed, a man of character, but one of – of an unsavoury reputation!' she snapped.

'Well, what an unhandsome thing to have done!' he said reproachfully. 'Doesn't she like me any more?'

Abby now made the discovery that it was possible, at one and the same time, to be furiously angry, and to have the greatest difficulty in suppressing an almost irresistible desire to burst out laughing. After a severe struggle, she managed to say: 'This – this is useless, sir! Let me assure you that you have no hope whatever of gaining the consent of Fanny's guardian to your proposal; and let me also tell you that she will not come into possession of her inheritance until she is five-and-twenty! That, I collect, is something you were not aware of!'

'No,' he admitted. 'I wasn't!'

'Until that date,' Abby continued, 'her fortune is under the sole control of her guardian, and he, I must tell you, will not, under any circumstances, relinquish that control into the hands of her husband one moment before her twenty-fifth birthday, if she marries without his consent and approval. I think it doubtful, even, that he would continue to allow her to receive any part of the income accruing from her fortune. Not a very good bargain, sir, do you think?'

'It seems to be a very bad one. Who, by the way, *is* Fanny's guardian?'

'Her uncle, of course! Surely she must have told you so?' replied Abby impatiently.

'Well, no!' he said, still more apologetically. 'She really had no opportunity to do so!'

'Had no – Mr Calverleigh, are you asking me to believe that you – you embarked on this attempt to recover your own fortune without first discovering what were the exact terms of her father's will? That is coming it very much too strong!'

'Who *was* her father?' he interrupted, regarding her from under suddenly frowning brows. 'You talk of her inheritance – You don't mean to tell me she's *Rowland* Wendover's daughter?'

'Yes – if it should be necessary for me to do so – which I strongly doubt!' said Abby, eyeing him with hostility. 'She is an orphan, and the ward of my brother James.'

'Poor girl!' He studied her appraisingly. 'So you are a sister of Rowland Wendover! You know, I find that very hard to believe.'

'Indeed! It is nevertheless true – though in what way it concerns the point at issue –'

'Oh, it doesn't!' he said, smiling disarmingly at her. 'Now I come to think of it, he had several sisters, hadn't he? I expect you must be the youngest of them. He was older than I was, and you are a mere child. By the by, when did he die?'

This question, put to her in a tone of casual interest, seemed to her to be so inapposite that the suspicion that he was drunk occurred to her. He showed none of the recognisable signs of inebriation, but she knew that her experience was limited. If he was not drunk, the only other explanation of his quite fantastic behaviour must be that he was slightly deranged. Unless he was trying, in some obscure fashion, to set her at a disadvantage? She found it impossible to understand what he hoped to gain by his extraordinary tactics, but the look of amusement on his face made her feel, uneasily, that he had an end in view: probably an unscrupulous end. Watching him closely, she said: 'My brother died twelve years ago. I *am* his youngest sister, but you are mistaken in thinking me *a mere child*. I daresay you wish I were!'

'No, I don't. Why should I?' he asked, mildly surprised.

'Because you might find it easier to flummery me!'

'But I don't want to flummery you!'

'Just as well!' she retorted. 'You wouldn't succeed! I am more than eight-and-twenty, Mr Calverleigh!'

'Well, that seems like a child to me. How much more?'

She was by now extremely angry, but for the second time she was obliged to choke back an involuntary giggle. She said unsteadily: 'Talking to you is like – like talking to an eel!'

'No, is it? I've never tried to talk to an eel. Isn't it a waste of time?'

She choked. 'Not such a waste of time as talking to you!'

'You're surely not going to tell me that eels find you more entertaining than I do?' he said incredulously.

That was rather too much for her: she did giggle, and was furious with herself for having done so.

'That's better!' he said approvingly.

She recovered herself. 'Let me ask you one question, sir! If *I* seem like a child to you, in what light do you regard a girl of seventeen?'

'Oh, as a member of the infantry!'

This careless reply made her gasp. Her eyes flashed; she demanded: 'How old do you think my niece is, pray?'

'Never having met your niece, I haven't a notion!'

'Never having – But – Good God, then you cannot be Mr Calverleigh! But when I asked you, you said you *were*!'

'Of course I did! Tell me, is there a nephew of mine at large in Bath?'

'*Nephew?* A – a Mr Stacy Calverleigh!'

'Yes, that's it. I'm his Uncle Miles.'

'*Oh!*' she uttered, staring at him in the liveliest astonishment. 'You can't mean that you are the one who – ' She broke off in some confusion, and added hurriedly: 'The one who went to India!'

He laughed. 'Yes, I'm the black sheep of the family!'

She blushed, but said: 'I wasn't going to say that!'

'Weren't you? Why not? You won't hurt my feelings!'

'I wouldn't be so uncivil! And if it comes to *black sheep* – !'

'Once you become entangled with Calverleighs, it's bound to,' he said. 'We came to England with the Conqueror, you know. It's my belief that our ancestor was one of the thatchgallows

43

he brought with him. There were any number of 'em in his train.'

A delicious gurgle of laughter broke from her. 'Oh, no, were there? I didn't know – but I never heard anyone claim a *thatch-gallows* for his ancestor!'

'No, I don't suppose you did. *I* never met any of us *came over-with-the-Conquest* fellows who wouldn't hold to it, buckle and thong, that his ancestor was a Norman baron. Just as likely to have been one of the scaff and raff of Europe. I wish you will sit down!'

At this point, Abby knew that it behoved her to take polite leave of Mr Miles Calverleigh. She sat down, offering her conscience a sop in the form of a hope that Mr Miles Calverleigh might be of assistance to her in circumventing the designs of his nephew. She chose one of the straight-backed chairs ranged round the table, and watched him dispose his long limbs in another, at right-angles to her. His attitude was as negligent as his conversation, for he crossed his legs, dug one hand into his pocket, and laid his other arm along the table. He seemed to have very little regard for the conventions governing polite conduct, and Abby, in whom the conventions were deeply inculcated, was far less shocked than amused. Her expressive eyes twinkled engagingly as she said: 'May I speak frankly to you, sir? About your nephew? I do not wish to offend you, but I fancy he is more the black sheep of your family than you are!'

'Oh, I shouldn't think so at all!' he responded. 'He sounds more like a cawker to me, if he's making up to a girl who won't come into her inheritance for eight years!'

'I have every reason to think,' said Abby frostily, 'that my niece is not the first heiress he has – as you phrase it! – *made up to*!'

'Well, if he's hanging out for a rich wife I don't suppose she is.'

Her fingers tightened round the handle of her parasol. 'Mr Calverleigh, I have not yet met your nephew. He came to Bath while I was away, visiting my sisters, and was called to London, on matters of business, I am told, before I returned. My hope is that he has realised that his – his suit is hopeless, and won't come back, but *your* presence in Bath quite dashes that hope, since I collect you must have come here in the expectation of seeing him.'

'Oh, no!' he assured her. 'Whatever put that notion into your head?'

She blinked. 'I assumed – well, *naturally* I assumed that you had come in search of him! I mean, – so close a relative, and, I understand, the only member of your immediate family still living – ?'

'What of it? You know, fiddle-faddle about families and close relatives is so much humbug! I haven't seen that nephew of mine since he was a grubby brat – if I saw him then, which very likely I didn't, for I never went near my brother if I could avoid it – so why the devil should I want to see him now?'

She could think of no answer to this, but it seemed to her so ruthless that she wondered, remembering that he had been packed off to India in disgrace, whether it arose from feelings of rancour. However, his next words, which were uttered in a thoughtful tone, and quite dispassionately, lent no colour to her suspicion. He said: 'You know, there's a great deal of balderdash talked about family affection. How much affection have you for *your* family?'

Such a question had never before been put to her; and, since it was one of the accepted tenets that one loved and respected one's parents, and (at the least) loved one's brothers and sisters, she had not previously considered the matter. But just as she was about to assure this outrageous person that she was devoted to every member of her family the unendearing images rose before her mind's eye of her father, of her two brothers, and even of her sister Jane. She said, a little ruefully: 'For my mother, and for two of my sisters, a great deal.'

'Ah, I never had any sisters, and my mother died when I was a schoolboy.'

'You are much to be pitied,' she said.

'Oh, no, I don't think so!' he replied. 'I don't like obligations.'

The disarming smile crept back into his eyes, as they rested on her face. 'My family disowned me more than twenty years ago, you know!'

'Yes, I did know. That is – I have been told that they did,' she said. She added, with the flicker of a shy smile: 'I think it was a *dreadful* thing to have done, and – and perhaps is the reason why you don't wish to meet your nephew?'

That made him laugh. 'Good God, no! What concern was it of his?'

'I only thought – wondered – since it was his father –'

'No, no, that's fustian!' he expostulated. 'You can't turn me into an object for compassion! I didn't like my brother Humphrey, and I didn't like my father either, but I don't bear them any grudge for shipping me off to India. In fact, it was the best thing they could do, and it suited me very well.'

'Compassion certainly seems to be wasted on you, sir!' she said tartly.

'Yes, of course it is. Besides, I like you, and I shan't if you pity me.'

She was goaded into swift retort. 'Well, that wouldn't trouble me!'

'That's the barber!' he said appreciatively. 'Tell me more about this niece of yours! I collect her mother's dead too?'

'Her mother died when she was two years old, sir.'

There was an inscrutable expression in his face, and although he kept his eyes on hers the fancy struck her that he was looking at something a long way beyond her. Then, with a sudden, wry smile, he seemed to bring her into focus again, and asked abruptly: 'Rowland did marry her, didn't he? – Celia Morval?'

'Why, yes! Were you acquainted with her?'

He did not answer this, but said: 'And my nephew is dangling after her daughter?'

'I am afraid it is more serious than that. I haven't met him, but he seems to be a young man of considerable address. He has succeeded in – in fixing his interest with her – well, to speak

46

roundly, sir, she imagines herself to be violently in love with him. You may think that no great matter, as young as she is, but the thing is that she is a high-spirited girl, and her character is – is determined. She has been virtually in my charge – and that of my eldest sister – from her childhood. Perhaps she has been too much indulged – granted too much independence. I was never used to think so – you see, I was myself – we all were! – brought up in such subjection that I vowed I wouldn't allow Fanny to be crushed as we were. I even thought – knowing how much I was used to long for the courage to rebel, and how bitterly I resented my father's tyranny – that if I encouraged her to be independent, to look on me as a friend rather than as an aunt, she wouldn't *feel* rebellious – would allow herself to be guided by me.'

'And she doesn't?' he asked sympathetically.

'Not in this instance. But until your nephew bewitched her she did! She's the dearest girl, but I own that she can be headstrong, and too impetuous.' She paused, and then said ruefully: 'Once she makes up her mind it is very hard to turn her from it. She – she isn't a *lukewarm* girl! It is one of the things I particularly like in her, but it is quite disastrous in this instance!'

'Infatuated, is she? I daresay she'll recover,' he said, a suggestion of boredom in his voice.

'Undoubtedly! My fear is that she may do so too late! Mr Calverleigh, if your nephew were the most eligible bachelor in the country I should be opposed to the match! She is by far too young to be thinking of marriage. As it is, I need not, I fancy, scruple to tell you that he is *not* eligible! He bears a most shocking reputation, and, apart from all else, I believe him to be a fortune-hunter!'

'Very likely, I should think,' he nodded.

This cool rejoinder made it necessary for her to keep a firm hand on the rein of her temper. She said, in a dry voice: '*You* may regard that with complaisance, sir, but I do not!'

'No, I don't suppose you do,' he agreed amiably.

She flushed. 'And – which is of even more importance! – nor does my brother!'

This seemed to revive his interest. A gleam came into his eyes. 'What, does he know of this?'

'Yes, sir, he does know of it, and nothing, I assure you, could exceed his dislike of such a connection! It was he who told me what had been happening here, in Bath, during my absence, having himself learnt of it through someone who chances to be a close friend of his wife. He posted up to London from Bedfordshire to apprise me of it. Pray do not think I exaggerate when I say that I have seldom seen him more profoundly shocked, or – or heard him express himself with so much violence! Believe me, sir, *nothing* could prevail upon him to give his consent to your nephew's proposal!'

'I do – implicitly!' he replied, the light of unholy amusement in his eyes. 'What's more, I'd give a monkey to have seen him! Lord, how funny!'

'It was not in the least funny! And –'

'Yes, it was, but never mind that! Why should you fall into a fuss? If the virtuous James forbids the banns, and if my nephew is a fortune-hunter, depend upon it he will cry off!' He saw the doubt in her face, and said: 'You don't think so?'

She hesitated. 'I don't know. It may be that he hopes to win James over –'

'Well, he won't do that!'

'No. Unless – Mr Calverleigh, I have reason – some reason – to fear that he might persuade her into an *elopement*! Thinking that once the knot was tied my brother would be obliged – ' She stopped as he broke into a shout of laughter, and said indignantly: 'It may seem *funny* to you, but I promise you –'

'It does! What a subject for a roaring farce! History repeats itself – with a vengeance!'

Wholly bewildered, she demanded: 'What do you mean? What can you *possibly* mean?'

'My pretty innocent,' he said, in a voice of kindess spiced with mockery, 'did no one ever tell you that *I* am the man who ran off with your Fanny's mother?'

Four

*I*t was a full minute before Abby could collect her startled wits enough to enable her to speak, and when she did speak it was not entirely felicitously. She exclaimed: 'Then I was right! And *you* are it!'

With every appearance of enjoyment, he instantly replied: 'Until I know what *it* signifies, I reserve my defence.'

'The skeleton in the cupboard! Only I told Selina it would prove to be no more than the skeleton of a mouse!'

'You lied, then! The skeleton of a black sheep if you wish, but *not* that of a mouse – even a black mouse!'

Her voice quivered on the edge of laughter. 'No, indeed! How – how *very* dreadful! But how – when – Oh, do, pray, *tell* me!'

'You shock me Miss Abigail Wendover! – you know, I *do* like that name! – Who am I to divulge the secret which has been so carefully guarded?'

'The skeleton, of course!'

'But skeletons don't talk!' he pointed out.

Preoccupied with her own thoughts, she paid no heed to this, but said suddenly: '*That* was why James flew into such a stew! Now, isn't it *like* James not to have told me the truth?'

'Exactly like him!'

'But why didn't George – No, you may depend upon it that he didn't know either! Because Mary doesn't, though she has always suspected, as I did, that there was something about Celia which was being kept secret. I wonder if Selina knew? Not the whole, of

49

course, for if she had she would never have encouraged your nephew, would she?'

'Oh, no! *She* wouldn't, and very likely *Mary* wouldn't either, but *George*, I feel, is another matter. Do enlighten me! Who *are* these people?'

She blinked. 'Who – ? Oh, I beg your pardon! I have been running on in the stupidest way! – talking to myself! Selina is my eldest sister: we live together, in Sydney Place; Mary is my *next* sister: next in age, I mean; and George Brede is her husband. Never mind that! *When* did you run off with Celia?'

'Oh, when she became engaged to be married to Rowland!' he answered, very much as if this were a matter of course.

'Good God! Do you mean that you *abducted* her?' she gasped.

'No, I don't recall that I ever abducted anyone,' he said, giving the matter his consideration. 'In fact, I'm sure of it. An unwilling bride would be the very devil, you know.'

'Well, that's precisely what I've always thought!' she exclaimed, pleased to find her opinion shared. 'Whenever I've read about it, in some trashy romance, I mean. Of course, if the heroine is a rich heiress the case is understandable, but – *Oh!*' Consternation sounded in her voice; painfully mortified, she stammered: 'I beg your pardon! I can't think what made me say –'

'Not at all!' he assured her kindly. 'A very natural observation!'

'Do you mean to tell me that that was why you – you ran off with Celia?' she asked incredulously.

'Well, no! But you must remember that I was very young in those days: halflings seldom have an eye to the main chance. It was All for Love, or the World Well Lost. We fell passionately in love – or, at any hand, we thought we did. You know, this is a damned sickly story! Let us talk of something else!'

'I think it is a sad story. But I don't perfectly understand how it was that Celia became engaged to my brother if she was in love with you?'

'Don't you? You should! Were you acquainted with Morval?'

She shook her head. 'I might perhaps have seen him, but I don't recall: I was only a child at that time. I know he was one of my father's closest friends.'

'Then you ought to be able to form a pretty accurate picture of him. They were as like as fourpence to a groat. The match was made between them. Celia was forbidden ever again to favour me with as much as a common bow in passing – mind you, I wasn't at all eligible – and ordered to accept Rowland's offer.'

'I understand her submission to the first order, but not to the second! I too submitted in a like case. It is not an easy matter to marry against the will of one's parents. But, with one's affections engaged, to accept another man's offer, merely because one's father wished it, is something I do *not* understand! If Celia was ready to elope with you she must have been a girl of spirit, too, and not in the least the meek, biddable creature we always thought her!'

'Oh, no, she hadn't an ounce of steel in her!' he said coolly. 'She was romantical, though, and certainly biddable: one of those pretty, clinging females who invariably yield to a stronger will! I hadn't the wit to perceive it, until the sticking point was reached, and she knuckled down in a flood of tears. And a very good thing she did,' he added. 'We might have carried it, if she had stood buff, and I should have been regularly in for it. I didn't think so at the time, of course, but I was never nearer to dishing myself. How did she deal with Rowland?'

He had stripped the affair of all its romantic pathos, but Abby could not help wondering whether his apparent unconcern hid a bruised heart. She answered his casual question reticently: 'I don't know. I wasn't of an age to know. She was always rather quiet, but she never appeared to be unhappy. I see now that she can't have *loved* Rowland, but I do know that she held him in the greatest respect. I mean, she depended wholly on his judgment, and was for ever saying *Rowland says*, as though that was a clincher to every argument!'

51

The slightly acid note on which she ended made him laugh. 'An opinion not shared by Abigail Wendover, I apprehend!'

'No!' she returned, her eyes kindling reminiscently. 'It was *not* shared by me! Rowland was a – ' She stopped, resolutely shutting her lips together.

'Rowland,' said Miles Calverleigh, stepping obligingly into the gap, 'was a pompous lobcock!'

'Yes!' said Abby, momentarily forgetting herself. 'That is exactly what he was! The most consequential, pot-sure –' Again she broke off short, adding hastily: 'Never mind that!'

'I don't – and it seems that Celia didn't either. No, she wouldn't, of course. You know, the more I think of it the more I feel that they must have been made for each other! Well, I'm glad to know she didn't fall into a green and yellow melancholy.'

Abby's brow was wrinkled. 'Yes, but – Did Rowland *know* of – of the elopement?'

'Oh, lord, yes!' He met her astonished look with a smile of pure derision. 'Come, come, ma'am! Where have your wits gone begging? Celia was an *heiress*! Consider, too, the scandal that would have attended a rupture of the engagement! People must have *talked*, and nothing could have been more obnoxious to a Wendover or a Morval! The affair had to be hushed up, and you must own that a very neat thing they made of it, between the four of them!'

'*Four* of them?'

'That's it: your father, Celia's father, my father, and Rowland,' he explained.

'Respectability!' she ejaculated bitterly. 'Oh, how much I have detested that – that god of my father's idolatry! Did *your* father worship at the same altar?'

'No, what he worshipped was good ton. I wasn't good ton at all, so he was glad of the chance to be rid of me, and I can't say I blame him. I was very expensive, you know.'

'From what I have heard, your brother was even more expensive!' she said. 'I wonder he didn't get rid of *him*!'

He smiled. 'Ah, but Humphrey was his heir! Besides, *his* debts were those of honour: quite unexceptionable, particularly when contracted in clubs of high fashion! He was used to move in the first circles, too, which I – er – didn't!'

'No doubt he would have taken no exception to *his* son's ruinous career!'

'Oh, that doesn't follow at all! Being badly under the hatches himself, he would probably have taken the most violent exception to it. However, he died before Stacy came of age, so we shall never know. Judging by my own experience, Stacy might have got himself into Dun territory at Oxford, but he could scarcely have gone to pigs-and-whistles – unless, of course, he was a regular out-and-outer, which, from what you've told me, he don't seem to be.'

'Were you up at Oxford?' she asked curiously.

'No, I was *down* from Oxford – *sent* down!' he replied affably.

She choked, but managed to say, after a brief struggle: 'What – whatever may have been your youthful f-follies, sir, I must believe that you have outgrown them, and – and I *cannot* think that you would wish your nephew – the head of your house! – to – to retrieve his fortunes by seducing a girl – oh, a *child*! – into a clandestine marriage!'

'But if the poor fellow is rolled-up what else can he do?' he asked.

She said through gritted teeth: 'For all I care, he may do anything he chooses, *except* marry my niece! *Surely – surely* you must perceive how – how *wrong* that would be!'

'I must say, it seems mutton-headed to me,' he agreed. 'He'd do better to fix his interest with a girl who is already in possession of her fortune.'

'Good God, is that *all* you have to say?' she cried.

'Well, what do you expect me to say?' he asked.

'Say! I – I expect you to *do* something!'

'Do what?'

'Put an end to this affair!'

'How?'

'Speak to your nephew – tell him – oh, I don't know! You must be able to think of something!'

'Well, I'm not. Besides, why should I?'

'Because it is your duty! Because he is your nephew!'

'You'll have to think of some better reasons than those. I haven't any duty to Stacy, and I don't suppose I should do it if I had.'

'Mr Calverleigh, you *cannot* wish your nephew to sink himself so utterly below reproach!'

'Wish? I haven't any feelings in the matter at all. In fact, I don't care a straw what he does. So if you are looking to me to rake him down, don't!'

'Oh, you are impossible!' she cried, starting up.

'I daresay, but I'm damned if I'll preach morality to oblige you! A nice cake I should make of myself! I like the way your eyes sparkle when you're angry.'

They positively flashed at this. One fulminating glance she cast at him before turning sharply away, and walking out of the room.

The Leavenings were forgotten; it was not until she had reached Laura Place that she remembered that the note she had written had been left on the writing-table. She could only hope that it would be found, and delivered to Mrs Leavening. By this time her seething anger had abated a little, and she was able to review her encounter with Mr Miles Calverleigh in a more moderate spirit. Slackening her pace, she walked on, into Great Pulteney Street, so deeply preoccupied that she neither acknowledged, nor even saw, the salutation directed towards her from the other side of the street by her clerical admirer, Canon Pinfold: an aberration which caused the Very Reverend gentleman to subject his conscience to a severe search, in an effort to discover in what way he could have offended her.

It was not long before Miss Abigail Wendover, no self-deceiver, realised that she was strangely attracted to the abominable Mr Miles Calverleigh. Out of his own careless mouth he had convicted himself of being a person totally unworthy of respect, but when she recalled the things he had said to her a most reprehensible bubble of laughter rose within her. A very little reflection, however, was enough to bring a blush to her cheeks. It was no laughing matter, and strangely depraved she must be to have felt the smallest inclination to laugh at the cool recital of his misdeeds. She knew that he had been expelled from Eton; he had told her in the most unconcerned way, that he had been sent down from Oxford; and it now appeared that he had crowned his iniquities by attempting to elope with a girl out of the schoolroom. Curiously enough she was less shocked by this escapade than by the rest: he could hardly, she supposed, have been much older himself, and it did seem that he had been desperately in love. It was bad, of course, but what was worse was his unblushing avowal of his sins. He had not mentioned them in a boastful spirit, but as though they had been commonplaces, which he regarded with amusement – even with ribaldry, she thought, once more obliged to suppress a reminiscent smile. When she remembered his callous refusal to intervene to save Fanny from his nephew's designs, however, she had no desire to laugh: she felt it to be unpardonable. He disclaimed any affection for Stacy; and, although he was certainly not in love with the memory of Celia, it was surely reasonable to suppose that enough tenderness remained with him to make him not wholly indifferent to her daughter's fate.

Recalling, exactly, the closing stage of her interview with him, contempt and indignation rose in Abby's breast, and she reached Sydney Place in a very uncomfortable state of mind: uncertain whether she most loathed Mr Miles Calverleigh, for his detestable cynicism, or herself, for succumbing to his wicked charm. Quite carried away, she uttered, aloud: 'No better than a wet-goose!' a savage self-apostrophe which considerably discomposed Mitton, opening the door at that inopportune moment.

Learning from him that Miss Butterbank was with her sister, she retired to her own room; and by the time she emerged from it she had in some measure recovered her accustomed equanimity, and had decided (on undefined grounds) that it would be wisest not to yield to her first impulse, which had been to pour the story of the morning's encounter into Selina's ears. She said nothing about it, merely assuring Selina that she had left a note at York House, to be delivered to Mrs Leavening upon her arrival. After all, one of the servants was bound to find it, and would no doubt give it to Mrs Leavening.

Fanny, returning from her expedition in time for dinner, seemed also to have recovered her equanimity: a circumstance which would have afforded Abby gratification had Fanny not art-lessly disclosed that Miss Julia Weaverham, included in the equestrian party, had told her all about the very civil letter her mama had received from Mr Stacy Calverleigh, heralding his return to Bath at the end of the week. 'And when you meet him you will see for yourself – you'll understand why – *won't* she, Aunt Selina?'

Thrown into disorder by the glowing, appealing look cast towards her, Selina lost herself in a tangle of disjointed phrases, from which she was rescued by her sister, who said calmly that she would be happy to make Mr Calverleigh's acquaintance, and added that Selina must not forget to send him a card of invi-tation to her evening-party. This, while it made Fanny bestow on her a shy, grateful smile which made her feel that she was a traitress, had the desired effect of luring Selina into an exhaus-tive discussion of the persons to be invited to meet the Leavenings, and of the arrangements for their entertainment which it would be necessary to make. Nothing more was said about Stacy Cal-verleigh, but Abby went to bed, later, in a mood of unusual depression, and spent a large part of the night mulling over a problem which grew greater and more insoluble as the minutes ticked past.

She awoke not much refreshed, but, as she sat before her dressing-table, it occurred to her that there was one person who might be able to offer her valuable advice. Mrs Grayshott, a woman of superior sense, not only held Fanny in affection but was the mother of a pretty daughter, and might be supposed to know better than a mere spinster-aunt how best to handle a girl in the throes of her first love-affair. At all events, it could do no harm to consult her, for Abby guessed her to be a safe repository for confidences, and felt herself to be in need of such a repository.

So she presently told Fanny that she would escort her to Queen's Square, in Mrs Grimston's stead, that morning, and occupy herself, while Fanny wrestled with Italian grammar under the aegis of Miss Timble, with some necessary shopping. After which, she said, she would pay Mrs Grayshott a visit, and remain with her until Fanny and Miss Lavinia Grayshott were released from the Italian class, and could, with perfect propriety, escort each other to Edgar Buildings.

Fanny, greeting this suggestion with acclaim, said: 'Oh, famous! Then I can purchase a new pair of silk stockings, in Milsom Street! I wanted to do so when you were away, but my aunt was feeling too poorly to go shopping, and nothing will prevail upon me ever again to go with Nurse! Well, you know what she is, Abby! If she doesn't say that the very thing one wants isn't *suitable* – as though one were still in the schoolroom! – she *sinks* one with embarrassment by saying that it is by far too dear, and she knows where it can be bought at half the price!'

Edgar Buildings, in George Street, were situated just within the fashionable part of the town, which extended northward from the top of Milsom Street to the exclusive heights of Upper Camden Place. Failing to discover an eligible lodging for his sister in the equally exclusive district which lay across the bridge and included Laura Place, Great Pulteney Street, and Sydney Place, Mr Leonard Balking would have chosen, had he consulted only his own pleasure, to have set Mrs Grayshott up in style there, even hiring an imposing house for her accommodation; but he had, besides his deep affection for her, a great deal of commonsense, and he realised that a large house would be a burden to her, and the long climb up to Camden Place not at all the thing for an invalid. So he had established her in Edgar Buildings, whence she could visit all the best shops, and even, without exhaustion, walk to the Pump Room, or to the Private Bath, in Stall Street. After condemning out of hand a set of apartments which he stigmatised as poky, he was fortunate enough to discover a first-floor suite which he thought tolerable, and everyone else described as handsome. Nearly all the lodgings in Bath were let in suites, and in the best part of the town these generally consisted of some four or five rooms, persons who wished for only two rooms being obliged either to look for them in an unfashionable quarter, or to endure all the disadvantages of one of Bath's numerous boarding-houses.

Mrs Grayshott's lodging was one of the most commodious sets of rooms to be had, providing her with bedrooms for herself, her daughter, her maid, and any chance visitor; and it had, besides a spacious drawing-room, a small dining-parlour. Mrs Grayshott, urgently assuring her brother that she and Lavinia could be perfectly comfortable in humbler lodgings, was silenced by his saying simply: 'You hurt me very much when you talk in that strain, my dear. You and your children are all the family I have, and surely I may be allowed to stand godfather to you?'

So Mrs Grayshott, whose circumstances were straitened, allowed herself to be installed in lodgings which were the envy of many of her acquaintances; and, since she made no secret of the fact that she owed her apparent affluence to the generosity of her brother, only such ill-natured persons as Mrs Ruscombe ever said that it seemed an odd thing that an impecunious widow should be able to live as high as a coach-horse.

Miss Abigail Wendover, admitted into the building by the very superior housekeeper, was informed that Mrs Grayshott was at home, and was about to mount the stairs when the housekeeper added, with an air of vicarious triumph: 'And Mr Oliver Grayshott, too, ma'am! Yesterday he arrived! I'm sure you could have knocked me down with a feather, and as for Madam it's a wonder she didn't suffer a spasm! But there! they say joy never kills!'

This news caused Abby to pause, feeling that her visit was ill-timed; but just as she was about to go away she heard her name spoken, and looked up to see that Mrs Grayshott was standing on the half-landing, smiling a welcome.

'Come up, Abby!' she said. 'I saw you from the window, and guessed you wouldn't stay when you knew what had happened! Oh, my dear, such a wonderful, wonderful surprise as it was! I can still hardly believe that I have him with me again!'

'No indeed!' Abby responded warmly. 'I am so glad – so happy for you! But you can't want to receive tiresome morning-visitors!'

'You could never be that! I have one, in the person of Mrs Ancrum, but I hope she may soon take her leave of us, for I most particularly want you to meet Oliver. And also to tell you of a very surprising circumstance – But that must wait until we are rid of Mrs Ancrum!'

She held out a coaxing hand as she spoke but even as Abby set her foot on the stair two more morning-visitors arrived: Lady Weaverham, accompanied by Miss Sophia Weaverham.

Escape was impossible; Mrs Grayshott had nothing to do but to beg the new arrivals to come upstairs, which they did, Lady Weaverham, an immensely stout individual, beaming good-nature as she heaved herself up the half-flight, and assuring her hostess, rather breathlessly, that she would not stay above a minute, but that upon hearing the news of the safe return of Mrs Grayshott's son she had felt that the least she could do was to call on her, just to offer her felicitations. 'And here, I see, is Miss Wendover, come on the same errand, I make no doubt!' she said, pausing to recover her breath, and holding out a hand tightly enclosed in lavender kid. 'Well, my dear, how do you do? Not that I need ask, for I can see that you're in high bloom, and if you didn't buy that delicious hat in London you may call me a chucklehead! Which Sir Joshua tells me I am, but I am more than seven, I promise you, and I can recognise town-bronze when I see it!' She then surveyed Mrs Grayshott out of her little, twinkling eyes, and said: 'And quite in your best looks *you* are, ma'am, which is not to be wondered at! So should I be, if my Jack had been restored to me when I was on the very brink of ordering my mourning-clothes! Now, tell me – how *is* he?'

'Not in such good point as I could wish, ma'am,' Mrs Grayshott replied, helping her to mount the rest of the stairs, 'but you will see how quickly he will recover! You will think, however, that I am presenting a skeleton to you, I daresay!'

If Mr Oliver Grayshott was not exactly a skeleton, he was certainly a very thin young man; and as he pulled himself up from his chair to greet the visitors Abby saw that he was also very tall. The cast of his countenance was aquiline; he had a keen pair of eyes, a mobile mouth, and a look of humour underlying the natural gravity of his expression. She thought, as she presently shook hands with him, that he looked to be older than his two-and-twenty years, but perhaps his disastrous sojourn in India might account for his hollow cheeks, and the tiny lines at the corners of his eyes. His manners were assured, but held a little of the diffidence natural to a boy of strict upbringing. He responded to Lady Weaverham's flood of questions and exclamations with the courtesy of an experienced man of the world, but betrayed his youth in the quick flush, and stammered disclaimer, with which he repulsed her entreaty to him to lie down upon the sofa.

Thinking that one voluble matron was enough for an invalid, Abby made it her business to engage Mrs Ancrum, almost as overpowering a visitor as Lady Weaverham, in trifling conversation. She was listening, with an air of spurious interest, to an account of the complications which had attended the birth of Mrs Ancrum's first grandchild, confided to her in an earnest under-voice, when the door opened, and Mr Calverleigh was announced.

Startled, she looked quickly over her shoulder, thinking for an instant that she must have misheard the servant. But she had not: standing on the threshold was Mr Miles Calverleigh, as carelessly dressed as when he had arrived at York House on the previous day, and entirely at his ease. His eyes, glancing round the room, rested for a moment on her face, and she thought that they narrowed in the suspicion of a smile, but he gave no other sign of recognition. Mrs Grayshott and Oliver had both risen, Oliver ejaculating: 'Sir!' in a tone of gratification, and Mrs Grayshott moving forward with both hands held out in a gesture of impulsive welcome. 'Mr Calverleigh, how kind of you!' she exclaimed. 'You grant me the opportunity to repair yesterday's omission!'

'No, do I?' he said. 'What was that?'

She smiled. 'You must know very well that I was too much overpowered to be able to find words with which to express my gratitude!'

'What, for dumping that young spider-shanks on your doorstep? I didn't expect to be thanked for *that*!'

She laughed. 'Didn't you? Well, I won't embarrass you by telling you how *deeply* grateful I am! I'll make you known to my friends instead! Lady Weaverham, you must allow me to introduce Mr Calverleigh to you – Mr *Miles* Calverleigh!' She waited, while he bowed with casual grace to her ladyship, and her eyes met Abby's for a pregnant moment, before she continued her presentation. She ended it by saying: 'I must tell you that Mr Calverleigh is our good angel! But for his exceeding kindness I shouldn't have had my *young spider-shanks* restored to me yesterday – or even perhaps, at all!'

'Very true, Mama,' intervened her son, 'but you are putting him to the blush! Take care he doesn't cut his stick!'

'Not at all!' Mr Calverleigh responded. 'Never have I won more gratitude with less effort! Continue, ma'am!' As he spoke, he thrust Oliver back into his chair, effectually bringing Mrs Grayshott's encomiums to an end by sitting down beside Oliver, and asking him if he felt any the worse for yesterday's journey. Oliver had barely time to assure him that he felt as fresh as a nosegay before Lady Weaverham claimed his attention, telling him how delighted she was to make his acquaintance, and how much she liked his nephew. 'Such a very amiable young man, and of the *first* stare! I am sure he has won all our hearts!'

'No, has he indeed?' he replied, with a smile as bland as her own. '*All* of them, ma'am?'

To all outward appearances blind to the quizzical gleam in Mr Calverleigh's eyes as they fleetingly met her own, Abby seethed with indignation. Only the recollection that she had appointed Fanny to join her in Edgar Buildings prevented her from following the example set by Mrs Ancrum, who rose at this moment to take her leave. It was evident, from what Mrs Grayshott had said, that he must have accompanied Oliver home from Calcutta; and equally evident that he had thereby conquered the widow's grateful heart. Mrs Grayshott had called him a guardian angel, which would have made Abby laugh if it had not instead made her so cross. He might have been carelessly kind to Oliver, but he was far from being an angel; and it would have given Abby much pleasure to have told Mrs Grayshott how mistaken she was. But detestable though he was – and never more so than at this moment, when he was all too obviously enjoying her discomfiture – this thought was a mere wistful dream. There could be no divulging the disreputable nature of his past history without running into danger, for once it became known, or even suspected, that he was what Mr George Brede termed a loose fish there was no knowing how much the scandal-mongers might discover. Besides, it would be a shabby thing to do: talebearers were odious; and one had to remember that he had paid for his youthful misdeeds by twenty years of exile. It might well be, Abby thought, rather doubtfully, that he had reformed his way of life.

Mrs Grayshott, coming back into the room from having escorted Mrs Ancrum to the head of the stairs, sat down beside Abby, saying softly: 'I had meant to have told you. I could see you were taken quite by surprise.'

'Yes, but it is of no consequence,' Abby assured her.

Mrs Grayshott looked as if she would have said more, but her attention was claimed by Lady Weaverham, and no further opportunity for private conversation offered itself, the arrival, a few minutes later, of the daughter of the house, accompanied by Miss Fanny Wendover, creating a lively diversion.

They came in, still sparkling with laughter at some

undisclosed joke, and a very charming picture they made: Lavinia, a pretty brunette, with innocent brown eyes, and a shy smile, providing Fanny with an excellent foil. Divinely fair, her beautiful features framed by a Villager straw hat with ribbons as blue as her eyes, Fanny made an instant hit with one at least of the assembled company: young Mr Grayshott, rising to his feet, stood gazing at her, apparently spellbound, until recalled from this trance by his mother, when he gave a little start, flushed darkly, and came forward to shake hands with Fanny.

Abby observed this without surprise: it was seldom that Fanny failed to rouse admiration, and she was looking particularly becoming today. Instinctively, Abby glanced at Mr Calverleigh, wondering how he was affected by the girl's resemblance to her mother, which was strong enough, she thought, to make him feel a reminiscent pang. If it did, he gave no sign of it. He was critically surveying Fanny; and when Mrs Grayshott made him known to her he caused Abby's heart to miss a beat by saying, as he took Fanny's hand: 'How do you do? So you are Celia Morval's daughter! I'm delighted to make your acquaintance: I was used to know your mother very well.'

Five

*F*or one awful moment Abby felt sick with dread of what he might say next. Then, just as she caught his eyes, a desperate appeal in her own, she realised that he was merely amusing himself at her expense, and was mischievously enjoying her discomfiture. Fright was succeeded by wrath, but not wholehearted wrath: there was apology as well as mockery in the smile directed at her over Fanny's head, and a disarming suggestion of fellowship, as though Mr Miles Calverleigh believed that in Miss Abigail Wendover he had discovered a kindred spirit.

Fanny, looking up, in her unaffected way, into his face, exclaimed: 'Oh, did you know my mother, sir? I never did – that is to say, I can't remember that I did!' She hesitated, and then asked shyly: 'Are you Mr Stacy Calverleigh's uncle? He is a particular friend of mine!'

If anything, thought Abby, could convince Miles Calverleigh that Fanny was a lamb to be guarded from stray wolves, the artlessness of this remark must have done so. She hoped, but could not be sure. His expression was that of a man listening with slightly bored indulgence to a child's prattle. He said: 'Then you will be able to introduce him to me, won't you?'

It was evident, from the look of surprise in Fanny's eyes, that Mr Stacy Calverleigh had told her nothing about his reprobate uncle: an omission for which, decided Abby, submitting the matter to dispassionate consideration, he could scarcely be blamed. Fanny said, on the edge of laughter: 'Oh – ! You are joking me, aren't you? Did I say something gooseish? Of course you must know Stacy much better than I do!'

'On the contrary! I don't know him at all – shouldn't recognise him if he walked into the room at this moment! When I left England he must have been in leading-strings.'

'Oh, *I see!*' said Fanny, her puzzled brow clearing.

'Well, I'll venture to say that you won't be disappointed in him!' said Lady Weaverham. 'Though I won't say you may not mistake him for a Bond Street Spark, for I did so myself, until I found he was no such thing. He's not above being pleased, and, what is more, his head hasn't been turned, which it might well have been for the caps that have been set at him in Bath!' She added, as Fanny blushed scarlet, and moved away from Mr Calverleigh: 'No, no, my dear, I don't mean *you!* The boot is quite on the other leg! Not a bit of heed will he pay to the other girls, and I'm sure I'm not surprised!' A fat chuckle shook her massive bosom; she completed Fanny's discomfiture by saying: 'Many's the time Sir Joshua has said to me that you bear the palm, my dear – not that he had any need to, because well do I know it!'

At this point, Oliver won Abby's approval by withdrawing Fanny a little away from the group, under pretext of pointing something out to her in the street. They sat down together, and were soon joined by Lavinia and Miss Sophia Weaverham, all four chatting happily until the party was broken up by Lady Weaverham, who heaved herself up from her chair, saying that she and Sophy must be off, or Sir Joshua would be wondering what had become of them. Abby would have followed her example, but received such an unmistakable signal from Fanny that she obediently postponed her leave-taking. The reason for the signal was disclosed as soon as the Weaverhams had departed, Lavinia eagerly asking her mama if Fanny might not stay to dine with them. 'Do say she may, Mama! I want to show her the *ravishing* things Oliver bought for me in India, particularly the shawl – no, *not* a shawl: I don't mean the Cashmere shawls, though they are the finest I ever saw in my life! – but the *other* thing –'

'Sari,' supplied her brother, smiling.

'Oh, yes! Sari!' said Lavinia, committing it to memory. 'And the sketches you drew of all those strange places, and natives, and things! Mama – ?'

'Why, certainly, my love!' Mrs Grayshott responded. 'If Miss Wendover permits!'

'Miss Wendover thinks, as I am persuaded you do too, ma'am, that the invalid has had enough visitors for one day,' said Abby. 'Another time, Fanny!'

Fanny nodded, and got up. 'Yes, of course. I did think it might not be quite the thing to do!'

This instantly drew protests and assurances from Lavinia and Oliver, under cover of which Mrs. Grayshott said: 'I wish you will let her stay! She is doing Oliver so much good! He does his best to hide it from me, but he is in very low spirits, feeling, I think, that he has failed to justify his uncle's confidence – oh, absurd, of course, but one knows how it is with boys! But dear little Fanny has *three times* made him laugh, quite in his old way! Let her remain with us! You know we keep country-hours! Martha shall bring her home before it is dark, I promise you.'

'My dear ma'am, if you do indeed wish it – ! But as for putting your Martha to the trouble of escorting her, most certainly not! I'll send the carriage for her, and only hope she may not be very much in your way!'

She then took leave of her hostess. So did Mr Miles Calverleigh: a circumstance which she regarded with mixed feelings. He followed her down the stairs, and it occurred to her that his object might be to apologise for having alarmed her so much half-an-hour before. But as she had by this time formed a very fair estimate of his character she was not much surprised when his first words to her, as soon as the street-door was shut behind them, were: 'Do tell me! – Who, and what, is Sir Joshua?'

'Sir Joshua,' she replied primly, 'is Lady Weaverham's husband, sir.'

'Yes, my pretty pea-goose, and Sophy's father too!' he said

outrageously. 'My powerful intellect has enabled me to assimilate those barren facts! Don't act the dunce!'

'Let me tell you, sir, that if you wish to be accepted into Bath society you will do well to mend your manners!' retorted Abby.

'I've none to mend, and not the smallest wish to be accepted into Bath, or any other, society. And if Bath society is composed of Lady Weaverham and her like –'

'Of course it isn't!' she interrupted impulsively. 'I mean – Oh, what a detestable man you are!'

'Well, if that's what you meant to say you must have a very hubble-bubble mind!' he commented. 'I may be detestable – in fact, I know I am – but what has that to say to anything?' He added, as she resolutely bit her lip: 'Yes, do laugh! You have a pretty laugh, and I like the way your eyes dance.'

Guiltily aware that this very improper speech had pleased rather than offended her, she said, as coolly as she could: 'We were discussing the Weaverhams, I think. They are very kind, worthy people, and although they are not – not the pink of gentility, they are generally well liked.'

'Full of juice, eh?' he said, showing at once his understanding and his disregard for polite ambiguities. 'Where did they pick up the title? In the City?'

'I don't know. Sir Joshua certainly was engaged in Trade, until he retired – they make no secret of that – but – but in a perfectly respectable way!'

'No need to defend him,' he said kindly. 'I've been engaged in trade myself, though I daresay you wouldn't say *respectably.*'

'I should be astonished if I discovered that you had done *anything* respectably!' declared Abby, goaded into retort. Shocked by her own lapse from propriety, she was thankful to see that they had reached York House, and added hastily: 'Our ways part here, sir, so I will say goodbye!'

'No, don't! it would be premature! I'm going to escort you to your home.'

'I am obliged to you, but it is quite unnecessary, I assure you!'

She had stopped by the entrance to the hotel, and held out her hand, repeating: 'Goodbye, Mr Calverleigh!'

'If you imagine that I am going to walk behind you, like a footman, all the way to Sydney Place, you are mightily mistaken, Miss Abigail Wendover!' he said, taking her hand, and drawing it within his arm. 'Is it now the established mode for young females to jaunter about the town unattended? It wasn't so when I lived in England!'

'I am not a young female, and I don't *jaunter*!' replied Abby hotly, pulling her hand away, but walking on beside him. 'Times have changed since *you* lived in England, sir!'

'Yes, alas, and not for the better!' he agreed, in a mournful tone. 'Bear with my foibles, ma'am! Being yourself stricken in years, that shouldn't be difficult!'

A chuckle escaped her. 'Don't be so absurd!' she admonished him. 'I may not be stricken in years, but I am no longer of an age when I need chaperonage. I don't care to let Fanny go out alone, though I know several mothers who see no objection to it *here*. Not in London, of course.' She paused, and said, after a moment: 'May I request you, sir, to take care what you say to Fanny? Since you have seen fit to inform her that you knew her mother *very well*, she may try to talk to you about Celia, and she is sufficiently needle-witted to add two and two together. I'm aware that you did it to put me in a quake, but, having succeeded, pray be satisfied!'

He laughed. 'No, no! just bantering you a little! You were looking such daggers at me that I couldn't resist!'

'Chivalrous!' she remarked.

'Not a bit! I warned you that there's no virtue in me.'

'Then why do you insist on escorting me home?'

'Because I want to escort you home, of course. What a birdwitted question!'

Her eyes began to dance, and her lips to quiver. 'You know, you are the most provoking creature I ever encountered!' she told him.

'Oh, come, now, that's doing it rather too brown!' he

expostulated. 'Remember, I was acquainted with your brother Rowland! I never saw much of James, but I shouldn't wonder at it if he's as bad. Or don't you find consequential bores provoking?'

'If I didn't believe you to be dead to all proper feeling,' said Abby, in a shaking voice, 'I should endeavour to point out to you that that is a – an *abominable* thing to say!'

'Well, thank God you do realise it!' he replied. 'Now we shall go on much more comfortably!'

'No we shan't. Not until you stop trying to hoax me into thinking you are uniformly odious! Pray, did you bring Oliver Grayshott home because you *wanted* to?'

'Yes, I like the boy. Don't you?'

'Yes, I daresay, but –'

'Now, don't run away with the notion that I came back to England on his account!' he admonished her. 'Nothing could be further from the truth! All I did was to take charge of him on the voyage: no very arduous task!'

'And subsequently put yourself to the trouble of bringing him down to Bath,' said Abby pensively.

'Oh, that was because –' he checked himself, but continued blandly, after an infinitesimal pause: '– because his uncle is a man of vast interests, and one never knows when the favour of such a man might stand one in good stead.'

'How quickly you made a recover!' said Abby admiringly. 'You were within an ace of telling me that you came to Bath to see your nephew, too!'

'Ah, I *did* tell you that I didn't know he was here! I rather thought I did,' he said, quite unperturbed. 'I hope he means to return: according to Lady Weaverham, he is a perfect paragon, and I *should* like to meet a Calverleigh who fitted that description.'

'You won't meet him in the person of your nephew!'

'How do you know? You've never clapped eyes on him!'

'No, but –'

'Furthermore, Selina likes him,' he pursued. 'You told me that yourself, and I have the greatest respect for her judgment.'

'Oh, have you indeed?' she said wrathfully. 'When *you* have never clapped eyes on *her* – !'

'Not to my knowledge,' he admitted. 'However, I understand her to be your eldest sister, and there's no saying but what I may have met her – before I was excluded from polite circles, of course. If I didn't, I look forward to making her acquaintance.'

They had reached the corner of Bridge Street, and Abby came to an abrupt halt. '*No!*' she said forcefully. 'I don't wish you to make her acquaintance! She knows nothing of what you disclosed to me – she doesn't even know that I met you yesterday! And I have no intention – none whatsoever! – of introducing you to her!'

'Haven't you? But you'll be made to look no-how if you don't, won't you? If Mrs Grayshott doesn't perform that office, would you wager a groat on the chance that Lady Weaverham won't?'

'No – or on the chance that you wouldn't instantly tell my sister of our previous meetings!' said Abby, with considerable bitterness. 'Without a blush!'

'Very likely,' he agreed.

Unable to think of any suitable rejoinder, she walked on in silence.

'And I promise you I won't blush,' he added reassuringly.

She choked, but managed to retort with tolerable gravity: 'I shouldn't suppose that you know how to!'

'No, I don't think I do,' he said, subjecting the matter to consideration. 'At my age, it is rather too late to acquire the accomplishment, don't you think?'

'Mr Calverleigh!' she said, turning her head to look up at him, 'let us be a little serious! It is true that I haven't yet met your nephew, but you have met my niece! You don't want for sense; you are not a green youth, but a – a man of the world; and you loved Fanny's mother! I don't doubt that, or that seeing Fanny must have given you a – a pang – brought it all back to you!'

'You know, the odd thing is that it didn't,' he interrupted. '*Is* she so like Celia?'

Astonished, she gasped: 'Her image!'

'No, is she indeed? What tricks memory plays one! I had thought that Celia had brown eyes.'

'Do you mean to say that you have *forgotten*?' demanded Abby, wholly taken aback.

'Well, it all happened more than twenty years ago,' he said apologetically.

'And no doubt your memory has confused her with some other lady!'

'Yes, that's very possible,' he acknowledged.

Miss Abigail Wendover decided, while she struggled with her emotions, that one of the worst features of Mr Miles Calverleigh's character was his obnoxious ability to throw her into giggles at quite the wrong moment. Being a woman of strong resolution, she mastered herself, and said: 'But you do remember that you once loved her, and I don't think you would wish her daughter to – to become the victim of a fortune-hunter – even if he is your nephew!'

'No. Not that I've considered the matter, but I don't wish anybody to become the victim of a fortune-hunter. Or, now I come to think of it, of any other predacious person. But I am of the opinion that you may be wronging my foolish nephew: he may well have tumbled into love with her, you know. Undoubtedly a piece of perfection!'

She looked up quickly, kindling to this praise of her darling. 'She *is* very pretty, isn't she?'

'Oh, past price! Which leads me to suspect that perhaps the poor fellow is in love with her!'

She frowned over this for a moment or two, before saying decidedly: 'It's of no consequence if he is: he is not a proper person for her! Besides, she's by far too young. Surely you must know that!'

'No, I don't. Her mother was about seventeen when she married Rowland.'

'Which *proves* she is too young!'

He grinned appreciatively, but said: 'You may be right, but

you can't expect me to agree with you. After all, I tried to marry Celia myself!'

'Yes, but you were only a boy then. You must be wiser now!'

'Much! Too wise to meddle in what doesn't concern me!'

'Mr Calverleigh, it should concern you!'

'Miss Wendover, it don't!'

'Then, if you've no interest in your nephew, why do you mean to linger in Bath? Why do you hope he means to return here?'

'I didn't say I had no interest in him. I own, I didn't think I had, but that was before I knew he was making up to your niece. You can't deny that that provides a very interesting situation!'

'Excessively diverting, too!'

'Yes, that's what I think.'

She said despairingly: 'I see that I might as well address myself to a gate-post!'

'What very odd things you seem to talk to!' he remarked. 'Do you find gate-posts less responsive than eels?'

She could not help smiling, but she said very earnestly: 'Promise me one thing at least, sir! Even though you won't intervene in this miserable affair, promise me that you won't *promote* it!'

'Oh, readily! I am a mere spectator.'

She was obliged to be satisfied, but said in somewhat minatory accents: 'I trust your word, sir.'

'You may safely do so. I shan't feel any temptation to break it,' he replied cheerfully.

Feeling that this remark showed him to be quite irreclaimable, Abby walked on in silence, trying to discover why she allowed herself to talk to him at all, far less to accept his escort. No satisfactory answer presented itself, for although he seemed to be impervious to snubs she knew that she could have snubbed his advances if she had made any real effort to do so. After a half-hearted attempt to convince herself that she endured his escort and his conversation with the sole object of winning his support in her crusade against his nephew she found herself to be under the shameful necessity of admitting that she enjoyed both, and – far worse! – would have suffered considerable disappointment had he announced his intention of leaving Bath within the immediate future. She could only suppose that it was his unlikeness to the other gentlemen of her acquaintance which appealed to her sense of humour, and made it possible for her to tolerate him, for there was really nothing else to render him acceptable: he was neither handsome nor elegant; his manners were careless; and his morals non-existent. He was, in fact, precisely the sort of ramshackle person to whom no lady of birth, breeding, and propriety would extend the smallest encouragement. He had nothing to recommend him but his smile, and she was surely too old, and had too much commonsense, to be beguiled by a smile however attractive it might be. But just as she reached this decision he spoke, and she glanced up at him, and realised that she had overestimated both her age and her commonsense. He was smiling down at her, and, try as she would, she was incapable of resisting the impulse to smile back at him. It was almost as if a bond existed between them, which was tightened by his smile. In repose his face was harsh, but the smile transformed it. His eyes lost their cold, rather cynical expression, warming to laughter, and holding, besides amusement, an indefinable look of understanding. He might mock, but not unkindly; and when he discomfited her his smiling eyes conveyed sympathy as well as amusement, and clearly invited her to share his amusement. And, thought Abby, the dreadful thing was that she did share it. He seemed to think that they were kindred spirits, and the shocking suspicion that he was right made her look resolutely ahead, saying: 'Yes, sir? What did you say?'

Quick to hear the repressive note in her voice, he replied meekly: 'Nothing, I assure you, to which you could take the least exception! In fact, no more than: *I wish you will tell me.* Upon which you turned your head, and looked up at me so charmingly that the rest went out of my mind! How the devil have you contrived to escape matrimony in all the unnumbered years of your life?'

An unruly dimple peeped, but she answered primly: 'I am very well content to remain single, sir.' It then occurred to her that this might lead him to suppose that her hand had never been sought in matrimony, which, for some reason unknown to herself, was an intolerable misapprehension, and she destroyed whatever quelling effect her dignified reply might have had upon him, by adding: 'Though you needn't suppose that I have not received *several* eligible offers!'

He chuckled. 'I don't!'

Blushing rosily, she said, trying to recover her lost dignity: 'And if that is what you wished me to tell you –'

'Oh, no!' he interrupted. 'Until you smiled so enchantingly I thought I knew. But you aren't old cattish – not in the least!'

'*Oh!*' gasped Abby. 'Old *cattish*? Oh, you – you – I am nothing of the sort!'

'That's what I said,' he pointed out.

'You didn't! You – you said –' Her sense of the ridiculous came to her rescue; she burst out laughing. 'Odious creature! Now, do, pray, stop roasting me! What do you really wish me to tell you?'

'Oh, I was merely seeking information! I don't recall that I ever visited Bath in the days of my youth, so I rely on you to tell me just what are its rules and etiquette – as they concern one desirous of entering society.'

'*You?*' she exclaimed, casting a surprised look up at him.

'But of course! How else could I hope to pursue my acquaintance with –' He paused, encountering a dangerous gleam in her eyes, and continued smoothly: 'Lady Weaverham, and her amiable daughter!'

She bit her lip. 'No, indeed! How shatterbrained I am! Lady Weaverham has several amiable daughters, too.'

'Good God! Are they all fubsy-faced?'

'A – a little!' she acknowledged. 'You will be able to judge for yourself, if you mean to attend the balls at the New Assembly Rooms. I am afraid there are no balls or concerts held at the Lower Rooms until November. You will find it an agreeable day promenade, however, and I expect there will be some public lectures given there. Concerts are given every Wednesday evening at the New Rooms. And there is also the Harmonic Society,' she said, warming to her task. 'They sing catches and glees, and meet at the White Hart. At least, they do during the season, but I am not perfectly sure –'

'I shall make it my business to discover the date of the first meeting. Meanwhile, my pretty rogue, that will do!'

Miss Wendover toyed for a moment with the idea of giving him a sharp set-down for addressing her so improperly, but decided that it would be wiser to ignore his impertinence. She said: 'Not fond of music, sir? Oh, well, perhaps you have a taste for cards! There are two card-rooms at the New Assembly Rooms: one of them is an octagon, and generally much admired – but I ought to warn you that hazard is not allowed, or *any* unlawful game. And you cannot play cards at all on Sundays.'

'You dismay me! What, by the way, are the unlawful games you speak of?'

'I don't know,' she said frankly, 'but that's what it says in the Rules. I expect it wouldn't do to start a faro bank, or anything of that nature.'

'I shouldn't wonder at it if you were right,' he agreed, with the utmost gravity. 'And how do I gain admittance to this establishment?'

'Oh, you write your name in Mr King's book, if you wish to become a subscriber! He is the M.C., and the book is kept at the Pump Room. Dress balls are on Monday, card assemblies on Tuesday, and Fancy balls on Thursday. The balls begin soon after seven o'clock, and end punctually at eleven. Only country dances are permitted at the Dress balls, but there are in general two cotillions danced at the Fancy balls. Oh, and you pay sixpence for Tea, on admission!'

'And they say Bath is a slow place! You appear to be gay to dissipation. What happens, by the way, if eleven o'clock strikes in the middle of one of your country dances?'

She laughed. 'The music stops! That's in the Rules too!'

They had reached Sydney Place by this time, and she stopped outside her house, and held out her hand. 'This is where I live, so I will say goodbye to you, Mr Calverleigh. I am much obliged to you for escorting me home, and trust you will enjoy your sojourn in Bath.'

'Yes, if only I am not knocked-up by all the frisks and jollifications you've described to me,' he said, taking her hand, and retaining it for a moment in a strong clasp. He smiled down at her. 'I won't say goodbye to you, but *au revoir*, Miss Wendover!'

She had been afraid that he would insist on entering the house with her to make Selina's acquaintance, and was relieved when he made no such attempt, merely waiting until Mitton opened the door, and then striding away, with no more than a wave of his hand.

She found, on going upstairs, that Selina had promoted herself to the sofa in the drawing-room, and had had the gratification of receiving a visit from Mrs Leavening. She was so full of Bedfordshire gossip that it was some time before Abby had the opportunity to tell her that Mrs Grayshott's son had at last been restored to her. She found it unaccountably difficult to disclose that Mr Miles Calverleigh had brought him to Bath, and when, after responding to her sister's exclamatory enquiries, she did disclose it, her voice was a trifle too airy.

Selina, fortunately, was too much surprised to notice it. She ejaculated: *'What?* Poor Mr Calverleigh's uncle? The one you told me about? The one that was sent away in disgrace? You don't mean it! But why did *he* bring the young man home? I should have thought Mr Balking would have done so!'

'I believe he took care of him on the voyage.'

'Good gracious! Well, he can't be so very bad after all! and very likely Mr Stacy Calverleigh isn't either! Unless, of course, he only came to find his nephew – not that there is anything bad about that: in fact, it shows he has very proper feeling!'

'Well, he hasn't!' said Abby. 'He didn't know his nephew was in Bath, and he hasn't any *family* feelings whatsoever!'

'Now, my love, how can you possibly – Don't tell me you've actually *met* him?'

'He came to call on Mrs Grayshott while I was there – and was so obliging as to escort me home. Quite Gothic!'

'I don't think it in the least Gothic,' asserted Selina. 'It gives me a very good opinion of him! *Just* like his nephew, whose manners are so particularly pleasing!'

'From all you have told me about his nephew, Mr Miles Calverleigh is nothing like him!' said Abby, with an involuntary choke of laughter. 'He is neither handsome nor fashionable, and his manners are deplorable!'

Selina, regarding her with real concern, said: 'Dearest, I am persuaded you must be yielding to prejudice, and indeed you should not, though, to be sure, dear Rowland was always used to say it was your besetting sin, but that was when you were a mere child, and *perfectly* understandable, as I told Rowland, because one cannot expect to find young heads – no, I mean *old* heads on *young* shoulders – not that I should expect to find heads on any shoulders at all, unless, of course, it was *a freak*! Which I know very little about, because you must remember, Abby, that dear Papa had the greatest dislike of *fairs*, and would never permit us to go to one. Now, what in the world have I said to cast you into whoops?'

'*Nothing* in the world, Selina!' Abby said, as well as she could for laughter. 'On – on the contrary! You've t-told me that in spite of all my f-faults I'm not a freak!'

'My dear, you allow your love of drollery to carry you too far,' said Selina reprovingly. 'There has never been anything like *that* in our family!'

Overcome by this comforting assurance, Abby fled, conscious of a wish that Mr Calverleigh could have been present to share her amusement.

Selina continued to speculate, in her rambling way, throughout dinner, on his probable character, what he had done to deserve being banished, and what had brought him back to England; but Fanny's arrival, just before the tea-tray was brought in, gave the conversation a welcome turn. Fanny was full of the quaint or the beautiful things Oliver Grayshott had brought home from India, and although Selina's interest in ivory carvings or Benares brass might be tepid, the first mention of Cashmere shawls, and lengths of the finest Indian muslin, aroused all her sartorial instincts; while a minute description of the sari caused her to wonder how long it would be before she dared venture out of doors, and to adjure Fanny to beg Lavinia not to have it made up until she had seen it. 'For you know, my dear, excellent creature though she is, dear Mrs Grayshott has *no* taste, and what a shocking thing it would be if such an exquisite thing were to be ruined!'

Fanny had spent a delightful day in Edgar Buildings, and she meant – if her aunts saw no objection – to repeat her visit. Lavinia, who was her dearest friend, had told her how low and oppressed poor Oliver was, and had asked her to come again, because funning with her, and making up charades, had quite got up his spirits. 'So I think I should, don't you?' Fanny said, frowning over her own thoughts. 'It isn't *me*, particularly, but being obliged to be polite and cheerful with a visitor, which does one a great deal of good when one has been ill, and feels dreadfully pulled.'

She had very little to say about Miles Calverleigh. It was plain that the only interest he had for her was his relationship to Stacy. She said that he was not at all like Stacy; and mentioned, as an afterthought, that he said he had known her mama well.

To Abby's relief, Selina accepted this without question, seeing in it an added reason for thinking he could not be as black as he had been painted. Having decided that it would be both unsafe and unkind to divulge to her the story of Miles Calverleigh and Celia Morval, Abby was thankful to be spared searching enquiries into the circumstances under which Miles Calverleigh had contrived to become intimately acquainted with a girl who had been married within two months of her come-out, and had lived thereafter in a Bedfordshire manor.

She retired to bed presently, devoutly hoping that Mr Calverleigh would have left Bath before Selina emerged from her self-imposed seclusion.

Six

*B*ut Mr Calverleigh called in Sydney Place on the following day. Mitton, recognising him as the gentleman who had escorted Miss Abby home on the previous afternoon, admitted him without hesitation, and took him up to the drawing-room, where Abby, under her sister's instruction, was engaged in directing cards of invitation to their projected rout-party. She was unprepared, and gave such a start that her pen spluttered. Turning quickly, and almost incredulously, she encountered the blandest of smiles, and the slightest of bows, before Mr Calverleigh advanced towards her sister. What excuse he meant to offer for his visit was a puzzle that was speedily solved: Mr Calverleigh, taking Selina's tremblingly outstretched hand in his, and smiling reassuringly down into her agitated countenance, told her that he had known her elder brother, and found himself unable to resist the impulse to extend his acquaintance with Rowland's family. 'Two of whom I had the pleasure of meeting yesterday,' he said, nodding with friendly informality at Abby. 'How do you do, Miss Abigail?'

She acknowledged this greeting in the frostiest manner, but so far from being abashed, he laughed, and said: 'Still out of charity with me? I must tell you, ma'am, that your sister was as cross as crabs with me for escorting her home. But in my day it was not at all the thing for girls of her quality to go out walking alone.'

Selina, already flustered by the style and manner of her unexpected visitor, lost herself in a tangle of words, for while on

79

the one hand, she shared his old-fashioned prejudice, on the other, she knew very well that to agree with him would be to incur Abby's wrath. So after floundering between a number of unfinished sentences, she begged him to be seated, and asked him where he had met her brother. Abby held her breath, but he returned a vague answer, and she let it go again.

'And you knew my sister-in-law too!' pursued Selina. 'It seems so odd that I never – not that I was acquainted with all their friends, of course, but I thought – that is to say – dear me, how stupid! I have forgot what I was going to say!'

He regarded her confusion with a twinkle. 'No, no, don't turn short about! You thought I had been sent packing to India before your brother was married, and you were perfectly right: I knew Celia when she was still Miss Morval.'

'A long time ago,' said Abby. 'Too long for me, I am afraid: you see, I didn't.'

The unmistakable boredom in her voice scandalised Selina into uttering a protesting: 'Abby *dear* – !'

Abby shrugged pettishly. 'Oh, well, it is so tedious to be obliged to discuss old times in which one played no part! Anecdotes, too! I have a surfeit of them from General Exford. I wish you will rather tell us of your Indian experiences, Mr Calverleigh.'

'But that would be merely to exchange one form of anecdote for another,' he pointed out. 'And *much* more boring, I assure you!'

'Oh, no! I am persuaded – so very interesting! All those Mahrattas, and things!' fluttered Selina, aghast at her sister's behaviour. 'Not that I should care to live there myself – and the climate *far* from salubrious – well, only think of poor young Mr Grayshott! But I daresay you had *many* exciting adventures!'

'Not nearly as many as I had in England!' He looked at Abby, wickedly quizzing her. 'No need to look so dismayed, Miss Abigail: I don't mean to recount them! Let us instead discuss the amenities of Bath! Do you mean to attend the concert this evening?'

For one sulphurous moment it was on the tip of her tongue to disclaim any intention of attending the concert, but the recollection that she was engaged to do so with a select party of friends checked her. She replied, with a glittering smile: 'Yes, indeed! The Signora Neroli is to sing, you know – a high treat for those of us who love music. You, I daresay, would find it a dead bore, for I believe you *don't* love music!'

'On the contrary: I find it wonderfully sopor – wonderfully soothing!'

A smile quivered at the corners of her mouth. 'I doubt if you will find the benches wonderfully sopor-soothing, sir!'

'That card takes the trick!' he said approvingly.

She chuckled, and then as she caught sight of her sister's face, blushed.

At that moment, Fanny came into the room, much to Abby's relief. She greeted Mr Calverleigh with unaffected pleasure: just as she would have greeted any other of her aunt's elderly admirers, Abby watched in some amusement, wondering how much Mr Calverleigh liked the touch of pretty deference which paid tribute to his advanced years. She was obliged to own that he took it with unshaken composure, responding in a manner that was positively avuncular. He did not stay long: a circumstance which caused Selina to say, when he had taken his leave, that although his manners were very odd, which was due, no doubt, to his having lived in India, he did know better than to remain for more than half-an-hour on a visit of ceremony.

'I warned you that his manners are deplorable!' said Abby. 'I shouldn't think he has the least notion of ceremony.'

'To be sure, it is not at all the thing to call on us in breeches and topboots – at least, gentlemen may do so in the country, of course, but not in Bath, without a horse, and it would have been more correct merely to have left his card – but I saw nothing in his manners to disgust me, precisely. He has a great deal of ease, but he is not at all vulgar. In fact, he has a well-bred air, and it would be very unjust to blame him for his complexion, poor man, because you may depend upon it *that* was India, and excessively unfeeling I think it of his father to have sent him there, no matter *what* he did!'

'Why, *did* he do something dreadful?' exclaimed Fanny, round-eyed with surprise.

'No, dear, certainly not!' said Selina hurriedly.

'But you said –'

'My love, I said nothing of the sort! How you do pick one up! It is not at all becoming! And that puts me in mind of something! Abby, *never* did I think to be put to the blush by a want of conduct in you! I declare, I was so mortified – so petulant and uncivil of you! And then, after placing yourself on *far* too high a form, besides snubbing him in the *rudest* way, you laughed in his face! As if you had known him for years!'

'Good God, why did no one ever tell me that I mustn't laugh at what a man says until I have known him for years?' countered Abby.

Before Selina could assemble her inchoate thoughts, Fanny said suddenly: 'Yes, but one has! I mean, one *feels* as if one has! For my part, I don't care a straw for his being shabbily dressed, and not having formal manners: I *like* him! I should have thought you would too, Abby, because he is just such a jokesmith as you are yourself! *Don't* you?'

'I must say,' interpolated Selina, 'that he was very diverting. And when he smiles –'

'Mr Calverleigh's smile must be reckoned as his greatest – if not his only – asset!' said Abby tartly. 'As to whether I like him or not, how can I possibly say? I am barely acquainted with him, Fanny!'

'That doesn't signify! He is barely acquainted with you, but anyone can see that he likes you very much!' retorted Fanny saucily. 'Do you think he will be at the concert this evening?'

'I haven't the least notion,' replied Abby. 'Certainly not, if riding-dress is his only wear!'

'Poor man!' said Selina, her compassion stirred. 'I daresay he may be sadly purse-pinched.'

However this might have been, Mr Calverleigh had either the means, or the credit, to have provided himself with the long-tailed-coat, the knee-breeches, and the silk stockings which constituted the correct evening-wear for gentlemen, for he appeared in the New Assembly Rooms, thus arrayed, a few minutes before the concert began, escorting Mrs Grayshott. But as he wore it as casually as his riding-dress, and appeared to set more store by comfort than elegance, no aspirant to fashion would have felt the smallest inclination to discover the name of his tailor.

Miss Abigail Wendover observed his arrival from under her lashes, and thereafter confined her attention to her own party. She was herself looking (as her niece very improperly told her) as fine as fivepence, in one of the new gowns made for her in London, of Imperial muslin, with short sleeves, worn low on her shoulders, a narrow skirt, and a bodice trimmed with a double pleating of ribbon. It became her slender figure to admiration, and it had not been her original intention to have wasted it on a mere out-of-season concert; but when she had looked more closely at her lilac crape she had realised that it was really too shabby to be worn again. This, at least, was the explanation that she offered to her surprised sister. As for her hair, which she had dressed in loose curls, with one shining ringlet disposed over her left shoulder, what did Selina think of it? It was all the kick in London, but perhaps it would not do in Bath?

'Oh, my dearest, I never saw you look so becoming!' said Selina, in a gush of sentimental tears. 'In such high bloom! I know you will be ready to eat me, but I must and I will say that no one would take you for Fanny's *aunt*!'

So far from showing a disposition to take umbrage, Abby laughed, cast an appraising look at her reflection in the mirror above the fireplace, and said candidly: 'Well, I never was a beauty, but I'm not a mean bit yet, am I?'

Certainly no one who was present at the concert that evening thought so. In the octagon room, where they waited for the rest of the party to assemble, Abby received quite as many compliments as Fanny; and on her way through the concert-room had the doubtful felicity of being ogled by a complete stranger.

During the interval, she did not immediately follow Mrs

Faversham into the adjoining room, where tea was being served, being waylaid by Mr Dunston, who came up with his mother on his arm. Civility obliged her to exchange commonplaces with Mrs Dunston, and when that amiable and platitudinous lady's attention was claimed by one of her acquaintances her son stepped instantly into the breach, saying simply: '*Fair as is the rose of May!* Do you know, that line has been running through my head ever since I set eyes on you this evening? You shine everyone else down, Miss Abby!'

'Flummery!' said an amused voice at Abby's elbow. 'You can't have seen her niece!'

'Sir!' uttered Mr Dunston, outraged. 'I believe I have not the pleasure of your acquaintance?'

'Let me make you known to one another!' said Abby hastily. 'Mr Dunston, Mr Calverleigh – Mr *Miles* Calverleigh!'

Mr Dunston executed a small, stiff bow, received in return a nod, and, for the first time in his stolid career, wished that the days of calling a man out on the slightest provocation did not belong to the past.

'I've come to carry you off to drink tea with Mrs Grayshott,' said Mr Calverleigh, taking Abby's hand, and drawing it within his arm. 'I left her guarding a chair for you, so come along!' He favoured Mr Dunston with another nod, and a brief smile, and led Abby inexorably away, saying: 'He did empty the butter-boat over you, didn't he? Who the devil is he?'

'He is a very respectable man, who lives with his mother a few miles distant from the town,' she replied severely. 'And even if he was talking flummery it was not at all handsome of you to say so!'

'I don't offer Spanish coin, if that's what you mean,' he retorted. 'Do you wish for it?'

'Surely, Mr Calverleigh, your wide experience of females must have taught you that compliments are always acceptable to us?' she said demurely.

'To nine out of ten females, yes! but not to you, Miss Abigail Wendover! You're more than seven! You know very well that in point of beauty you don't shine every other lady down: there are at least three real diamonds here tonight, leaving Fanny out of the reckoning.'

'My dear sir, only point them out to me, and I'll present you! I expect I'm acquainted with them – indeed, I've a shrewd notion I know who they are!'

He shook his head. 'No. I prefer to admire them from a distance. My wide experience warns me that they lack that certain sort of something which you have in abundance.'

'My – *sufficiently* wide experience of you, Mr Calverleigh, warns me that you are about to say something outrageous!'

'No, I assure you! Nothing derogatory! Charming girls, all of them! Only I don't want to kiss them!'

She gave a startled gasp. 'You don't want – Well, upon my word! And if you mean me to understand from that –'

'I do,' he said, smiling down at her. 'I should dearly love to kiss you – here and now!'

'W-well you can't!' said Abby, rocked off her balance.

'I know I can't – not here and now, at all events!'

'*Ever!*' she uttered, furiously aware of flaming cheeks.

'Oh, that is quite another matter! Do you care to wager a small sum on the chance?'

Making a desperate recovery, she said: 'No! I never bet on certainties!'

He laughed. 'You know, you are a darling!' he said, completing her confusion.

'Well, what *you* are is a – a –'

'Hedge-bird?' he suggested helpfully, as she stopped, at a loss for words opprobrious enough to describe him. 'Gullcatcher? Bermondsey boy? Rudesby? Queer Nabs?'

She broke into laughter, and threw at him over her shoulder, as she went before him into the tea-room: 'All of those – and worse! In a word, infamous! Mrs Grayshott! How do you do? And – which I know you will think more important! – How does your invalid do?'

She sat down beside Mrs Grayshott as she spoke, wholly withdrawing her attention from the infamous Mr Calverleigh, who lounged away to procure her a cup of tea. Mrs Grayshott said: 'My invalid is not as stout as I could wish, nor as docile! Dr Wilkinson has seen him, however, and assures me that I have no need to fear that any permanent damage has been done to his health. He recommends a course of hot baths, which, he tells me and, indeed, I know from my own experience – do much to restore a debilitated frame. Abby, my dear, you must let me compliment you on this new way you have of dressing your hair! You look delightfully – and have set a new fashion in Bath, if I am any judge of the matter! Yes, I know you only care for compliments on Fanny's appearance, so not another word will I say in your praise! I imagine you have had a surfeit of compliments already – if not from Mr Dunston, who appeared to me to be quite moonstruck, certainly from Mr Calverleigh!'

'Not at all!' replied Abby. 'Mr Calverleigh thinks me a candle in the sunshine of three veritable diamonds present tonight! Four, including Fanny!'

'Does he, indeed?' replied Mrs Grayshott, a good deal amused. 'I suspect he is what Oliver calls *a complete hand*! You know, my dear, I must own that I am glad to see you on such good terms with him, for it has been very much on my conscience that I almost *forced* him upon you, which, as I hope you know, I never meant to do!'

'Oh, I know you didn't, ma'am! I wish you won't give it another thought. Sooner or later I must have met him, you know.'

'And you like him? I was afraid that his free-and-easy manners might offend you.'

'On the contrary! They amuse me. He is certainly an original!'

Mrs Grayshott smiled, but said rather wistfully: 'Why, yes! But not only that! He is so very *kind*! He makes light of the services he rendered Oliver throughout that weary voyage, but I've heard the truth from Oliver himself. But for Mr Calverleigh's unremitting care I don't think that my poor boy would have survived, for he tells me that he suffered a recrudescence of that horrible fever within two days of having been carried aboard! It was Mr Calverleigh, rather than the ship's surgeon, who preserved his life, his long residence in India having made him far more familiar with the disorder than any ship's surgeon could be! I must be eternally obliged to him!' Her voice shook; she overcame the little surge of emotion, and said, with an effort at liveliness: 'And, as though he had not done enough for me, what must he do but procure tickets for this concert tonight, and positively *bully* me into accompanying him! Something I must have said gave him the notion that I should very much like to hear Neroli, and I think it particularly kind in him to have given me the opportunity to do so, because I am afraid he is not himself a music-lover.'

Having very good reason to suppose that Mr Calverleigh's kindness sprang from pure self-interest, Abby was hard put to it to hold her tongue. It was perhaps fortunate that he rejoined them at this moment, thus putting an end to any further discussion of his character. She accepted the tea he had brought, with a word of thanks and a charming smile, but could not resist the impulse to ask him if he was not ravished by Neroli's voice.

He replied promptly: 'Not entirely. A little too much *vibrato*, don't you agree?'

'Ah, I perceive that you are an expert!' said Abby, controlling a quivering lip. 'You must enlighten my ignorance, sir! What does that mean, if you please?'

'Well, my Latin is pretty rusty, but I should think it means to tremble,' he said coolly. 'She does, too, like a blancmange. And much the same shape as one,' he added thoughtfully.

'Oh, you *dreadful* creature!' protested Mrs Grayshott, bubbling over. 'I didn't mean *that*, when I said I thought she had rather too much *vibrato*! You know I didn't!'

'I thought she had too much of everything,' he said frankly.

Mrs Grayshott cried shame upon him; but Abby, caught in the act of sipping her tea, choked.

When he presently restored her to her own party, she was spared the necessity of introducing him to Mrs Faversham by that lady's greeting him by name, and with a gracious smile:

Lady Weaverham had already performed that office, in the Pump Room that morning.

Mr Faversham said, taking his seat beside Abby: 'So that's young Calverleigh's uncle!' He looked critically after Mr Calverleigh's tall, retreating figure. 'Got the look of a care-for-nobody, but I like him better than his nephew: too insinuating by half, that young man!'

'You don't like him, sir?'

'No, I can't say I do,' he replied bluntly. 'Fact of the matter is I set no store by these young sprigs of fashion! My wife calls me an old fogey: daresay you will too, for the ladies all seem to have run wild over him! Haven't met him yet, have you?'

'No, that pleasure hasn't been granted me,' she said, in a dry tone.

It was to be granted her on the following day. Mr Stacy Calverleigh, coming down from London on the mail-coach, arrived at the White Hart midway through the morning, and stayed only to change his travelling-dress for the corbeau-coloured coat of superfine, the pale pantaloons, and the gleaming Hessian boots of the Bond Street beau, before setting out in a hack for Sydney Place.

The ladies were all at home, Abby, who had just come in from a visit to Milsom Street, submitting to her sister's critical inspection some patterns of lace; Selina reclining on the sofa; and Fanny wrestling with the composition of an acrostic in the back drawing-room. She did not immediately look up when Mitton announced *Mr Calverleigh*, but as Stacy advanced into the room he spoke, saying in a rallying tone: 'Miss Wendover! What is this I hear about you? Mitton has been telling me that you have been quite out of frame since I saw you last! I am so very sorry!'

His voice brought Fanny's head up with a jerk. She sprang to her feet, and almost ran into the front room, exclaiming with unaffected joy: 'Stacy: oh, I thought it was only your uncle!'

She was holding out her hands to him, and he caught them in his, carrying first one and then the other to his lips with what Abby, observing her niece's fervour with disapprobation, recognised as practised grace. 'You thought I was my uncle? Now, I begin to suspect that it is you rather than Miss Wendover who must be out of frame!' he said caressingly. 'Indeed I am not my uncle!' He gave her hands a slight squeeze before releasing them, and moving forward to drop on his knee beside the sofa. 'Dear Miss Wendover, what has been amiss? I can see that you are sadly pulled, and my suspicion is that you have been trotting too hard!'

The demure laughter in his voice robbed his words of offence. Selina all too obviously succumbed to the charm of a personable and audacious young man, scolding him for his impertinence, in the manner of an indulgent aunt, and favouring him with an account of her late indisposition.

Abby was thus afforded an opportunity to study him at her leisure. She thought that it was easy to see why he had made so swift a conquest of Fanny: he was handsome, and he was possessed of ease and address, his manners being distinguished by a nice mixture of deference and assurance. Only in the slightly aquiline cast of his features could she detect any resemblance to his uncle: in all other respects no two men could have been more dissimilar. His height was not above the average, but, in contrast to Miles Calverleigh's long, loosely knit limbs, his figure was particularly good; he did not, like Miles, look as if he had shrugged himself into his coat: rather, the coat appeared to have been moulded to his form; the ears of his collars were as stiff as starch could make them; his neckcloths were never carelessly knotted, but always beautifully arranged, whether in the simple style of the Napoleon, or the more intricate folds of the Mathematical; and he showed exquisite taste in his choice of waistcoats. Such old fashioned persons as Mr Faversham might stigmatise him as a tippy, a dandy, a bandbox creature, but their instinctive dislike of the younger generation of dashing blades on the strut carried them too far: Stacy Calverleigh was a smart, but not quite a dandy, for he affected few of the extravagances of fashion. His shirt-points might be a little too high, his coats a trifle too much padded at the shoulder and nipped in at the waist, but he never overloaded his person with jewellery, or revolted plain men by helping himself to snuff with a silver shovel.

His profile, as he knelt beside the sofa, was turned towards Abby, and she was obliged to acknowledge that it was a singularly handsome profile. Then, when Fanny seized the opportunity offered by a pause in Selina's garrulity to present him to her other aunt, and he turned his head to look up at Abby, she thought him less handsome, but without quite knowing why.

He jumped up, exclaiming, with a boyishness which, to her critical ears, had a false ring: 'Oh! This is a moment to which I've been looking forward – and yet dreading! Your very humble servant, ma'am!'

'Dreading?' said Abby, lifting her brows. 'Were you led to suppose I was a gorgon?'

'Ah, no, far from it! A most beloved aunt!'

His ready smile curled his lips as he spoke, but Abby, looking in vain for a trace of the charm which awoke instant response in her when the elder Calverleigh smiled, realised that it did not reach his eyes. She thought they held a calculating look, and suspected him of watching her closely to discover whether he was making a good or a bad impression on her.

She said lightly: 'That doesn't seem to be a reason for your dread, sir.'

'No, and it's moonshine!' Fanny said. 'How can you talk such nonsense, Stacy?'

'It isn't nonsense. Miss Abigail loves you, and must think me unworthy of you – oh, an impudent jackstraw even to dream of aspiring to your hand!' He smiled again, and said simply: 'I think it too, ma'am. No one knows better than I how unworthy I am.'

A sentimental sigh and an inarticulate murmur from Selina showed that this frank avowal had moved her profoundly. Upon Abby it had a different effect. 'Trying to take the wind out of my eye, Mr Calverleigh?' she said.

If he was disconcerted he did not betray it, but answered

immediately: 'No, but, perhaps – the words out of your mouth?'

Privately, she gave him credit for considerable adroitness, but all she said was: 'You are mistaken: I am not so uncivil.'

'And it isn't true!' Fanny declared passionately. 'I won't permit anyone to say such a thing – not even you, Abby!'

'Well, I haven't said it, my dear, nor am I likely to, so there is really no need for you to fly up into the boughs! Tell me, Mr Calverleigh, have you made the acquaintance of your uncle yet?'

'My uncle?' he repeated. He glanced at Fanny, a question in his eyes. 'But what is this? *You* said, when I came in, that you thought I was my uncle! The only uncle I possess – if I do still possess him – lives at the other end of the world!'

'No, he doesn't,' replied Fanny. 'I mean, he doesn't do so now! He brought Lavinia Grayshott's brother home from Calcutta, and he is here, at the York House!'

'Good God!' he said blankly.

'He is not at all like you, but *very* agreeable, isn't he, Aunt Selina?'

'Yes, indeed,' agreed Selina. 'He is quite an oddity – so informal, but I daresay that comes of having lived for so long in India, which does not sound to me at all the sort of place anyone would *wish* to live in, but that, after all, was not his fault, poor man, and he is *perfectly* gentlemanly!'

'I'm glad to know that at least!' Stacy said ruefully. 'I never met him in my life, but I heartily wish him otherwise, for I fear he may destroy what little credit I may have with you! Alas, the round tale is that he is the black sheep in my family!'

'Oh, I fancy you have met him!' said Abby, showing hackle. 'He has no recollection of having done so, I own, but thinks he might have seen you when you were, as he phrased it, *a grubby brat*!'

He shot a quick look at her, but said, smiling again: 'Ah, very likely! I can't be blamed for having forgotten the circumstance, can I? I wonder what has brought him back to England?'

'But I told you!' Fanny reminded him. 'He brought poor Mr Oliver Grayshott home! And such good care did he take of him that Mrs Grayshott feels she cannot be sufficiently obliged to him! As for Oli – as for Mr Grayshott, he says he is a *trump*, and won't listen to a word in his disparagement!'

'Worse and worse!' he declared, with a comical grimace. 'A male attendant, in fact! A faint – a very faint – hope that he might have made his fortune in India withers at the outset!'

'Much might be forgiven in the prodigal son who returned to the fold with well-lined pockets, might it not?' said Abby, bestowing upon him a smile as false as she believed his own to be.

'Oh, everything!' he assured her gaily. 'That's the way of the world, ma'am!'

'Very wrong – most improper!' interpolated Selina, trying, not very successfully, to assemble her inchoate ideas into comprehensible words. 'I mean – I mean, money ought not, and *cannot* re-establish character! And to expect a man who had been cast off in a perfectly inhuman way (for so it seems to me, and I don't care what *anyone* says!) to come home to – to *shower* guineas on his *most* unnatural relations, is – is *monstrous*! Or, at any rate,' she temporised, 'absurd!'

'Bravo, Selina!' exclaimed Abby.

Faintly blushing under this applause, Selina said: 'Well, so it seems to me, though it had nothing to do with you, Mr Calverleigh, so you must not be thinking that I mean to censure *you*, and in any event poor Mr Miles Calverleigh hasn't made his fortune – at least, he doesn't look as if he had, because he wears the shabbiest clothes! On the other hand, he is putting up at York House, and that, you know, is by no means *dagger-cheap*, as some dear friends of ours, who are staying there, tell me.'

'The reverse!' he said. 'You terrify me, ma'am! He had always the reputation of being excessively expensive, and with never a feather to fly with! I only hope he doesn't tip them the double at York House, leaving me to stand the reckoning!' He saw that this speech had shocked Selina, and had made Fanny look gravely at him, and quickly and smoothly retrieved his position, saying:

'The truth is, you know, that he caused my grandfather, and my father too, a great deal of embarrassment, so that I never heard any good of him. I own, however, that I have often wondered if he could be quite as black as he was painted to me. Indeed, if *you* do not dislike him, Miss Wendover, he cannot be! I shall lose no time in making his acquaintance.' He turned towards Fanny, his smile a caress. 'Tell me all the latest Bath-news!' he begged. 'Has Lady Weaverham forgiven me for having been obliged to cry off from my engagement to dine with her? Has Miss Ancrum summoned up the courage to have that tooth drawn, or is she still wearing a swollen face? Did – oh, tell me everything! I feel as if I had been absent for a twelvemonth!'

Since the most interesting event which had lately occurred in Bath was the return of Oliver Grayshott to his mother's fond care it was not long before Fanny was telling him all about this, and demanding his help with the acrostic she was composing for Oliver's amusement. 'You see, I am doing what I may to entertain him,' she explained. 'Poor boy, he is so dreadfully pulled that he can't join in any of our expeditions, or attend the assemblies, or *anything*, so when Lavinia asked me to lend her my aid in keeping up his spirits *of course* I said I would!' She added, to her younger aunt's suppressed indignation: 'I thought you could not object?'

He responded suitably, but Abby, who was rapidly taking him in strong dislike, received (and welcomed) the impression that he did not regard the intrusion on the Bath scene of Mr Oliver Grayshott with favour.

Seven

Mr Stacy Calverleigh, having partaken of a light nuncheon in Sydney Place, strolled back towards the centre of the town, but instead of turning left at the end of Bridge Street, into High Street, he hesitated at the junction of the roads, and then, with a shrug of his shoulders, walked on, along Borough Wall to Burton Street. Turning northward up this he soon reached Milsom Street, at the top of which, in George Street, the York House Hotel was situated.

This hostelry was the most exclusive as well as the most expensive to be found in Bath; and it vaguely irritated Stacy that his ne'er-do-well uncle should be staying in it. Not that he had any wish to stay there himself, for however much money he might owe his tailor, and a great many other London tradesmen, he had no intention of damaging his reputation in Bath by going on tick there. In fact, the White Hart suited him very well, situated as it was in Stall Street, with many of its rooms overlooking the Pump Yard. The quiet of York House was not at all to his taste: he liked to be at the hub of things, and had no objection to the noise and bustle of a busy posting-house.

The weather had been uncertain all day, and by the time he reached York House it had begun to rain again. There was a damp chill in the air which made the sight of a small fire, burning in Mr Miles Calverleigh's private parlour, not unwelcome. Mr Calverleigh was seated on one side of it, his ankles crossed on a stool, and a cheroot between his fingers. He was glancing through a newspaper when the waiter announced Stacy, but after lowering it, and directing a critical look at his nephew, he threw it aside, saying, in a tone of tolerant amusement: 'Good God! Are you my nephew?'

'So I've been led to believe, sir,' replied Stacy, bowing slightly. '*If* you are indeed Miles Calverleigh?'

'I am, but you mustn't let it worry you,' said Miles kindly. 'You don't favour your father much: for one thing, he wasn't such a dapper-dog. Hadn't the figure for it. I collect that yellow calf-clingers are now all the crack?'

'Oh, decidedly!' said Stacy, whose primrose pantaloons were indeed of the first stare. He laid his hat, and his gloves, and his clouded cane down on the table. 'I have been absent from Bath or I should have visited you earlier, sir. You must forgive my seeming remissness.'

'Well, there's no difficulty about that: I hadn't the least expectation of seeing you.'

'One would not wish to be backward in any attention to so close a relative,' said Stacy, a trifle haughtily.

'What, not even to such a loose screw as I am? Come, come, nevvy! that's doing it rather too brown! You are wondering what the devil brings me here, and wishing that nothing had done so!' He laughed, seeing that he had taken Stacy aback, and said: 'Come down from your high ropes, and don't try to stand on points with me: I've no taste for punctilio. You don't owe me respect or observance, you know. Sit down, and empty your budget!'

'Well, sir – what *has* brought you home to England?' asked Stacy, with a forced smile.

'Inclination. Cheroot?'

'Thank you, no!'

'A snuff-taker, are you? You'll end with yellow stains all round your nose, but I daresay you may have caught your heiress before that happens, so it don't signify.'

Stacy said quickly, on the defensive: 'I don't know what you – who has told you –'

'Don't act the dunce! Miss Wendover told me – Miss Abigail Wendover – and I don't fancy your suit will prosper.'

'Not if she has anything to say in the matter!' Stacy said, his brow darkening. 'I believe her to be my enemy. I met her for the first time today, and it is very plain she'll knock me up if she can!'

'Not a doubt of it. I can tell you of another who is likely to bum squabble you, and that's James Wendover.'

'Oh, him!' Stacy said, shrugging. 'He may try to do so, but he won't succeed. Fanny doesn't care a rush for him. But this curst aunt is another matter. Fanny –' He broke off, realising suddenly that he had been betrayed into indiscretion, and summoned his boyish smile to his aid. 'The thing is that Fanny *is* an heiress. One can't blame her family for wishing her to make a great match, but when one is deep in love considerations of wealth or rank don't signify.'

'Well, at seventeen a girl may fancy herself to be deep in love, but in my experience it isn't a lasting passion,' commented Miles cynically. 'You aren't going to tell me that considerations of wealth don't signify to you, are you?'

The smile died under that ironic gaze; Stacy said angrily: 'Damn it, how could I marry a girl without fortune?'

'I shouldn't think you could. According to what I hear, your windmill has dwindled to a nutshell.'

'Who told you that?' Stacy demanded suspiciously. 'I wasn't aware that you had any acquaintance in England!'

'How should you be? I have, but it was Letty who told me you're monstrously in the wind.'

'Do you mean my great-aunt Kelham?' Stacy said incredulously. 'Are you asking me to believe that you have visited *her*?'

'Oh, no! I don't give a straw what you believe. Why should I?' said Miles, with unabated affability.

Flushing, Stacy stammered: 'Beg pardon! It was only that – well, she's such a devil of a high stickler that I shouldn't have thought – that is to say, –'

'*I* see!' said Miles encouragingly. 'What you would have thought is that she'd have shut the door in my face!'

Stacy burst out laughing. 'Well, yes!' he admitted. 'If I don't owe you respect, I need not wrap it up in clean linen, I collect!'

'Oh, no, not the least need to do that!' Miles assured him. 'The thing is that your great-aunt – lord, to think of Letty's being a great-aunt! She's no more than a dozen years older than I am! – well, the thing is that she was used to have a kindness for me. That might have been because she detested my father, of course. Come to think of it, *your* father wasn't first oars with her by any means. Or it might have been because most females are partial to rakes,' he added thoughtfully.

'Was *that* why you were sent abroad?' Stacy asked. 'I've never known precisely – you see, my father never spoke of you, except to say that you were *not* to be spoken of!'

'Oh, I was shockingly loose in the haft!' responded his uncle cordially. 'I started in the petticoat-line at Eton: that's why they expelled me.'

Stacy regarded him in some awe. 'And – and at Oxford?'

'I don't recall, but I should think very likely. The trouble then was that I was too ripe and ready by half: always raising some kind of a breeze. Nothing to the larks I kicked up in London, though. A peep-of-day boy, that was me – and a damned young fool! I crowned my career by trying to elope with an heiress. That was coming it rather too strong for the family, so they got rid of me, and I'm sure I don't blame them.' He smiled mockingly at his nephew. 'The luck didn't favour you either, did it?'

Stacy stiffened. 'Sir?'

'Tried to leap the book yourself, didn't you?'

'That, sir, is something I prefer not to discuss! It was an unfortunate episode! We were carried away by what we believed to be an unalterable passion! The circumstances – the whole truth – cannot be known to you, and – in short, I don't feel obliged to justify myself to you!'

'Good God, I trust you won't! It's no concern of mine. I may be your uncle, but I've really very little interest in you. You're too like me, and I find myself a dead bore. The only difference I can discover is that you're a gamester. That's the one vice I never had, and it don't awake a spark of interest in me, because I find gaming a dead bore too.'

'I suppose you're trying to gammon me – or know nothing of gaming, and that I don't believe!'

'Oh, no! I tried gaming, but it held no lure for me. Too slow!'

'Slow?' Stacy gasped.

'Why, yes! What have you to do but stake your blunt, and watch the turn of a card, or the fall of the dice? Same with horse-racing. Now, if I'd ever been offered a match, to ride my own horse against another man's, that would have been sport, if you like! But I ride too heavy, and always did.'

'But they said – I was given to understand – that you cost my grandfather a fortune!'

'I *was* expensive,' admitted Miles, 'though I shouldn't have put it as high as a fortune. But I got a deal of amusement out of my spendings. What the devil is there to amuse one in hazard or faro?'

It was evident that Stacy found this incomprehensible. He stared, and said, after a moment: 'I should envy you, I suppose! But I don't. It's in my blood, and surely in yours too! Father – my grandfather – great-uncle Charles – oh, all of them!'

'Yes, but you must remember that I was a sad disappointment to the family. My father even suspected me of being a changeling. A delightful theory, but without foundation, I fear.' He threw the butt of his cheroot into the fire, and got up, stretching his long limbs. His light eyes looked down at Stacy, their expression hard to interpret. 'Have you lost Danescourt yet?' he enquired.

Stacy laughed shortly. 'Good God, what would any man in his senses stake against that damned barrack? It's mortgaged to the hilt, and falling into ruin besides! It was encumbered when my father died, and *I* can't bring it about. I hate the place – wouldn't waste a groat on it!'

'Shades of our ancestors!' said Miles flippantly. 'They must all be turning in their graves. Perhaps *you* are a changeling! Or did you come to visit me in the hope that I might be able to restore your fallen fortunes?'

'Hardly!' Stacy said, flicking a glance at his uncle's person. 'I'm told you came home bear-leading Mrs Grayshott's son, which doesn't lead me to suppose you're swimming in lard! I hope to God that won't leak out!'

'Oh, I don't think so!' said Miles reassuringly. 'But you have it wrong: I wasn't bear-leading him. I was combining the duties of sick-nurse and valet.'

'Good God! If *that* should become known – ! I wish you will consider *my* position, sir!'

'But why should I?'

'Well, damme, I *am* your nephew!' Stacy said indignantly. 'And you are, after all, a Calverleigh!'

'Yes, but not at all high in the instep, I promise you. As for our relationship, no one can blame you for being my nephew – I don't myself – but if it irks you, don't acknowledge me!'

'It may seem to you to be a funning matter,' returned Stacy, reddening, 'but I shall beg leave to tell you, sir, that it is no very pleasant thing for me to have you here, looking like – oh, dash it, like a regular rough diamond!' He rose, and picked up his hat. 'I don't know how long you mean to remain in Bath, but I trust you are aware of what the charges are in this hotel!'

'Don't give them a thought!' said Miles. 'I won't chalk 'em up to you. If I find myself at a stand, I can always shoot the crow.'

'Vastly diverting, sir!' snapped Stacy, collecting his gloves and his cane. ''Servant!'

He executed a slight bow, and left the room. He was so much ruffled that he had reached the White Hart before his anger had cooled enough to allow him to consider whether he had acted wisely in letting his temper ride him. He was not naturally an even-tempered man, but he had cultivated an air of smiling good-humour, knowing that it was as great an asset to anyone living precariously on the fringe of society as his handsome countenance. It was rarely that he betrayed irritability, or lost his poise, even under the severe provocation of receiving a set-down from some out-and-outer into whose circle he had tried to insinuate himself, or a high-nosed stare from a great lady whose favour he wanted to win. He began to be vexed with himself, and to wonder what quality it was in his uncle which had set up his bristles; but it was not for some time, and then with reluctance, that it dawned on him that he had been made to feel small. This had nothing to do with Miles's superior height, and even less with his manner, which had not been that of a man talking to his nephew, but that of a man talking to a contemporary whom he regarded with indifference. Recalling how Miles had lounged at his ease, looking as though he had dressed all by guess, in an outmoded coat, his neckcloth loosened, and an abominable cheroot between his long brown fingers, he felt resentment stir again. He, and not his disreputable uncle, should have been master of the situation, but in some mysterious way he had been made to feel awkward. He had expected to have been received, if not with gratification, at least with pleasure: it had been a piece of condescension on the part of the head of the family to have visited its reprobate, but the reprobate was apparently unaware of this. He had been neither pleased nor displeased, and certainly not gratified; and the only interest he had shown in his nephew was of the most casual order. Stacy found this so galling that he almost wished himself back at the York House, for the purpose of giving the impudent fellow a well-deserved set-down.

It soon occurred to him, however, that it behoved him to tread warily: even, if he could do it, to make a friend of Miles. Miles knew of his courtship of Fanny Wendover, and there could be small doubt that he had learnt of it from her aunts. He had shown no sign of disapproval: indeed, he had taken as little interest in that as in the disclosure that Danescourt was heavily encumbered, but if he was on terms with Miss Abigail Wendover it might be worth while to make a push to gain his support.

Marriage had few attractions for Mr Stacy Calverleigh, but it had been forcibly borne in upon him that only by a rich marriage could he escape from embarrassments which had become extremely pressing; and he was determined to marry Fanny, even if he were forced to persuade her to elope with him. But it would be infinitely preferable to marry her with the consent of her aunts and her uncle. Selina he could bring round his thumb, but he had guessed from the outset that Selina was of less importance than Abigail, and that it was Abigail's influence which was the more likely to weigh with Mr James Wendover.

He had no illusions about James. He had never known James's father, or his elder brother, far less his grandfather, but he knew that they had been bywords in their day, and that James was commonly held to be the epitome of a Wendover. He was ruled by two passions: a determination to advance the interests of the family, and an even stronger determination to avoid at all costs anything savouring remotely of the scandalous. He could be depended on to oppose Fanny's marriage to an impecunious young man of slightly damaged reputation, but once the knot was tied he could also be depended on to hush up the resultant scandal. And if he did not immediately make suitable provision for his wealthy ward he would very soon be obliged to do so, for fear of *what people would say*. This (according to the malicious) was the dread which governed his conduct. And if Stacy showed himself to be a reformed character people would certainly say very rude things indeed, unless James put Fanny in possession of at least the income from her large fortune, and of her ancestral home. Particularly, thought Stacy, if the clandestine marriage were blessed with an heir. For himself, he had every intention of behaving with the utmost propriety, even of resigning himself for quite some time to living for several months of the year at Amberfield. It would be boring, but once it was known that he was married to an heiress whose property would become his within a few years he would be able to exist comfortably on the expectation. It should be possible for him to settle with his most pressing creditors, and although he would still be in Dun territory there would be no longer any fear of finding himself locked up for debt. Not the most avaricious bluntmonger would proceed to extremes against a man who was heir (by marriage) to a handsome fortune.

It was not, of course, the ideal marriage. He would have preferred – and, indeed, had preferred – a bride who had attained her majority; but heiresses were few and far between, and since his abortive attempt at an elopement his chances of being allowed to come within speaking distance of one had lessened to vanishing point. On the other hand, Fanny was a little beauty, and he thought that if he must become leg-shackled he would as lief marry her as any other. But he wanted to do so with the approval of her aunts; and, having made a conquest of Selina, he had been hopeful of achieving a like success with Abigail. Five minutes in her company had been enough to shatter optimism: Abigail was made of sterner stuff than her sister, and had plainly set her face against him. Probably James Wendover was to blame for that; perhaps another man's influence could be brought to bear with advantage. She seemed to be on friendly terms with Miles, which made it desirable to lose no time in enlisting Miles's support.

So when he attended the ball at the Upper Rooms that evening, and found that his uncle was present, talking to Mrs Grayshott, he seized the first opportunity that offered of greeting him with every sign of pleasure. He was relieved to see that Miles did at least possess knee-smalls and a swallow-tailed coat, but his fingers itched to rearrange a necktie which he thought deplorable, and to brush into a more fashionable style his uncle's raven locks. His own were beautifully pomaded, and swept into a Brutus; his coat exactly fitted his trim figure; a fob dangled at his waist; a quizzing-glass hung round his neck; the subtle fragrance of Steek's lavender water clung to his person; and a diamond pin nestled in the folds of his Oriental tie. In fact, as Lady Weaverham observed to Mrs Slinfold, he had the unmistakable London touch. Mrs Slinfold, concurring, added that in her opinion he was the first in elegance of all the gentlemen present; but Mrs Ruscombe, overhearing, said with her shallow laugh: 'Oh, do you think so? Such a fribble! My husband – so naughty of him! – calls him a positive coxcomb!'

But since everyone knew not only that it was Mrs Ruscombe's custom to attribute her more damaging criticisms to her meek spouse, but also that she had made every effort to throw the eldest of her five daughters in Mr Stacy Calverleigh's way, this remark was received in stony silence. Mr Stacy Calverleigh might be too much of a bandbox creature for everyone's taste, but he was not a coxcomb, for he neither strutted, nor played off the airs of an exquisite. His manners were very agreeable, so that even the most censorious of his elders were obliged to admit that he was pretty-behaved enough.

When Miss Abigail Wendover arrived, chaperoning her lovely niece, it was seen that she was wearing another of her London gowns, and agreed amongst her friends that she was in quite her best looks, only Mrs Ruscombe advancing the opinion that it was easy to appear to advantage if one was prepared to squander a fortune on one's back.

This estimate was an exaggeration, but, being comfortably endowed, Abby was not obliged to study economy, and had had no hesitation in purchasing an extremely costly gown of figured lace, worn over a satin robe, which hung in soft folds to her feet, and ended in a demi-train. This, as much as the diamond aigrette in her hair, proclaimed to the knowledgeable that she had no intention of dancing; but Mr Miles Calverleigh was not of their number, and presently made his way to where she was sitting, and begged to have the honour of leading her into the set which was then forming.

She smiled, but shook her head, saying: 'Thank you, but I don't dance.'

'I'm glad of that,' he said. Then, as surprise and quick amusement leapt into her eyes, he laughed, and added: 'I'm a shocking bad hand at it, you see! May I sit down, and talk to you instead?'

'Pray do!' she responded. 'I have been wishing for the opportunity of talking to you, sir. Have you yet made the acquaintance of your nephew?'

'Yes, he was so obliging as to pay me a visit today.'

'What do you think of him?' she demanded.

'Why, nothing! Must I?'

'I wish you won't be so provoking!' said Abby.

'I wouldn't provoke you for the world. But what would you have me say? He was with me for less than an hour, and I can't recall that he said anything that interested me to the point of *thinking* about him.'

'You are a most unnatural uncle!' she told him, with a severity at variance with the dimple that peeped in her cheek.

'Am I?' He reflected for a moment. 'No, I don't think so. I'd three uncles, and none of 'em took the smallest interest in me. After all, why should they?'

'For no reason at all, I daresay! Are you trying to make me – oh, what is it the hunting men say? – fly from a scent? Yes, that's it. Well, you won't do it! I also made the acquaintance of your nephew today, and I don't scruple to tell you that I like him even less than I had expected I should!'

'No, did you? Your expectations must have been much higher than you led me to suppose!'

'No, but – oh, I suppose I did expect him to be a man of charm! I don't find him charming at all, and I can't conceive how Fanny came to fall in love with him! Now, tell me to my head, can you?'

'Oh, easily!' he replied. 'He is a very pretty fellow, you must allow! Turns out in excellent trim, too, and has both air and address.'

'Oh, yes!' she said bitterly. 'Playing off his cajolery! He tried to turn me up sweet, but it's my belief he is one who hides his teeth. And when he smiles there's no smile in his eyes: only – only a *measuring* look! Surely you must have seen it?'

'Well, no!' he confessed. 'But that might be because he didn't smile very often when he was with me. Or perhaps because he saw no need to – er – measure me!'

She said quickly: 'You didn't like him either, did you?'

'Oh, no! But how many people does one like?'

She frowned over this, momentarily diverted. 'Upon first

acquaintance? I don't know: not very many, perhaps. But one need not *dis*like them, and I *do* dislike Mr Stacy Calverleigh!'

'Yes, I thought you did,' he said gravely.

'And I don't believe, for all his protestations and caressing ways, that he *truly* loves Fanny, or would have made the least push to engage her affections had she not been possessed of a large fortune!'

'Oh, lord, no!'

She turned her head, looking up into his face with pleading eyes, and laying one of her expensively gloved hands on his arm. 'If you too think that, won't you – oh, Mr Calverleigh, *won't* you do *anything* to save my poor Fanny?'

He was regarding her with the smile which, unlike his nephew's, sprang to life in his eyes, but all he said was: 'My dear girl – No, no, don't poker up! It was a slip of the tongue! My dear Miss Wendover, what do you imagine I *could* do?'

Never having considered this, she was at a loss for an answer. She said lamely: 'Surely you must be able to do *something*!'

'What leads you to think so?'

'Well – well, you are his uncle, after all!'

'Oh, that's no reason! You've told me already that I am an unnatural uncle, and if that means one who don't meddle in the affairs of a nephew over whom he has no authority, and who might, for aught he cares, have been any other man's nephew, you are undoubtedly right!'

'Not authority, no! But whatever you may say the relationship exists, and you must have *influence*, if you would but exert it?'

He looked down at her in some amusement. 'You know, you have some remarkably hubble-bubble notions in that charming head of yours! How the devil should I have influence over a nephew who met me for the first time this afternoon?'

She perceived the force of this argument, but the conviction that he could drive off Stacy, if he chose to do it, remained with her. It was irrational, to be accounted for only by the strength she believed she had detected in his harsh-featured countenance, and by a certain ruthlessness which underlay his careless manners. She said, with a tiny sigh: 'I suppose you can have none. And yet – and yet – I think you *could*, if you but wanted to!'

'For my part,' he retorted, 'I think you are very well able to button it up yourself, without any assistance from me.

There did not seem to be anything more to be said, nor was she granted the opportunity to pursue the subject, her attention being claimed just then by Mr Dunston, who had been watching her jealously for some minutes, and now came up to beg for the privilege of taking her into the tea-room presently.

They met again, two days later, in Edgar Buildings; and however little pleased Abby may have been to find Mr Stacy Calverleigh in Mrs Grayshott's drawing-room, making himself agreeable to his hostess, and winning Fanny's favour by the engaging solicitude with which he treated Mr Oliver Grayshott, she was undoubtedly pleased to see his uncle, and betrayed it by the sudden smile which lit her eyes, and the readiness with which she put out her hand.

She discovered that her arrival had interrupted a lively discussion. Mr Grayshott's medical adviser, visiting him earlier in the day, had professed himself very well satisfied with his progress, and had endorsed a somewhat recalcitrant patient's belief that it would do him a great deal of good to abandon the sofa, and to get out for a little air and exercise. A drive up to Lansdown, and a gentle walk there, enjoying the view of the Bristol Channel, was what he recommended; but when Mr Grayshott took exception to this programme, saying, very improperly, that he would be damned if he allowed himself to be driven to Lansdown or anywhere else, as though he were dying of a deep decline, the doctor laughed, and said: 'Well, well, go for a ride, if you choose! It won't do you any harm, provided you don't go too far, or exhaust yourself.'

This was by no means what Mrs Grayshott wanted. She believed Oliver to be a long way from complete recovery, unable to forget how grey and worn he had looked after the journey from London; and she could not like his scheme of riding out of Bath with his sister as his only companion. Lavinia was a nervous horsewoman, requiring constant surveillance: not at all the sort of escort one would choose to send out with an invalid; and Fanny, instantly offering to accompany the Grayshotts, was no more acceptable to the widow. Fanny was not nervous. Mrs Grayshott, herself no horsewoman, had heard her described by one of her admirers as a clipping rider, a regular good 'un to go, which was an encomium to strike dread into a mother's anxious heart. And then, to make matters worse, Stacy Calverleigh, who had met the two girls in Queen's Square, and accompanied them to Edgar Buildings, proffered his services, laughingly assuring Mrs Grayshott that he would engage himself to bring the party back to her in good time, and none the worse for wear.

This question was instantly approved of by the girls, if not by Oliver, which made it difficult for Mrs Grayshott to decline it. She was floundering amongst some rather lame excuses when Abigail was announced.

'In a good hour! Come in, my dear, and lend me your support!' she exclaimed going forward to greet Abby. 'Here is my wilful son determined on riding up to Lansdown, and these other young people bent on making up a party to go with him! I am persuaded you cannot like the scheme any more than I do, for although Mr Stacy Calverleigh has very kindly offered to go with them I fear that he would find the task of preventing three such harum-scarum children from going much too far quite beyond his power!'

'No, indeed we wouldn't!' cried Fanny. 'We mean to take the greatest care of Oliver, and I promise you it wouldn't be at all hard for Stacy to prevent us from going too far, even if we wished to do so, ma'am!' She turned impulsively towards Abby. '*You* don't object to it, do you, Abby?'

Misliking the scheme, yet unable to think of any other reason for placing a veto on it but the inclusion of Stacy in the party, Abby hesitated. Rescue came from an unexpected quarter. 'Do you ride, Miss Wendover?' asked Mr Miles Calverleigh, smiling across the room at her with such complete understanding in his eyes that an answering smile was won from her.

'Why, yes!' she replied.

'In that case, you may be easy, ma'am,' said Miles, to Mrs Grayshott. 'Between us, Miss Wendover and I should be able to control the activities of the younger members of this hazardous expedition.'

The only objection raised to this unexpected augmentation of the party came from Oliver, who said, with feeling, that he had not yet received notice to quit, and was very well able to take care of himself. He added that if he had had the least apprehension that his wish to hack out of Bath would have caused such a commotion he would never have uttered it.

'Silence, halfling!' said Miles, in shocked accents. 'You are leading Miss Wendover to suppose that you don't want her to go with you!'

This intervention naturally cast Oliver into confusion, and he hastened to reassure Abby. She laughed at him, telling him that she had not the smallest intention of enacting the role of dry-nurse; and was herself much heartened by Fanny's instant approval of the revised scheme.

'Oh, capital!' Fanny exclaimed. 'You will come, won't you, *Best* of my aunts?'

Eight

Since Oliver showed no signs of exhaustion, and Stacy, behaving with great circumspection, made no attempt to monopolise Fanny's attention, nothing occurred to spoil Abby's enjoyment of this mild form of exhilaration. Miles Calverleigh rode beside her for most of the time, and made himself so agreeable that she forgot her anxieties in listening to what he had to tell her of India, and the customs of its people. He had to be coaxed to talk, saying at first that persons who gabbed about their foreign experiences were dead bores, but the questions she put to him were intelligent, and her interest in his replies so real that he soon dropped his reserve, painting a vivid picture for her, and even recounting some of his experiences. These ranged from the adventurous to the comical, but it was not long before he brought them to an end, saying: 'And that is enough about me! Now tell me of yourself!'

'Alas, there's nothing to tell! I've done nothing, and have been nowhere. You don't know how much I envy you – how often I have wished I were a man!'

'Have you, indeed? You must be alone in that wish!'

'Thank you! But you are wrong: my father wished it too! He wanted another son.'

'What, with Rowland and James as grim examples? Or because he hoped that a third son might be less of a slow-top?'

'Certainly not! And although I didn't like him I must in common justice say that Rowland, at least, was not a slow-top. He was hunting-mad, you know, and a very hard goer.'

'I wasn't talking about that. Intellectually a slow-top!'

'Oh, yes, but so was my father! Naturally he didn't count his stupidity a fault in Rowland. In fact, he had the greatest dislike of clever people.'

He chuckled appreciatively, which made her say, in a conscience-stricken voice: 'I ought not to have said that. My wretched tongue! I do *try* to mind it!'

'Then don't! I like the way you have of saying just what comes into your head.'

She smiled, but shook her head. 'No, it is my besetting sin, and I ought long since to have overcome it.'

'From what I recall of your father, I should suppose that he made every effort to help you to do so. Did he dislike you as much as you disliked him?'

'Yes, he – Oh, how dare you? You are quite abominable! You know very well that it would be the height of impropriety for me to say that I disliked my father! Every feeling must be offended!'

'Well, none of mine are,' he responded imperturbably. 'You did, didn't you?'

'Yes, but it is one of the things which must never be said. And if he disliked me I am bound to own that it was quite my own fault. I was a sad trial to him, I fear.'

'Yes, of course: too clever by half!'

'I'm not clever – or only if you compare me with the rest of my family,' she said reflectively. 'I love them dearly, but Selina and Mary are perfect widgeons, and although my sister Jane has a good deal of commonsense she never thinks of anything but her children, and the failings of her servants. My father merely thought I was bookish, which was the worst he could say of anyone! He ascribed all my undutiful conduct to it.'

'Now, I should have said that you had an all too lively sense of your duty,' he remarked.

'Not when I was a girl. I was for ever rebelling against the restrictions imposed upon me, and oh, how much I detested that hateful word, *propriety*! That's why I was used to wish I were a man: so that I could have escaped from it! Girls can't, you know. We are always shackled – hedged about –'

'*Cabin'd, cribb'd, confined,*' he supplied, adding grandiloquently: 'I'm bookish too.'

A ripple of laughter broke from her. 'So I perceive! And that is just how it was in my family.'

'Was? Still is!'

She turned her head, startled. 'No! Why, what can you mean?'

He nodded towards the four younger members of the party, riding ahead. 'Fanny, of course. Don't you cabin, crib, and confine her?'

'Indeed I don't!' she said warmly. 'She enjoys far, far more liberty than ever I did!' A quizzically raised eyebrow brought the blood rushing to her cheeks. She stammered: 'It's true! You – you are thinking that I don't permit her to go anywhere without me, but that is *not* true! I have never, until your odious nephew came to Bath, accompanied her on such expeditions as this – and if *he* had not been in question, and young Grayshott had invited her to go with him, she might have done so with my goodwill!' She paused, and, after considering for a moment, said frankly: 'No. Not alone. *I* should have no qualms, but where she is concerned I must take care that she does nothing to provide all the Bath quizzes with food for gossip! You see, my brother entrusted her to my guardianship, and however nonsensical I may think many of the conventions which hedge us about I must, for her own sake, compel her to abide by them. Pray try to understand! What I, at my age, might choose to disregard, she, on the verge of her come-out, must not!'

'Poor girl!' he said lightly. 'How many nonsensical conventions are *you* ready to flout?'

'Oh, a great many, if I had only myself to consider!'

'We'll put that to the test. Will you go with me to the play on Saturday?'

She hesitated, in equal surprise and doubt. After a moment, she said: 'Are you inviting me to form one of your party, sir?'

'Good God, no! I haven't a party.'

'Oh!' She relapsed again into silence. 'I collect you mean to invite Fanny as well?' she hazarded at last.

'Oh, no, you don't!' he retorted. 'You know very well that Fanny is engaged to go with the Grayshotts to Mrs Faversham's waltzing-party! I wonder you will let her!'

'Do you, indeed? Well, if you think me so – so *stuffy*, *I* wonder that you should suppose I would go to the theatre with you alone! The waltz is not danced in the Rooms, but Bath is a very old-fashioned place, and, in London, waltzes, and quadrilles too, are extensively danced. I am very happy that Fanny should be given the opportunity of – of getting into the way of it, before her come-out in the spring! But when it comes to going to the theatre –' She paused, frowning over it.

He waited, regarding her profile with a derisive smile, until she said, struck by a sudden inspiration: 'If you were to invite my sister as well! That would make it perfectly unexceptionable!'

'No doubt!'

She could not help laughing. 'Yes, I know, but – Well, it is quite absurd, but there is a difference – or there is thought to be – between escorting a lady to – oh, to a concert, in the Assembly Rooms, and to the theatre! I think it is because the concerts, being held by subscription, are more private. Then, too, one doesn't sit apart, and one mingles with –'

'Oh, if that's all, we can sit in the pit!'

' – with one's friends!' finished Abby severely.

'And at the end of the first act, when your escort hopes to enjoy your company, some impudent fellow snabbles you from under his nose, and takes you off to tea – just as I did, when that mooncalf who paid you slip-slop compliments thought you were his own!'

'Well! At least you have the grace to own your impudence!' she retaliated. 'However gracelessly you may do so! But Mr Dunston is not a mooncalf, and the compliments he paid me were very pretty.'

'Any man who could tell you that you shone down every other

woman present, and said you were as fair as a rose in May can't help but be a mooncalf. Trying it on much too rare and thick!'

Piqued, she said: 'I am not a beauty, and I never was, but I am not an *antidote*, I hope!'

He smiled. 'No, you are neither the one nor the other. What that dunderheaded admirer of yours hasn't the wit to perceive is that you've something of more worth than mere beauty.'

Miss Wendover was well aware that it behoved her to give the audacious Mr Calverleigh a cold set-down, or, at the very least, to ignore this remark; but instead of doing either of these things she directed a look of shy enquiry at him. 'Have I? Pray tell me what it may be!'

He looked her over critically, the amusement lingering in his eyes. 'Well, you have a great deal of countenance, and an elegant figure. I like your eyes too, particularly when they laugh. But that's not it. What you have in abundance is charm!'

She blushed rosily, and stammered: 'I am afraid, sir, that it is now you who are offering me Spanish coin!'

'Oh, no! Your nose is indifferent, and your mouth a trifle too large, and your hair, though it grows prettily, is an unremarkable brown.'

She broke into laughter. 'I acquit you!'

'So I should hope! I might have added that you had also courage, but I doubt it.'

She fired up at that. 'Then you are mistaken! I collect that's a jibe, because I hesitated to accept your invitation! Very well, I will go to the play with you!'

'Good girl!' he said approvingly. 'Pluck to the backbone! But I won't take you if you really feel that it would damage your reputation.'

'No,' she said, in a resolute tone. 'Not at my age!'

'Just what I was thinking myself,' he agreed.

She looked sharply at him, but he was perfectly grave. 'Would it be proper for you to dine with me first, at York House?' he asked.

'Thank you, but I should prefer you to dine in Sydney Place,' she replied. 'My sister will be very happy to further her acquaintance with you.'

He bowed a meek acceptance, and, as they had by this time reached their goal, which was the monument erected to the memory of one Sir Basil Grenville, killed in the Civil Wars, their conversation came to an end.

Nor was it resumed; for after the remains of a Saxon fortification, situated near by, had been shown to the Calverleighs, one of whom affected a civil but artificial interest in it, and the other no interest at all, it was judged to be time to turn homeward; and upon the return journey the party split up into a different order, Mr Stacy Calverleigh contriving that Abby should ride with him instead of with his uncle.

'Do, pray, allow me to be your escort, ma'am!' he said. 'I have been seeking an opportunity to talk to you, and – I hope – to better my acquaintance with you.'

'By all means,' she answered, in a cool voice. 'What is it you wish to say to me, sir?'

He bestowed his flashing smile upon her. 'Ah, you know what I wish to say! And I, alas, know that I am addressing myself to an ear little inclined to listen to me!'

'If you mean to address yourself to me in rehearsed periods, you are perfectly right!' she told him. 'Without roundaboutation, you wish to obtain my consent to Fanny's becoming engaged to you. I am afraid you haven't understood the case: Fanny isn't my ward, but my brother's. You must apply to him, not to me. In fact,' she added thoughtfully, 'you should have done so before making Fanny an offer. To form a connection with a girl of seventeen without the knowledge of her guardian is really not at all the thing, you know.'

He looked a little discomposed. 'Had I known – I thought, at first, that she was Miss Wendover's ward! Naturally, if I had known –'

'Then what prevented you from asking my sister's permission before you declared yourself to Fanny?' asked Abby, in an interested voice.

He bit his lip. 'I should have done so, of course, but I had no reason to suppose – that is to say, I believed she was aware – did not look upon my suit with disfavour! Then, too, conscious as I am of my unworthiness I did not intend – Ah, Miss Abby, you don't understand! You make no allowance for the violence of my feelings, which, I confess, carried me beyond the bounds of propriety!'

'No, I don't think I do,' agreed Abby.

He shot a challenging look at her, which she met with a faint bland smile. 'From the moment I saw her I was lost!' he said dramatically. 'Oh, I have fancied myself in love before, many times – you see, I don't attempt to deceive you, ma'am! – but when I met Fanny I knew that it had never been more than fancy, and bitterly did I regret the past – all my follies and indiscretions! Yes, and determined to become worthy of that beautiful angel!'

'Well, you have plenty of time to achieve your ambition,' said Abby cordially. 'There is no saying but what, if you were to succeed, my brother might look more kindly upon you, when Fanny reaches her majority.'

'Four years! Miss Abby, neither she nor I could endure it! We hoped – Fanny was fully persuaded that you – her favourite aunt, as she calls you! – would stand our friend! *Your* support must weigh with Mr Wendover!'

'My dear sir, if I were to lend my support to such an unsuitable and improvident marriage, Mr Wendover would suppose me to have run mad, and would be more likely to have me placed under restraint. And I must say that I shouldn't blame him!'

'Improvident!' he exclaimed, catching at the word. 'Ay, that is the obstacle! Believe me, I feel it as keenly as you do! My inheritance was wasted before I came into it, and when I tell you that my father died before I was of age you may judge how unripe I was, how little able to restore what had been squandered! I hope I am wiser now.'

'I am sure,' said Abby politely, 'that all your friends must share that hope. I fear, however, that my brother will require some rather more solid proof.'

Nettled, he said: 'You misunderstand me, ma'am! When I spoke of my inheritance having been wasted, I did not mean that I am reduced to penury! Between my fortune and Fanny's I fear there may be disparity, but although my lands are not in such good heart as I could wish they are extensive, and I am, after all, the head of my family! There have been Calverleighs at Danescourt since I don't know when!'

'Since the Conquest,' she supplied, with a reminiscent chuckle. 'According to your uncle, the founder of your house was in all probability one of the – the *thatchgallows* in the Conqueror's train.'

'My uncle is fond of cutting jokes,' he replied, with a forced smile. 'Even Mr James Wendover can scarcely find fault with my lineage! As for fortune, I don't know what Fanny's may be, nor do I care – except that if it is to form an insuperable barrier between us I wish it at Jericho!'

'Well, for the next eight years it might as well be,' she said prosaically. 'It was left to my brother to be held in trust for Fanny until she reaches the age of five-and-twenty, you know.'

'Five-and-twenty!' he ejaculated, the smile wiped suddenly from his lips. He recovered himself in a flash, saying: 'I didn't know it, and am agreeably surprised. Under those circumstances I must surely escape the stigma of being thought a fortune-hunter.'

This seemed to her so disingenuous that she was too much disgusted to answer him. She rode on at a quickened pace, so that the rest of the party was soon overtaken, and Stacy was obliged to bring his confidences to an end.

Whatever discomfiture he might feel, no sign of it was to be detected, either in his face or in his manner. He seemed, rather, to be in spirits, full of liveliness and wit, keeping Lavinia in giggles, and causing Fanny to ask her aunt, when they rode down Great Pulteney Street together, if she did not find him as charming as he was handsome.

'Why, as to that – he has agreeable manners, but – do you think him *charming*, Fanny?' said Abby, on a note of surprise.

'Good gracious, Abby, *everyone* does so!' Fanny cried.

'Oh!'

Ruffled, Fanny said: 'This must be prejudice! Pray, what fault do you find in him?'

Abby smiled. 'If I were to tell you, love, you would be ready to pull caps with me!'

'Yes – if you said what I believe to be in your mind! You think him a fortune-hunter, don't you?' She waited for a moment, but as Abby said nothing, continued hotly: 'It is false, and – and unworthy of you, Abby! I beg your pardon, but I won't allow you to abuse him! He didn't know about my fortune when he fell in love with me, and later, when he learned of it from some odious tattle-box, he was utterly cast down – talked of his *presumption*, said his case was hopeless, and that he would never, never have approached me if he had known the truth! Such stuff! I verily believe he would have gone away if I hadn't been able to tell him that it will be four whole years before I have a penny more than the pin-money my uncle doles out to me!'

'I am afraid you misled him a little, dearest, and that the blame rests on my shoulders,' said Abby apologetically. 'I thought you knew – at least, that's what I should have supposed, had I thought about it all. I'm ashamed to say that I didn't. My excuse is that we have never discussed money-matters, have we? You won't come into possession of your fortune until you are five-and-twenty.'

Fanny looked very much taken aback, and exclaimed heatedly: 'You don't mean it! Well, of all the shabby things to do – ! Why, *already* I need more than my uncle gives me, and I shall need *much* more when I go to London for my come-out!'

'Of course you will!' agreed Abby, considerably heartened by this naïve speech. 'Your uncle knows that – indeed, we had some discussion about it when I was in London. You won't find him ungenerous, I promise you. He wishes you to present what he calls a creditable appearance!'

'Not ungenerous if I am meek and obedient! But if I don't submit to his tyranny – what then?'

'Really, Fanny!' Abby protested. 'What cause have you ever had to talk of his tyranny?'

'None – *yet*! But if he tries to part me from Stacy it *will* be tyranny! And I'll tell you this, Abby! – I don't care a rush for my hateful fortune, or even if my uncle cuts off my allowance, and Stacy won't care either! No, and I don't care if I don't go to London – not a bit!'

'I wish you will not talk in that skimble-skamble style!' said Abby, with asperity. 'Anyone would take you for a perfect zero! Do you, in all seriousness, expect your uncle to allow you to be married out of the schoolroom?'

'He would, if Stacy were wealthy, and were an Earl, or some such thing!' said Fanny, on an angry sob.

'Oh, no, he would not!' replied Abby. 'He would have me to reckon with! Do, for heaven's sake, try for a little commonsense, child! You have tumbled into love, and you believe it to be a lasting attachment – '

'I *know* it is!' Fanny declared passionately.

'Very well! It may be as you say, and if it should prove to be so you may rest assured of my support. Young Calverleigh has told me that he means to become worthy of you, and if he succeeds in reforming his way of life –'

'He has done so!'

'In that case, I see no reason at all for you to fall into affliction. Neither your uncle nor I are monsters of cruelty, and if, when you have seen a little of the world, you still prefer Calverleigh to all the other men you will meet, and he shows himself to be equally constant, we shall not oppose the marriage.'

'What, wait for nearly a whole year?' cried Fanny, aghast. 'Oh, no, no, no! If you had ever been in love you *could* not be so heartless!'

'I see nothing very heartless in wishing you to enjoy at least one London season before you embark on eight years of poverty,' said Abby dryly.

'That isn't what you wish!' Fanny said, her voice trembling. 'You wish to take me away from my beloved Stacy! I know just how it would be if I consented! You, and my Aunt Mary, would take good care n-never to let me so m-much as *see* him! I daresay you think I should soon forget him, but I shan't! Oh, Abby, Abby, I thought you loved me!'

'You know very well that I do.'

But Fanny, swallowing her tears, shook her head, and rode on in silence.

Meanwhile, Stacy, having begged for the honour of entertaining his uncle to dinner that evening, was taking great pains to order such dishes and wines as would be most likely to put Mr Miles Calverleigh in a mellow mood. Having scrutinised the bill of fare, and bored the waiter by changing his mind three times, he decided at last in favour of a soup, to be removed with a loin of veal, and followed by partridges, accompanied by broiled mushrooms and French beans, with a dressed crab, fat livers in cases, and some artichoke bottoms in sauce, as side-dishes. This elegant repast was served in his private parlour, and although Miles, a sparing eater, could not have been said to do full justice to it, toying with the veal, and refusing the crab and the livers, he ate two partridges, and raised no demur at having his glass constantly refilled.

Until the covers were removed, and a bottle of brandy set upon the table, Stacy confined his conversation to everyday chit-chat, which consisted largely of anecdotes of ton, and the latest titbits of London scandal, but when the waiter left the parlour Miles Calverleigh, pushing his chair back, and stretching his legs out before him, one ankle crossed over the other, yawned, and said: 'Cut line, nevvy! You didn't invite me here to regale me with on-dits. What do you want of me?'

'Good God, sir, nothing! Why, what should I want?'

'I've no idea. Or what you imagine I could – or would – do for you.'

This was not encouraging, but Stacy persevered. 'Don't you feel that we should get to know one another, sir?'

'No, why?'

Stacy blinked at him. 'Well – our relationship!'

'Don't give it a thought! Relations are a dead bore.'

'Not you, sir!' said Stacy, with his ready laugh. 'Indeed, far from it! I can't tell you how many times in the past week I've heard your praises sung!'

'Well, don't try. Are you hopeful of borrowing money from me?'

'Much good that would do me! I daresay your pockets are as much to let as mine!' Stacy said, tossing off the brandy in his glass, and stretching out his hand for the bottle.

Miles, who was warming his own glass in his cupped hands, said: 'As I don't know to what extent your pockets are to let –'

He was interrupted. 'Wholly!' Stacy said, with yet another laugh, this time one devoid of mirth. 'I'm all to pieces!' He waited for a moment, but as he won no other response than a polite look of enquiry from his unfeeling relative continued jerkily: 'The devil's been in the cards! Yes, and in the bones too! I've only to rattle them and they fall crabs! If I can't contrive to fly a kite, I shall be gutted!'

Mr Miles Calverleigh, having warmed his glass to his satisfaction, and savoured the aroma of the brandy, sipped it delicately. 'I daresay you'll come about,' he said.

Anger rose in Stacy, and, with it, his colour. 'Not if that curst aunt of Fanny's has anything to say to it! And now she tells me that Fanny don't come of full age until she's five-and-twenty!'

'You will have to look for another kite to fly, won't you?'

Stacy disposed of his second glass of brandy. 'Do you suppose I haven't done so? Damn it, I thought it was all hollow! But when a man's luck is out it's ames-ace with him, whatever he sets his hand to! I've been punting on tick for weeks past – hardly dare show my face in town!'

'I should go abroad, if I were you.'

'Pray, what should I subsist on?' snapped Stacy.

'Oh, on your wits!' said Miles cheerfully.

'I collect that's what you did!'

'Yes, of course.'

'They don't seem to have served you very well!'

Miles laughed. 'Better than an apron-string hold would have done, I promise you!'

There was just enough contempt in his voice to put Stacy, already embarking on a third glass, in a flame. He exclaimed: 'I don't know what right you have to hold up your nose, sir! It's what you did – or tried to do – yourself!'

'Is it?' said Miles. 'You seem to be remarkably well informed!'

'You as good as told me so,' Stacy muttered. 'In any event, I've always known that you ran off with some heiress or another.'

'So I did,' agreed Miles, without the smallest sign of discomposure. 'I shouldn't recommend you to follow my example: you would do better to regard me in the light of a grim warning.'

'I don't wish to run off with Fanny! It was never my intention, until that archwife returned to Bath to thrust a spoke in my wheel!'

'That *what*?'

The astonishment in his uncle's voice recalled to Stacy's mind his reason for having invited him to dinner, and, with an abrupt change of front, he said: 'I should not abuse her! No, or blame her either, I suppose. But when one's hopes are cut up – She has set her face against the marriage, sir!'

'Well, you certainly can't blame her for that.'

'I have said I don't! I've done my utmost to bring her about – assured her of my determination to be worthy of Fanny – all to no avail! She is unmoved! Nothing I could say had the least effect on her!'

'You can't tell that. The chances are you made her feel damned queasy.'

'But it's true!' Stacy declared, flushing hotly. 'I'll be a pattern-husband, I swear!'

'Hornswoggle!' said his uncle, not mincing matters.

'No, I tell you!'

'Well, don't! What the devil's the use of telling me that, or anything else? *I'm* not the girl's guardian!'

'You could help me, if you chose to do it!'

'I doubt it.'

'Yes, yes, I'm certain of it!' Stacy said eagerly, once more refilling his glass. 'Miss Abigail likes you – you're wondrous great with her! I heard how she was talking to you today, and laughing at the things you said to her! If you were to support me, plead my cause –'

'Yes, you're a trifle disguised!' interrupted Miles.

'No such thing! I'll have you know, sir –'

'Oh, not ape-drunk!' said Miles reassuringly. 'Just about half-sprung!'

'I'll engage to see *you* out, sir!'

Miles looked amused. 'You'd be obliged to knock under! However, I'd as lief you made the attempt rather than talk any more balderdash! *I* plead your cause? What the devil gave you the notion that I plead any causes but my own? Believe me, it's wide of the mark!'

'You *can't* be such a – such a care-for-nobody as to refuse to lift as much as a finger to assist me!' said Stacy indignantly.

'Oh, you're quite mistaken! I am precisely such a care-for-nobody.'

'But I'm your nephew! You can't want me to be rolled-up!'

'It's a matter of indifference to me.'

'Well, upon my soul!' Stacy exploded.

'As it would be to you if that fate befell me,' said Miles, slightly smiling. 'Why should either of us care a straw for what becomes of the other?'

Stacy gave an uncertain laugh. 'Damme if ever I met such a queer-card as you are!'

'Don't let it distress you! Comfort yourself with the reflection that it would do you no good if I did choose to recommend you to Miss Abigail Wendover.'

'She would listen to you,' Stacy argued. 'And if *she* could be brought to consent to the marriage I don't doubt that

Wendover would do so too. He doesn't concern himself with Fanny – never has done so! – and his wife don't like her. *She* isn't going to bring her out next year! I'll lay you a guinea to a gooseberry she'd be glad to see Fanny safely buckled before she brings out her own daughter!'

'Then why waste your eloquence on me? Address yourself to Mrs James Wendover!'

'With Miss Abigail against me?' Stacy said scornfully. 'I'm not such a clunch!'

'My good boy, if you imagine that James Wendover could be persuaded by his sister, or by anyone else, to consent to Fanny's marriage to a basket-scrambler, you're a lunatic!' said Miles brutally.

Stacy drained his fourth glass. 'What'll you wager against the chance that he'll find himself forced to consent?' he demanded, his utterance a little slurred. 'Got to force him to – nothing else to be done to bring myself about!'

'What about Danescourt?'

Stacy stared at him rather owlishly. 'Danescourt?'

'Why don't you sell it?' asked Miles coolly.

'Sell it! I'm going to save it! Before they can foreclose!'

'As bad as that?'

'Yes, damn you! Besides – I don't want to sell it!'

'Why not? You told me you hated it!'

'Yes, but it means something. Gives one consequence. Place in the country, you know: Calverleigh of Danescourt! No substance without it – bellows to mend with me!'

'It appears to be bellows to mend with you already,' said his uncle caustically.

Nine

*M*r Stacy Calverleigh, having slept off the result of his potations, awoke, far into the following day, with only the haziest recollections of what might have passed between himself and his uncle. So much did he plume himself on his ability to drink all other men under the table that he ascribed the circumstance of his having been put to bed by the boots to the vile quality of the brandy supplied by the White Hart; and when he encountered Mr Miles Calverleigh in Milsom Street, two days later, he laughingly apologised for it, and for its effect upon himself, describing this as having been rendered a trifle above oar. He spoke gaily, but under his insouciance there lurked a fear that he might have been betrayed into indiscretion. He said that he hoped he had not talked a great deal of nonsense, and was reassured by his uncle's palpable lack of interest. He then ventured to express the hope that Miles would not betray him to the ladies in Sydney Place, saying: 'I should find myself in the briars if Miss Abigail even suspected that I do, now and then, have a cup too much!'

'What a good thing you've warned me not to do so!' responded Miles sardonically. 'Entertaining females with accounts of jug-bitten maunderings is one of my favourite pastimes.'

He left Stacy with one of his careless nods, and strode on down the street, bound for the Pump Room. Here he found all the Wendovers: Abby listening with an expression of courteous interest to one of General Exford's anecdotes; Fanny making one of a group of lively young persons; and Selina, with Miss

Butterbank in close attendance, receiving the congratulations of her friends on her emergence from seclusion. After an amused glance in Abby's direction, Miles made his way towards Selina, greeting her with the ease of long friendship, and saying, with his attractive smile: 'I shan't ask you how you do, ma'am: to enquire after a lady's health implies that she is not in her best looks. Besides, I can see that you are in high bloom.'

She had watched his approach rather doubtfully, but she was by no means impervious to flattery, or to his elusive charm, and she returned the smile, even though she deprecated his compliment, saying: 'Good gracious, sir, at my age one doesn't talk of being in high bloom! *That* is quite a thing of the past – not that I ever was – I mean, no more than *passable*!'

'Oh, my dear Miss Wendover, how can you say so?' exclaimed Miss Butterbank throwing up her hands. 'Such a farradiddle I declare I never heard! But you are always so modest! I must positively beg Mr Calverleigh to turn a deaf ear to you!'

Since he was at that moment asking Mrs Leavening how she had prospered that morning in her search for lodgings, he had no difficulty in obeying this behest. The only difficulty he experienced was how to extricate himself from a discussion of all the merits, and demerits, of the several sets of apartments Mrs Leavening had inspected. But having agreed with Selina that Axford Buildings were situated in a horrid part of the town, and with Mrs Leavening that Gay Street was too steep for elderly persons, he laughed, and disclosed with disarming candour that he knew nothing of either locality. 'But I believe people speak well of Marlborough Buildings,' he offered. 'Unless you would perhaps prefer the peace and quiet of Belmont?'

'Belmont?' said Selina incredulously. 'But that would never do! It is uphill all the way! You can't be serious!'

'Of course he isn't, my dear!' said Mrs Leavening, chuckling. 'He hasn't the least notion where it is. Now, have you, sir?'

'Not the least! I shall make it my business to find out, however, and I'll tell you this evening, ma'am,' he promised.

He then bowed slightly, and walked away. Selina, taking umbrage at the suggestion that there was any part of Bath with which she was not fully acquainted, exclaimed: 'Well, I must say I think him a very odd creature! One might have supposed – not that I know him at all well, and one shouldn't judge anyone on a single morning-visit, even in his riding-dress, which I cannot like – though Abby assures me he won't *dine* with us in it – but his manners are very strange and abrupt!'

'Oh, he is certainly an original, but so droll!' said Mrs Leavening. 'We like him very much, you know, and find nothing in his manners to disgust us.'

'Exactly what I have been saying to dear Miss Wendover!' interpolated Miss Butterbank. 'Anyone of whom Miss Abby approves cannot be other than gentlemanlike!'

'Yes, but it is not at all the thing for her to be going to the play in his company. At least, it doesn't suit *my* sense of propriety, though no doubt my notions are antiquated, and, of course, Abby is not a girl, precisely, but to talk as if she was on the shelf is a great piece of nonsense!'

Mrs Leavening agreed to this, but as her husband came up at that moment Selina did not tell her old friend that Abby, not content with accompanying Mr Calverleigh to the theatre, had actually invited him to dine in Sydney Place.

This bold stroke had quite overset Selina. The news that Mr Calverleigh had been so kind as to invite Abby to go to the play she had received placidly enough, if with a little surprise: it seemed very odd that a single gentleman should get up a party, but no doubt he wished to return the hospitality of such ladies as Mrs Grayshott, and Lady Weaverham. Were the Ancrums going as well?

Abby was tempted, for a craven moment, to return a non-committal answer, but she overcame the impulse, and replied in an airy tone: 'Oh, it is not a party! Do you think I ought not to have accepted? I did hesitate, but at my age it is surely not improper? Besides, the play is *The Venetian Outlaw*, which I particularly want to see! From some cause or another I never have seen it, you know: once I was ill, when it was put on here, and once I was away from home; but you went to see it twice, didn't you? And were in raptures!'

'Yes, but not with a *gentleman*!' Selina said, scandalised. '*Once*, I went with dear Mama, only you were too young then; and the second time Lady Trevisian invited me – or was that the *third* time? Yes, because the *second* time was when George and Mary were with us, and you had a putrid sore throat, and so could not go with us!'

'This time I am determined *not* to have a putrid sore throat!'

'No, indeed! I hope you will not! But Mr Calverleigh must invite some others as well! I wonder he shouldn't have done so. It argues a want of conduct in him, for it is not at all the thing, and India cannot be held to excuse it, because there are no theatres there – at least, I shouldn't think there would be, should you?'

'No, dear. So naturally Mr Calverleigh couldn't know that he was doing anything at all out of the way, poor man! As for telling him that he must invite others as well as me, I hope you don't expect *me* to do so! That would indeed be improper! And, really, Selina, what possible objection can there be to my going to the play under the escort of a middle-aged man? Here, too, where I am well known, and shall no doubt meet many of our friends in the theatre!'

'It will make you look so – so *particular*, dearest! You would never do so in London! Of course, Bath is a different matter, but worse! Only think how disagreeable it would be if people said you were encouraging Mr Calverleigh to dangle after you!'

This thought had already occurred to Abby, causing her to hover on the brink of excusing herself from the engagement; and had Selina said no more she might possibly have done so. But Selina's evil genius prompted her to utter fatal words. 'I am persuaded that James would tell you to cry off, Abby!'

'Are you indeed?' retorted Abby, instantly showing hackle. 'Well, that settles the matter! I shall do no such thing! Oh, Selina, pray don't fly into a great fuss! If you are afraid of what the quizzes may say, you have only to tell them that since you don't yet venture out in the evening Mr Calverleigh very kindly offered to act as your deputy. And once it becomes known that he dined with us here, before escorting me to the theatre –'

'Nothing – *nothing*! – would prevail upon me to do anything so unbecoming as to invite a single gentleman to dine with us!' declared Selina, with unwonted vigour.

'No, dear, but you are not obliged to do so,' said Abby mischievously. 'I've done it for you!'

'*Abby!*' gasped Selina, turning pale with dismay. 'Asked a *man* to dine with us *alone*? You can't be serious! *Never* have we done such a thing! Except, of course, James, which is a very different matter!'

'Very different!' agreed Abby. 'Mr Calverleigh may be an oddity, but he's not a dreadful bore!'

'I was never so mortified!' moaned Selina. 'So brass-faced of you, as though you knew no better, and *exactly* what dear Papa deplored, and what he would say to it, if he were alive, which I am *devoutly* thankful he is not, I shudder to think!'

It had taken time, patience, and much tact to reconcile Selina but in the end she consented to entertain Mr Miles Calverleigh, persuaded by the horrid suspicion that if she refused to do so her highty-tighty young sister was quite capable of setting the town in an uproar by dining with him at York House. She had then devoted the better part of the afternoon to the composition of a formal invitation, written in her beautiful copper-plate, and combining to a nicety condescension with gracious civility. Mr Miles Calverleigh responded to this missive with commendable promptness, in a brief but well-expressed note, which conveyed to Selina's mind the impression that he had invited her sister to go with him to the play in a spirit of avuncular philanthropy. She was thus able to meet him in the Pump Room with a modicum of complaisance; and although, when he left her side, he joined the group round Abby, she had no apprehension of danger. It was not at all remarkable that he should show a preference for her: a great many gentlemen did so; but if it had been suggested to Selina that Abby was quite as strongly attracted to him as he to her she would have thought it not so much remarkable as absurd. Abby enjoyed light flirtations, but Selina had almost ceased to hope that she would ever discover amongst her suitors one who was endowed with all the perfections she apparently demanded. They were certainly not to be found in Mr Miles Calverleigh, with his swarthy countenance, his casual manners, and his deplorable want of address.

Nor was Abby apprehensive that in pursuing her acquaintance with him she might be running into danger. She was by no means sure that she liked him. He was amusing, and she enjoyed his company; but he frequently put her quite out of temper, besides shocking her by his unconcerned repudiation of any of the virtues indispensable in a man of principle. He was undoubtedly what her brother-in-law succinctly described as a loose screw, and so hopelessly ineligible that it never so much as crossed her mind that in him she had met her fate. Nor did it occur to her that in encouraging his advances she was influenced by anything other than the hope that she might be able to persuade him to send his nephew to the rightabout. He had refused unequivocally to meddle, but the hope persisted, and, with it, the growing conviction that if he wished to bring Stacy's schemes to fiddlestick's end he would know just how it could be done. To inspire him with such a wish was clearly her duty; if it had been suggested to her that her duty, in this instance, had assumed an unusually agreeable aspect, she would have acknowledged readily that it was fortunate that she did not find Mr Calverleigh repellent; but she would have been much amused by a further suggestion that she was rapidly losing her heart to a black sheep.

So she was able to greet him, when he descended upon her in the Pump Room, with calm friendliness; and when he presently detached her from her circle, inviting her, with his customary lack of finesse, to take a stroll about the Room, in the accepted manner of those who made the Promenade their daily business, she was perfectly willing to walk off with him.

'I've received an invitation from your sister,' he told her. 'She hopes that I will give you both the pleasure of dining in Sydney Place on Saturday, but I'm not deceived: her hope is that I may break a leg, or be laid low of a severe colic, before I can expose you to the censure of all your acquaintance. Shall I be doing so?'

She laughed. 'Good God, no! I hope my credit is good enough to survive a visit to the theatre in your company! Much I should care if it proved otherwise! I've a great desire to see this particular play, and have never yet done so. It has always been popular in Bath, you know.' Her eyes danced. 'If only you had had the good sense to have been a *widower*, I daresay Selina wouldn't have raised the least objection! She saw no harm in my attending the races with General Exford: there is something very respectable about widowers! *Single* gentlemen, in her view, are surrounded by an aura of impropriety.'

'What, even the turnip-sucker who pays you extravagant compliments?'

'If,' said Abby, a trifle unsteadily, but with severity, 'you are speaking of Mr Dunston, Selina knows him to be a very worthy man who has far too much conduct to transgress the bounds of propriety by as much as an inch!'

'He *is* a slow-top, isn't he? Poor fellow!'

'He may be a slow-top, but that's better than being ramshackle!' retorted Abby, with spirit.

'No, do you think so indeed? Was that a cut at me, by the way, or at Stacy?'

'Well, it was at you,' said Abby frankly. 'I don't think Stacy *ramshackle*: I think him a shuffling rogue! Mr Calverleigh, if you had heard him trying to cut a wheedle, when we rode back from Lansdown, you must have been disgusted!'

'Very likely. The wonder is that Fanny seems to be not at all disgusted.'

'She is very young, and had never, until that wretch came here, known any men but those who reside here: Selina's and my friends, or the schoolboy brothers of her own friends! You must know that she has only lately begun to go out into society a little;

and although, during the winter, a number of London-visitors come to Bath, she has met none of them. I saw to that!'

'Why let yourself be blue-devilled?' he asked. 'She'll recover!'

'I don't doubt she would do so, if he were removed from her sight!'

'Or even if she were to be removed from his,' he suggested.

She frowned over that for a moment, and then said, with a sigh: 'I've thought of it, of course, but I believe it wouldn't answer. James talked of removing her to Amberfield, and that would be fatal: she would run away! And if my sister Brede were to invite her to stay with her in London she would know that it was at my instigation, and to separate her from your nephew. What is more, he would follow her, and you may depend upon it that it would be easier for them to meet in London than it is here, where everyone knows her. I think, too, that if it were possible to prevent this she *wouldn't* recover – or, at any hand, not for a long time. Towards me she would be bound to feel resentment: oh, she's resentful already!' She hesitated, before saying, with a faint smile: 'I was used to think, you know, that we stood upon such terms as would make it a simple matter for me to guide her – even to check her! That my influence was strong enough to – But I seem to have none at all. I suppose I've gone the wrong way to work with her: nothing I could urge would carry the least weight with her! I wish – oh, how much I wish – that her eyes might be opened to what I am persuaded is his true character! That would be the best thing that could happen! It would be painful for her, poor child, but she wouldn't wear the willow for long: she has too much pride! And above all she wouldn't fancy herself a martyr! That's *very* important, because if one thinks oneself the victim of tyranny there is every inducement to fall into a lethargy.'

'I should imagine that that would make life very uncomfortable for you. But hasn't it occurred to you that my nephew has a rival?'

'Oliver Grayshott?' She shook her head. 'I don't think it. She says he is like a brother to her! And although I fancy *he* has a strong tendre for *her* he has done nothing to attach her.'

'Well, if you think it nothing to send her laudatory verses masquerading as acrostics, and to ransack all the libraries for the works of her favourite poets, you must be as green as she is!' he said caustically.

She could not help laughing. 'Does he do so? I thought they were his favourites too: he is certainly very well read in them.'

'Pea-goose! So would you be, if you made it your business to study them!'

'Poor young man! But even if Fanny did prefer him to your nephew it wouldn't do, I'm afraid.'

'Why not?'

'Because – as you very well know! – James would consider him to be almost as ineligible as Stacy!'

'I know nothing of the sort. Your brother James whistle a fortune down the wind? Gammon!'

'But he has no fortune!' she protested. 'He is connected with trade, too, which James would very much dislike.'

'Oh, would he? My sweet simpleton, let James get but one whiff of an East India merchant's heir in Bath, and he won't lose a moment in setting snares to catch such a prize!'

She disregarded this, exclaiming: 'You must be mistaken! Oliver has no such expectations! Indeed, he feels that he has miserably disappointed his uncle.'

'Not he! Balking thinks the world of him, means to take him into partnership as soon as he's in good point again.'

'No, does he indeed? I am so glad! But as for thinking of his marrying Fanny, that's moonshine! I own, I should be thankful if she did fall in love with him – though she is much too young for marriage – but there's no likelihood of her doing so while she's besotted of your odious nephew.'

'You know, if you mean to talk of nothing but your totty-headed niece and my odious nephew I *shall* have a colic,' he informed her.

'Well, of all the detestably uncivil things to say – !' she gasped.

'If it comes to that, what a detestably boring thing to talk about!'

'I beg your pardon!' she said icily. 'To me, it is a subject of paramount importance!'

'Yes, but it isn't so to me.'

Since Miss Butterbank came up at that moment, to tell her that dear Miss Wendover was ready to go home, she was prevented from uttering the retort that rose to her lips; but when her graceless tormentor presented himself in Sydney Place on Saturday she received him with a good deal of chilly reserve. As far as she could discover, this had no effect on him whatsoever. He devoted himself largely to Selina, listening good-naturedly to her rambling discourse, until she embarked on a catalogue of the various illnesses suffered by herself and several of her friends when he retaliated by telling her of the terrible diseases rife in India. From there it was a small step to a description of such aspects of Indian life, climate, and scenery as were most calculated to hold spellbound a middle-aged lady of enquiring mind and credulous disposition. Selina mellowed perceptibly under this treatment, and told Abby, when they had withdrawn from the dining-room, leaving their guest to enjoy a glass of port in solitary state, that really Mr Calverleigh was a most interesting man. 'I declare I feel as if I had actually been to India myself!' she said. 'So vivid, and droll – all those strange customs! Tigers and elephants, too – not that I should care to live with tigers, and although I believe elephants are wonderfully docile I don't think I could ever feel myself at ease with them. But so *very* interesting – quite like a fairy story!'

Abby, who thought that some of Mr Calverleigh's tales were exactly like fairy stories, was able to agree to this with perfect sincerity. She had every intention of maintaining her punctilious civility, and might have done so had he not said, as he took his seat beside her in the carriage he had hired for the evening: 'I wish I had ordered a hot brick to be provided.'

'Thank you, but there was not the least need to do so: I don't feel at all cold.'

'I daresay icebergs don't feel cold either, but I do!'

She was betrayed into a smothered choke of laughter,

whereupon he added: 'From having lived so long in a hot climate, you understand.'

'I understand you perfectly, sir, and shall take leave to tell you that there's neither truth nor shame in you!'

'Well, not *much*, perhaps!' he owned.

Since this quite overset her gravity, she was obliged to relent towards him, and by the time Beaufort Square was reached their former good relationship had been so well restored that she was able to look forward to an evening of unalloyed enjoyment, which not even the surprised stares of several persons with whom she was acquainted seriously disturbed. Mr Calverleigh proved himself to be an excellent host: not only had he hired one of the handsomely appointed first-tier boxes, but he had also arranged for tea and cakes to be brought to it during one of the intervals. Abby said appreciatively: 'How comfortable it is not to be obliged to inch one's way through the press in the foyer! You are entertaining me in royal style, Mr Calverleigh!'

'What, with cat-lap and cakes? If I entertained you royally I should give you pink champagne!'

'Which I shouldn't have liked half as well!'

'No, that's why I didn't give it to you.'

'I expect,' said Abby, quizzing him, 'it is invariably drunk in India – even for breakfast! Another of the strange customs you described to my sister!'

He laughed. 'Just so, ma'am!'

'Well, if she recounts your Canterbury tales to young Grayshott you will have come by your deserts! *He* will refute them, and *you* will look no-how!'

'No, no, you wrong the boy! He's not such a clodpole!'

'Incorrigible! It was a great deal too bad of you to make a May-game of poor Selina.'

'Oh, I didn't! It was made plain to me that she has a very romantical disposition, and delights in the marvellous, so I did my best to gratify her. Turning her up sweet, you know.'

'Trying how many brummish stories you could persuade her to swallow is what you mean! How many did you tell me?'

He shook his head. 'None! You should know better than to ask me that. I told you once that I don't offer you Spanish coin, and I'll tell you now that I don't offer you Canterbury tales either.' He saw the startled look in her eyes, the almost imperceptible gesture of withdrawal, and added simply: 'You wouldn't believe 'em.'

This made her laugh again, but for a moment she had indeed been startled, perceiving in his light eyes a glow there could be no mistaking. She had felt suddenly breathless, and embarrassed, for she had hitherto suspected him of pursuing nothing more serious than an idle flirtation. But there had been a note of sincerity in his voice, and his smile was a caress. Then, just as she was thinking: *This will never do!* he had uttered one of his impishly disconcerting remarks, which left her wondering whether she had allowed her imagination to mislead her.

His subsequent behaviour was irreproachable, and there was so little of the lover in his manner that her embarrassment swiftly died. She reflected that he was really a very agreeable companion, with a mind so much akin to her own that she was never obliged to explain what she meant by some elliptical remark, or to guard her tongue for fear of shocking him. He was attentive to her comfort, too, but in an everyday style: putting her shawl round her shoulders without turning the office into an act of homage; and neither pressing nor retaining her hand when he assisted her to enter the carriage. This treatment made her feel so much at her ease that when he asked her casually if she would join an expedition to Wells, and show him the cathedral there, she had no hesitation in replying: 'Yes, willingly: going to Wells, to see the knights on horseback, has always been a high treat to me!'

'What the deuce are they?' he enquired.

'A mechanical device – but I shan't tell you any more! You shall see for yourself! Who else is to join your expedition?'

'I don't know. Yes, I do, though! We'll take Fanny and young Grayshott!'

She smiled, but said: 'You should invite Lavinia too.'

'Oliver wouldn't agree with you. Nor do I. There will be no room in the carriage for a fifth person.'

'She could take my place. Or even Mrs Grayshott. She would enjoy the drive.'

'She would find it too fatiguing. Can't you think of anyone else to take your place?'

'Yes, Lady Weaverham!' she said instantly, a gurgle of merriment in her throat.

'No, I think, if I must find a substitute for you, I shall invite your sister's bosom-bow – what's her name? Buttertub? Tallow-faced female, with rabbit's teeth.'

'Laura Butterbank!' said Abby, in a failing voice. 'Odious, *infamous* creature that you are!'

'Oh, I can be far more odious than that!' he told her. 'And if I have any more wit and liveliness from you, Miss Abigail Wendover, I'll give you proof of it!'

'*Quite* unnecessary!' she assured him. 'I haven't the least doubt of it!'

She could not see his face in the darkness of the carriage, but she knew that he was smiling. He said, however, in stern accents: 'Will you go with me to Wells, ma'am, or will you not?'

'Yes, sir,' said Abby meekly. 'If you are quite sure you wouldn't prefer Miss Butterbank's company to mine!'

The carriage had drawn up in front of her house. Mr Calverleigh, alighting from it, and turning to hand her down, said: 'I should, of course, but having already invited you I feel it would be uncivil to fob you off.'

'Piqued, repiqued, and capoted!' said Abby, acknowledging defeat.

Ten

*T*he visit to the theatre produced its inevitable repercussions. Only such severe critics as Mrs Ruscombe saw anything to shock them in it, but it was surprising how quickly the word sped round Bath that Mr Miles Calverleigh was becoming extremely particular in his attentions to Miss Abigail Wendover. There was nothing in this to give rise to speculation, for Abby had never lacked admirers; but considerable interest was lent to the affair by what was generally considered to be her encouragement of the gentleman's pretensions.

'Only think of her going to the play with him all by herself! When Lady Templeton told me of it I could only stare at her! I'm sure she has never done such a thing before!' said Mrs Ancrum.

'Mark my words,' said Lady Weaverham, 'it's a Case! Well, I'm sure I wish them both very happy!'

'Quite a new come-out!' said Mrs Ruscombe, with her thin smile. 'It doesn't astonish me: I have always thought her a trifle bold.'

Abby was well aware that she had become overnight an object for curiosity; and so, within a couple of days, was Selina, who was thrown into what she called a taking by the arch efforts of one of her acquaintances to discover whether dear Miss Abigail was about to contract an engagement.

'I was never so much provoked in my life!' she declared. 'Such impertinence! I gave her a sharp set-down, as you may suppose! You and Mr Calverleigh – ! If I hadn't been vexed to death, I could have laughed in her face! Why, he isn't even well-favoured, besides being *quite* beneath your touch – not, of course, by *birth*, but a man of *most* unsavoury reputation, though *that* Mrs Swainswick knows nothing about, and you may depend upon it I didn't breathe a *syllable* to her. But how she could have the impudence to imagine – not but what I knew how it would be from the start, and I must *beg* you, dear Abby, to keep him at a proper distance!'

Abby was quite as much vexed as Selina, but her indignation took a different form. 'What a piece of work about nothing!' she said contemptuously. 'I should rather think you would give that vulgar busy head a sharp set-down! What *would* be quite beneath my touch would be to pay the smallest attention to anything she, or others like her, may choose to say of me!'

If more than the vulgar Mrs Swainswick's sly question had been needed to rouse the spirit of rebellion slumbering in her breast, it was provided by Mr Peter Dunston, who told her that he was afraid his mother had been quite shocked by the news of her escapade. 'She is old-fashioned, you know. I need hardly assure you that *I* do not share her sentiments! What *you* do could never be wrong, Miss Abigail. Indeed, if I had as little regard for your good name in Bath as Calverleigh I should have ventured to invite you to go to the play in *my* company!'

This put Abby in such a flame that if Mr Calverleigh had asked her to jaunter off to Wells with only himself as escort she would instantly have agreed to it. Not being informed of her state of mind, he did not do so; but as the two younger members of his party soon wandered off together, when they reached Wells, he did, in fact, become her only escort for a large part of the day, the only flaw to this agreeable arrangement being that none of the Bath quidnuncs knew anything about it. But this regret was soon forgotten in the pleasure of introducing, to a Cathedral she loved, one who was quick to appreciate its beauty, needing no prompting from her. She thought, in touching innocence, that in Miles Calverleigh she had found a friend, and a better one by far than any other, because his mind moved swiftly, because he could make her laugh even when she was out of charity with him, and because of a dozen other attributes which were quite frivolous – hardly attributes at all, in fact – but which added up to a charming total, outweighing the more important faults in his character. She was aware of these, but she could find excuses for his cynicism, and even for the coldness of heart which made him look upon the problems or the troubles besetting other people with a detachment so profound as to seem inhuman. It was no wonder that twenty years of exile had made him uncaring: the wonder was that he was not embittered. As for the life he had led during those years, she did not suppose that virtue had played a noticeable part in it, but she felt it to be no concern of hers. Nor did she wish to know how many mistresses he had had, or what excesses he might have committed: the past might keep its secrets, leaving her to the enjoyment of the present.

If she spared a thought for her niece, whom she had so reprehensibly allowed to escape from her chaperonage, it was merely to hope that Fanny was enjoying the day as much as she was. The child had not been in spirits at the start of the expedition. She had tried to hide it with rather more than her usual vivacity, but her gaiety had had a brittle quality. Abby dared not hope that she had quarrelled with Stacy; probably she was downcast because she had begun to despair of winning her family's consent to her projected engagement. Perhaps Oliver would succeed in coaxing her out of the dumps; perhaps, if Lavinia, who had not yet learnt to withhold confidences from those she loved, had told him the story of Fanny's infatuation, he might even venture to offer her a little advice. Abby had no doubt that it would be good advice, and very little that advice from a man with whom Fanny stood on friendly terms would be listened to far more readily than advice from an aunt.

Oliver did know the story, but the only advice he gave was addressed to his sister. He had listened to her sentimental outpourings in silence, disappointing her by saying quietly, when she had done: 'Lavvy, you shouldn't repeat what Fanny tells you.'

'Oh, no! Only to you – and Mama, of course!'

'Well, to Mama, perhaps, but not to me. I let you do so only because I already knew, from Mama, that Fanny had formed an – an attachment which her aunt dislikes. And because I fancy you are much in sympathy with her.'

'Yes, indeed I am!' she said earnestly. 'It is the most affecting thing imaginable, for they fell in love the first time they met! He is so handsome, too, and has *such* an air! And merely because he hasn't the advantage of fortune – as though it signified, when Fanny is positively *rolling* in riches! –'

'It isn't that,' he interrupted, hesitating a little. 'Not wholly that.'

'Oh, you are thinking that he was used to be very wild, and expensive, but –'

'No, I'm not, Lavvy. I know nothing about him, except that –' Again he hesitated; and then, as she directed a look of puzzled enquiry at him, said, with a little difficulty: 'He isn't a halfling, you know, or a greenhorn. He must be a dozen years older than Fanny, and a man of the world into the bargain.'

'Yes!' said Lavinia enthusiastically. '*Anyone* can see he is of the first stare, which makes it so particularly romantic that he should have fallen in love with Fanny! I don't mean to say that she isn't ravishingly pretty, because she is, but I should think there must be *scores* of fashionable London-girls on the catch for him, wouldn't you?'

'Listen, Lavvy!' he said. 'The thing is that he hasn't behaved as he ought! A man of honour don't flummery a girl into meeting him upon the sly, and, he don't pop the question to her without asking leave of her guardian!'

'Oh, Oliver, you are repeating what Mama says! How can you be so stuffy? Next you will be saying that Fanny ought to wait meekly until her guardian bestows her on a man of *his* choice!'

'I shan't say anything of the sort. But I'll tell you this, Lavvy: if Calverleigh had made *you* the object of his havey-cavey attentions I'd knock his teeth down his throat!'

Startled, and rather impressed, she said: 'Good gracious! Would you? *Well!*'

'Try to, at all events,' he said, laughing. 'It's what any man would do.'

She did not look to be entirely convinced. He put his arm round her, and gave her a brotherly hug. 'It isn't for me to interfere: I haven't the right. But you'll be a poor friend to Fanny if you don't make a push to persuade her not to throw her cap over the windmill. That's the way to return by Weeping Cross.'

He had said no more, and how much of what he had said was repeated to Fanny he had no means of knowing, because he was wary of betraying to his sister that he took far more than a neutral interest in the affair, and so would not ask her. Between himself and Fanny it was never discussed, and much as he longed to beg her not to throw herself away on a court-card who, in his view, was an ugly customer if ever he saw one, it did not come within his province to meddle in the affairs of a girl who would never be more to him than an unattainable dream, or within his code of honour to cry rope upon a fellow behind his back. Given the flimsiest of excuses – if only he had been even remotely related to Fanny! – he would speedily have cut the fellow's comb for him; for although he was not yet in high force he had no doubt of his ability to draw the elegant Mr Stacy Calverleigh's cork, besides darkening both his daylights, before tipping him a settler. His hands clenched themselves instinctively into two bunches of purposeful fives as he allowed his fancy to dwell for a moment on the pleasing vision of a regular set-to with Stacy. He was innately chivalrous, but he would have no compunction whatsoever in milling down this sneaking rascal, who, if he had ever come to handy-blows in his life (which Mr Grayshott doubted) was certainly no match for one whose science, and punishing left, had won fame for him in the annals of his school and college. But only for a moment did the vision endure: even the excuse of rivalry was denied him. Mr Grayshott, setting out for India in high hope, and eager determination to prove himself worthy of his uncle's trust, had been defeated by his constitution, and saw himself as a failure. Mr Balking had told him not to tease himself about the future, and not to take it so much to heart that his health had broken down. 'For how could you help it? I wish I'd never sent you to Calcutta – except that the experience you've gained will stand you in good stead. I've a place for you in the London house, but time enough to talk of that when you're on your pins again.'

Mr Balking had been kindness itself, but Oliver, his spirits as much as his gaunt frame worn down by recurrent fever, foresaw that he was destined to become a clerk in the counting-house, from which lowly position he was unlikely to rise for many dreary years. He had set no store by Uncle Leonard's assurances that he was very well satisfied with his work in Calcutta: that was the sort of thing that an affectionate uncle might be expected to say. He had reached Bath in a state of deep depression, but as his health improved so did his spirits, and he began to think that it might not be so very long before he worked his way up to a position of trust. When he was able to look back dispassionately over the two years he had spent in India, he thought that perhaps his uncle really was satisfied with his progress there. He had found his work of absorbing interest, and knew that he had a talent for business. In fact, if he had been a windy-wallets, boasting of his every small success, he would have said that he had done pretty well in the Calcutta house. As he was a diffident, and rather reticent young man, he maintained a strict silence on the subject, and waited, in gradually increasing hopefulness, for the day when his doctor should pronounce him well enough to apply himself once more to business.

But his optimism did not lead him to the length of supposing that the Wendovers would ever consider him to be an eligible husband for Fanny. Older than his years, he recognised in Fanny's passionate attachment to Stacy a schoolgirl's brief, violent infatuation. He was reminded of the throes into which Lavinia, at the age of fifteen, had been cast when she fell suddenly, and inexplicably, in love with one of the visiting professors at Miss Timble's Seminary. It had made her remarkably tiresome for several weeks, but there had been no harm in it, her passion being unrequited, and the professor a respectable man, with a wife, and five children, to all of whom he was devoted. Neither Oliver nor Mrs Grayshott had set any store by the event; Oliver thought that he would have set as little by Fanny's present bewitchment had she but lost her foolish heart to a man of character. As it was, he was pretty sure that she had walked into a snare set for her by a handsome fortune-hunter, and he was extremely uneasy. Something Lavinia had let slip from her tongue, and hastily retracted, had given rise in his mind to the incredible suspicion that a runaway marriage was in contemplation. He found that his mother shared this suspicion, and was only partly reassured when he learned that she had warned Miss Abigail Wendover of a possible danger. Miss Abigail was no fool, but he felt that the situation demanded a man's hand. Failing her brother, who did not seem to be one on whom Miss Abigail placed any reliance, the obvious man to intervene was Mr Miles Calverleigh. But Miles showed no disposition to do so, or even to take any interest in his nephew's activities. That did not surprise Oliver: he had not spent several weeks in Mr Calverleigh's company without discovering that he never did take any interest in persons he didn't like. It was inconceivable that a man of his cut could like Stacy, and useless to suppose that regard for the good name of his family would impel him to exert himself to preserve it: he had no such regard. On the other hand, there could be no doubt that he liked Miss Abigail Wendover very much indeed. Oliver, naturally precluded from discussing Stacy with Stacy's uncle, could only hope that his tendre for her would move him to come to her assistance. He was a strange man, so cold, and yet so kind; there was no understanding him, but one thing was sure: if he did befriend one, there were no limits to the help he would, in his unconcerned way, extend. It was possible, of course, that Miss Abigail, like himself, would feel all the awkwardness of broaching the matter to him. Oliver thought that perhaps his mother might prevail upon her to overcome such scruples, and decided to nudge her into making the attempt.

During the drive to Wells he realised, as quickly as her aunt, that Fanny was doing her best to hide some inward care under a mask of gaiety. His heart went out to her, the sweet, silly baby that she was. He felt almost sick with the longing to gather her into his arms; but that desire must be repressed: not only did his circumstances make it impossible for him to declare himself, but Fanny did not want his love, but only his friendship. She had said once, when his mother had reproved him for calling her by her name: 'Oh, but I begged him to do so, ma'am! Because Lavvy and I have always been like sisters, so Oliver must be my brother!'

Half a loaf was better than no bread: he didn't know who had been responsible for that silly proverb, only that he must have been a cod's head. It wasn't better; when the lovely, darling girl you would have given your soul to possess invited you to be her brother it was infinitely worse.

But if a brother was what Fanny wanted, a brother she should have; and perhaps, adopting that distasteful rôle, he might, at least, be admitted into her confidence, and be granted the opportunity to offer her wiser counsel than she would get from his foolish sister.

So when they had stayed for some time in the chapel in the north aisle of the Cathedral, where the famous clock had been placed, and had watched the little knights endlessly tilting at each other across the barrier which surmounted it, he detained Fanny, as she was preparing to follow her aunt and Mr Calverleigh to another part of the Cathedral, and suggested that they might go and sit down outside for a while. She agreed readily to this, causing his heart to melt by looking up at him in quick anxiety, and saying: 'Yes, to be sure we'll do that, if you wouldn't liefer go back to the Swan? There's nothing so fatiguing as Cathedrals! You are tired already, aren't you?'

'No, I promise you I'm not – or only a very little!' he answered. 'I think I might be, however, if I were obliged to go all over this place, because that would mean standing to gaze at tombs, and screens, and windows! I don't know why it should be so, but standing is a thing I can't yet do, though I am beginning to walk with the best of you.'

'Well, you shan't stand. If it is not too chilly for you, we'll go and sit by the moat round the Palace, and watch the swans. And if my aunt should ask you what you think of the figures on the West Front you may say that you've never seen anything so truly exquisite. That wouldn't be a fib, do you think?'

His eyes were full of tender amusement; he said gravely: 'No, just *suggestio falsi*! Ought I to see them?'

'Good gracious, no! There are tiers and tiers of them!'

'In that case, I'm ready to tell any number of fibs – even a real bouncer!'

She laughed, and then fell silent for a minute or two. He made no attempt to break into her abstraction, but presently she seemed to recall herself, and embarked on some light, everyday chit-chat, rather in the manner of a hostess trying to entertain a difficult guest. It was plainly an effort, and he stopped her, saying involuntarily: 'Ah, don't, Fanny!'

Startled, she looked quickly up at him, a question in her big eyes. 'Don't?'

'Don't think yourself obliged to make conversation! That's not treating me as though I were your brother!'

'Oh – !' She blushed, and turned her head away.

'Is something troubling you?' he asked gently.

'No – oh, no! Of course not! Look, there are two of the swans! If only we had brought some bread to throw to them! I do think swans are the most beautiful birds in the world, don't you? Or do you prefer peacocks?'

'No,' he replied baldly, leading her to a conveniently placed bench. Sitting down beside her, he said: 'What is it, Fanny? Don't say you're not blue-devilled! That *would* be a bouncer – almost a *plumper*!'

She gave a nervous little laugh. 'It's nothing. Well, nothing very much! Just that I'm at outs with Abby – at least, not precisely at outs with her, but –' She paused, and her eyes darkened. 'I thought – But people – grown-up people –' she said, betraying her youth, 'don't *understand*! They don't care for anything but consequence, and propriety, and respectability, and – and eligibility, and whenever you wish to do anything *they* don't wish you to do, they say you are far too young, and will soon forget about it!'

'Yes, and also that one day you will thank them for it!' he agreed sympathetically. 'And the worst of it is that, in general, they are right!'

'Not always!'

'No, but odiously often!'

'*When you are as old as I am* – !' said Fanny, in bitter mimicry.

'Don't tell me that Miss Abigail has ever uttered those abominable words!'

'No. No, she hasn't done that, but she doesn't enter into my feelings, and I thought she would! I never *dreamed* she would be just like my uncle! Worldly, and – and prejudiced, and not thinking it signifies if you are unhappy, as long as you don't do anything your horrid uncle doesn't approve of!' She added, with strong indignation: 'And she doesn't even *like* him!'

He said nothing for a few moments, but sat frowning ahead at the embattled wall beyond the moat. Fanny, pulling a handkerchief out of her reticule, defiantly blew her nose. Oliver drew a resolute breath, and said, picking his words with care: 'If someone who is very dear to you – as you are to Miss Abigail – seems to be set on taking what you believe to be a false step, you must try to prevent it, don't you agree?'

'Yes, but I am not taking a false step!' said Fanny. 'And I am not too young to know my own mind! I have always known it! And I won't let them ruin my life, even if I have to do something *desperate*!'

'Don't!' he said. 'How could you be happy if you did what must pretty well break Miss Abigail's heart? Forgive me, Fanny, but I fancy I know what the trouble is, and I wish there was something I could do to help you.' He paused. 'Have you ever met my uncle? Not, I'm thankful to say, at all like *your* uncle! He's very kind, and very wise, and he once told me never to make important decisions hastily – not to do what couldn't be *un*done until I was perfectly sure that I should never *wish* to undo it.'

'Of course not!' said Fanny simply. She got up. 'Are you rested? Would you care to stroll about the town for a little while? I don't think it *is* warm enough here, do you? We'll go through the Dean's Eye into Sadler Street: I expect you will like to see that.'

Her confidences were at an end; and since she had so unmistakably drawn to the blinds against prying eyes there was nothing for him to do but to acquiesce. He won a laugh from her by saying that while he placed himself unreservedly in her hands he could not help feeling that they ran a grave risk of being clapped into prison for such irreverence; and expressed great relief when she explained that the Dean's Eye was merely an old gateway. This mild joke did much to restore her to ease; he set himself thereafter to divert her, and succeeded well enough to make her say, when they joined their elders at the Swan, to partake of an early dinner there before driving back to Bath, that she had spent a charming afternoon. A little nervously, she added: 'And you won't regard anything I said, will you? It was all nonsense! I daresay you know how it is when one falls into a fit of the dismals: one says things one doesn't mean.'

He reassured her, but could not refrain from saying: 'Even though I'm only a pretence-brother, will you tell me if ever you are in any kind of a hobble, or – or are not quite sure what you should do?'

'Oh, thank you! You are very good!' she stammered. 'But there's no need – I mean, it was only being blue-devilled, as you said! Nothing is *really* amiss!'

He said no more, but this speech, far from allaying his anxiety, considerably increased it. He wished grimly that he could know what had occurred to agitate her, but it was perhaps as well that his suspicion received no confirmation, since he had neither the right nor, as yet, the physical strength to deal appropriately with Mr Stacy Calverleigh, and would have found it impossible to control his instinct. For Mr Calverleigh, living in imminent danger of foreclosure, and seeing the shadow of the King's Bench Prison creeping inexorably towards him, had abandoned the hope of winning his heiress by fair means, and had decided (with a strong sense of ill-usage) that there was nothing for it but to elope with her.

But Fanny, who had so enthusiastically pictured herself in such a romantic adventure, had suddenly been brought to realise that it was one thing to declare one's readiness to cast off the shackles of one's upbringing, and to divorce oneself from home and family, and quite another actually to do it.

Stacy had urged his desperate proposal on her in Bath Abbey, a circumstance which made her feel nervous and uncomfortable at the outset. When he had appointed this rendezvous, she had been almost shocked. It was surely not at all the thing! But he had laughed at her scruples, calling her his adorable little prude, and she had agreed to the assignation – if only to prove to him that she was no prude. It had been made hurriedly, in Meyler's Library, and it had entailed some difficult, and what she could not but feel horridly deceitful, planning. However, she had done it, and had been rewarded for her hardihood by having her hands passionately kissed, and her bravery extolled. But she was feeling far from brave, and looked round nervously in dread of seeing someone she knew. It was not, of course, very likely that any resident of Bath would be found in the Abbey at an hour when no service was being held, but there was no telling but what someone might be entertaining a guest who wished to visit it. She whispered: 'Oh, pray take care!' and pulled her hands away. 'If I were to be recognised – ! I am in such a quake! I don't *think* anyone saw me on the way, but how can one be sure? Grimston went with me to Miss Timble's, and she will call for me later at Mrs Grayshott's, but, oh, Stacy, I was obliged to pretend to Miss Timble that I had mistaken the day for my singing lesson, and it made me feel a *wretch*!'

'No wonder!' he agreed warmly. 'It is intolerable that we

should be obliged to stoop to subterfuge: I feel it as acutely as you do, beloved! But since your aunt returned to Bath I've been granted no opportunity to snatch as much as five minutes alone with you. How can I talk to you at a concert, or in a ballroom? And talk to you I must!'

'Yes – oh, yes! I have longed so much to be with you! If only I had a veil! Who are those people over there?'

'Only a parcel of trippers,' he replied soothingly. 'Don't be afraid, my sweet one! There is no one here who knows you. We will sit down over there, where it is dark, and there's nothing of interest to attract the trippers. That I should be forced into *stealing* a meeting with you! It is of all things the most repugnant to me, but what other course is open to me? Only one! – to renounce you wholly, and that I *cannot* bear to do!'

'Stacy, *no!*' she gasped, clutching his arm.

He laid his other hand over hers, clasping it firmly. 'I shall never win your aunt's support: she has made that abundantly plain to me! She will take care that we never see one another, except in company, or as we have done today. Dearest, how can we go on in such a way?' He took her hand and mumbled kisses into its palm. 'If you knew how much I long to take you in my arms, to call you my own!'

'I want that too,' she said shyly.

'Then come away with me, as we planned! Dare you snap your fingers in the face of the world? Tell me!'

'Yes, indeed I dare!' she said, with a sparkling look.

'How shall I ever be able to prove to you how much I adore you? Let us put a period to this hateful situation into which we have been driven, and let us do it as soon as may be contrived! Tomorrow!'

'*Tomorrow?*' Fanny echoed blankly. 'Oh, *no,* Stacy! I – I couldn't! I mean, it is too soon!'

'The next day, then!'

It was at this moment that Fanny began to perceive the difference between dreams and reality. She shook her head, saying pleadingly: 'I wish I could, but – you don't perfectly understand, Stacy! It would be too difficult. I have so many things to attend to!'

'It must be soon!' he urged. 'At any moment you may be swept from me! I suspect that your aunt is contemplating doing so already. If that were to happen, our tale would be told!'

'No, it wouldn't!' she objected. 'Besides, she isn't contemplating it! How could she, when we are holding a rout-party next week? And that's another reason why I couldn't possibly run away immediately. I daresay you may have forgotten about it, but – '

'What do I care for rout-parties?' he exclaimed. 'Our happiness is at stake!'

Fanny had no objection to Mr Calverleigh's dramatic utterances, for they bore a close resemblance to the impassioned speeches of her favourite heroes of romance, but a strong vein of commonsense underlay her imaginings, and she replied, in an alarmingly practical spirit: 'No, no! How should that be? It means only a little put-off!'

'Only – ! When every hour that I am apart from you seems a week, and every week a year!'

No arithmetician, she found no fault with this mathematical progression. The sentiment thus expressed made her blush rosily, and slide her hand into his again. 'I know. It's so with me too, but you haven't considered, my dearest one! How *could* I run away before Aunt Selina's party? It would be the most infamous thing to do, because she is looking forward to it so much, poor darling, and it would destroy all her pleasure in it if – Good God! she wouldn't be able to hold it at all! Only think what an uproar there will be!'

Exasperation seized him, and for an instant she caught a glimpse of it in his face. It was gone so quickly that she could not be sure that it had ever been there at all. He saw doubt in her widening eyes, and said ruefully: 'That I should be willing to consign Aunt Selina to perdition! Isn't it shocking? So kind as she is, and – as I believe – so much my friend! For how long must I wait before I can call you my own – to cherish and protect?'

Had she been privileged to hear these noble words, Miss Abigail Wendover would have informed Mr Calverleigh, in explicit terms, that Fanny needed to be protected only from himself. Their effect on Fanny was to make her blush still more vividly, and to whisper: 'Not long! I promise!'

He had seldom felt less amorous, for he considered that she was being irritatingly capricious, but he responded at once with one of his lover-like speeches. His fear was that she might, if she were given time for reflection, draw back from the proposed elopement. It had not escaped his notice that she had recoiled from his suggestion of an immediate flight. He set himself to the task of winning her back to her former mood of eager acceptance, employing all the arts at his command. He did not doubt his power over her, but he reckoned without the streak of obstinacy her aunts knew well: she responded deliciously to his love-making; she listened in soft-eyed rapture to the idyllic picture he drew of the life they would lead together; but she would not consent to elope with him before her aunts' party. He dared not persist, for there was a mulish look in her face, and his fear was that if he pressed her too hard she might cry off altogether. He assured her that he had no other wish than to please her, and hoped to God that she did not often fall into distempered freaks.

Eleven

The clandestine meeting in the Abbey was undetected; but although Fanny was relieved to find her aunts quite unsuspicious she was also made to feel guilty, and ashamed. Nor did she any longer feel quite so happy in her love. It was not that she did not most ardently desire to pass the rest of her life in Stacy's protective arms, but she could not help thinking how very much more pleasant it would be if she could be married to him with the blessing of her family. There was a flavour of high adventure about an elopement; she had been quite sincere when she had said that she neither shrank from taking so bold a step, nor cared a button for the inevitable censure of the world. It had not occurred to her, until she had recollected her aunts' rout-party, that her elopement would pitchfork them into a very disagreeable situation. Floating in a dream of love and heroism, she had scarcely considered any but the broader aspects of the case, and even those only as they concerned herself. The opinion of the world was of no consequence; she and Stacy would be blissfully indifferent if the world cast them off, for they needed only each other for perfect happiness. As for her aunts, they would be very much shocked at first, even angry, but when they saw how right she had been to marry Stacy they would come round, and end by doting as fondly upon him as upon her. Not until Stacy urged her to fly with him immediately did she begin to perceive some of the minor objections attached to an elopement. Such things as rout-parties were quite unimportant, of course: Stacy said so, and it was so. But they were not unimportant to two maiden ladies who had been numbered for years amongst Bath's most respected residents. Not one of the invitations sent out on Aunt Selina's gilt-edged cards had been declined, for an invitation to attend one of the Misses Wendover's select parties was considered to confer distinction on the recipient. It had flashed through Fanny's mind as soon as Stacy had made his proposal that to subject her aunts to the humiliation of being obliged to cancel their party would be conduct too base ever to be pardoned. It would be even worse if they decided to hold it, as though they had not been plunged into a scandal (and it was stupid to suppose that the news of the elopement would not spread through Bath like wildfire), for if they did that they would find their big double drawing-room woefully thin of company. Several other minor objections occurred to her, but she resolutely banished them. One could not be expected to sacrifice the happiness of one-self and one's beloved merely to save one's aunts from embarrassment.

There was yet another objection which she found oddly daunting. Never having formed any very clear picture of the actual ceremony, who was to perform it, and where it was to take place, it came as a shock to her when Stacy described in romantic detail a flight to the Border. Innocent as she was, she yet knew that nothing could be more improper. Even her closest friends would find it hard to excuse conduct so indelicate: she had as well tie her garter in public! 'You cannot mean *Gretna Green*?' she had exclaimed incredulously. 'No, no! I know people do so in novels, but not – *real* people, like us! It is not at all the thing, Stacy! Why, I daresay it would take us two or three days to reach the Border! You can't have considered! We must be married in London, or – Bristol, or somewhere much nearer to Bath!'

So Stacy had had to explain to her that there were certain difficulties attached to the clandestine marriages of minors. He had done it very well, so that by the time they had parted at the door of the Abbey she was convinced that there was no other way open to them, and that it was as repugnant to him as it was to her. He would be no more than her courier until the knot was tied. 'But I will not press you,' he had said. 'If your courage fails you – if you cannot trust me enough – tell me! I'll go away – try to forget you!' He had added with a melancholy smile: 'You will forget me more easily!'

She had cried out against this. She was not so fickle, or so hen-hearted, and as for her trust in him, it was infinite!

She had promised to fly with him as soon after the rout-party as could be contrived; and, in the heat of an impassioned moment, had done so with enthusiasm. It was only later that an unacknowledged doubt began to trouble her.

Then had come the expedition to Wells, and her conversation with Oliver. He had said that he wished he could help her, but the things he had said to her had not helped her at all: in fact, they had increased her discomfort.

Abby, recognising the signs of inward turmoil, tried in vain to win her confidence. She could not discover that there had been any falling-out between the lovers, and the fear that Stacy was trying to persuade Fanny to elope with him began to haunt her. She told Mr Miles Calverleigh, when he drove her to Stanton-Drew, to inspect the Druidical monument there, that she lived in dread of waking one morning to find Fanny gone.

'Oh, I shouldn't think that at all likely!' he replied. 'Speaking as one who is not without experience, it's not as easy to elope at dead of night as you might think.'

She could not suppress her responsive dimple, but she said austerely: 'You are perfectly shameless! Why isn't it easy? I should have supposed it to be much easier than to do it during the day.'

'That's because you haven't applied your mind to it.'

'Very true! It so happens that the need to do so has never come in my way.'

'Oh, I can see that! It wouldn't surprise me to learn that you imagine a rope-ladder to be employed in the business.'

'It would surprise *me* very much to learn that it was! You know, I have never been able to understand how anyone *could* escape by means of a rope-ladder, particularly a female. It's all very well to talk of throwing it up to the window, but the chances are one wouldn't be able to catch it, or would fall out of the window, trying to do so. And what would you attach it to, if you *did* catch it?'

'I can't think.'

'No, and even if it was attached I have a strong notion that it is not at all easy to come down a rope-ladder. Depend upon it, it requires a great deal of practice.'

'Hampered by your petticoats, too,' he said thoughtfully. 'I see that you *have* applied your mind to the problem: tell me all about it!'

She laughed. 'No, I won't allow you to divert me. This is not a funning matter. I know that you think it a great bore, but –'

'Well, don't you?'

'How could I? I think it *vexatious* – indeed, I could slap Fanny for being such a wet-goose! – but one cannot be *bored* by what nearly concerns anyone to whom one is very much attached, and for whom one is responsible, can one?'

'As I have never found myself in such a position, I can't say.'

She said, with quick sympathy: 'I know that, and I pity you! You told me once – you said that you were not an object for compassion, but you are, Mr Calverleigh!'

'Yes, I've come to that conclusion myself,' he said unexpectedly. 'I was used not to think so, but ever since I came to Bath I have been growing steadily more convinced that I was mistaken.'

Taken by surprise, feeling very much as if she had suffered an electric shock, Abby gave a gasp. After a brief, but perceptible, pause, she said with as much composure as she could summon to her aid: 'You might not have felt the want of family ties whilst you were abroad, I daresay. But we were speaking of Fanny, and you were about to explain to me why I need not be afraid that she will run away in the night, when we fell into an absurd digression on the subject of rope-ladders. I should be very glad to believe you, but – but why?'

'Oh, it would be much too dangerous! The poor girl would be obliged to get up and scramble on her clothes in the dark, in case some other member of the household should be wakeful, and see the light under her door. After which, she must grope her way down two pairs of stairs, and if their creakings didn't rouse you the approach of a chaise over the cobblestones at that hour of night would certainly do so. Then, too, she must draw back the bolts on the front-door, take off the chain, and lastly, most difficult task of all, shut the door behind her – all without a sound! Of course, she might choose to leave the house open to any chance marauder, but I feel sure that you will tell me she is not so lost to all sense of what is due to you as *that*!'

'Yes!' said Abby, perceiving the force of these objections. 'And her room is at the back of the house, so how could she know that your horrid nephew was punctual to his appointment? Something might have happened to detain him, and only think how awkward it would be for her! She would be bound to consider that possibility. Anyone would! Furthermore, Grimston – our old nurse – sleeps in a little room next to hers, and although *I* may believe that nothing less than a trumpet-blast in her ear would wake her, you may depend upon it that Fanny would be in a quake! Oh, I think you are undoubtedly right! She won't make the attempt at night, and I'll take good care she has no opportunity during the day, even if I must accompany her everywhere, like the dragon I vowed I never would be.'

'That might become a trifle tedious. Are you so sure that she is planning to elope with my horrid nephew?'

'No,' she replied at once. 'Sometimes I tell myself that I am suffering from a stupid irritation of nerves: that however much she might fancy herself in love she would never do anything so improper, so unprincipled! And then I think that he has taken such strong possession of her mind that she will do whatever he wishes. But she has been in low spirits lately, in a worry, I conjecture. It might be that she can't bring herself to do what she knows is very wrong. I *did* entertain the hope that she had quarrelled with Stacy, but she hasn't.' She sighed. 'He was at the concert last night, and she looked at him as if he were her whole dependence and delight.'

'No, did she? I envy him. Not, of course, that I've the smallest desire that *Fanny* should bestow such a look upon me, but I wish that you would.'

She was aware suddenly that her heart, in general a very reliable organ, was behaving in a most alarming way, first trying to jump into her throat, and then beginning to thump so violently that she felt breathless, and uncomfortably hot. It was an effort to speak, but she managed to do so, saying: 'Mr Calverleigh – I am in no mood – for flirting!'

'Now, when have I ever tried to flirt with you?' he protested.

She felt herself impelled to steal a look at him, which she instantly realised was a very imprudent thing to have done, because he was smiling at her, and in a way which made her heart beat still more violently.

'I love you, you know,' he said conversationally. 'Will you marry me?'

The manner in which he made this abrupt proposal struck her as being so typical of him that a shaky laugh was dragged from her. 'Of all the graceless ways of making me an offer – ! No, no, you are not serious! you cannot be!'

'Of course I'm serious! A pretty hobble I should be in if I weren't, and you accepted my offer! The thing is that it is such a devil of a time since I proposed marriage to a girl that I've forgotten how to set about it. If I ever knew, but I daresay I didn't, for I was always a poor hand at making flowery speeches.' He smiled at her again, a little ruefully. '*That I should love a bright particular star!*'

'Oh – !' she breathed. 'Oh, pray don't say such things!'

'I won't, if you dislike it,' he said obligingly.

'Dislike it! How could anyone dislike to have such a thing said to her? But it won't do! You mustn't say any more on this head! *Pray* do not!'

'No, that's quite unreasonable,' he said. 'I won't pay you any compliments, but you can't expect me not to say any more! I've asked you to marry me, Abigail!'

'You must know I can't – how impossible it would be!'

'No, I don't. Why should it be?'

'The – the circumstances!' she uttered, in a stifled voice.

He looked to be a good deal puzzled. 'What circumstances? Mine? Oh, I'm perfectly well able to support a wife! You must have been listening to my horrid nephew.'

'I've done no such thing!' she said, much incensed. 'And if I had I shouldn't believe a word he said! What's more, considerations of that nature wouldn't weigh with me, if – if I returned your regard!'

'Don't you? Not at all?'

'I – No! I mean – I mean, it isn't *that*!'

'Well, if it isn't that – Good God, you don't mean to tell me it's because I made a cake of myself over Celia Morval twenty years ago? No, really, my sweet life, that's doing it much too brown! What had it to do with you? You must have been in the nursery!'

'Yes, but – Oh, *surely* you can perceive how impossible it would be for me to marry you? She was my brother's wife!'

'No, she wasn't.'

'She was engaged to be married to him, at all events, and she *became* his wife! And, if it hadn't been hushed up, there would have been a shocking scandal – of your making!'

'But it *was* hushed up,' he pointed out.

She looked helplessly at him. 'How can I make you understand?'

'Oh, I do understand! You don't care a straw for all that ancient history, but you know that James would, and you're afraid he'd kick up the devil of a dust. He wouldn't, but I daresay he'd wear you to death, trying to heckle or cajole you into giving me up. However, you needn't let that worry you: I can deal with James.'

She said, in a low tone: 'I'm not afraid of James. If – if I knew that I was doing right. But it wouldn't be James only. My sisters – all my family – would be thrown into such an uproar! I only wish I might not be wholly cast off!' She glanced up fleetingly, and tried to speak more lightly. 'I shouldn't like that, you know. They may not know about Celia – indeed, I am very sure they don't, though I suppose Cornelia might, being James's wife – but, alas, they *do* know that you are the prodigal son!'

'Alas? What if they didn't know it? Would my disreputable past weigh with *you?*'

Her head was down-bent; she shook it slightly. 'Not if I loved you enough.'

'That sounds to me remarkably like a leveller. Don't you?'

She said frankly: 'I don't know. That's to say, it is so easy to mistake one's feelings: that I *do* know, for I cut my eye-teeth years ago. I hadn't any thought of marriage, and I didn't think that you had either, so – so I've had no time to consider. I own that if the circumstances had been different I – I should have been sorely tempted! But to marry – and at my age, too! – to disoblige one's family ought *not* to be considered. Do you understand?'

'Well, I understand that you've the devil of a lot of scruples, but it's no use expecting me to enter into them,' he replied. 'Family ties don't mean anything to me: didn't I tell you so once? As for making a sacrifice of yourself to suit your family's notions of respectability, I call it addlebrained!'

She smiled reluctantly. 'You would, of course! But it isn't quite that. I don't think I can explain it, because it's all tangled in my head – making me addlebrained! Do I seem odiously missish?'

'Yes, but I wasn't going to say so,' he assured her.

The laughter sprang into her eyes. '*Obnoxious* creature! If only you didn't always make me laugh! Sometimes I wonder if you have any proper feelings at all!'

'Almost none, I fear. Would you marry me if I had?'

She ignored this. 'Or any sense of shame either! But you have a great deal of quickness, and I'm persuaded you must see how outrageous it would be if I were to do the very thing I am trying to prevent Fanny from doing!'

'O my God!' he ejaculated. 'These Calverleighs – !'

'Exactly so!'

'Do you think *exactly*?' he asked diffidently. 'Would you object to it if I were to point out to you certain differences between the Calverleighs?'

She put out her hand impulsively. 'Oh, I know, I know! There is no comparison between you!'

He took her hand, and held it lightly on his knee. 'Oh, there is *some* comparison! Shocking fellows, both of us! I was one of the roaring-boys when I was on the town: they used to say of me that I was a hell-born babe – too rackety by half! But what no one ever said of me, not even my loving family, was that I was a bounce, or a queer-nabs!'

'Do they say that of Stacy?' she asked anxiously.

'So I've been informed, and I don't find it at all difficult to believe. Well, to continue our respective histories, each of us eloped with an heiress – or, rather, attempted to do so.'

'But you were in love with Celia! You didn't care for her fortune!' she interpolated swiftly.

'No, nor was I nine-and-twenty. I'm in love with you, and I don't care for *your* fortune.'

'You need not tell me that! Besides, I haven't a fortune. Not like Fanny! I think you would call it an *independence*, perhaps, or an easy competence.'

'Well, that's one objection disposed of: no one would be able to say that I married you for your fortune.'

'You wouldn't care if they did!' she said shrewdly.

'No, but you would.' There was a good deal of amusement in his eyes as they rested on her face. 'Just what do you imagine I've been doing during the past twenty years, dear innocent?'

'I don't know. How should I? You have never told me!'

'I'll tell you now. I've been making *my* fortune, of course.'

She laughed. 'So now you are a nabob! How stupid of me not to have guessed it!'

An odd smile flickered at the corners of his mouth. 'Just so!' he said. 'You aren't even interested, are you?'

'Well, no!' she confessed. 'Except that I did think you were perhaps a trifle purse-pinched, and I collect that this isn't the case, which I'm glad of, for your sake.'

'Thank you,' he said meekly.

'You know, if you *were* a rich nabob, your nephew might look to you rather than to Fanny to rescue him from his embarrassments,' she said.

'Not unless he was touched in his upper works! That would be rainbow-chasing, my dear!'

She smiled, but her own words had recalled her overriding anxiety to her mind. She drew her hand away, which had been resting snugly in his clasp, and gave a sigh. 'Wouldn't you do it, if it lay within your power? No, I suppose you wouldn't. Isn't there *anything* you might do to save my poor Fanny?'

'I thought it wouldn't be long before we came back to your poor Fanny. You are determined to embroil me in her affairs, aren't you?'

'Don't be vexed with me!' she begged. 'It is so very important! Perhaps you couldn't do anything, but you *might* be able to – if not for Fanny's sake, for mine?'

'Yes, well, let us now emerge from this pretty fairy-story!' he said, with a touch of astringency. 'If you imagine that I have the smallest desire to receive your hand as a reward for having performed a difficult task to your satisfaction you're beside the bridge, my child! I've no fancy for a reluctant wife. I want your love, not your gratitude.'

'I didn't say that!' she faltered. 'Indeed, I didn't!'

'You came mighty near it, didn't you?' he said quizzically. He got up, and held out his hands to her.' Come! If we don't make our way back to that inn, and get the horses put-to again, we shall be devilish late, and Miss Wendover will be thinking that *you* have eloped, not Fanny!'

She allowed him to pull her to her feet. As she walked beside him, towards the inn where they had left the curricle, she said tentatively: 'I hope you are not offended?'

He glanced down at her, and she was relieved to see that he was smiling again, very tenderly. 'No, not a bit. I was trying to decide whether I love you most when you're awake upon every suit, or when you're a pea-goose.'

Her eyes sank, as her colour rose; she said, with an uncertain laugh: 'I must seem like a pea-goose, I know. It is your fault, for – for putting windmills into my head! It doesn't seem so to you, but you have set me a problem, which I must solve, I think, by myself – if you understand me?'

'Well enough, at all events, not to press you further today. When I *do* press you further, I'll take care I don't do so here! Or in any other place where there's a hoary legend to take possession of your mind!'

'Hoary legend?' she repeated, momentarily puzzled. Her brow cleared suddenly. 'Oh, the bride and her attendants being turned into those stones! I had forgotten it.'

This interlude did much to lessen her constraint. During the drive back to Bath he talked on indifferent topics, so that she was very soon at her ease. She was careful not to introduce Fanny's name into her conversation, and was considerably surprised when he did so, saying abruptly: 'Don't tease yourself too much over Fanny! Have you any reason for fearing that she means to run away with Stacy? I'm inclined to doubt it, you know.'

She replied calmly: 'I don't know. She doesn't mean to do so before Thursday, I believe. She was discussing which of her new gowns she should wear for the party only this morning, so I think myself reasonably safe for the present. Afterwards – well, if she does mean to elope, she will find it a more difficult adventure than she bargained for!'

'I should think you would be more than a match for her,' he said. 'But that puts me in mind of something! I must make my excuses to your sister: I shan't be in Bath next week.'

She was conscious of feeling a disproportionate degree of disappointment, and a little disquiet. She said: 'My sister will be sorry. Are you – do you expect to be away for long?'

'Not longer than I need. There's some business I must attend to, and it won't do to put it off.'

'No, of course not,' she replied sedately. Then, as a thought occurred to her, she uttered an exclamation of annoyance, and said: 'Now, if only I had known, we need not have sent a card to Stacy!'

'Did you do so? Why?'

'Oh, because Selina *would* have it that if you were to be invited, Stacy must be too!'

'No! Did she really wish to invite me so much that she was prepared to receive Stacy? I must have made a bigger hit with her than I knew!' he remarked, in gratified accents.

Abby bit her lip, and replied with great dignity: 'My sister – I regret to say! – doesn't hold him in dislike. She thinks him very pretty-behaved, so it isn't a hardship to her to be obliged to entertain *him*!'

Twelve

*T*he news that Mr Calverleigh had left Bath was brought to Sydney Place by Miss Butterbank on the following morning. She was a little disappointed to find that Miss Wendover was already aware of it, having received a brief note from him excusing himself from attending her rout-party; but as he had not divulged his reason for leaving Bath, his destination, or the means by which he proposed to travel, she was quickly able to repair two of these omissions. She was known, behind her back, as the Bath Intelligencer, but although she could tell Miss Wendover that Mr Calverleigh had set out on the London Mail Coach, at five o'clock on the previous evening, she had not discovered the nature of his business, and could only advance a few conjectures.

Miss Wendover heard of the departure with relief, and indulged the hope that Mr Calverleigh did not mean to return to Bath. Foolish she might be, but it had not escaped her notice that he and Abby had become wondrous great, which was a circumstance which filled her with misgiving. He was an interesting man, and one who had been, in her opinion, hardly used, but no more ineligible husband for Abby could have been imagined. When the suggestion had first been slyly made to her that Abby was encouraging his advances she had been as incredulous as she was indignant, but when Abby, not content with accompanying him to the theatre, took to driving about the neighbouring countryside with him, she became very uneasy, and disclosed to the faithful Miss

Butterbank that she wished neither of the Calverleighs had ever come to Bath.

Their coming had certainly cut up her peace. First, there had been Stacy (poor young man!), whose very understandable attentions to Fanny had brought down James's wrath upon her head, and even, to some extent, Abby's; and who had turned out to be sadly unsteady, if James and George were to be believed, though it would not surprise her to find that they had grossly exaggerated Stacy's failings, for there was something so particularly winning about his graceful manners, and the deference he used towards his elders. He was the head of his family, too, and the owner of a considerable estate in Berkshire. She had never visited Danescourt, but she had looked for it in an old volume entitled *Seats of the Nobility and Gentry*, and there, sure enough, it was, with an illustration depicting a large, sprawling house of obvious antiquity, and a quantity of interesting information about its history, and that of the Calverleighs, who seemed to have owned it for an impressive number of centuries. If it was true, as George had told Abby it was, that it was so grossly encumbered that it was in imminent danger of passing out of Calverleigh hands, it could not be regarded as an asset, of course, for its loss must diminish Stacy's consequence to vanishing point, and transform him from a desirable *parti* into a scapegrace who had wasted his inheritance, and reduced himself to penury. But how could she have known this, when she had welcomed Stacy to Sydney Place? It was most unjust of James to have sent her such a scold; and for her part she would find it hard to believe that, whatever the poor young man's misfortunes might be, he had come to Bath in search of a rich wife. As for the shocking suspicion Abby had, that he meant to elope with Fanny, *that* she never would believe; and she wondered how Abby could suppose dear little Fanny to be so dead to all feelings of shame, or how she herself could be so regardless of her sister's precarious health as to put such ideas into her head as must give rise to the sort of agitating reflections calculated to throw her nerves into disorder.

And then, as though all this were not bad enough, Mr Miles Calverleigh had descended upon them, and lost no time at all in attaching himself particularly to Abby! There was no doubt about *his* reputation, for, however much one might pity him for the harsh treatment meted out to him by his father, the fact remained that not the most rigorous father would pack his son off to India without good reason. And if James thought he could lay the blame for this black sheep's intrusion into Abby's life at her door he was never more mistaken, and so she would tell him. Who, in the world, could have thought that Abby, rejecting the offer of the noble lord who addressed himself to her surrounded by the aura of dear Papa's approval, holding up her nose at such admirable suitors as Mr Peter Dunston, would succumb to the advances of a man who had nothing whatsoever to recommend him to one so notoriously picksome as she was? He was not at all handsome; he had none of his nephew's address; his manners were the reverse of graceful; and his raiment, so far from being elegant, showed neither neatness nor propriety. Not only did he pay morning-visits in riding-breeches and indifferently polished top-boots, but, more often than not, he looked as though he had dressed all by guess, tying his neckcloth in a careless knot, and shrugging himself into his coat. Anyone would have supposed that Abby, herself always precise to a pin, would have held such a shabrag in disgust – even if he had been unrelated to the Calverleigh she held in positive abhorrence! She had always been capricious, but to allow the uncle to make up to her while she refused to countenance the nephew's courtship of her niece carried caprice into the realm of distempered freakishness. And one had thought that she had outgrown what dear Rowland had called the odd kick in her gallop!

Abby, well aware that Selina was watching her with misgiving, betrayed none of her own misgivings. Away from Miles Calverleigh's disturbing presence, she could be mistress of herself; and she pursued her usual avocations without a sign that her cheerful calm concealed a heart and a mind suffering from a serious disorder. Mr Calverleigh's shortcomings were as obvious to her as to Selina, and as little as Selina did she know why, after so many fancy-free years, she should have fallen in love with one so hopelessly ineligible and so totally unlike any of the gentlemen with whom she had enjoyed passing flirtations. She had been attracted by his smile, but no smile, however fascinating it might be, could cause a cool-headed female of more than eight-and-twenty so wholly to lose her poise and her judgment that she felt she had met, in its owner, the embodiment of an ideal. Fumbling for an explanation, she thought that it was not Miles Calverleigh's smile which had awakened an instant response in her, but the understanding behind the smile. She had been conscious, almost from the start of their acquaintance, of an intangible link between them, as though he had been her counterpart; and nothing he had said, no disclosure of cynical unconcern, or total disregard of morals, had weakened the link. He could infuriate her, he frequently shocked her, but still she felt herself akin to him.

She had told him that she was not sure that she loved him, but she had done so not in doubt of her love for him, but in dismay at the realization that she did love him, whatever he was, or whatever he had done. If she had been a besotted schoolgirl, like her niece, she would have melted into his embrace, and have thought the world well lost. But at eight-and-twenty one did not, on an impulse, cast aside all the canons of one's upbringing; and still less did one lightly ignore the duty owed to one's family. Miles Calverleigh did not recognise family claims, and what shocked her most in this was the discovery that she was not shocked, but had experienced instead a pang of envy.

She wondered whether it was the rebellious streak in her, so frequently deplored even by her mother, which had drawn her irresistibly to Miles Calverleigh; but when she considered this, as dispassionately as she could, she thought that it could hardly be so. It might lead her to throw her cap over the windmill, but it found no answering chord in Miles. He was not a rebel. Rebels fought against the trammels of convention, and burned to rectify what they saw to be evil in the shibboleths of an elder generation, but Miles Calverleigh was not of their number. No wish to reform the world inspired him, not the smallest desire to convert others to his own way of thinking. He accepted, out of a vast and perhaps idle tolerance, the rules laid down by a civilised society, and, when he transgressed these, accepted also, and with unshaken good-humour, society's revenge on him. Neither the zeal of a reformer, nor the rancour of one bitterly punished for the sins of his youth, awoke a spark of resentment in his breast. He did not defy convention: when it did not interfere with whatever line of conduct he meant to pursue he conformed to it; and when it did he ignored it, affably conceding to his critics their right to censure him, if they felt so inclined, and caring neither for their praise nor their blame.

Such a character should have been alien to a Wendover. Abby knew it, and tried to convince herself that she was suffering from much the same adolescent madness which had attacked her niece, and from which she would soon recover. She met with no success: she was not an adolescent, but she could remember the throes of her first, frustrated love-affair, and she knew that her present condition was quite unlike the joys and agonies experienced ten years earlier. Like Fanny, she had fallen in love with a handsome countenance, and had endowed its owner with every imaginable virtue. Looking back in amusement upon this episode, she thought how fortunate it was for the undesirable suitor that her father had sent him packing before he had had time to tumble off the pedestal she had built for him. But she had built no pedestal for Miles Calverleigh: the very thought of setting him upon one appealed irresistibly to her lively sense of humour, and made it necessary for her explain to Selina that her sudden laugh, breaking a long silence, had been caused by the recollection of an old joke, too foolish to be repeated. The discovery that her first suitor had feet of clay would have shattered her infatuation; she had known from the beginning that Miles Calverleigh was no paladin, but his sins were of as little importance to her as his sallow, harsh-featured face. If she married him, it would be with her eyes open to his faults, and in the knowledge that, in consulting only her own ardent desire, she would be subjecting every member of her family to varying degrees of shock, dismay, and even, where Selina and Mary were concerned, to grave distress.

It was a hard problem to solve, and none of the arguments that dashed endlessly in her brain brought her any nearer to a decision, though they nagged at her all day, and kept her awake long into the night.

But no one, watching her as she moved amongst her guests on Thursday evening, would have suspected that anything had occurred to ruffle her serenity; and not the keenest eyes could detect in her face any sign that she was labouring under the pangs of love. So much in command of herself was she that she was even able, when Lady Weaverham enquired archly when they might expect to see Mr Miles Calverleigh in Bath again, to reply smilingly: 'I don't know, ma'am. We miss him, don't we? My sister thinks him much too free and easy, but for my part I find him most entertaining. One never knows what he will say next!'

'Which, to my mind,' Lady Weaverham told Mrs Ancrum, 'isn't the way a young woman talks about a gentleman she's nutty upon! And never a blush, or a conscious look either! Well, I did think it was a case between them, but I daresay it wouldn't have done, so it's as well that it ain't.'

Though nobody suspected that there was anything amiss with Abby, several people noticed that Fanny was not in her best looks. She was a little flushed, and decidedly heavy-eyed, but when Mrs Grayshott asked her kindly if she was feeling quite well she assured her that indeed she was, except for a slight headache. 'Don't say anything to Abby about it, ma'am!' she begged. 'It would spoil the party for her if she knew, and I promise you it is *very* slight!' She added, before flitting away to greet some fresh arrivals: 'You know how it is, when one holds a large party! However carefully you may plan it, there seem always to be such a number of things to do at the last moment that you can't help but be rather tired by the time the party begins!'

It was true that she had been busy for most of the day, but neither fatigue nor a slight headache would, under normal circumstances, have much impaired her enjoyment of the party. But she too was faced with a difficult problem; and although she had made up her mind that if the choice lay between eloping with Stacy to Scotland and losing him for ever, Scotland it must be, the decision had not put an end to her heart-searchings, and it had certainly not raised her spirits. When Selina chatted happily of winter plans, and discussed the numerous dresses she must have for her come-out in the spring, she felt an absurd desire to burst into tears; yet when she tried to imagine what it would be like to bid Stacy goodbye, her impulse was to fly to him immediately, just to assure him that she meant to keep her promise. The trouble was that she had been granted no opportunity since their stolen meeting in the Abbey to exchange more than a few words with him, and those only in public. It was no wonder that she should be feeling low. Once she was with him, and no longer lived in dread of being separated from him, everything would be right: it was only the actual severing of the ties which bound her to Sydney Place which made her feel wretched, and she must naturally be sad at wrenching herself from her home. After all, she had been miserable for days before she had gone, once, to spend a month with her Uncle James and her Aunt Cornelia. She had been extremely homesick, too, but she had recovered from this in a week. And if she could do so when staying with her uncle, who was so precise and prosy, and her aunt, who was detestable, how much more rapidly would she recover when she was in the arms of a husband whom she adored!

Her heart leaped up when she saw Stacy bowing over Selina's hand. How handsome he was! how elegant! how easy and polished were his manners, and how gracefully he made his bow! He made every other man in the room look dowdy and clumsy. He was top-of-the-trees – the Real Thing – and from amongst all the fashionable beauties who must surely have cast out lures to him he had chosen her – little Fanny Wendover, who hadn't even made her come-out! She felt a rush of pride in him, and wondered how she could have hesitated for a moment to go away with him.

Yet when, presently, he made his way to her side, and tried to draw her apart, she would not allow it, saying in an urgent undervoice: 'No, no, not here! not now!'

'But, my darling – !' he expostulated caressingly.

She was terribly nervous, fancying that at least a dozen pairs of eyes were on her; a stab of pain shot through her head; and suddenly she was shaken by a wave of irritation, and whispered quite fiercely: '*Don't!*'

He looked to be a good deal taken-aback. 'But, Fanny, I must talk to you!'

'Not now!' she repeated. 'I can't – All these people – ! Oh, pray don't tease me! I have *such* a headache!'

The smile faded from his lips. He said: 'I see what it is: your courage has failed you, or your love is not as strong as I believed it to be.'

'No, no, I *promise* it isn't so! Only we cannot talk here! Surely you must perceive the danger?'

'Then where?'

'Oh, I don't know!' She saw the frown gathering on his brow, and said hurriedly: 'Tomorrow – in the Gardens! At – at two o'clock! Aunt Selina will be resting on her bed, and Abby always visits old Mrs Nibley on Fridays. I'll contrive to join you there without Grimston's knowing. No more now: Abby is looking at us!'

She turned away on the words. The stabs of pain in her head were increasing, making her feel sick, and almost blinding her. A couple of uncertain steps brought her into collision with someone. She stammered: 'Oh, I beg your pardon! I didn't see!'

Her hand was caught, and held in a sustaining grasp; Oliver Grayshott's voice sounded above her head. 'Fanny, what it is? You are ill!'

'Oh, it's you!' she said, clinging gratefully to his hand. 'I'm not ill. It is only that my head aches so dreadfully! I shall be better directly.'

'Yes, but not in this squeeze,' he said. 'You must go to bed at once!'

'Oh, no, how can I? It would break up the party, and create a horrid fuss!'

'No, it won't,' he said calmly. 'No one will notice it, if you slip out of the room. I think you have a *migraine*, and I know, because I've had 'em myself, that there's only one thing for it, and that's to lie down on your bed. Shall I fetch Lavinia to go with you?'

'No, pray don't! It isn't as bad as *that*! Nurse will know what to do for me. Only don't say anything to frighten my aunts!'

'Of course not,' he replied.

'Thank you,' she sighed. 'I'm *very* much obliged to you!'

He watched her go unobtrusively out of the room, and then made his way to where his mother was seated, talking to Canon Pinfold. He soon found an opportunity to tell her that Fanny had retired with a headache, and was anxious that her aunts should not be alarmed. She said reassuringly that she would convey the news to Abby, who would be neither alarmed nor even surprised. 'She told me, when I said I thought Fanny not looking quite the thing, that she was pretty sure she had the headache, only the silly child wouldn't own to it.'

In point of fact, Abby had observed Fanny's departure. She said: 'Yes, I saw her go, and I was excessively grateful to Oliver for persuading her to do so. What a kind young man he is! I shall take a peep at her when I go upstairs to bed, but I need never be in a worry about her when Grimston has her in charge! I expect she will be quite restored by tomorrow.'

She was mistaken. While she was still sipping a cup of chocolate on the following morning, she received a visit from Mrs Grimston, who came to request her, ominously, to take a look at Miss Fanny as soon as might be convenient.

'It's no more than I expected, miss,' said Mrs Grimston, with the peculiar satisfaction of the devoted retainer who has detected incipient illness in one of her nurslings. '"Yes," I said to myself, when she came up to me last night, "there's more to this than a headache. If I know anything about it," I said, "what you've got, poor lamb, is the influenza!" Which she has, Miss Abby.' She took the empty cup from Abby, and added: 'And, if I was you, ma'am, I would send the footboy to fetch the doctor to her, because she's in a high fever, and there's no saying but what she may throw out a rash presently, though the measles it *can't* be!'

'No, of course it can't!' said Abby, throwing back the bedclothes. 'I don't doubt it's nothing more than influenza, just as you say!'

'If it's not the scarlet fever,' said Mrs Grimston, depressing optimism. She held up Abby's dressing-gown for her. 'For I shouldn't be doing my duty, Miss Abby, if I didn't tell you that she's been complaining for the past hour and more that she has a sore throat!'

'Very likely,' Abby returned. 'So did I, when I was laid up for a sennight with the influenza, last year!'

Balked of her wish to allay anxiety by her superior knowledge and commonsense, Mrs Grimston threw in a doubler. 'Yes, Miss Abby, and if it *is* the influenza, it's to be hoped Miss Selina hasn't taken it from her!'

'Oh, Grimston, you – you *wretch*!' Abby exclaimed ruefully. 'If she has, we *shall* be in the suds! Well! all my dependence is upon you!'

Mollified by this tribute, Mrs Grimston relented, and said, as she accompanied Abby to the sickroom: 'And so I should hope, ma'am! They say that there's a lot of this influenza going about, so I daresay Miss Fanny hasn't taken anything worse. But you know what she is, Miss Abby, and if you'll take my advice, you'll send for the doctor!'

Abby did indeed know what Miss Fanny was, and she gave a ready consent to the footboy's being sent off immediately on this errand. Fanny, though rarely ill, was a bad patient. If any seasonal ailment, or epidemic disease, attacked her, it invariably did so with unprecedented violence. None of her school-friends had been as full of the measles as she had been; none had whooped more distressingly; or had been more tormented by the mumps; so it came as no surprise to Abby, upon entering a room redolent with the fumes of burning pastilles, to find her in a high fever, and complaining in a miserable wail that she was hot, uncomfortable, aching in every limb, and hardly able to lift her eyelids.

'Poor Fanny!' Abby said softly, lifting the folded handkerchief from her brow, and soaking it afresh with vinegar. 'There! is that better? Don't cry, my pet! Dr Rowton is coming to see you, and he will soon make you more comfortable.'

'I don't want him! I'm not ill! I'm not, I'm not! I want to get up! I *must* get up!'

'To be sure, and so you shall, just as soon as you feel more the thing,' Abby said soothingly.

'I *do* feel the thing! It's only that my head hurts me, and I can't hold my eyes open, and everything aches all over me!' wept the sufferer. 'Oh, Abby, *please* make me better *quickly*!'

'Yes, darling, of course I will.'

This assurance seemed to calm Fanny. She lay still for a while, dropping into an uneasy doze; but within a very few minutes she became restless again, insisting that she was better, trying to get up, and bursting into tears when Abby gently pressed her back on to her pillows.

Having had considerable experience of her mercurial temperament, and knowing that whenever she was condemned to lie in bed it took much to persuade her that her ills would not be instantly alleviated by her getting up, and going for a walk, Abby set no particular store by her agitation. Leaving Mrs Grimston to sit with her, she withdrew, to dress, and – when fortified by breakfast – to break the news to Selina.

She found that Fardle, Selina's maid, had been before her, carrying such an unpromising account of Fanny's condition that Selina's appetite had been destroyed. When Abby came into her room, she was sitting up in bed, eating pieces of toast dipped in weak tea: a melancholy diet to which it was her custom to resort in times of stress. She greeted her sister with a moan, and a demand to be told whether the doctor had been sent for.

'Yes, dear, an hour ago! I daresay he will be here directly,' replied Abby cheerfully. 'Not that I think there is much to be done for her, but I hope he may be able to make her more comfortable at least. Grimston gave her a fever powder at seven o'clock but it hasn't answered, so I have told her not to repeat it.'

'No, no, don't let Grimston quack her! Oh, Abby, if she should be beginning in the smallpox – !' uttered Selina, staring fearfully at her.

'Beginning in the *smallpox*?' echoed Abby, in astonishment. 'Good God, no! How can you be so absurd, Selina? Why, surely you haven't forgotten that Dr Rowton persuaded us all to be inoculated last year? Besides, where could she have contracted it? There are no cases of it in Bath that I've heard of!'

'No, dear, very likely not, but one never *knows*, and Fardle has been telling me –'

'Fardle!' exclaimed Abby. 'I might have guessed as much! I am perfectly sure that she has a sister, or an aunt, or a cousin, who nearly died in the smallpox, and that her symptoms precisely resembled Fanny's, for we've never yet had an illness in this household, but what one of Fardle's relations had had it too, only *far* worse! Pray don't fly into a fuss, dear! I shall own myself surprised if Dr Rowton finds Fanny to be suffering from anything more serious than influenza.'

'Oh, my love, why didn't you send for Dr Dent? I have no great opinion of Rowton, though an excellent man in his way, of course, but *not* clever! You know how well Dr Dent understood my case when *I* had influenza!'

'Yes, dear, but I was persuaded you would wish me to send for Rowton, because he is familiar with her constitution,' said Abby diplomatically. 'Do you mean to drive into town this morning? Will you buy a bottle of lavender water, if you please?'

'Fardle must procure it,' said Selina, in a failing voice. 'I shall rest quietly in bed this morning, for I have already felt a spasm, and heaven forbid *I* should be ill at this moment! Such a dreadful shock to be roused with such news! Yes, and she must bring me some camphor, for I don't believe there is any in the house, and you know how susceptible I am to colds and influenza!'

Abby agreed to this, but ventured to suggest that not the most susceptible person would be very likely to contract influenza twice within the space of a month.

'No, dearest,' replied Selina, directing a look of patient reproach at her. 'I daresay an ordinary person might not, but, alas, I have never enjoyed high health, and as for not contracting influenza twice in a month, I had *three* epidemic colds last winter, one after another! And I recall that you said exactly the same when you came home from Lady Trevisian's card-party, sneezing and snuffling, and I begged you not to come *near* me, but to go up to your bed immediately! You said *I* could not catch it from you, because I had not been out of *my* bed above a sennight! But I did!'

Abby begged pardon, kissed her cheek, and left her to the enjoyment of her mild triumph.

In the sickroom, she found Fanny tossing restlessly, and alternately expressing her determination to get up, and complaining of the various aches and pains which assailed her. Her pulse was rapid, and her skin very hot and dry, and it was obvious that her fever was mounting.

Mrs Grimston, drawing Abby out of the room, said that if anyone were to ask her she would feel herself impelled to say that they were regularly in for it. 'As nasty an attack as any I've nursed her through!' she said. 'Well, I'm sure it's not to be wondered at, the way she's been gallivanting to parties all over, and her no more than a baby! Burnt to the socket, that's what she is, Miss Abby, and so full of crotchets and nonsense as is enough to put one quite out of patience! First she must get up, and the moment my back's turned so she did! Only that turned her so dizzy she was glad enough to be put back into bed. Then she began to cry, but I soon put a stop to that, ma'am, for we don't want her to get into one of her ways, for, as I told her, *that* won't make her feel better!

Then nothing will do for her but what she must speak to Betty about mending a frill on her blue muslin. "There'll be time enough for that, Miss Fanny," I said, "and no need to bring Betty into the room to take the influenza, for I'll speak to her about it myself." '

The arrival of Dr Rowton brought this monologue to a close. He was a sensible-looking man, with a latent twinkle in his eye, but it was not difficult to see why Selina thought poorly of him. He had cheerful, matter-of-fact manners, and had been known to tell ladies in failing health that their mysterious ailments arose from want of occupation, or from thinking too much about themselves. He said, as he shook hands with Abby: 'And how is Miss Wendover? I hear she has my old friend, Dent, attending her now. I thought it wouldn't be long before she gave poor Ockley the go-by: not her style at all!'

He did not take a very serious view of Fanny's case; but when he left her he told Abby that she would probably be laid up for some little time. 'Oh, yes, it's influenza right enough,' he said. 'It's running very much about, you know, and unusually virulent. A pity Fanny should have caught it. Now, had it been you, Miss Abby, I should have said you'd be as bobbish as ever in a week but we both know what Fanny is, don't we? Always the way with girls of her cut! You'll have to keep her quiet – as quiet as you can! I was used to call her Miss Quicksilver, when she was a child, and she hasn't altered much. I'll send my man round with some medicine for her to take, and we'll see how she goes on tomorrow.'

He was a favourite of Fanny's, ranking amongst her oldest friends, and Abby had hoped that his visit would do her good. She did indeed manage to conjure up a wan smile, when he walked up to the bedside, saying: 'Well, Miss Quicksilver, and pray what's all this?' but the voice in which she responded: 'Oh, *dear* Dr "Wowton", make me well again quickly!' was very lachrymose; and when he told her, in his blunt way that she would certainly not be able to get up that day, or for several days, she burst into tears.

When Abby returned to the sickroom, however, she seemed to be resigned to her fate, and to be inclined to sleep.

She did drop off into an uneasy doze from time to time, but her dreams were haunted by Stacy, either waiting for hour upon hour in Sydney Gardens, or accusing her of being false to him; and more than once she woke with tears on her cheeks, and a jumble of words on her feverish lips.

She retained no very clear memory of what had happened at the previous night's party, but she did remember that she had promised to meet Stacy, and that he had been angry with her for not talking to him. He had said that he could see she didn't love him, and now he would be sure of it. She had racked her brains to hit upon some way of conveying a message to him, but Abby and Nurse were in league against her; they would not even let her see Betty Conner, who could have done it for her. Perhaps he would think that she had stayed away on purpose, to show him that she didn't want to run off with him after all. Perhaps he would leave Bath, as he had threatened to do, and she would never see him again, never be able to tell him that it hadn't been her fault, or that she did love him, and wasn't afraid to elope with him to Scotland.

These agitating reflections did nothing to improve her condition; and as her fever mounted they became even more lurid, until they included visions of her own death-bed, and Stacy's remorse at having so misjudged her. But towards evening Dr Rowton's paregoric medicine began to take effect, and she grew calmer, emerging from the state of semi-delirium which had kept Abby hovering on the verge of sending a second, and far more urgent, summons to the doctor. She felt so ill, and so much exhausted, that she no longer wanted to get up, or even to exert herself sufficiently to try once more to think how she might send a message to Stacy. It must be too late by now, she thought apathetically. Her whole life was ruined, but it didn't seem to matter nearly as much as her aching body, and the stabbing pain in her temple, and her terrible thirstiness. When Abby raised her, she leaned her head gratefully on Abby's shoulder, murmuring her name.

'Yes, my darling, I'm here,' Abby said tenderly. 'Nurse is going to shake up your pillows while you have a cool drink of lemonade. There, is that better?'

'Oh, yes!' she sighed, her thirst for the moment assuaged. She opened her eyes, and they fell on a big bowl of flowers. 'Oh!' she breathed.

'Looking at your beautiful flowers?' Abby said, laying her gently down again. 'Oliver and Lavinia brought them, when they came to enquire how you did. They left their love to you, and were so sorry to hear that you're so poorly. Go to sleep again now, darling: I won't leave you.'

The spark of hope that had flickered in Fanny's breast died, but as she lay dreamily looking at the flowers it occurred to her that if the Grayshotts knew that she was ill they would be very likely to tell other people, and so, perhaps, the news would reach Stacy's ears, and he would know why she had broken her word to him. With a deep sigh of relief, she turned her head on the pillow, snuggling her cheek into it, and drifted back into sleep.

Thirteen

*I*t was not long before the news reached Stacy Calverleigh, but when it did it brought no relief to his anxieties, which were rapidly becoming acute. He had not supposed, when he kicked his heels in the Sydney Gardens, that Fanny had failed him from intention, nor did it occur to him that she might be ill. Not being endowed with the perception which distinguished Mr Oliver Grayshott, he had failed to notice her flushed cheeks and heavy eyes, and had ascribed the headache of which she had complained to a tiresome fit of missishness. The likeliest explanation that presented itself to him was that she had been prevented from keeping her assignation by the vigilance of her aunt. It had at first exasperated him; but, upon reflection, he had come to the conclusion that the frustration of her plan might well prove to be all that was needed to cause such a wilful, headstrong girl as Fanny to throw herself into his arms in a fury of indignation. Confident that she must be pantingly eager to tell him why she had been unable to meet him, and equally eager to escape from her shackles, he paraded the Pump Room on the following morning; and, when neither she nor Miss Wendover put in an appearance, wasted considerable time in taking a look-in at the libraries, strolling up such fashionable streets as Fanny would be most likely to visit on a shopping expedition, and loitering interminably in Queen's Square. No balls or concerts took place at the Assembly Rooms on Fridays, and as he had received no invitation to any private party it was not until Saturday that he learned of Fanny's indisposition.

It struck him with dismay. It must mean delay, even if she made a quick recovery, and delay was what he could not afford. It was not in his nature to envisage disaster. He had the true gamester's belief in his luck, and experience had encouraged him to think that when this failed him some unexpected stroke of Providence would rescue him from his predicaments. But several unpleasant communications, which not the most hardened of optimists could have failed to recognise as the precursors to writs, had reached him; and a most disquieting letter from his man of business had conveyed to him the intelligence that foreclosure on his estates was now imminent. For perhaps the first time in his life, he knew panic, and for a few wild moments entertained thoughts of a flight to the Continent. While these endured, his spirits rose: life abroad held out its attractions. A clever gamester, one who knew what time of day it was, could make a fortune if he set up a gaming establishment in any one of half a dozen cities which instantly leaped to his mind. Not Paris: no, not Paris. Now that Napoleon was marooned on St Helena Island, far too many Englishmen were to be found disporting themselves in Paris: he had as well – or as ill – set up such an establishment in London. But there were other promising cities, rather further afield, where the chances of his being recognised by an English traveller were negligible.

This was important. Mr Stacy Calverleigh, eyed askance by the society into which he had been born, even being obliged, since his disastrous attempt to secure an heiress, to endure more than one cut direct, bent on seducing yet a second heiress to elope with him, was not so lost to a sense of his obligations that he did not recoil from the thought of transforming himself, openly, into the proprietor of a gaming-house. He had often thought what a capital hand he would have made of it, had it been possible for him to join the company of these gentry; he had never regarded his estates as anything other than a coffer into which he could dip his hand at will; but the inculcated precepts of his breeding remained with him. There were some things a Calverleigh of Danescourt must never do; and high on the list of these prohibitions ranked the only profession at which he felt he might have excelled.

But if one could enter it without the knowledge of those who would most contemptuously condemn him? As his fancy played with the possibilities of such a situation, his eyes brightened, and he began to picture a future rosier, and far more to his secret taste, than any that had yet presented itself to him.

Only for a few, fleeting moments, however. To embark on such a career, it was necessary that the dibs should be in tune, and the dibs were not in tune. There was no other solution to his difficulties than a rich marriage. Marriage to Fanny was not the ideal solution, but a notice (he had already drafted it) sent to the *Gazette*, and the *Morning Post*, of his marriage to the only daughter of the late Rowland Wendover Esquire, of Amberfield, in the County of Bedfordshire, would stave off his creditors, and might, at the least, make it very difficult for Mr James Wendover to repudiate the alliance.

A visit of enquiry and condolence to Sydney Place did not strengthen this more hopeful view. He was received by the elder Miss Wendover; and although she welcomed him with rather guilty kindness, her account of her niece's illness was not encouraging. Mr Miles Calverleigh, with his dispassionate yet shrewd ability to sum up his fellow-creatures, would have appreciated it at its true value; Mr Stacy Calverleigh, absorbed in his own entity, only noticed the peculiarities of the persons with whom he came in contact when their idiosyncrasies directly affected him, and so made no allowance for the exaggerations of an elderly lady whose paramount interest lay in the ailments of herself, or of anyone attached to her. He left Sydney Place with the impression that if Fanny were not lying at death's door she was so gravely ill that it must be many weeks before she could hope to be restored to health. Miss Wendover said that she had often feared that Fanny's constitution too closely resembled her own, and embroidered this statement with some instances which, had he been listening to her with as much attention as his solicitous expression indicated, might well have led him to conclude that Fanny, for all her looks and vitality, was a frail creature, supported by her nerves, which too frequently betrayed her.

He was not listening. The delicacy of Fanny's constitution was a matter of secondary importance. What was of the first importance was the apparent likelihood that her recovery from her present disorder would be too slow to admit of her being able, or even willing, to undertake the long journey to the Scottish Border for several weeks.

He maintained his smile, and his air of courteous concern, but when he took his leave of Miss Wendover, consigning to her care the tasteful bouquet he had ventured to bring with him for the invalid, he was as near to despair as it was possible for anyone of his temperament to be. He walked slowly back to the centre of the town, trying in vain to think of some other means of recruiting his fortunes than marriage. A run of luck might save him from immediate ruin, but a prolonged run of damnable ill-luck had made it impossible for him to continue punting on tick. If his vowels were still accepted in certain circles, it was with reluctance; and he had been refused admittance – in the politest way – to two of the exclusive hells which had for several years enjoyed his patronage. For the first time in his life he knew himself to be at a stand, and without any hope of deliverance.

But Providence, in whom he had for so long reposed his careless trust, had not forgotten him. Providence, in the guise of Mrs Clapham, was at that very moment entering the portals of the White Hart, preceded by her courier, accompanied by her female companion, and followed by her maid, and her footman.

He did not immediately realise that Providence had intervened on his behalf. By the time he had reached the White Hart, Mrs Clapham had been reverently escorted to the suite of rooms bespoken by her courier, and the only signs of her presence which were observable were the elegant travelling-chariot which had brought her to Bath, and was still standing in the yard, and the unusual state of bustle prevailing amongst the various servants employed at the hotel.

There were those who considered the situation of the White Hart to be too noisy for comfort, but it was patronised by so many persons of rank and consequence that the stir created by the arrival of Mrs Clapham was remarkable enough to arouse Stacy's interest. He enquired of the waiter who brought a bottle of brandy to his room who the devil was Mrs Clapham, and why were they all tumbling over themselves to administer to her comfort? The waiter replied, with strict civility, but repressively, that she was the lady who had engaged the largest and most luxurious set of apartments in the house. The boots was more informative, and from him Stacy gathered that Mrs Clapham was a widow-lady, full of juice, and flashing the rags all over. Everything of the best she had to have, and ready to pay through the nose for it. Very affable and pleasant-spoken, too, which was more than could be said of her companion. Top-lofty *she* was, giving her orders as if she was a duchess, and saying that first this and then that would not do for her mistress, and her own sheets and pillows must be put on her bed, and her own tea served to her, and dear knows what more besides!

Stacy's curiosity was only mildly tickled by this description. It was not until he encountered Mrs Clapham on the following morning that the thought that Providence might once more have come to his rescue darted through his brain. A widow, travelling with a large entourage, and bringing with her her own bedlinen, suggested to him a turbaned dowager, the relict of a bygone generation. Mrs Clapham might be a widow, but she was no dowager. She was quite a young woman: past her girlhood, but not a day older than thirty, if as old. She was remarkably pretty, too, with an inviting mouth, and a pair of brown eyes which were as innocent as they were enormous, until she dropped demure eyelids over them, and looked sidelong from under the screen of her curling lashes. Then they became unmistakably provocative. She was dressed with great elegance, but in a subdued shade of lavender, which seemed to indicate that, while she had cast off her weeds, her bereavement was of fairly recent date. When Stacy saw her first, she was tripping down the stairs, trying to

184

button one of her gloves, without dropping the prayer-book she was holding. As Stacy looked up at her, it slipped from her imperfect grasp, and fell almost at his feet.

'Oh – !' she exclaimed distressfully. Then, as he picked it up, and straightened its crumpled leaves: 'Oh, how very obliging of you! Thank you! So stupid of me! It is all the fault of these tiresome gloves, which *will* come unbuttoned!'

Her companion, following her down the stairs, clicked her tongue, and said: 'Pray allow me, Mrs Clapham!'

Mrs Clapham held out her wrist helplessly, repeating, with a rueful smile cast at Stacy: 'So *stupid* of me! Oh, thank you, dear Mrs Winkworth! I don't know how I should go on without you!'

Stacy, presenting her prayer-book to her, bowed with his exquisite grace, and said: 'One or two of the pages a little crumpled, ma'am, but no irreparable damage, I fancy! May I beg leave to make myself known to you? – Stacy Calverleigh, wholly at your service!'

She gave him her tightly gloved hand. 'Oh, yes! And I am Mrs Clapham, sir. This is Mrs Winkworth, who takes such good care of me. We are on our way to Church, in the Abbey. The *feel* it gives me! I have never attended a service in an abbey before: isn't it absurd?'

'Your first visit to Bath, ma'am?' he enquired, bestowing a modified bow upon her companion.

'Oh, yes! I was never here before in my life, though I have been to Tunbridge Wells. But I have been living retired lately, in the country, only it was so *very* melancholy that I was quite moped. So the doctor advised me to come to Bath, and take the Hot Bath, and perhaps drink the waters.'

'They are very nasty!'

'Mrs Clapham, the bell has stopped ringing,' interposed Mrs Winkworth.

'So it has! We must make haste!'

She smiled, bowed, and hurried away. Mrs Winkworth also bowed, very slightly, but she did not smile.

His spirits much improved, Stacy retired to his own room to

consider the possibilities of this new and unexpected event. Mrs Clapham was obviously wealthy, but the presence of Mrs Winkworth argued that a careful watch was being kept over her. Mrs Winkworth was a middle-aged woman, who must have been handsome in her youth, for she had good features, and fine, if rather hard, grey eyes. Stacy thought, from her forbidding mien and the somewhat authoritative manner she used towards Mrs Clapham, that she had been hired rather as a chaperon than as a companion, and this indicated that the widow's relations were jealously guarding her from gentlemen hanging out for rich wives. Neither lady, he was quick to realise, was of the first stare. Mrs Winkworth was plainly of Cockney origin: her refined accents were superimposed on that unmistakable twang; Mrs Clapham he wrote down as a provincial, whose husband had almost certainly made his fortune in trade.

If there was a fortune, which was not yet certain. It was not unknown for a pretty widow, desirous of contracting a second, and more genteel, marriage, to invest a modest competence as Mrs Clapham might be doing: rigging herself out in style, and visiting a fashionable watering-place in the hope of attracting, and ensnaring, an eligible suitor. Not that Bath was any longer a resort of high fashion, but very likely she did not know that its visitors nowadays were rarely smart bachelors, but for the most part elderly persons, who wintered there for the sake of its mild climate; or invalids who came to drink the waters, or to take a course of Vapour Baths. On the other hand, the employment of a courier and a footman, not to mention her insistence on having her bed furnished with her own linen, seemed excessive; and the presence of a dragon-like companion lent no colour to the suspicion that she might be an ambitious female on the catch. Nor did her dress, which was costly but unostentatious. He recalled that she had been wearing large pearl drops in her ears, and round her throat a necklace of pearls which, if they were indeed pearls, must have cost the late Mr Clapham a pretty penny. But in these days one never knew: the most convincing pearls could be made out of glass and fish-scales. He had purchased one of these sham necklaces himself once, to gratify the lightskirt at that time living in his keeping, and the sheen on those trumpery beads would have deceived anyone but a jeweller.

He decided, coldly considering Mrs Clapham, that he must make it his business to ingratiate himself with her companion, and did not doubt his ability to do so: elderly females – witness Miss Wendover! – could easily be bamboozled. It would do no harm to bring Mrs Winkworth round his thumb; and, if he could be satisfied that Mrs Clapham was as wealthy as she appeared to be, it would be of the first importance to do so.

Another possibility suggested itself to him: all too frequently the wealth inherited by widows was so tightly tied up that they might as well have been paupers. Not so long since, he had himself been as near as a toucher to being completely taken-in. Within ames-ace of offering for the hand of a widow in affluent circumstances, he had discovered that the better part of her very handsome independence would be lost to her if she embarked upon a second marriage. A very near-run thing that had been, and he meant to take good care he did not again court such a risk.

In these calculations Fanny was not forgotten. If Fanny had been of full age, he would not have considered for a moment Mrs Clapham's claims to his attention, for although (had it been possible for him to consult only his inclination) he would not have chosen such a high-spirited and self-willed bride as Fanny, she was a lovely little creature, and marriage to her would do much to rehabilitate him in the eyes of society. The Wendovers did not figure amongst the members of the *haut ton*, but they might have done so, had they so wished. The family, though not of such ancient lineage as the Calverleighs, was of undoubted gentility, and had been for long established in the county of Bedfordshire. It was also extremely well connected. When Mr James Wendover, who had no taste for town-life, was constrained by his equally well-connected spouse to hire a house in London for his eldest daughter's come-out, it would require no effort on his part to introduce Miss Albinia into the first circles. Everyone knew the Wendovers, and a surprising number of distinguished persons acknowledged some sort of relationship with the family. Frivolous people might make game of Mr James Wendover's prejudices, but marriage to his niece, the heiress to Amberfield, could be depended on to restore the bridegroom to respectability.

But Fanny was not of full age; and while Stacy knew enough of her uncle to be tolerably sure that he would be obliged, by his dread of scandal, to condone her runaway marriage, and, at the least, put her in possession of the income derived from her estates, – if not immediately, certainly when she became seized with the effects of matrimony – it had been rudely borne in upon him that there was no time to be wasted in extricating himself from his embarrassments. He had hoped to have carried Fanny off within a day of her aunts' curst rout-party, but she had contracted influenza, and it might now be weeks before she was well enough even to contemplate an elopement. Nor could he be sure that he could bring her to the sticking-point when she was restored to health. It had taken much coaxing to overcome her unexpected recoil from a Gretna Green marriage – if he had overcome it, which was doubtful. He had thought that he had done so, but she had almost repulsed him at the rout-party. It seemed all too probable that still more precious time would be wasted in bringing her under his spell again.

But if Mrs Clapham was indeed in untrammelled possession of a handsome fortune; if she could be swept off her feet by the attentions of a personable man of birth and fashion – and one, moreover, who owned a seat which was mentioned, if not minutely described, in any Guide Book to Berkshire – Badbury, his man of business, would not find it impossible to persuade his mortgagees to grant him a few more weeks' grace before instituting forfeiture proceedings. There would be no question of an expensive elopement – and that, when the proprietors of the old-established house with whom one's family had banked since time out of mind were indicating, sorrowfully but implacably, that unless one's debt to them was substantially reduced they would be forced to dishonour any further drafts upon their resources, would be an advantage. Mrs Clapham was not a minor, and the notice of his engagement to her, coupled with a disclosure to Badbury of her circumstances, would be enough to fob off his creditors.

There was very little doubt in his mind that the conquest of Mrs Clapham would not be difficult. He had instantly recognised the invitation in her eyes, and the widening look which betrayed admiration; and what, in her ingenuous way, she had already divulged, informed him that she was heartily bored by the decorous conduct imposed upon her by her widowhood. She might be the daughter and the relict of respectable trades-men, but experience made it easy for Mr Stacy Calverleigh to detect in her the signs of the Approachable.

It was possible that she had come to Bath merely in search of diversion, and that when she threw him that tantalising glance from under her sweeping lashes she had nothing more serious in mind than flirtation; but he thought it unlikely. She might have the instincts of a straw damsel, but he judged her to be sprung from middle-class parents, and to be too much imbued with the boring, shabby-genteel notions obtaining amongst the depressing and regrettably increasing members of this class to encourage the advances of any gentleman unable, or unwilling, to offer her the security of marriage.

He would have preferred, of course, to have become leg-shackled to a female of his own order, but the exigencies of his position made it impossible for him to be too nice in his choice. She seemed, at all events, to be a simple creature, who could be groomed into the semblance of a woman of quality. Her simplicity had led her to Bath, which was at once fortunate, and a trifle ticklish. Passing under review the numerous acquaintances he had made in Bath, he could discover no rival amongst them. But for weeks past the eyes of the residents had been interestedly watching his courtship of Fanny, and however little he might regard the censure of such as Mrs Ancrum, or Lady Weaverham, he would find himself in the suds if that determined pursuit came to the ears of Mrs Clapham. If he decided that it would be worth his while to transfer his attentions to her, he would be obliged to seek a way out of an obviously awkward situation. Well, it would be time enough to think how best to deal with trouble when he was brought face to face with it: that had always been his rule, and, on the whole, it had answered pretty well. Meanwhile, his first and most pressing need was to enquire more precisely into Mrs Clapham's circumstances.

From his window, he was able to observe her return to the White Hart; and thus it came about that just as she had begun to mount the stairs he rounded the turn in the first pair, and came running lightly down. At sight of her, he checked, and, with a startled apology, retreated to the half-landing.

'Oh, pray don't – why, if it isn't you, Mr Calverleigh!' she exclaimed. 'Don't tell me you're putting up here too!'

He laughed. 'Must I not? I'm afraid I am! I'm sorry if you should object to it, but I was here before you, you know! What is to be done?'

She went into a trill of mirth. 'As though I meant anything so uncivil! You're bantering me, sir! No, indeed, I'm sure I'm glad you are putting up here, for I've no other acquaintance in Bath. I was only saying to Mrs Winkworth, a couple of minutes past, how much I wished I knew someone here who could tell me how to find my way about, or where to go to purchase an umbrella, which I can see is what I shall be needing!'

'What, have you come to Bath without an umbrella, ma'am? Oh, that will never do! I will certainly direct you to the nearest shop which sells them! You will be wishing to write your name in Mr King's subscription book too, I daresay.'

'Ought I to do so? You'll think me a regular zany, but I don't perfectly understand. Who – who is Mr King?'

'He is the Master of Ceremonies at the New Assembly Rooms – the Upper Rooms, as they are often called. They hold balls and concerts there, and card-parties.'

'Balls! Oh, no, I don't think I ought! Not *yet*! You see, it is not *quite* a year since Mr Clapham died, and although I have put off my blacks, because he never liked me to wear black, I shouldn't care to show disrespect. I'm sure it wouldn't be seemly for me to go to balls. Not but what I will become a subscriber, if it is the thing, which is what Mr Clapham would have wished, for *never* did he behave scaly, even when there was no good to be got by paying down his dust! So you must tell me – oh, dear, there are so many things I want to know!' She paused, and then said shyly: 'I wonder – Would you care to drink tea with us in my private parlour? We should be very happy – shouldn't we, Mrs Winkworth?' A thought seemed to occur to her; she added: 'Unless, of course – no, I don't mean that! I mean – I mean, you might, perhaps be engaged with your own party? Or – if you should chance to be a *married* man, we should be honoured to receive Mrs Calverleigh too!'

'No, I'm not married,' he replied. 'I shall be delighted to drink tea with you, ma'am!'

Her face brightening, she said: 'Oh, then, pray come whenever you choose! This evening?'

Far too astute to jump at an invitation, he excused himself, but, after a little hesitation, allowed her to persuade him to accept one for the following evening. He fancied that he read a certain measure of approval in Mrs Winkworth's expression, and took his leave of both ladies, feeling that a promising start had been made in his new venture.

The tea-drinking was very successful. He found her seated on one side of a small fire, dressed all in grey, with no ornaments but her pearls, and one fine diamond ring, which he judged to have sentimental associations, since she gazed at it, from time to time, with wistful fondness.

It was not at all difficult to draw her out, for she was of a chatty and confiding disposition. Her tongue might run on wheels, but he was able to gather various important pieces of information from amongst the chaff of her conversation. He learned that she had lived almost her whole life in Birmingham, until Mr Clapham had bought a house a few miles outside the town, and had bestowed it upon her, just because he knew she had always hankered after a house in the country. Well, *house* – ! It was more of a Property.

'But that was Mr Clapham all over,' she said. 'He was quite elderly, you know, but I was excessively attached to him.'

'So you should have been,' dryly interpolated Mrs Winkworth. 'The way he doted on you!'

'Oh, you mean to say that he spoiled me!' Mrs Clapham pouted. She threw a laughing, rueful glance at Stacy. 'That's what she is for ever telling me, unkind thing! I'm afraid it's true; I've always been sadly spoiled. You see, I was Papa's only child, and my mama died when I was very young. And then, when he died, Mr Clapham was so *very* kind, settling everything for me, and looking after all my affairs, and trying to make me understand about horrid things like *Consols*, only I never did, and I don't think I ever shall, except that Papa had a great many of them. Business makes my head ache! So when Mr Clapham asked me to marry him I was truly thankful. Oh, he was so kind to me! He was used to say nothing was too good for me, and that after having nobody to care for so many years – for his sister, who kept house for him died, and so he was the only one left – he *liked* to give me things. If ever I took a fancy to something, he would buy it, not saying a word to me, and there it would be the very next day, for a Surprise! Oh, I do wish I could show you my rubies! They are my favourite jewels, but Mrs Winkworth *would* have me lock them up in the Bank before we came to Bath, because it isn't proper to wear coloured stones until one is out of black gloves, and she thinks they would be stolen if I kept them in a hotel.'

'My dear ma'am, how you do run on!' said Mrs Winkworth, frowning at her.

She was instantly penitent. 'I never *could* learn to bite the tongue! It is very bad! Papa was used to say it ran like a fiddlestick, but Mr Clapham liked my silly bibble-babble. But you are very right: I have been boring on for ever! I won't do so any more. Tell us about yourself, Mr Calverleigh! Do you live in London, or in the country?'

'Oh, in London – though I was bred up in the country.'

'I thought you did,' she said artlessly. 'I mean to live there myself, for I'm sure I couldn't bear to continue living at the

Towers without Mr Clapham. He took me there once, and I liked it excessively. We stayed at a very comfortable hotel – I can't remember what it was called, but Mr Clapham always stayed there when he was obliged to go to London, because he said they served the best dinners of all the hotels.'

'Then I collect it was the Clarendon.'

She clapped her hands together. 'Yes, that was it! How clever of you to guess! Only I shouldn't wish to *live* in a hotel. I mean to buy a house.'

'*Hire* a house, ma'am,' corrected Mrs Winkworth.

'Well, perhaps – if that's what they do in London,' said Mrs Clapham doubtfully. She looked at Stacy. 'Is it? Do you hire *your* house?'

He smiled, and said, with a great air of frankness: 'No, I have a lodging merely.'

'Oh!' She considered this for a moment. 'I daresay a lodging is less trouble to you – being a gentleman.'

'Much less trouble!' he said, with a comical grimace.

'Yes, but – but a house of one's own is more agreeable, I think. More homelike!'

'Not my house!' he said humorously.

'But you said you had only a lodging!'

'In London! I have a place in Berkshire: my family has owned it for generations. I daresay you know the style of thing: very historical, very inconvenient, and needs an army of servants to keep it in order. Quite beyond my touch! I'd sell it, if I could.'

'Can't you? If you don't wish to live in it?'

He threw up his hands in mock horror. 'Sell Danescourt? My dear ma'am, never let any member of my family hear you suggest such a thing! I promise you, they would think it little short of blasphemy!'

He judged that he had said quite enough (and rather neatly, too) to impress her, and soon took his leave. Mrs Winkworth bestowed quite an approving smile upon him, which showed him that his candid avowal of his straitened circumstances had had its calculated effect on her.

Fourteen

*T*he acquaintance, so promisingly begun, ripened quickly, but the difficulties foreseen by Mr Stacy Calverleigh soon began to loom large. Within the walls of the White Hart it was an easy matter to pursue his delicate courtship; outside this hostelry, it became perilous. He had known that it would be; and his forebodings were confirmed when (at her request) he escorted Mrs Clapham to the Pump Room, and instantly attracted unwelcome notice. It had been impossible to evade that public appearance. 'Oh, Mr Calverleigh!' had uttered the widow, in a flutter of shyness. '*Pray* go with me! For I don't know a soul, and that is so very uncomfortable!'

He had been obliged to accompany her, and even to introduce her to such ladies of his acquaintance as he could not avoid; but although he fancied he had carried it off pretty well ('Your la'ship must allow me to present Mrs – Mrs Clapham to you. She is a stranger to Bath – putting up at the White Hart!') he was well aware that he had become the subject for every kind of inquisitive conjecture. He realised, too late, what a gudgeon he had been to have devoted himself so exclusively to Miss Fanny Wendover, and did what he could to allay suspicion by replying to the demand of a matron, famed for her blunt manners, to be told who, pray, was this Mrs Clapham? with his engaging air of boyish candour: 'I haven't the least notion, ma'am, but *perfectly* respectable, I believe! Yes, I know what you are thinking, but I won't have her abused! Not, perhaps, quite up to the rig, but – but excessively amiable!'

The droll look that went with this conveyed volumes, but he could not be sure that these had been read with understanding. He was thankful that Mrs Clapham's scruples forbade her to attend any balls, and wished that these had included concerts. But Mrs Winkworth had said that concerts were unexceptionable, and he was obliged to accept, with every sign of pleasure, an invitation to accompany both ladies to one which held out, as an apparently irresistible lure, the promise of a performance, by four distinguished instrumentalists, of Mozart's Quartet in G Minor. Mr Stacy Calverleigh was not musical, and nor, judging by the infelicitous nature of her remarks, was Mrs Clapham; but when he entered the concert-room, with the widow leaning on his arm, it seemed, to his jaundiced eyes, that not one of the Bath residents with whom he was acquainted shared his indifference to classical music. The room was packed as full as it could hold. He felt, as he escorted his ladies past the benches, to the chairs provided for such well-inlaid persons as Mrs Clapham, that the entire genteel population of Bath was present. Amongst the company, were Mrs Grayshott, with her son and daughter, and when he glanced in their direction, Stacy encountered a long, unsmiling look from Oliver. It made him rage inwardly, for he read into it contempt and condemnation. He thought that it would not be long before the insufferable puppy found the means to communicate with Fanny; and wondered if there was any fear that when she next met him she would subject him to a painful scene. He spent the better part of the evening trying to hit upon some means of detaching Mrs Clapham from Bath. It was not until they emerged from the Rooms into a mizzle of rain that a possible solution occurred to him. Then, as Mrs Clapham asked despairingly if it was *always* raining in Bath, he expressed surprise that she should not have chosen to go to Leamington Priors rather than to Bath. No doubt she must know that it was a spa enjoying notoriously good weather, and offering visitors, besides beneficial waters, every amenity, from Pleasure Gardens to Assembly Rooms as elegant as any in the country. No, Mrs Clapham, strangely enough, had never been there, for all it was so close to Birmingham. She accused him archly of wishing to be rid of her. '*That*, ma'am, is an absurdity which neither merits, nor will obtain, notice!' he replied. 'To own the truth, I have a strong notion of going there myself!'

'I wonder,' said Mrs Clapham demurely, 'if drinking the waters there would do me good?'

It was as well that this question was merely rhetorical, for, never having visited the spa, he had no idea for what the Leamington Waters were held to be beneficial, and could scarcely have answered it. Nor, when he procured, on the following day, a guide book to the Principal Watering and Sea-bathing places, was he any better equipped to do so. The guide book was not reticent on the subject: it presented him with a list of the diseases for which the waters were known to be efficacious, but as these consisted of such distressing disorders as Obstinately Costive Habits, Scrofulous Tumours, White Swellings of the Knee, and Intestinal Worms, Mr Calverleigh could only hope that Mrs Clapham would not enquire more closely into the matter.

He told Mrs Winkworth that Bath was a hotbed of scandal, warning her, with his ready laugh, that it was enough for an unattached gentleman to offer his arm to a single lady for the length of a street to set all the quizzes tattling that he was dangling after her. That, he hoped, would drive a spoke in the wheel of any mischief-maker who might seek to convince her that he was a fickle and desperate flirt.

Mrs Winkworth had relented towards him, and no longer directed suspicious looks at him. She even apologised for having been, as she phrased it, a trifle starched-up when she had first made his acquaintance. 'You wouldn't wonder at it, if you knew how many burrs and downright fortune-hunters I've had to drive off, Mr Calverleigh,' she said. 'Sometimes I wish to goodness I hadn't agreed to live with Nancy, when Clapham died, but I've known her since she was a child, and I hadn't the heart to say no to her. No more than anyone ever has had, more's the pity! Not that she isn't a sweet little thing, but she'd let any scamp come over her, because she hasn't a particle of nous. And as for being fit to manage her affairs – well, there!'

'I expect her trustees will take care she doesn't fritter away her fortune,' Stacy said.

But Mrs Winkworth replied, with a snort: 'Yes, I daresay they might, if she had any!'

It appeared that Mr Clapham had died, leaving all he possessed to his beloved wife, in a Will written on an odd scrap of paper: an aberration which Mrs Winkworth ascribed partly to his having been carried off very suddenly, and partly to his besottedness. 'And a harder-headed man of business you'd be hard put to it to find!' she told Stacy. 'Well, they say there's no fool like an old fool, don't they?'

Inevitably, it was Miss Butterbank who bore the news of Mrs Clapham's arrival in Bath to Sydney Place. She was able to tell Miss Wendover how many times Mr Stacy Calverleigh had been seen in her company, how many trunks the lady had brought to Bath, and was even able to disclose, in a shocked whisper, that she had twice dined with him at the *table d'hôte*, and that it was *said* that he took tea with her, in her private parlour, every evening.

'Which I cannot bring myself to believe!' Selina told Abby. 'Not that I mean to say that poor Laura Butterbank is not a very truthful woman, but you may depend upon it she must have been misinformed.'

Abby had had little leisure for visiting, but she had chanced to meet Mrs Grayshott at the chemist's a few days earlier, and had received from her a less high-coloured account of the affair.

'A wealthy widow!' she had exclaimed. 'Nothing could be better! I wish he may run off with her tomorrow!'

She had not mentioned the matter to Selina, but she did so now, saying: 'I believe it to be quite true – that Calverleigh is now bent on fixing his interest with this Mrs Clapham; at least Mrs Grayshott told me of it a day or two ago, but she can't be as well-informed as Laura Butterbank, for she didn't mention the tea-drinking, or the *table-d'hôte*. My dear, why look so dismayed? You don't *still* want him to marry Fanny, surely!'

No, Selina did not want that, but it was so very shocking, so distressing to think that a young man with such agreeable manners should turn out to be a monster of duplicity! She had never been so much deceived in her life. 'And when I think of poor little Fanny – if it *is* true, not that I am at all convinced, because very likely it is nothing but a Banbury story, and I do implore you, not to breathe a *word* to her!'

'Certainly not! She will discover it soon enough, poor child! It may not come as quite such a shock to her as we fear. You must have noticed, Selina, that amongst all the bouquets, and the bunches of grapes, which are handed in by her admirers, only one bunch of flowers bore young Calverleigh's card, and he has only once called to enquire how she goes on. If you haven't noticed it, I am persuaded that she has. She says nothing, but it is painful to see how eagerly she looks for the card attached to each new posy that is carried up to her room, and how her face falls when she finds that it is *only* from Oliver – or Jack Weaverham – or Peter Trevisian!'

Miss Abigail Wendover was looking tired, as well she might. Fanny's attack had been severe; the fever had lasted for longer than even Dr Rowton had pessimistically foretold; and although she was now allowed to lie on the sofa in the drawing-room for a few hours each day, and even to receive visits from her particular friends, her temperature still showed a tendency to rise towards evening, and it was evident that she was sadly pulled by her illness. The bulk of the nursing had fallen to Abby's lot, for Fanny could scarcely endure Mrs Grimston's brisk ministrations. She complained that her hands were rough, that the floor shook every time she stumped across it, that she could not come near the bed without knocking against it, and that she never stopped scolding and fussing. These grievances, whether real or imaginary, made her cross, restless, and recalcitrant; she reverted to her childhood's cry of: 'I want *Abby*!' and Abby, just as she had always done, instantly responded to it.

She was reasonably docile with her aunt, but constant attendance on her, coupled as it was with a certain degree of anxiety, were beginning to take their toll. Selina, bemoaning the fragility of her own constitution, which prevented her from sharing the task of nursing Fanny, told Abby that she was looking positively hagged, and begged her, at all the most unseasonable moments, to lie down on the sofa, if only for an hour.

It might have been supposed that Abby would have had no time or thought to spare for her own troubles, but they seemed always to be at the back of her mind until she retired to bed, when they immediately leaped to the fore, and kept her awake, tossing and turning almost as restlessly as Fanny. She might tell herself that it was a very good thing that Miles Calverleigh had left Bath, but the melancholy truth was that she missed him so much that it was like a physical ache. No word had come from him; he had been absent for longer than she had anticipated; and the fear that perhaps he did not mean to return to Bath at all was a heavy weight on her spirits. She found herself continually wondering where he was, and what he was doing, and wishing that she could at least know that no accident had befallen him.

None had. He was in London, but while Abby would have considered a visit to his aunt, several to the City, and some prolonged conferences with his lawyer unexceptionable it was as well that one at least of his activities was unknown to her.

Lady Lenham greeted him with a tart demand to be told when he meant to furbish himself up.

'I don't know. Must I?' he replied, lightly kissing her cheek.

'It's no use expecting me to bring you back into fashion if you don't adonise yourself a trifle.'

'Then I won't expect it,' he said amiably. 'I never was one of your dapper-dogs, and it's too late to change my habits, and if you're thinking I should look well in a wasp-waisted coat, and with the points of my collars reaching half-way up my cheeks, you are letting your imagination run off with you, Letty – take my word for it!'

'There's reason in all things,' she retorted. 'Where have you been all these weeks? Don't tell me you've been getting into mischief again!'

'No, no, I've been behaving very decorously!' he assured her. 'You have to, in Bath. A devilish place!'

She stared at him. 'You've been in *Bath*?'

'That's it. I took Leonard Balking's nephew there, you know.'

'Yes, you told me you were going to do that, but what in the world kept you there?' she asked suspiciously.

'Just circumstances!'

'Oh! Philandering, I collect! Well, what do you mean to do now?'

'Become a tenant-for-life. You told me it was what I ought to do: remember?'

'What!' she exclaimed. 'Are you trying to play off your tricks on me? Who is she?'

'Abigail Wendover,' he replied coolly.

She gave a gasp. 'You're not serious? One of the *Wendovers*? Miles, she's never accepted an offer from you?'

'No, but she will.'

'Well, either you've windmills in the head, or she's very very different from the rest of her family!'

'Of course she is! You don't suppose I'd have fallen in love with her if she hadn't been, do you?'

'No, and I don't suppose her family would countenance it for an instant!'

'Lord, Letty, what's that got to say to anything?'

She laughed. 'You don't change much, Miles! You always were a care-for-nobody, and you always will be! I wish you may succeed with your Abigail. She's the youngest sister, isn't she? I never met her, but I'm acquainted with Mary Brede, and have been avoiding James Wendover and his odious wife for years.'

'Yes, that's what I mean to do,' he said.

His next visit was to a slightly portly gentleman, residing in Mount Street, who stared unbelievingly at him for a moment, before ejaculating: '*Calverleigh!*' and starting forward to wring his hand. 'Well, well, well. After all these years! I hardly recognised you, you old devil!'

'No, I had to look twice at you, too. You're as fat as a flawn, Naffy!'

'Well, at least no one would take me for a dashed blackamoor!' retorted Mr Nafferton.

After this exchange of compliments, the two middle-aged gentlemen settled down, with a bottle between them, to indulge in reminiscences which, had they been privileged to hear them, would have startled Mr Nafferton's wife, and considerably diminished his credit with his heir.

'Lord, how it takes me back, seeing you again!' said Mr Nafferton a trifle wistfully. 'Those were the days!'

'Nights, mostly,' said Mr Calverleigh. 'How many times did *you* end up in a lighthouse? *I* lost count! What became of the Dasher, by the way?'

'Dolly!' uttered Mr Nafferton. 'To think I should have forgotten she was used to be your peculiar!' He chuckled. 'You'd never recognise her! She set up a fancy-house a dozen or more years ago! Drives in the park in a smart barouche, with one or two of her prime articles, and looks like a duchess! Behaves like one, too! No Haymarket ware in *her* house: all regular Incognitas! Or so I'm told!' he added hastily.

Mr Calverleigh grinned, but merely said: 'Became an Abbess, did she? Yes, she always was as shrewd as she could hold together. Where's this fancy-house of hers?'

Armed with this information, his next visit was to a house in Bloomsbury, where he sent in his card. Miss Abigail Wendover would certainly not have approved of this excursion.

Mr Calverleigh, ushered into a saloon, was still inspecting the elegance of its furnishings with deep appreciation when the lady upon whom he had come to call entered the room, his card in her hand, and exclaimed: 'It *is* you! Good God! I couldn't believe it!'

Mr Calverleigh, laughter in his eyes, took two long strides

towards her, caught her in his arms, and heartily embraced her.

She returned the embrace, but said: 'Now, that's quite enough! I'll have you know I'm a respectable woman now!'

Mr Calverleigh, most reprehensibly, gave a shout of mirth.

'Well, you know what I mean!' said the lady, bridling a little.

'Yes, to be sure, I do. Who gave you the gingerbread, Dolly?'

'Oh, he was a regular rabshackle!' she disclosed. 'You wouldn't have known him, for he was long after your time. I never liked him above half, but he was full of juice, and I'm bound to say he bled very freely. What I mean is, he was very generous to me,' she amended, suddenly attacked by a fit of alarming primness.

Mr Calverleigh was unimpressed. 'No, is *that* what you mean? Come down from your high ropes! Do you remember the night a party of us went on a spree to Tothill Fields, and you broke a bottle of Stark Naked over the head of the fellow that was trying to gouge my eyes out?'

'No, I don't!' she said sharply. 'And if you hadn't got into a mill with a bruiser and a couple of draymen because you was as drunk as Davy's sow I wouldn't have had to demean myself! *If* I did do anything of the sort, which I don't at all remember!'

'I must be thinking of someone else,' said Mr Calverleigh meekly. 'What was the name of that towheaded bit of game Tom Plumley brought along with him?'

'*That* fussock!' she exclaimed, in a voice vibrant with scorn. 'Why, she hadn't enough spunk to hit a blackbeetle on the head! Now, give over, Miles, do! I don't say I'm not glad to see you again: well, it's like a breath of old times, but that's the trouble! Seeing you makes me forget myself, and start talking flash, which is a thing I haven't done in years! What's more, you didn't come here to crack about old revel-routs! And if, Mr Calverleigh,' she added, with another transition into gentility, but with a twinkle in her sharp eyes, 'you have come here in search of *a bit of game*, I must warn you that you will find no cheap molls in *this* establishment, but only young ladies of refinement.'

'That's very good, Dolly!' he approved. 'Did it take you long to learn to talk like that?'

'Out with it! What is it you want?' she demanded, ignoring this sally.

'Just what you said, of course,' he replied. 'A young lady of refinement!'

Fifteen

*T*he Leavenings had hired lodgings in Orange Grove. Not an ideal situation, perhaps, admitted Mrs Leavening, when Selina pointed out to her its several disadvantages, but it was a fine, open place, and no need at all to summon up a chair every time she wanted to visit the Pump Room, or do a little shopping. As for the Abbey bells, she didn't doubt that they would soon grow to be so accustomed to them that they would scarcely notice them. 'Well, my dear,' she told Selina placidly, 'when you get to be of our age, you must have learnt that you won't find anything that's exactly what you want, so, if you've a particle of commonsense, you'll take the best that's offered you.' She then said, with a chuckle: 'Mr Calverleigh will laugh when he hears of it! He *would* have it, only because I like looking out of the window at what's passing in the street, that I should never be happy but in the centre of the Town!'

Abby had been taking no more than a polite interest in the Leavenings' plans, but these words affected her powerfully. She said: 'If he ever does hear of it! Does he mean to return to Bath, ma'am?'

She spoke with studied nonchalance, but Mrs Leavening was not deceived. The quizzical gleam in her eye brought the blood into Abby's cheeks, but all she said was: 'Well, my dear, as his rooms are being kept for him at the York House, it's to be supposed he does!'

That was the only ray of sunlight permitted for many days to break through the clouds surrounding Miss Abigail Wendover.

She was enduring a time of trial, for which not Miles Calverleigh alone was responsible, but also her dear sister, and her cherished niece.

Influenza had left Fanny irritable and depressed. It was quite unnecessary for Dr Rowton to say that this uncharacteristic mood was attributable to her illness, and only what was to be expected. Abby knew that, but neither her own good sense nor the doctor's reassurance made it easier for her to bear patiently the extremely wearing demands made upon her spirits by a convalescent who, when not sunk in gloom which affected everyone in her vicinity, peevishly found fault with everything, from the strength of the tea carried up to her room on her breakfast-tray, to the intolerable dullness of the books so hope-fully chosen by Abby at Meyler's Library; or stared resentfully out of a rain-spotted window at a leaden sky, and sighed: 'If only it would stop raining! If only I could go out!'

Poor little Fanny, said Selina, was quite unlike her merry self: an understatement which kindled a spark of amusement in Abby's shadowed eyes. Dr Rowton told Abby, in his blunt way, that the sooner she stopped indulging Fanny the better it would be for herself, and Fanny too; but Dr Rowton did not know that there was another and deeper cause of Fanny's crotchets than influenza. Abby did know, and even when she most wanted to slap her tiresome darling her heart went out to her. She was herself suffering from much the same malady, and if she had been seventeen, instead of eight-and-twenty, no doubt she would have abandoned herself to despair, just as Fanny was doing.

Fanny's megrims might impose a severe strain upon Abby's nerves, but it was Selina who rasped them raw, and broke down her command over herself.

Selina had seen Mrs Clapham, and she knew that it was all Too True. She had seen her in the Pump Room, whither a twinge of rheumatism had sent her (braving the elements in her carriage, with the hood drawn up) that morning. She had not at first known who she was, for how should she? She had merely been thinking that the bonnet she was wearing was in excellent

205

style (though she had realised rather later that it bore too many plumes, and was of a disagreeable shade of purple, besides being a most unsuitable hat for a widow), when dear Laura Butterbank had whispered that she was Mrs Clapham.

'Which was a most unpleasant shock, as you may suppose, and almost brought on one of my distressing spasms. Fortunately, I had my vinaigrette in my reticule, for just when I was thinking that I did not at all like the look of her (not that I saw her face, for she had her back turned to me, but one can always tell), whom should I see but young Calverleigh, making his way towards her, with that hoaxing smile on his face, all delight and cordiality, as though he hadn't been dangling after Fanny for weeks! *And*, Abby, he had the impudence to *cut* me! It's of no use to say that he didn't see me, because I am persuaded he did, for he took very good care not to look in my way again, besides going off with that vulgar creature almost immediately. When I recall the way he has been running tame in this house, inching himself in – at least, he did so until you came home and snubbed him, and although I thought it a little unkind in you at the time, you were perfectly right, which I *freely* own – well, dearest, I was almost overpowered, and I trembled so much that I don't know how I was able to reach the carriage, and if it hadn't been for Mr Ancrum, who gave me his arm, very likely I never should have done so.'

She was obviously much upset. Abbey did what she could to soothe her agitation, but there was worse to come. That Woman (under which title Abby had no difficulty in recognising the odious Mrs Ruscombe) had had the effrontery to come up to her to commiserate her, with her false, honeyed smile, on poor little Fanny's humiliating disappointment. And not one word had she been able, in the desperation of the moment, to utter in crushing retort. Nothing had occurred to her!

Unfortunately, all too many retorts occurred to her during the succeeding days, and whenever she was alone with Abby she recalled exactly what Mrs Ruscombe had said, adding to the episode the various annihilating things she herself might have said, and reminding Abby of the numerous occasions when Mrs Ruscombe had behaved abominably. She could think of nothing else; and when, for the third time in one evening, she broke a brooding silence by saying, as though they had been in the middle of a discussion: 'And *another* thing . . . !' Abby's patience deserted her, and she exclaimed: 'For heaven's sake, Selina, don't start again! As though it wasn't bad enough to have Fanny saying: "If only it would stop raining!" a dozen times a day! If you don't wish to drive me into hysterics, *stop* talking about Mrs Ruscombe! What she said to you I have by heart, and as for what you *might* have said to her, you know very well you would never say any such things.'

She repented immediately, of course: indeed, she was horrified by her loss of temper. Begging Selina's pardon, she said that she thought she was perhaps overtired.

'Yes, dear, no doubt you must be,' said Selina. 'It is a pity you wouldn't rest, as I *repeatedly* recommended you to do.'

Selina was not offended, oh, dear me, no! Just a little hurt, but she did not intend to say any more about that. She was sure Abby had not meant to wound her: it was merely that she was a trifle lacking in sensibility, but she did not intend to say any more about that either.

Nor did she, but her silence on that and every other topic was eloquent enough, and soon provided Abby with all that was needed to make her long passionately for Miles Calverleigh to come back, and to snatch her out of the stricken household without any more ado.

But it was not Miles Calverleigh who made an unexpected appearance in Sydney Place shortly before noon one morning. It was Mr James Wendover, carrying a small cloak-bag, and wearing the resentful expression of one forced, by the inconsiderate behaviour of his relations, to endure the discomforts of a night-journey to Bath on the Mail Coach.

It was Fanny, seated disconsolately by the window in the drawing-room, who saw him first. When the hack drew up, the hope that it had brought Stacy Calverleigh to her at last soared in her breast for one ecstatic moment, before it sank like a plummet at the sight of Mr Wendover's spare, soberly clad figure. She exclaimed, startling Abby: 'It is my uncle! No, no, I won't – I can't! Don't let him come *near* me!'

With these distraught words, she rushed from the room, leaving Abby to make her excuses as best she might.

Forewarned, Abby betrayed neither perturbation nor astonishment when Mr Wendover presently entered the room, though she did say, as she got up from her chair: 'Well, this is a surprise, James! What brings you to Bath, I wonder?'

Bestowing a perfunctory salute upon her cheek, he replied, in acrid accents: 'I must suppose that you know very well what has brought me, Abby! I may add that it has been most inconvenient – *most* inconvenient! – but since you have apparently run mad I felt myself compelled to undertake the journey! Where is Selina?'

'Probably drinking the waters, in the Pump Room,' replied Abby calmly. 'She will be here directly, I daresay. Did you come by the Mail? What made it so late?'

'It was not late. I arrived in Bath punctually at ten o'clock and have already accomplished *part* of my mission. Why it should have been *necessary* for me to do so I shall leave it to your conscience to answer, Abby! If,' he added bitterly, 'you *have* a conscience, which sometimes I am compelled to doubt!'

'It certainly seems as though I can't have. However, I console myself with the reflection that at least I'm not as buffle-headed as the rest of my family!' said Abby brightly. 'I collect that you came to try whether you could put an end to Fanny's rather unfortunate flirtation with young Calverleigh. Now, if only you had warned me of your intention you would have been spared the journey! You have wasted your time, my dear James!'

His eyes snapped; he said, with a dry, triumphant laugh: 'Have I? Have I indeed? I have already seen the young coxcomb, and I made it very plain to him that if he attempted to persuade my foolish niece into a clandestine marriage he would find himself taken very much at fault – *very* much at fault! I informed him that I should have no hesitation – none whatsoever! – in taking steps to have such a marriage annulled, and that under *no* circumstances should I disburse one penny of her fortune if she contracted an alliance without my sanction! I further informed him that he would have eight years to wait before deriving any benefit from that fortune!'

'I said you had wasted your time,' observed Abby. 'I, too, informed him of these circumstances. I don't think he believed me, and I am very sure he didn't set much store by all this bluster of yours. I have no great opinion of his intelligence, but I fancy he is sufficiently shrewd to have taken your measure before ever he decided to make a push to captivate Fanny. Good God, if he *had* succeeded in eloping with Fanny you would have gone to any lengths to hush up the scandal, and so, depend upon it, he very well knows!'

An angry flush mounted into Mr Wendover's thin cheeks. 'Indeed? In-deed! You are very much mistaken, my dear sister! I am aware that you fancy yourself to be awake upon every suit, but in *my* humble opinion you are as big a wet-goose as Selina! I don't doubt for a moment that he paid little heed to anything you may have said to him: only a gudgeon could have failed to take *your* measure! When, however, he was confronted by *me*, the case was altered! I am happy to be able to inform you that this lamentable affair is now at an end!'

'Yes, it came to an end when Fanny took ill. You had really nothing to do with it, you know. According to all accounts, Stacy Calverleigh, for the past fortnight, has being laying determined siege to a rich widow – a far more desirable conquest than Fanny, I assure you! I have not myself had the felicity of meeting the lady, but I understand that she is much inclined to succumb to his attractions.'

He was so much surprised that his anger was instantly quenched. He exclaimed: 'You don't mean it! Is it indeed so? Well, upon my word! Nothing could be better! A widow, you say? Well! They say he is all to pieces, you know – quite gutted! And Danescourt falling to ruin! I was never more shocked in my life! Fanny is to be congratulated!'

'Very true, but I fear you won't be able to do so. She is still far from well. In fact, I think it would be wiser if she doesn't come downstairs today – in case she should still be infectious.'

Since James, as she knew well, shared Selina's dread of contracting any infectious complaint, he agreed hastily that it would be wisest for Fanny to remain in her room. He said that there was now no need for him to see her: a remark hardly calculated to endear him to his sister. He continued for several minutes to animadvert on Stacy Calverleigh's character; but suddenly he fell silent, and the pleased expression vanished from his face. He began to fidget about the room, twice began to say something, and apparently thought better of it, and finally came to a halt in front of Abby's chair, and said portentously; 'Abby! There is something I must say to you!'

She could guess what was coming, but she merely raised her brows enquiringly.

'Something of more importance than Fanny's frippery affair – of far graver importance! It has upset me very much. It made me bilious for two days. You must know that I have always been subject to stomach disorders, and nothing brings on one of my attacks more surely than shock! I suffered a severe shock, sister, when it came to my knowledge that not only was young Calverleigh in Bath, but also his uncle! I had not thought it to have been possible!'

'Why not?' asked Abby.

He seemed to find it difficult to answer this, for after glaring down at her for a moment, he ejaculated, somewhat lamely: 'Here! In Bath! I had supposed him to be in India!'

'Well, so he was, but he has now returned to England. I believe it is quite customary for people to do so.'

'Customary! Ay, for *some* people! And here – here of all unlucky places! That I might be obliged actually to meet the fellow – !'

'Don't let it distress you!' she said, in a deceptively kind voice. 'I don't wish to seem unfeeling, but you cannot be laid up with a bilious-attack in this house! I hope, since there is no likelihood of your meeting Miles Calverleigh, that *that* trial at least may be spared us. It so happens that he is *not* in Bath.'

'He is not?' he said eagerly. 'Then where is he?'

'I have no notion where he may be,' she responded coldly.

He regarded her out of narrowed, suspicious eyes. 'Does he mean to return?'

'Oh, I hope so!' she said, smiling in a way which should have warned him of danger.

'You hope so! Then it is true, is it? Not only has the fellow had the effrontery to make you the object of his *gallantry*, but you *have* encouraged him to do so! You have *not* outgrown that – unsteadiness of character, which my father was used to fear would one day lead you into serious imprudence. You still have what Cornelia has always believed to be a love of singularity. You still –'

'Do you know, James, I can't but believe that you would be happier if you paid rather less heed to the reports Mrs Ruscombe so regularly sends to Cornelia?' she interrupted. 'If you lived here, you would pay none at all!'

He reddened. 'If you tell me that there is no truth in the intelligence she thought it her duty to send Cornelia, I must naturally accept your word.'

'The only thing I have to tell you is what I have already told you: you are wasting your time! I am not a child, and what I do is my own concern! Now, if you please, let us discuss some other subject before we come to dagger-drawing!'

She spoke quite quietly, but she was by this time very angry. He seemed to realise it, for when he had taken another turn about the room he said, in a more moderate tone: 'I do not mean to set up your back. Recollect that although I have no authority over you I am your brother! What you do cannot but be of concern to me. I beg you will tell me – have you indeed a partiality for this man?'

She looked at him without speaking, but it was Miles Calverleigh's face she saw, not his. A smile crept into her eyes;

she turned them away from her brother, and sat looking into the fire. 'Oh, yes!' she said softly.

He groaned. 'And he? Has he had the imp – has he made you an offer?' She nodded, and again he groaned. 'My poor girl! I do most sincerely pity you! Rest assured that not one word of what you have divulged to me shall ever pass my lips! You cannot marry Calverleigh. Good God, one would have thought that at your age –' He broke off, and said, with what was meant for an indulgent smile: 'Well, well, you are not so old, after all, and one may fancy oneself in love at any age, eh? But you are old enough to reflect before you abandon yourself to folly – to an act of such madness as must ruin your life! You must allow me to speak plainly to you, little though I may relish the task. I own that I look upon it with repulsion: indeed, I never thought to be obliged to discuss such matters with any of my sisters! Calverleigh is a ne'er-do-well. His reputation –'

'Very bad, wasn't it?' she agreed.

'Yes, my dear sister, it was! I shall not sully your ears with the details of his career – Abigail! Do you find it a matter for *laughter*?'

'Oh, I beg your pardon!' she said, choking on a giggle. 'It is most uncivil to laugh in a person's face, but I couldn't help but do so! I suddenly thought how much Miles Calverleigh would enjoy hearing you talk such fustian, and wondered what he would say! Though I have a very good notion of that! It would certainly be outrageous, so perhaps it is as well that he isn't here, for he would shock you very much – quite enough to make you bilious, I daresay! Don't s-sully my ears any more, James! Remember that I came out of leading-strings a long time ago! I find that I don't care a straw for his reputation.'

'You are hysterical!' he exclaimed. 'You do not know what you are saying! He is a man without principles, without regard for any of the virtues *you* have been taught to revere!'

'Oh, quite without regard for *them*!' she said cordially. 'He hasn't any regard for family obligations either, and I am fast coming to the conclusion that he is perfectly right.'

He said repressively: 'I make all allowance for the freakish things you delight in saying, but such wild, unthinking talk as this is very unbecoming in you. When you say that you don't care a straw for Calverleigh's reputation, you don't understand what you are saying, for you know nothing about it. It would be shocking if you did.'

'Well, you don't know anything about it either, do you?' she said. 'You can't have known very much before he was sent to India, for you are younger than he is, and he was only twenty at that time; and you can know nothing at all about him from that date onward.'

He found himself obliged to take another turn about the room, his hands clasped behind his back, and his fingers working convulsively. Coming to a halt again, he drew an audible breath, and said: 'Abby! There are circumstances which render any alliance between a Wendover and a Calverleigh impossible – unthinkable! I cannot say more: you must believe me when I tell you that it *is* so!'

'There is no need for you to say more,' she replied, with composure. 'I know what happened – twenty years ago!'

'*What?*' He looked, for a moment, horrified, and then incredulous. 'You cannot know!'

'Oh, yes! He eloped with Celia, didn't he? But it was all hushed up, after the manner of her family and ours, and she married Rowland after all.'

'Who told you this?' he demanded, thunderstruck.

'Why, he did, of course – Miles Calverleigh!'

His jaw dropped. He seemed to find it difficult to speak, and stuttered: '*C-Calverleigh* t-told you? C-Calverleigh himself? Good God!' Words failed him. While she watched him in some amusement, he pulled out his handkerchief, and wiped his brow. Regaining a measure of control over his emotions, he said: 'It is worse than I had thought it possible it could be! He must be dead to shame! Lost to every vestige of propriety!'

'I shouldn't think he ever had a vestige of propriety to lose,' she said reflectively. 'As for shame, I don't know, but he is not

213

ashamed of running off with Celia. I see little reason why he should be. It was imprudent – and, of course, improper – but he was very young, and when her father forced Celia to become engaged to Rowland, I daresay it seemed to him to be the only thing to be done. I don't blame him. Those whom I do blame, and from the bottom of my heart despise, are Papa, and Morval, and Rowland!'

He looked fixedly at her, and, lowering his voice, said, in apocalyptic accents: 'You do not know all! They were not overtaken *until the following day*!'

She tried not to laugh, but his awful aspect was too much for her. Quite appalled by such depravity, he said sharply: 'Upon my soul! I begin to think you are well matched, you and that scoundrel!'

'Yes, James: I begin to think so too!' she agreed, between irrepressible outbreaks of laughter.

It was perhaps fortunate that they were interrupted at this moment by Selina, who came into the room in a flutter of welcome. To Selina, family ties were all-important; her affections, though not deep, were sincere and enduring, and she was genuinely glad to see James, forgetting, as she fondly embraced him, that the last letter she had received from him had roused her to considerable indignation.

'James! *Well!* Such a surprise! I hadn't the least notion – and only a fricassee of rabbit and onions for dinner! Now, if only I had known! But Betty or Jane can go into town, and procure some partridges, or perhaps a haunch of venison, which Fletching dresses very well, and is something you were always partial to.'

But James was not staying to dine with his sisters. He was returning to London on the Mail Coach.

Dismayed, Selina faltered: 'Not staying? But, James – ! You brought your cloak-bag! Mitton has carried it up to your room, and means to unpack it as soon as the bed has been made up!'

'Desire him to bring it down again, if you please. It *was* my intention to have put up here for a night, but what I have learnt since I entered this room has shocked me so much – I may say, appalled me! – that I prefer to return to London!'

'Good God!' uttered Selina, casting a wildly enquiring look at Abby. 'You cannot mean – oh, but Abby has told you, *surely*, that we believe there is no danger to be apprehended now? There has been no continued observance: the *wretch* has only *once* called since dear Fanny took ill, and with my own eyes I have seen the Creature he is making up to!'

'I am not referring to young Calverleigh,' said James stiffly. 'I came to Bath in the hope of discovering that the very disturbing rumours which have reached me had little foundation in truth. Instead, I learn that your sister has become infatuated with a man who should never have been permitted to cross your threshold!'

'No, no! Oh, pray do not say such things, James!' begged Selina faintly. 'He is perfectly respectable, though I cannot like the way he dresses – so very careless, and coming to pay us a formal visit in top-boots! – and, of course, he must have been sadly rackety when he was young, to have been sent away to India – not that I think it was right to do such a cruel thing, for I don't, and I never shall, and I consider it to be most unjust to say that he ought not to have been allowed to cross the threshold after all these years of being condemned to live in India, which may be a very interesting place, but is *most* unhealthy, and has burnt him as brown as a nut! And Abby is as much your sister as mine!'

'If Abby is so lost to propriety, to all sense of the duty she owes her family, as to marry Calverleigh, she will no longer be a sister of mine!' he said terribly.

'That's no way to dissuade me!' said Abby.

'No, no, dearest!' implored Selina. 'Pray don't – ! James didn't mean it!'

'When you have heard what I have to say, Selina –'

'Yes, but not now!' said Selina, much agitated. 'Mitton is fetching up the sherry, and I must take off my hat and my pelisse, and then it will be time for luncheon, which we always have, you know – just a baked egg, or a morsel of cold meat – and afterwards, when you are *calmer*, and we shan't be interrupted, which is always so vexatious when one is enjoying a serious discussion. No, I don't mean that! Not *enjoying* it, because already I am beginning to feel a spasm!'

James eyed her a little uneasily, and said, in a milder voice: 'Very well, I will postpone what I have to say. I do not myself partake of luncheon, but I should be glad of a cup of tea.'

'Yes, dear, of course, though I am persuaded it would do you good to eat a mouthful of *something* after your journey!'

'Don't press him, Selina! he's bilious,' said Abby.

'Bilious! Oh, then, no *wonder* –!' cried Selina, her countenance lightening. 'I have the very thing for you, dear James! I will fetch it directly, but on no account sherry!'

She then fled from the room, paying no heed to his exasperated denial of biliousness.

'Take care, James!' said Abby maliciously. 'You will find yourself in the suds if you throw Selina into strong convulsions!'

He cast her a repulsive glance. 'Spare me any more of your levity, Abigail! I shall say no more until after luncheon.'

'You won't say any more to me at any time,' replied Abby. 'You have already said too much! You may not have noticed it, but the sun came out half-an-hour ago. What *I* am going to do after luncheon, dear James, is to take Fanny out for a drive!'

With these words, accompanied by a smile of great sweetness, she went away to inform Fanny of the treat in store for her.

Fanny was also suffering from agitation. She turned an apprehensive, suspicious face towards her aunt, and said: 'How long does my uncle mean to remain here? I don't want to see him!'

'Have no fear, my love!' said Abby cheerfully. 'Your uncle is equally reluctant to see you! I told him you were still infectious.'

Fanny gave a spontaneous laugh. 'Oh, *Abby*! What a fib!'

'Yes, it weighs heavily on my conscience, but I don't grudge a fib or two to save you from what I cannot myself endure. Grimston will bring a tray to you. I must send a message to the stables now.'

But in the end it was not Abby who took Fanny for her drive, but Lavinia Grayshott. Just as Abby was preparing to take her place in the barouche beside Fanny, Lavinia came running up, and exclaimed breathlessly: 'Oh famous! Going out at last! *Now* you will soon be better! Oh, Miss Abby, I beg your pardon! – how do you do? I was coming to see Fanny, just to bring her this book! Oh, and, Fanny, take care how you open it! There's an acrostic in it, from Oliver!'

Abby saw the brightening look in Fanny's face, and realised that Fanny would prefer Lavinia's company to hers. The knowledge caused her to feel a tiny heartache, but she did not hesitate. She said, smiling at Lavinia: 'Why don't you go with Fanny in my place? Would you like to?'

The answer was to be read in Lavinia's face. 'Oh – ! But you, ma'am? Don't *you* wish to go with her?'

'Not a bit!' Abby said. 'I have a thousand and one things to do, and shall be glad to be rid of her! The carriage shall take you home, so if Martha sees no objection I shall resign Fanny into your charge.'

Martha, following more slowly in Lavinia's wake, readily consented to the scheme; so Lavinia jumped into the carriage. Before it drew out of sight, Abby saw the two heads together, and guessed that confidences were already being exchanged. She stifled a sigh, as she turned back into the house. Between herself and Fanny there was constraint, for Fanny knew her to be hostile to Stacy Calverleigh. Well, perhaps she would unburden herself to Lavinia, and feel the better for it.

Sixteen

*B*elatedly following Selina's advice, Abby retired to her bedroom, to lie down. Contrary to her expectation, she fell asleep almost at once, and was still sleeping when James left the house. When she awoke it was almost five o'clock, and the house was very quiet. She encountered Mrs Grimston on the landing, and learned from her that Miss Fanny was in the drawing-room, and seemingly none the worse for her drive; and that Miss Selina had gone up to rest as soon as Mr James had taken himself off. These words had a sinister ring, but as they were not followed by any mention of spasms or palpitations, and no distressing sounds could be heard emanating from Selina's room, Abby hoped that they had been inspired merely by Mrs Grimston's dislike of James. She went on down the stairs, and found Fanny with her head bent over the novel Lavinia had bestowed on her. She glanced up when Abby came into the room, and it struck Abby immediately that she was looking pale, and that her perfunctory smile was forced.

'Not tired, my darling?' she asked.

'No, thank you. No, not at all! I am reading the book Lavvy brought me: it is the most exciting story! I can't put it down!'

But it did not seem to Abby, as she occupied herself with embroidery, and covertly observed her niece between the setting of her stitches, that the book was holding Fanny absorbed. She was using it as a shield. The suspicion that Lavinia's indiscreet tongue had been at work crossed Abby's mind. As she presently folded her work, she said: 'Going to sit up for dinner, Fanny?'

'Oh!' Fanny gave a little start. 'Oh, is it dinner-time already? Yes – I don't know – Oh, yes! I'm not ill now!'

Abby smiled at her. 'Of course you're not, but you have been out for the first time today, and it wouldn't surprise me to learn that Lavinia has chattered you into a headache! A dear girl, but *such* a little gabster!'

She was now sure that Lavinia had been tattling. Fanny's chin came up, and her eyes were at once challenging and defensive. 'Oh, I don't regard her!' she said, with a pathetically unconvincing laugh. 'She is always full of the marvellous, but – but very diverting, you know!'

Yes, thought Abby, Lavinia has poured the tale of Stacy's perfidy into her ears, and although she does not quite believe it, she is afraid it may be true.

Her impulse was to take Fanny in her arms, petting and comforting her as she had so often done in the past, but a new and deeper understanding made her hesitate.

'If you please, Miss Abby,' said Fardle ominously, from the doorway, 'I should wish to have a word with you, if convenient!'

'Why, certainly!' Abby said, with a lightness she was far from feeling. She followed Fardle out of the room, and asked: 'What is it?'

The eldest Miss Wendover's devoted handmaid fixed her with an eye of doom, and delivered herself of a surprising statement. 'I feel it to be my duty to tell you, Miss Abby, that I don't like the look of Miss Selina – not at all I don't!'

'Oh!' said Abby weakly. 'Is – is she feeling poorly? I will come up to her.'

'Yes, miss. I was never one to make a mountain out of a molehill, as the saying is,' stated Fardle inaccurately, 'but it gave me quite a turn when I went to dress Miss Selina not ten minutes ago. It is not for me to say what knocked her up, Miss Abby, and I hope I know my duty better than to tell you that it's my belief it was Mr James that burnt her to the socket. All I know is that no sooner had he left the house than she went up to her room, saying she was going to rest on her bed, which was only to be expected. But when I went up to her she wasn't on her bed, nor hadn't been, as you will see for yourself, miss. And hardly a word did she speak, except to say she wouldn't be going down to dinner, and didn't want a tray sent up to her. Which is not like her, Miss Abby, and can't but make one fear that she's going into a Decline.'

On this heartening suggestion, she ushered Abby into Selina's room.

Kindly but firmly shutting the door upon her, Abby looked across the room at her sister, who was seated motionless beside the fire, with a shawl huddled round her shoulders, and a look in her face which Abby had never seen there before.

'Selina! Dearest!' she said, going quickly forward, to drop on her knees, gathering Selina's hands into her own.

Selina's eyes turned towards her in a stunned gaze which alarmed Abby far more than a flood of tears would have done. 'I have been thinking,' she said. 'Thinking, and thinking . . . It was my fault. If I hadn't invited her to our party she wouldn't have written such things to Cornelia.'

'Nonsense, dearest!' Abby said, gently chafing her hands. 'Now, you know you promised me you wouldn't say another word about That Woman!'

She had hoped to have coaxed a smile out of Selina, but after staring at her uncomprehendingly Selina uttered: 'It was because I was cross! *That* was why you said you would marry him, wasn't it? But I didn't mean it, Abby, I didn't mean it!'

'Goosecap! I know you didn't!'

Selina's thin fingers closed round her own like claws. 'James said – But I told him it was no such thing! He put you all on end, didn't he? I guessed how it must have been. I told him. I said that there was no question of – I said you would never dream of marrying Mr Calverleigh. And you wouldn't, would you, Abby?'

Meeting Selina's strained, searching eyes, Abby hesitated, before saying: 'My dear, why put yourself into such a taking? I thought you *wished* me to marry?'

'Not Mr Calverleigh! I never *wished* it, except for your sake, but I thought, if you married Mr Dunston – so kind – in every way so suitable – and everyone would have been pleased, and you wouldn't have gone away from me, not *quite* away from me, because I might have seen you every day –'

'Selina, I shall never go quite away from you,' Abby said quietly. 'This is the merest agitation of nerves! You have let James talk you into high fidgets. In spite of his top-boots, and his careless ways, you don't dislike Mr Calverleigh. Why, it was you who first said how unjust it was to condemn him for the sins of his youth!'

'But I didn't know that you meant to marry him,' said Selina simply.

'Well, nor did I, at that time. Come, my dear, there is no occasion for this despair!'

But by the time Selina, still clutching her hand, had enumerated the ills which would result from such a marriage there seemed to be every reason for despair. The list was a long one, and it ranged over a wide ground, which included the mortification which would be suffered by the family at the marriage of one of its members to a black sheep; the sneers of Mrs Ruscombe; the impossibility of Selina's remaining in Bath, where she was so well known; the harm that would be done to Fanny, on the verge of her come-out; of Fanny's unhappiness at being separated from her dearest aunt; of her own misery at being estranged from James, and Jane, and perhaps even Mary.

At this point, Abby was moved to expostulate: 'But you wouldn't be, stoopid!'

'James warned me. He left me in such anger! Because I told him that I should never give you up, whatever you did, which I never, never would! And he said that if I supported you I should cut myself off from the family – so *dreadful*, Abby! – so that I should do well to consider carefully before I made my choice, only there *is* no choice, so what a silly thing to say, and how could he suppose I would choose anyone but you, if there were? And as for not looking to see his face again, I said that if he was unkind to you he need not look to see *my* face, which is true, only I can't bear to think of it, because we have always been so happy, and even if we don't very often see the others they are our *family*!'

Abby was so much touched by this unexpected championship that tears started to her eyes. 'Oh, my dearest! How brave of you – how *loyal*! Do you indeed love me so much?'

'But of course I do!' said Selina.

Abby kissed her. 'Best of my sisters!' she said, mistily smiling. 'But as for James – ! How *dared* he talk to you like that? I wish very much that *I had* been present!'

'Oh, no, Abby! It would have been much, much worse! And I couldn't blame him. Not when he told me!'

'Told you what?' asked Abby sharply.

Selina turned her face away, shuddering. 'Celia . . . !'

'So he told you that, did he? Of all the chuckleheaded *dummies!*' Abby exclaimed wrathfully.

'He felt himself obliged to tell me, and, of course, I quite see – because I thought it was just that Mr Calverleigh had been very wild when he was young, which is not what I could *like*, but still – ! So he had to tell me the truth, and it has sunk me utterly, and I can't help wishing that he hadn't, for it would have been so much more comfortable, only very wrong, but I shouldn't have known it was!'

'Put it out of your mind!' said Abby. 'If it doesn't concern me, it need not concern you! To be sure, it would be a little awkward if people knew of it, but they don't, and, in any event, Celia wasn't Rowland's *wife* when it happened!'

Selina stared at her in horror. 'Abby, you *could* not! A man who – Abby, *think*! No, no, *promise* me you won't do it!' Tears began to roll down her cheeks. 'Oh, Abby, don't leave me! How could I live without you?'

'Hush, Selina! Nothing is decided yet. Don't, I beg of you, fall into one of your – into a fuss! Come, let me put you into bed! You're tired out. Fardle shall bring up your dinner to you, and –'

'Rabbit and onions!' uttered Selina, breaking into sobs of despair. 'I couldn't, I couldn't!'

'Oh!' A wry smile twisted Abby's lips. 'No, I don't think I could either.'

This was perhaps fortunate, for no opportunity was offered her to partake of this or any other dish. Selina's sobs were the prelude to one of her dreaded fits of hysteria, and as this was accompanied by spasms and palpitations it was long before Abby could leave her. When Selina at last fell into an exhausted sleep, the only thing her equally exhausted sister wished for was her bed.

The morning brought confirmation of her suspicion that Lavinia had indeed been tattling. Mrs Grayshott came to Sydney Place to see Abby.

'For I could do no less than tell you, Abby, and beg your pardon! I have never been so vexed with Lavinia! And the worst of it is that she did it on purpose, and is not sorry for it! She told me what she had done the instant she came home yesterday, knowing, of course, that I should be extremely displeased, but saying that she was Fanny's friend, and that she knew she had been right to warn her.'

'Perhaps she was,' said Abby. 'I don't know. I don't think Fanny quite believes it.'

'No, that also Lavinia told me. But Oliver thinks that even if she does not the shock of discovering that it is true will have been lessened for the poor child. But it was not Lavinia's business to have meddled! My dear, how tired you look!'

'I *am* a little tired,' owned Abby. 'My sister is not quite well today, so . . .'

She left the sentence unfinished, but she had said enough to send Mrs Grayshott back to Edgar Buildings in a state of such seething and impotent indignation that she informed her son, with unusual venom, that the sooner Miss Wendover's numerous ailments carried her off the better it would be for Abby.

Hardly had she left Sydney Place than a sealed letter was delivered at the house. It was directed to Fanny, and brought to her in the drawing-room by Mitton. She took it with a shaking hand, made as if to tear it open, and then, with an inarticulate excuse, went out of the room.

She did not return. Abby, who had guessed that the missive must have been sent by Stacy Calverleigh, waited in growing disquiet for a full hour, and then went up to her room.

Fanny was seated by the window. She looked at Abby, but said nothing, and her face was so stony that Abby hesitated. Then she saw the helpless suffering in Fanny's eyes, and went to her, not speaking, but folding her in her arms, and holding her close. Fanny did not resist, but for perhaps a minute she was as rigid as a statue. Stroking the bright curls, Abby said huskily, as though to a much younger Fanny, who had tumbled down, and grazed her knees: 'Never mind, my darling, never mind!'

She could have cursed herself for the inadequacy of these foolish words; but a quiver ran through Fanny, a rending sob broke from her, she turned in Abby's arms, and clung to her, torn and shaken by the pent-up emotions of the past fortnight.

It was long before she could be calm again, but gradually the sobs dwindled into pathetic hiccups, and she lay limply in Abby's embrace, her head on Abby's shoulder, and her lashes wet on her cheeks. When Abby would have fetched some water for her to drink, she said brokenly: 'Oh, no! This is so comfortable!' Presently she said: 'You knew, didn't you?'

'I knew, but I haven't known how to tell you.'

'Lavinia told me. I wouldn't believe her. But it was true. It was just my fortune, wasn't it?'

'I am afraid so, darling.'

Another silence fell, before Fanny said: 'I've been very stupid. Wicked, too. I meant to elope with him.'

'I don't suppose you would have done so, however.'

Fanny sighed. 'I don't know. Sometimes I thought I couldn't, but when I was with him –' Her voice failed, and it was a moment or two before she could speak again. 'Then I was ill, and he didn't come, or – or write to me, even when other people came to visit me. I tried to believe it was because he was afraid you might not let him see me, but I think I knew . . . Only I went on hoping, and when Lavinia told me about Mrs Clapham I felt at first that it *couldn't* be true, and then I wasn't quite sure, and then – and then the letter came.' A shudder ran through her. 'Abby, it made me feel *sick*! *Really* sick!'

'He told you that he had changed his mind?'

'No. I – I think I could have borne that. People *do* fall out of love, don't they? If he had told me that he had met someone he liked better than me – But he didn't. I was only a silly schoolgirl before I was ill, but I'm grown up now, and I shall never be taken-in again.'

Abby was not tempted to smile. She said: 'I hope no one will ever try to take you in again, dearest.'

'No, for I don't feel that I shall ever fall in love again. My uncle saw him yesterday, didn't he? Abby, *you* didn't send for him, did you?'

'I not only didn't send for him, but I came to cuffs with him before he had been in the house above ten minutes.'

'I thought you could not have done so. Oh, Abby, I beg your pardon! I've been horridly cross and unkind, but I didn't mean it! I love you more than anyone in the world!'

'Then I shall try my *very* hardest to forgive you!'

A watery chuckle greeted this sally. 'I'm so glad I've got you still. For always, Abby!' She lifted Abby's hand to her cheek, and cuddled it there. 'I love Aunt Selina too, of course, but in a – dutiful way. I couldn't bear to go on living here, if there was *only* my Aunt Selina.'

Abby heard this with mixed feelings. Though it warmed her heart it also caused it to sink. Miles Calverleigh's image seemed to be drawing further and further away.

'I burned the letter,' Fanny said abruptly. 'And the lock of hair. Do you think I might write to tell him so?'

'Oh, I shouldn't do that! Far more dignified to pay no heed to him at all!'

'Y-yes, only –' Her breast heaved. 'He says he shall keep mine to the day of his death, in memory of the only girl he ever truly loved! *That* was what made me feel sick!'

'I'm not surprised. It is making me feel sick too.'

'And he pretends that he is giving me up for my own sake, because he realises, since he has talked to my uncle, that he has no hope of winning his consent, and it would be very wrong for us to be married without it, and he fears I should regret it, and – Abby, it was *false*, every word of it! I could not have believed that he could write me such stuff! And to think I was widgeon enough to be taken-in! Because he knew from the very start that my uncle wouldn't consent, and he knew you wouldn't either, and that was why he wanted me to elope with him!' She sat up, her eyes and cheeks aflame with indignation, and her hands clenched. 'I hate him! I can't *think* how I ever came to fall in love with him!'

Abby was happy to encourage her in this frame of mind. Fanny raged for several minutes, but the mood could not last. Suddenly she flung herself back into Abby's arms in a fresh passion of grief, wailing: 'What shall I *do*? Oh, Abby, I'm so unhappy! What shall I *do*?'

'Well, I think the best thing to do is to follow Dr Rowton's advice,' replied Abby.

'Go away? Oh, no! I don't want to go away! I can't! I won't!'

'To be sure, when he first told me that you ought to go to the sea-side, to set you up again, I own that I felt doubtful, for in my opinion there is nothing more melancholy than the sea-side in November. But when he suggested Exmouth I remembered how delighted the Trevisians were with the place – and they, you know, were there in December. They stayed at the Globe, and Lady Trevisian almost persuaded your aunt to go there, when she was so sadly out of frame last winter, for she said they had been as comfortable there as in their own home. The climate is excellent, too, and there are several charming walks, besides I know not how many interesting expeditions to be made. I have been wondering whether, if we decided to try how we liked it, Mrs Grayshott would spare Lavinia to us. Do you think she might?'

The bait failed. Fanny was vehement in her entreaties not to be taken away from Bath. 'Everyone would think it was because I have been *jilted*!'

'Well,' said Abby dryly, 'when I consider that poor Mitton is worn out with plodding to the front-door to take in flowers, and fruit, and books from your army of admirers, my love, I think it very much more likely that *you* will be held to have been the jilt!'

She did not press the matter; but derived a certain amount of comfort from the belief that Fanny's pride had received almost as severe a blow as her heart.

Fanny meant to be good, not to be cross, or to allow it to be seen that she was in great affliction, but although she tried very hard, every now and then, to appear cheerful, her spirits remained low and oppressed, and, like her eldest aunt, she could not forbear discussion of her trouble with Abby. Hoping that she might soon talk herself out of her despair, Abby listened patiently, diverting her mind whenever an opportunity presented itself but never withholding her sympathy.

Selina, on the other hand, made no attempt to appear cheerful, but as she kept her bed for three days after her brother's disastrous visit, and complained when she left it of a great many aches and ails, perhaps only Fardle and Mrs Grimston ascribed her rather lachrymose condition to anything other than one of the disorders which so frequently attacked her. She spent most of her time on the sofa, wincing at the slamming of a door in the distance, or the postman's horn in the street; infuriating her excellent cook by thinking, in the morning, that she could fancy a particular dish, and by laboriously eating three mouthfuls of it when it made its appearance on the dinner-table; and trying by every means known to her to keep Abby by her side. 'Let me enjoy your company while I still may!' she said, shedding tears.

Between her sister and her niece, Abby's lot was not enviable, and might well have driven her to distraction had it not been eased by Mr Oliver Grayshott, who came nearly every day with Lavinia to visit Fanny, to divert her with parlour-games, if the weather was inclement, or, on fine days, to accompany her on her drives, or to take her for gentle walks in the Sydney Gardens. It was noticeable that she was always more cheerful after these visits, and if Abby grew to dread the two words: *Oliver says*, she had the comfort of knowing that Oliver's sayings were distinguished by their good sense. It was a little galling to discover that Fanny would accept Oliver's advice rather than hers – particularly when his advice tallied exactly with hers – but she suppressed such ignoble feelings. She wondered what would be the outcome of this close friendship. Fanny was not in love with Oliver. She continued to regard him as a brother, and almost certainly confided in him, and sought his guidance; but Abby could not help feeling that he was too quiet a man to appeal to her. Still, one never knew: perhaps, in a year or two's time, her trust and liking would have grown into love. One knew of many cases of a lively woman's finding happiness with a husband who was cast in a more sober mould than her own. There was no doubt that Oliver loved Fanny, though he treated her just as he treated Lavinia. It was only when he looked at her that he unconsciously betrayed himself. One could always tell, Abby thought, and instantly tried to decide when it was that she had first seen in Miles Calverleigh's very different eyes just that inner glow.

Seventeen

*M*eanwhile, Mr Stacy Calverleigh's star had been in the ascendant, and this in spite of his uncomfortably diminishing resources. He had been obliged to hang up his shot at the White Hart for several weeks; and he knew that only his increasing intimacy with the wealthy Mrs Clapham was restraining the proprietor of this establishment from indicating that the settlement of his bill would be appreciated. His efforts to persuade the widow to remove to Leamington had failed, and he had been obliged to show himself in public with her more often than was prudent; but these were small evils when compared with Mrs Clapham's coquettish encouragement of his advances. He had not enjoyed his session with Mr James Wendover, but he had been swift to turn it to good account. He had taken great pains over the letter he had written to Fanny, and by the time he had polished its well-turned phrases, and copied the whole out fair, he really felt that in renouncing her he was behaving as nobly as he expected her to believe. He was a little afraid that she might address a passionate reply to him, or even accost him in public, and silently cursed the obstinacy of Mrs Clapham in refusing to withdraw from Bath; but when he received no letter from Fanny, and was accorded only a slight, distant bow from her when her carriage was held up by the usual press of traffic in Cheap Street, his mind was relieved of care, and he felt himself to be at liberty to pop the question to Mrs Clapham.

It had not occurred to him that he might meet with a refusal, nor did her response to his proposal alarm him.

'Marry you?' said Mrs Clapham, laughing. 'Me? Good gracious no!'

He took this for coyness, and was rather impatient of it, but he said, in his most caressing voice: 'I think it was your sportive playfulness which made me tumble headlong in love with you. And I had believed myself to be case-hardened!'

Her next words were disturbing. 'Well, by what I'm told, you weren't so case-hardened but what you were making up to that pretty little girl who bowed to you in Cheap Street, before I came to Bath!'

It was the manner in which she spoke which disturbed him more than her words. There had always been a danger that she might discover how particularly he had attached himself to Fanny, and he knew just how to deal with that. He was unprepared for the change in her voice, and in her demeanour, and it startled him. He had hitherto supposed her to be a silly, fluttering little *ingénue*, but she was not looking at all ingenuous, and her voice was not only decidedly tart, but it had lost some of its gentility. It disconcerted him, but only momentarily: he realised that she was suspicious of a rival, and jealous of her. He laughed, flinging up his hands. 'What, little Fanny Wendover? Oh, Nancy, Nancy, you absurd and adorable witch! My dear, do you know how old she is? Seventeen! Not out of school yet!'

'More shame to you!' she said.

'Yes, indeed, if I *had* made up to her. Oh, these Bath quizzes! I warned you how it would be! But I own I did not think that at my age I should be suspected of dangling after a mere child only because I took notice of her, and indulged her with a little very mild flirtation!'

He trod over to her chair, and dropped gracefully on to his knee, and possessed himself of her hands, smiling up into her face. 'I have had many flirts, but never a true love till now!' he said whimsically.

'Well, you haven't got one in me!' said Mrs Clapham. 'I've had many flirts too, but I've no wish for a husband, so you may as well stop making a cake of yourself! Going down on your knees, as if you was playing Romeo!'

'I know how unworthy of you I am, but I dared to hope you were not indifferent to me!' he persevered.

'Get up, do!' responded the lady unromantically, pulling her hands away.

He obeyed her, looking remarkably foolish, and shaken quite off his balance. He stammered: 'How is this? It cannot be that you have been trifling with me! I cannot believe you could be so heartless!'

'Oh, can't you?' she retorted, getting up, and shaking out her skirt. 'Now, you listen to me, Mr Flat-catching Calverleigh! It don't become you to talk of hearts, and it isn't a particle of use pitching me any more of your gammon, because I'm up to all the rigs! We've had an agreeable flirtation, and the best thing you can do now is to own yourself beaten at your own game, and take yourself off! Otherwise you might hear a few things you wouldn't relish. Taking notice of a school girl! Cutting a sham with an heiress is what *you* were doing, and not for the first time, I'll be bound! Well, I don't want to say anything unladylike, *but*,' she ended, overcoming this reluctance, 'you're one as would marry a midden for muck, and that's the truth!'

He was white with mingled shock and rage. He opened his mouth to speak, but shut it again, for there was nothing he could say. He turned, and walked out of the room.

His was not a sensitive nature. He could shrug off a snub; he could listen with indifference to the strictures of Mr James Wendover. But Mr Wendover's contempt had been expressed with icy propriety. No one had ever torn his character to shreds with the crude vulgarity favoured by Mrs Clapham, and it was some time before he could in any way recover from his fury. It was not the truth of what she had said that provoked this fury: it was her incredible insolence in daring to address him – a Calverleigh! – in such terms.

When his rage abated, it was succeeded by fear, a more deadly fear than he had ever before experienced, for it was unattended by even a glimmer of optimism. There was no way left to him of staving off his creditors; he would be forced to pawn his few pieces of jewellery to enable him to pay his shot at the White Hart, and to buy himself a seat on the stage-coach to London. He tried to think of someone from whom he might be able to borrow a hundred pounds, or even fifty pounds, but there was no one – certainly no one in Bath.

He had reached the point of entertaining wild thoughts of abandoning his luggage, and escaping from the White Hart with his bill unpaid, when he was interrupted by the entrance of one of the waiters, who presented him with a letter, which had been brought, he said, by one of the servants employed at the York House Hotel.

Stacy did not recognise the careless scrawl, but when he spread open the single sheet he found that it was from his uncle, and briefly invited him to dine at York House that evening.

His first impulse was to send back a refusal. Then it occurred to him that he might be able to induce Miles to lend him some money, even if it was only a pony. He must be fairly flush in the pocket, he thought, for although he bore none of the signs of being well-inlaid he was again putting up at the most expensive hotel in Bath, which he could not have done had he left his shot unpaid when he went off to London so suddenly. He bade the waiter stay a moment while he wrote a reply to his uncle's letter, and was considerably provoked when he learned that the messenger had departed, having been told that no answer was expected. Coupled with the curt nature of the invitation, which might well have been mistaken for a command, this amounted to an affront, and set up Stacy's bristles. He decided to overlook it: his uncle's manners were deplorably casual, and probably he had had no intention of offending.

Upon arrival at York House, he was taken to Miles Calverleigh's sitting-room, where the table had already been laid for dinner. Determined to please, he exerted himself to be an affable, conversable, and even deferential guest. He praised the excellence of the dishes set before him; he said that it was not often that he was offered burgundy of such rare quality; he recounted such items of Bath-news as might be supposed to be of interest; he tried to draw Miles out on the subject of India. Miles regarded him with an amused eye, contributed little to the conversation, but outdid him in affability.

When the cloth had been removed, and the brandy placed on the table, Stacy said, with his air of rueful frankness: 'I must tell you, sir, that I was devilish glad to get your letter! I've been drawing the bustle a trifle too freely, and find myself on the rocks. Only temporarily, of course, but I've no banking accommodation in Bath, which puts me in a stupid fix. I don't like to ask it of you but I should be very grateful if you could lend me a trifle – just to keep me in pitch and pay over an awkward period, you know!'

His uncle removed the stopper from the decanter in his leisurely way, and poured brandy into the glasses. 'No, I won't lend you money,' he said.

He spoke with his usual amiability, but there was something in his voice which Stacy had never heard before. It was almost an implacable note, he thought. Surprised, and slightly nettled, he said: 'Good God, sir, I don't want any considerable sum!'

Miles shook his head. Without quite knowing why, Stacy felt a stir of alarm in his breast. He forced up a laugh. 'If you must have it, sir, it's damned low water with me – until I can bring myself about! I haven't sixpence to scratch with!'

'I know you haven't.'

The placidity with which this was uttered made Stacy flame into anger. He jumped up, his hands clenching and unclenching.

'Do you indeed? Well, let me tell you, my very dear uncle, that unless I can be given time to find some means of raising the recruits there will be a writ of forfeiture served on me!'

'Oh, it needn't come to that!'

'Needn't come to it? Are you *quite* blubber-headed? Don't you –'

Miles laughed. 'No, no, I'm not at all blubber-headed!'

'I beg pardon!' Stacy said, choking down his rage. 'I didn't mean to say that! The thing is –'

'No need to apologise,' said Miles kindly. 'No need to tell me what the thing is either.'

'I am afraid, sir,' said Stacy, trying to speak politely, 'that owing, no doubt, to your long residence abroad you are not familiar with the – the various conditions attached to mortgages. I must explain to you –'

'You are in arrears with the interest, and you have no possible means of paying up. Sit down!' He picked up his glass, and sipped some of the brandy in it. 'That's why I sent for you.'

'*Sent* for me?' interrupted Stacy.

'Did I say sent for you? It must have been a slip of the tongue. Begged for the honour of your company!'

'I cannot imagine why,' muttered Stacy resentfully.

'Just on a matter of business. I want two things from you: one is an equity of redemption; the other is Danescourt – by which is to be understood the house, and the small amount of unencumbered land on which it stands. For these I am prepared to forgo the interest owing on the existent mortgages, and to pay you fifteen thousand pounds.'

Stacy was so thunderstruck by these calmly spoken words that his brain whirled. He almost doubted whether he had heard his uncle aright, for what he had said was entirely fantastic. Feeling dazed and incredulous, he watched Miles stroll over to the fire, and take a spill from a jar on the mantelpiece. He found his voice, but only to stammer: 'B-but – equity of redemption – why, that means – Damn you, is this your notion of a joke?'

'No, no, I never cut jokes in business!' replied Miles. He came back to his chair, a lighted cheroot between his fingers, and sat down again, stretching his long legs out before him, with one ankle crossed over the other, after his usual fashion. He regarded his stunned nephew with mild amusement, and said: 'I'm a very rich man, you know.'

Since Stacy knew nothing of the sort, he felt more strongly than before that he had strayed into a world of fantasy. 'I don't believe it!' he blurted out.

'I am afraid,' said Miles, apologetically, 'that you have been misled into thinking that because I've no fancy for rigging myself out in the first style of elegance, cutting a dash, or saddling myself with a multitude of things I haven't the least wish to possess, I must be as cucumberish as you are yourself. You should never judge by appearances, nevvy!'

It seemed monstrous to Stacy that his uncle should not have informed him that he was in affluent circumstances. He exclaimed hotly: 'You have been deceiving me, then! Deliberately deceiving me!'

'Not at all. You deceived yourself. That isn't to say that I wouldn't have deceived you, had it been expedient to do so. But, to own the truth, it was of no consequence to me whether you thought me a nabob or a Church rat. Except, of course,' he added reflectively, 'that if you had known I was full of juice I should have found you an intolerable nuisance. You see, I never lend money without security.'

Stacy reddened, but said: 'If you can indeed afford to buy up the mortgages – if you don't wish to see Danescourt pass out of our hands – if you are willing to help me to bring myself about – we could come to some agreement! We could –' He broke off, encountering his uncle's eyes, and seeing in them a look as implacable as the note he had detected in his voice. There was no smile in them, and no warmth; nor could he perceive in them anger, impatience, contempt, or any human emotion whatso-ever. They were coldly dispassionate, and as hard as quartz.

'You know, you labour under too many misapprehensions,' said Miles pleasantly.

'But – Good God, you can't dispossess me!'

'What makes you think so?'

'You wouldn't! We are both Calverleighs! You are my *uncle!*'

'You have a remarkably false notion of my character if you think that that circumstance will prevail upon me to maintain Danescourt for your benefit. I can't think where you came by it.'

The brief, vague vision of being able once more to draw upon his estates for his needs faded. Miles had spoken amiably, but with finality. Stacy was conscious of an unreasoning resentment. He said: 'What is it to you? Much you care for being Calverleigh of Danescourt! Or *is* that it?'

'Oh, lord, no! I care for Danescourt, that's all.'

'That's what I said!'

'It's not what you meant, or what I mean. I want Danescourt because I'm fond of it, and for the same reason I won't see it fall into ruins. If I weren't, I wouldn't lift a finger to save it. All that fiddle-faddle you talk about being Calverleigh of Danescourt don't mean a thing to me.'

'Coming it too strong, uncle! And just as well if it *were* true, for *I* am the head of the family, and while I'm alive *I* am Calverleigh of Danescourt!'

'Yes, yes!' said Miles, on a soothing note. 'You can go on calling yourself Calverleigh of Danescourt, or anything else you like: I've no objection.'

'How the devil can I do so if I don't own even the house?' demanded Stacy hotly. 'I'll sell you an equity of redemption, but I'll not sell the house or the demesne!'

'Well, once I foreclose, you won't have any choice in the matter, will you? You'll be glad to sell it to me at any figure I name.'

Stacy stared at him, very white about the mouth. 'You'd do that? Foreclose on me – your own nephew! – force me out of my very birthplace? My God, is that what you've been doing all these years? Waiting for the chance of revenge?'

'No, I've been far too busy. I wish you would rid your mind of its apparent conviction that I think myself hardly used. I don't, and I never did. I didn't like your grandfather, or your father either, but I've often been grateful to them for the good turn they didn't know they'd done me. India suited me down to the ground. What's more, if they hadn't sent me there I might never have discovered that I had a turn for business. But I had, Stacy, and you'd do well to bear it in mind. When you prate to me about our relationship, you're wasting your time. Sentiment has no place in business, even if I had any, which I haven't. As for your talk about *revenge*, it's balderdash! I don't like you any more than I liked your father – in fact, less – but why the devil should I want to be revenged on you?'

'On him! Because I am his son!'

'Good God! You must have watched the deuce of a lot of melodramas in your time! Until I met you, I'd no feeling for you of any kind: why should I? If I had found Danescourt as I'd left it – or if I'd even found you making a push to restore it – I shouldn't have interfered. But I didn't. I had been warned of it, which was why I decided to come home, but I wasn't prepared –'

'It wasn't my fault!' Stacy said quickly, his colour surging into his face. 'It was my father who granted the first mortgage! He was in Dun territory when he died, and how the devil could I –'

'Don't excuse yourself! It makes no odds to me which of you let it fall into decay.'

'I should have been glad enough to set it in order, but I hadn't the means!'

'No, and as you wouldn't have spent a groat more than you were obliged to on it if you had had the means, and would sell it tomorrow, if you could find a fool willing to purchase a place which you described to me, on the occasion of our first meeting, as a damned barrack, mortgaged to the hilt, and falling into ruin besides, I am now going to relieve you of it.'

'You'd be better advised to leave it in my possession! What do you imagine will be said of you, if you – you usurp my place?'

'Well, according to Colonel Ongar, my arrival will be regarded in the light of a successful relieving force. You seem to have made yourself odious to the entire county.'

'Exactly as you did, in fact!'

'No, no, I was never *odious*! Merely a scapegrace! My youthful sins will be forgiven me the moment I remove the padlock from the main gate, and cut down that hayfield of yours. I must say, I don't at all care for it.'

'*Hayfield?* What the devil – ?'

'In my day it was the South Lawn.'

There was an uncomfortable silence. 'So you've been there, have you?' Stacy said sullenly.

'Yes, I've been there. I thought poor old Penn was going to burst into tears. Mrs Penn did. Fell on my neck, too, and went straight off to kill a fatted calf. The return of the Prodigal Son was nothing to it. No, I don't think I shall be shunned by the county, Stacy.'

Another silence fell, during which Stacy sat scowling down at the table. He said suddenly: 'Fifteen thousand? Paltry!'

'Perhaps,' suggested Miles, 'you are forgetting the little matter of the mortgages.'

Stacy bit his lip, but said: 'It's worth more – much more!'

'It is, in fact, worth much less. However, if you believe you can sell it for more, by all means make the attempt!'

'With you holding all the rest of the estate? Who the devil would buy a place like Danescourt with no more land attached to it than the gardens, and the park?'

'I shouldn't think anyone would.'

'Brought me to Point Non-Plus, haven't you?' said Stacy, with an ugly laugh.

'You're certainly there, but what I had to do with it I don't know.'

'You could help me to make a recover – give me time!'

'I could. I could also ruin you. I don't choose to do either – though when I saw Danescourt I was strongly tempted to let you take up residence in the King's Bench Prison, and leave you to rot there! Which is what you will do, if you refuse my offer.'

'Oh, damn you, I can't refuse it! How soon can I have the blunt?'

'As soon as the conveyance is completed. The necessary documents are being prepared, and you will find them with my lawyer. I'll furnish you with his direction. You had better take your own man with you, to see all's right, by the way.'

'I shall certainly do so! And I shall be very much obliged to you if you'll advance me a hundred, sir, at once!'

'I'll make you a present of it,' said Miles, drawing a roll of bills from his pocket.

'You're very good!' said Stacy stiffly. 'Then, if there's nothing more you wish to say, I'll bid you goodnight!'

'No, nothing,' replied Miles. 'Goodnight!'

Eighteen

Since Miss Butterbank, after a night and the better part of a day enduring the agonies of violent toothache, was closeted with the dentist when Mr Miles Calverleigh returned to Bath, the news of his arrival was not carried to Sydney Place until several hours after he had made an unexpected descent upon Miss Abigail Wendover.

He took her entirely by surprise. Not only did he present himself at an unusually early hour, but when Mitton admitted that he rather thought Miss Abigail was at home he said that there was no need to announce him, and ran up the stairs, leaving Mitton in possession of his hat and malacca cane, and torn between romantic speculation and disapproval of such informal behaviour.

Abby was alone, and engaged on the task of fashioning a collar out of a length of broad lace. The table in the drawing-room was covered with pins, patterns, and sheets of parchment, and Abby had just picked up a pair of shaping scissors when Mr Calverleigh walked into the room. She glanced up; something between a gasp and a shriek escaped her; the scissors fell with a clatter; and she started forward involuntarily, with her hands held out. 'You've come back! Oh, you *have* come back!' she cried.

The unwisdom, and, indeed, the impropriety of this unguarded betrayal of her sentiments occurred to her too late, and did not seem to occur to Mr Calverleigh at all. Before she could recover herself she was in his arms, being kissed with considerable violence. 'My bright, particular star!' uttered Mr Calverleigh, into her ear.

Mr Calverleigh had very strong arms, and a shoulder most conveniently placed for the use of a tall lady. Abby, gasping for breath, gratefully leaned her cheek against it, feeling, for a few brief moments, that she had come safely to harbour after a stormy passage. She said, clinging to him: 'Miles! Oh, my dear. I've missed you so dreadfully!' But hardly had she uttered these words than all the difficulties of her situation rushed in upon her, with the recollection of the decision she had so painfully reached, and she said, trying to wrench herself free: 'No! Oh, I can't think what made me – ! I can't, Miles, I can't!'

Mr Calverleigh, that successful man of affairs, was not one to be easily rocked off his balance. 'What can't you, my heart's dearest?' he enquired.

Abby quivered. 'Marry you! Oh, Miles, *don't!*'

She broke from him, and turned away, groping blindly for her handkerchief, and trying very hard not to let her emotion get the better of her.

'Well!' said Mr Calverleigh, in stunned accents. 'This is beyond everything! After what has just passed between us! I wonder you dare look me in the face!'

Abby, was not, in fact, daring to look him in the face: she was occupied in drying her wet cheeks.

'Has no one ever told you that it is the height of impropriety to kiss any gentleman, unless you have the intention of accompanying him immediately to the altar?' demanded the outraged Mr Calverleigh. 'It will not do, ma'am! Such conduct –' He broke off abruptly, as she looked up, between tears and laughter, and said, in quite another voice: 'Now, what's this? Let me look at you!'

As he took her face between his hands as he spoke, and turned it up, she was obliged to let him. She dared not meet his eyes, however, and very nearly broke down again when he said, after a moment's scrutiny: 'My loved one, I left you in a high state of preservation! What has been happening here?'

She moved away, saying: 'Do I look hagged? I am – I am rather tired. Fanny has been ill. And there have been other things.' She smiled, with an effort, and made a gesture towards a chair. 'Won't you sit down? I must tell you – explain to you – why I can't marry you.'

'Yes, I think you must do that,' he said, drawing her to the sofa. 'I can think of only one reason: that you find you don't love me enough.'

She allowed him, though reluctantly, to push her gently down on to the sofa, and sat there, primly upright, with her hands tightly folded in her lap. 'I meant to tell you that that was it,' she said, keeping her eyes lowered. 'I – thought it would be best to say just that. I never, never meant to –' She stopped, as a thought occurred to her, and looked up, a sparkle of indignation in her eyes. 'I should like to know what Mitton was about to let you walk in on me, without coming first to ask me if I was at home to visitors, and not even announcing you!' she said, with a strong suggestion of ill-usage in her voice.

He had taken his place at the other end of the sofa, seated sideways, with one arm lying along the back of it: a position which enabled him to keep his eyes on her profile. He seemed to be quite at his ease; and there was nothing in his demeanour to suggest that he was suffering from any of the chagrin natural to a gentleman whose suit had been rejected. He said: 'Oh, you mustn't blame the poor fellow! I told him I would announce myself.'

'You had no business to do so!' scolded Abby. 'If you hadn't startled me – if I had had a *moment's* warning – I shouldn't have – it wouldn't have happened!'

'Well, you might not have kissed me, but I had every intention of kissing you, so it's just as well he didn't announce me,' said Mr Calverleigh. 'Do you always kiss gentlemen who walk in unannounced? I'll take good care none is allowed to do so when we are married!'

A smile trembled on her lips, and she blushed faintly, but also she shook her head, saying: 'We are not going to be married.'

'I was forgetting that,' he apologised. 'Why are we not going to be married?'

'That is what I feel I must explain to you. I didn't mean to, but after behaving so very improperly it wouldn't be any use to tell you that I don't love you, would it?'

'No, none at all,' he agreed.

'No. Well – you must try to understand, Miles! I know you don't enter into my feelings on this subject, so it is very difficult to explain it to you. I have thought and thought – argued with myself until my head aches – but in the end I've realised that I cannot marry you – ought not to do so!'

'What brought you to this conclusion?' he asked conversationally.

She began carefully to pleat her damp handkerchief. 'I suppose you might say it was Mrs Ruscombe. She is Cornelia's bosom-bow – James's wife, you know – and she makes it her business to spy on us, and to send a record of all our doings to Cornelia.' She raised her eyes to his for an instant, smiling wryly. 'I am afraid we were not very discreet, Miles, for she told Cornelia that I was encouraging your advances, and that brought James down upon us, as you may imagine. Of course we came to points – we always do – but even though I was in the most shocking pelter I couldn't keep from laughing. You never heard such pompous fustian in your life! I found myself wishing you could have been there to enjoy it!'

'I rather wish that too,' acknowledged Mr Calverleigh. 'Did he forbid the banns?'

'Heavens, yes! He said that if I married you I should be cast out of the family, and he would have divulged the Awful Truth about you and Celia if I hadn't told him that I knew it already, and that shocked him so much that he said he began to think we – you and I – were well matched!'

'You know, he's not such a bad fellow after all!' remarked Miles.

'He is a toad. It wasn't anything he said which made me realise how impossible it is. Nothing he said to me. But he said it

242

all over again to Selina, and, I daresay, a great deal more.' She fell silent, deeply troubled. At last, she sighed, and said: 'I never knew how much Selina loved me. James told her she would have to choose between me and the family, and, oh, Miles, she said that she would never give me up, whatever I did! Selina! But she was dreadfully upset – she made herself ill, and she is still quite overpowered, and – and can scarcely bear to let me out of her sight. She says over and over again that she doesn't know what she will do when I'm gone, and that – has made me realise how wrong – how heartless – it would be if I were to marry you. If you had been the sort of dull, respectable man of whom the family would have approved I think she would have grown accustomed – though sometimes I feel I ought not to leave her, no matter who asked me to marry him. You see, we have been together all my life, and for years – ever since my mother died – I've managed everything for her, and taken care of her. But if you had been Peter Dunston, whom she has been trying to persuade me to marry these three years, she would have been pleased, and that would have helped her to bear the loneliness she dreads. She would have known I was near at hand, and she wouldn't have been estranged from the family, or – Oh, I can't explain it to you! So – so many evils would result from our marriage! If you think it wouldn't become known that I had married you against the wishes of my family, you cannot know Bath! They might seem insignificant to you; they seem so to me; but not to Selina. And then there is Fanny!'

'I wondered when we were going to come to Fanny,' remarked Miles chattily.

'We must come to her. I can't desert her, Miles. She is in great affliction poor child, for she has discovered what is your vile nephew's true character!'

'Just as you hoped she might,' he interpolated.

'Yes, indeed, and I am thankful for it! But it has quite overset her, and – and she too needs me. It would never do to leave her here with Selina – wholly separated from me! For she would be, you see. James wouldn't permit me even to write to her. When

243

she knew about Stacy, she told me that she was glad she had me – for always. She won't want me always, of course, but perhaps for some years to come she will.'

'Would it be of any use for me to suggest that there are answers to all these problems?' he said.

She shook her head. 'No. You see, one can argue – one can persuade oneself that none of these things matter, but one knows, all the time, that they do matter. Miles, I *could* not, deliberately, and selfishly, for the sake of my own happiness, plunge my whole family into so much trouble, and the two I love most into misery as well! I beg of you, don't try to convince me! I'm worn out with thinking!'

Her voice cracked; she put up her hand to shield her eyes; and felt her other taken into a sustaining clasp. 'No, I won't try to convince you,' said Miles reassuringly.

Someone must have told Selina that her sister was closeted with Mr Calverleigh. Since James Wendover's visit she had not left her room until noon, yet here she was, entering the drawing-room with a nervous cough, and looking far less trim than usual, as if she had dressed in a hurry. 'Oh!' she exclaimed, in rehearsed surprise. 'Mr Calverleigh! Dear me, I had no notion you were in Bath! So civil of you to call! Such a wretched day too!'

Abby sprang up and walked over to the window; Mr Calverleigh, rising more leisurely, showed no sign of discomfiture, but shook hands with Selina, and in the calmest way enquired after her health. He remained only for a few minutes longer, and when he took his leave it was with unruffled composure.

Hardly was the door shut behind him than Selina said in an agitated voice: 'He was holding your hand! Oh, Abby, why did he come? Do not keep me in suspense! I can't bear it!'

'I imagine you must know why he came,' said Abby, in a level voice.

'I guessed it!' moaned Selina, pressing a hand to her heart. 'What was your answer? *Tell* me, Abby!'

'Don't distress yourself!' Abby said wearily. 'I have refused his offer.'

'Oh!' cried Selina, suddenly radiant. 'Oh, how glad I am! Dear, dear Abby, now we can be happy again!'

Feeling quite unable to respond to this, Abby left the room without a word, and sought the seclusion of her bedchamber. She remained there for some considerable time, and was thus spared the account of Mr Calverleigh's arrival in Bath, which Miss Butterbank, with a scarf still wrapped round her face, brought to Sydney Place. Selina said nothing about this when she later told Abby the rest of the news Miss Butterbank had poured into her ears. This was of a startling and an intriguing nature: Mrs Clapham, accompanied by her retinue, had left Bath on the previous evening; and Mr Stacy Calverleigh had undoubtedly followed her, for he had boarded one of the post coaches that very morning, and without, said Miss Butterbank, a word of warning to anyone.

Abby was relieved to know that he had removed himself from Bath, but although she made an effort to enter into Selina's speculations on the various possible causes of these separate departures, she felt no flicker of interest. The next piece of Bath news came from Mrs Leavening, and interested her too much.

Mrs Leavening, now established in Orange Grove, had called at York House for any letters which might have been sent there, and she had learnt of Mr Calverleigh's return. She had also learnt that he had remained for only one night before disappearing again, like a perfect will-o'-the-wisp. 'There's no knowing what freakish thing he'll do next!' chuckled Mrs Leavening. 'What in the world made him come all the way from London only for one night? It seems he's set up his own chaise, too, but where it has taken him off to goodness knows! He is quite in my black books, as I shall tell him, for he promised to give us a look-in when he came back to Bath, and never a glimpse of him did we get. However, they say he means to return, so I daresay I shall have an opportunity to give him a scold.'

Abby, knowing that it would be better for her not to see Mr Calverleigh again, tried to school herself into hoping that he would not call in Sydney Place, but failed. Their parting had been too abrupt; there had been so much left unsaid; and to have been obliged to say goodbye to him as to the merest acquaintance was too painful to be borne.

Nothing more was heard of him for three interminable days. Selina, miraculously restored to health and spirits, wrote a surreptitious letter to James, informing him, in the strictest confidence, that all was at an end between Abby and Mr Miles Calverleigh, and that she had known from the start that the affair had been grossly exaggerated by Mrs Ruscombe. She added that she hoped dear Cornelia would not, in future, allow herself to pay so much heed to That Woman's malicious gossip.

Her expression of dismay, when, upon the fourth day, Mitton announced the arrival of Mr Calverleigh was almost ludicrous. It caught Fanny's attention, and made her look quickly at Abby, a sudden suspicion entering her mind.

Mr Calverleigh, with his customary disregard for the conventions governing polite circles, had chosen a most unseasonable hour for his visit. The ladies had only ten minutes earlier left the breakfast-parlour. He seemed to be quite unaware that he was committing a social solecism, but entered the room as though sure that he must be welcome, and cheerfully greeted its occupants. He said that he was glad to have found them at home, congratulated Fanny on her recovery from her illness, and, turning to Abby, said, smiling at her: 'I've come to take you for a drive.'

Selina seethed with indignation. What Abby found to like in this abrupt, mannerless creature was a matter passing her comprehension! She hurried into speech. 'So obliging of you, sir, but it would be *most* unwise for my sister to venture out in an open carriage! The weather is so unsettled – it will come on to pour in another hour, I daresay, for at this season there is no depending on it! Besides, I wish her to go with me to the Pump Room!'

Forgetting her own troubles in the liveliest curiosity, Fanny said brightly: 'I'll go with you, Aunt Selina. A drive is just what will do Abby good, after being cooped up in the house for so long!'

Mr Calverleigh, smiling at her, said: 'Good girl!' which made her giggle, and told Abby to go and put on her bonnet. He added a recommendation to bring a tippet, or a shawl, with her. 'So that you may be easy!' he said, addressing himself to Selina. 'I don't think she will take cold, if she wraps herself up well, and if it should come on to rain we can always find shelter, you know.'

He then engaged Fanny in idle conversation, while Selina sought in vain for further reasons why Abby should not drive out with him.

When Abby came back into the room, suitably attired for the expedition, Selina made a last attempt to convince her that she was running the gravest risk of contracting a heavy cold, if not an inflammation of the lungs, but Fanny, giving Abby an impulsive kiss, interrupted her very rudely, saying: 'Fiddle! It is the finest day we have had for weeks! I'll come and tuck you up in *quantities* of shawls, Abby!'

'Thank you!' Abby said, laughing. 'I fancy one will be enough! Goodbye, Selina: there is no need for you to be in a fidget, I promise you.'

Mr Calverleigh watched her go out of the room, and turned to take leave of Selina. 'Don't worry!' he said. 'I shall take great care of her.'

Five minutes later, leaving Fanny waving farewell on the doorstep, he drove off at a smart trot, and said darkly: '*Indian* manners, my dear!'

Abby chuckled. '*Rag*-manners! Poor Selina!'

'I was afraid you might yield to her entreaties.'

'No. I hoped I might see you again. It was so uncomfortable – saying goodbye as we did. I never told you about Fanny, either. We – we won't discuss that other matter, for there is nothing to be said, and I know you won't distress me by trying to persuade me, will you?'

'No, no, I won't try to persuade you!' he promised.

This ready acquiescence was unexpected, and not altogether welcome; but after a few moments Abby said, with determined cheerfulness: 'Stacy *did* mean to elope with Fanny, you know.

247

She told me the whole. If she hadn't contracted influenza, heaven knows what might have happened! But she did, and while she was laid up we had the most amazing stroke of good fortune befall us!'

He laughed. 'No, did you?'

'Yes, for who should arrive in Bath but a rich widow! *Fabulously* rich, by all accounts! I never saw her myself, but I believe she is quite young, and very pretty. And she put up at the White Hart!'

'No!'

'Yes! With a companion, and a maid, and a footman – oh, and a courier as well! You wouldn't have believed it!'

'Oh, wouldn't I!' said Mr Calverleigh.

'And she hadn't been there for a day before Stacy was busy fixing his interest with her! Would you have thought it possible?'

'Not only possible, but certain.'

'Well, I must say I didn't, when I first heard of it. I never supposed him to be as – as shameless as that!'

'My odious nephew, I regret to say, is entirely shameless.'

'He must be. I can't help pitying the widow, for I think she must have found him out. She left Bath quite suddenly, and although I was excessively thankful that Stacy *did* attach himself to her, it must have been very painful for her.'

'Set your mind at rest, my love! It wasn't at all painful for her.'

'You can't know that!' objected Abby.

'Oh, yes, I can!' he retorted. 'I sent her here!'

'*You?*' she gasped.

'Yes, of course. Didn't you guess it? I rather thought you would.'

'Good God, no! But who was she? *How* did you contrive to send her to Bath? And what a *shocking* thing to do! Exposing her to – Miles, it was *monstrous*! How *can* you laugh?'

'You shouldn't make me laugh. My precious pea-goose, I hired her to bamboozle Stacy! As far as I can discover, her performance was most talented – though she seems to have broken down a trifle before she rang down the final curtain. As

248

to who she is, I really don't know, except that she was at one time an actress.'

Miss Abigail Wendover, having digested this information, said, in accents of stern disapproval: 'I collect, sir, that she is not a – a respectable female?'

'Let us rather say, ma'am, that you are unlikely to meet her in the first circles.'

'*You* seem to have done so!'

'No, no, not in the first circles!'

Her dimple quivered, but she suppressed it. 'And are you very well acquainted with her?' she enquired politely.

'Oh, no! I only met her once – to rehearse her in her rôle, you know. Dolly found her for me. Dolly was Mrs Clapham's companion. I was extremely well acquainted with *her* – some twenty years ago,' he explained outrageously. 'She used to be known as the Dasher, and a very dashing little barque of frailty she was! She is now engaged in – er – a different branch of the profession, and has become alarmingly tonnish. However, she consented, at an extortionate price, to take part in my masquerade. In fact, she insisted on doing so. She never could resist a spree.'

'You,' said Abby, in a shaking voice, 'are the most disreputable person I have ever encountered!'

'Well, that's not saying much! Except for my odious nephew, I don't suppose you've encountered any disreputable persons at all.' He turned his head, and added: 'You never knew me in my disreputable days, Abigail. They are all in the past.'

Her eyes fell. After a minute, she said: 'It must have cost you a great deal, I fear. The masquerade, I mean. When I asked you to rescue Fanny, I never intended –'

'Oh, I had an axe of my own to grind as well!' he assured her.

'Oh!' she said doubtfully. 'Well, –' She stopped suddenly, recognising a landmark. 'Good gracious, we are on the London road! Where are we going?'

'Reading,' he replied.

'*Reading?*' she echoed blankly. 'Don't be so absurd! It must be sixty miles away!'

'Sixty-eight.'

She laughed. 'Just a gentle drive, to exercise the horses! Seriously, where are we going?'

'I am perfectly serious.'

'Oh, are you, indeed?' she retorted. 'And we shall be back in good time for dinner, no doubt!'

'No, my darling, we shall not,' he said. 'We are not going back at all.'

She stared incredulously at him. 'Not – Miles, stop bantering me! It is too ridiculous! You cannot suppose I'm such a ninny as to believe we could drive all the way to Reading in a curricle-and-pair!'

'Oh, no, of course I don't! We are only going as far as to Chippenham in the curricle. My post-chaise is waiting there, to carry us the rest of the way.'

She still felt that he must be trying to hoax her, but she began to be uneasy. 'And what do we do when we reach Reading?' she asked.

'We get married, my very dear.'

'Have you run mad?' she demanded.

'Well, I don't *think* so!'

'Miles – Miles, you *are* joking me, aren't you?'

'I promise you I was never more in earnest. I can't show it to you at the moment, but I have a special licence in my pocket.'

'Oh, how dare you?' she gasped. 'Stop *at once*! If you think I am going to elope with you –'

'No, no!' he said. 'This isn't an elopement! I'm abducting you!'

She tried to speak, but dared not trust her voice.

'I thought it would be the best thing to do,' he explained.

That was too much for her self-control; for the life of her she could not help bursting into laughter. But when she managed to stop laughing, she said: 'Oh, do, please, take me home! How *could* you think I would consent to such a shocking thing?'

'My dear girl, you don't consent to an abduction! You consent to an *elopement*, and I knew you wouldn't do that.'

'You told me once that you thought an unwilling bride would be the very devil!' she reminded him.

'If I had thought that you were unwilling you wouldn't be sitting beside me now,' he replied.

'But I am unwilling! Miles, I won't – I can't! Oh, I believed you understood!'

'I did. You said you wouldn't marry me for a great many reasons which were most of them quite idiotish, but you also said that you couldn't seek your own happiness at the cost of Selina's and Fanny's. Well, you have the right to make a sacrifice of yourself, but I'll be damned if I'll let you sacrifice me!'

After a moment's stricken silence, Abby said remorsefully: 'I never thought of that! Would it – would it be – ?'

'Yes,' he said. 'It would!'

'Oh, if only I knew what I ought to do!' she cried wretchedly.

'You don't, but I do. So don't argue with yourself any more! You haven't any choice in the matter, you know. That's why I've forcibly carried you off. It makes it much easier for you, don't you think?'

'Miles, you are the most impossible, disgraceful – Only think what a scandal there would be!'

'What, you don't imagine that any member of your family would breathe a word about it, do you? No, no! The marriage was private, of course! I expect James will think of some excellent reason for that.'

'James! He will utterly disown me!'

'No hope of that,' he said. 'I daresay he may hold off for a few months to save his dignity, but it won't be for long. You, my loved one, little though it interests you, are about to become an extremely wealthy woman. You are also going to become the mistress of Danescourt.'

'Danescourt? But doesn't that belong to Stacy?'

'No, it belongs to me: I've bought it from him. I am taking you there tonight. It's in a deplorable state, but I threw an army into

251

it last week to put it into some kind of order, and told our old housekeeper to hire some servants, so I hope you won't find it too uncomfortable. We won't stay there above a day or two, but I want you to inspect it, and decide what you wish for in the way of curtains and things of that nature. Where would you like to go after that?'

She said helplessly: 'I don't know. Oh, this is too fantastic! For heaven's sake, take me home! Only think of poor Selina!'

'Nothing would prevail upon me to take you home. You may write a note to poor Selina from Chippenham: I'll send it by a post-boy: but you are not going to see her again until you are firmly riveted, my girl, and it is too late for her to cling round your neck!'

'But what will she *do*?' said Abby distractedly.

'She will in all probability find a substitute for you in Miss Butterbank,' he replied calmly. 'What's more, they will deal extremely together. Fanny, I daresay, will go to your sister in London. By the by, do you wish for a London house?'

'No, of course I don't! Miles, do you realise that I haven't even a *toothbrush*?'

'Do you know, I believe you're right?' he said. 'And I thought I had remembered everything! What a fortunate thing that you mentioned it! We must buy one in Reading.'

'Have you had the audacity to – Oh, you are too abominable! I won't marry you! I will *not*! Take me home!'

Mr Miles Calverleigh brought his horses to a halt at the side of the road, and turned, and smiled at her. 'Tell me that that is what, *in your heart*, you want me to do, and I will!'

She looked into his eyes, and what she saw in them made her pulses race.

'Tell me, Abby!'

'You may be able to abduct me,' said Abby, with dignity, 'but you can't force me to tell lies! . . . *Miles!* there's a coach coming, and a man staring at us over the hedge! For heaven's sake – !'